Gyorgy's snarli... caught a glimp... belonged to the planet's largest carnivore, short fur and baleful eyes. The impression was one of total obedience emitting total viciousness, of stumpy, pig-like legs and pointed ears, of foul breath and utter, soul-devouring horror . . .

He glimpsed the fur, which was flying apart. He glimpsed the wicked canines and incisors as they shattered. He caught a brief impression of something unearthly ripping into shreds and tatters of synthetic, dying flesh, veering in mid-spring to crash heavily and messily against the doorframe.

Also by Bernard King in Sphere Books:

VOLUME I OF THE CHRONICLES OF THE KEEPER:
THE DESTROYING ANGEL

TIME-FIGHTERS

VOLUME II
OF THE CHRONICLES
OF THE KEEPER

Bernard King

SPHERE BOOKS LIMITED

SPHERE BOOKS LTD

Penguin Books Ltd, 27 Wrights Lane, London w8 5tz (Publishing and Editorial)
and Harmondsworth, Middlesex, England (Distribution and Warehouse)
Viking Penguin Inc, 40 West 23rd Street, New York, New York 10010, USA
Penguin Books Australia Ltd, Ringwood, Victoria, Australia
Penguin Books Canada Ltd, 2801 John Street, Markham, Ontario, Canada l3r 1b4
Penguin Books (NZ) Ltd, 182–190 Wairau Road, Auckland 10, New Zealand

Published by Sphere Books Ltd 1987

Copyright © by Bernard King 1987
All rights reserved

Made and printed in Great Britain by
Richard Clay Ltd, Bungay, Suffolk
Filmset in Monophoto Sabon

This particular box o' demons is for Donald Hickling,
in part-payment of an impossible debt.

Faust climbed the steps of the temple. Above
the door, a carved motto caught his eye:
Neither God nor Devil. For a second, he
hesitated, with upraised hand. Then he
pushed in the door, which offered no resistance.

— Claude Farrère

CONTENTS

PART ONE: Seeking the Immortals   1

   27 JULY 869   3

   14 APRIL 939   9

   3 AUGUST 1540   13

   20 SEPTEMBER 1540   18

   11 JUNE 1732   26

   3 AUGUST 1871   31

   21 JULY 1884   39

   27 JULY 1884   48

   13 APRIL 1978   59

   MONDAY 23 MARCH LAST YEAR   62

   THURSDAY 30 APRIL LAST YEAR   68

   SATURDAY 2 MAY LAST YEAR   74

PART TWO: The Skull Meditation   81

PART THREE: The Guardian of the Relic   213

PART ONE

Seeking the Immortals

27 JULY 869

Late afternoon

It was all Naddodd Gamlesson's fault. If he hadn't got blown off course on a voyage from Norway to the Faeroes he'd never have found this strange new land of ice and fire. As it was the silly old fart couldn't keep the news to himself. He had to return with it, to tell everybody about the place. Immensely inconsiderate.

If Grim Haddingsson had been left there with Naddodd he would have cut the blood eagle on the old bugger's back, no doubt about it. And next in line would have been Gardar Svarsson's mother, the old witch! Really, it was more than flesh and blood ought to have to cope with.

Gardar had sailed from Trondheim in Norway a few weeks before, following Naddodd's original course. His mother, Heidi, now old and wrinkled and with her reputation for second sight reinforced by every extra seam in her raddled old face, had heard Naddodd's account of his discovery and decided to use her powers to help her son. There were good reasons, Grim conceded. There always were.

The political situation in Scandinavia had worsened since the Yngling dynasty, the royal house allegedly founded by the god Odin himself, had declined and been finally extinguished after the death of Ingjald Onundsson. Expeditions to find new lands for conquest and settlement were no longer uncommon. A Norse king had already established himself at Dublin and Naddodd's tale of a new land to the north-west was being taken seriously by quite a number of Vikings. Gardar Svarsson, out of favour at the court of Halfdan the Black, had decided upon this expedition because his mother also believed Naddodd's story.

From Trondheim they had followed the original course to the Faeroes, where their longboats had taken on fresh water and provisions. After resting for a few days and feasting to improve their spirits they had continued west-north-west, following nothing more tangible than old Heidi's interpretation of Naddodd's account.

Yet the old witch had got it right. Ten days later they had made land at Hornafjord in the south-east of what eventually would be called Iceland, in a shallow fjord with broad gravel-sand banks and a gentle green landscape beyond. At its mouth was a small, rocky island and once past that Gardar's ships found themselves in a natural harbour. There they disembarked and made camp whilst they discussed the implications of their find.

The land appeared deserted, and Gardar determined upon sailing along the coast to establish the extent of this new country. Grim and a few others were instructed to remain behind at the camp, and Grim insisted that Gardar should leave him a longship and sufficient men to crew it, in case the others failed to return. After an appropriate amount of haggling Gardar agreed, on condition that Heidi stayed behind at Hornafjord as well.

Grim Haddingsson and his men watched Gardar set out on his expedition with mixed feelings. Despite the confinement of their ocean voyaging the men were mostly good friends, and some of those who remained behind had brothers and other relatives setting off into the unknown.

The days passed slowly, with those men not detailed to guard the camp setting off to explore inland. The strangest thing about this new country was the length of the nights. Grim had heard about the midnight sun before, but only as a traveller's tale from merchants who had penetrated as far north as Bjarmaland. To see it for himself was both unnerving and wonderful. The land was never totally dark, but for a few brief hours each night the dusk was deeper than at other times. At first it puzzled them, but after a while, when no evil crept out of the protracted twilight, they grew to accept the simple fact of nature.

And now they had been there almost a fortnight. The eastern bank of the fjord was fully explored and charted, and something of the true rugged grandeur of the land was beginning to emerge. Even Grim was forced to admit that the countryside held a strange beauty, with its moss-covered rocks and low, almost stunted, woodland. And the climate itself was mild and welcoming, as if it had warmed to their presence and decided to greet them in its own way.

They sat about their fires in the long evening and sang songs and told stories, boasting of their valour and their deeds. For the grizzled veterans who made up most of Gardar's crews it was almost a holiday, a pleasant rest in lives which had seen their share of fighting and sorrow. The only thorn in their flesh was old Heidi, Gardar's mother, who would go off on her own and sit by herself, lost in those strange trances which were the root of her sorcerous reputation.

'She's a strange old crow,' Grim once remarked, out of her hearing, for he would never have dared to say it had she been present. 'I don't know whether to be grateful for her powers, for getting us here in one piece, or to curse them for getting us here at all. After all, lads, we've an uncertain future ahead of us. Mother Ran didn't cast her net for a shipwreck on the way here, but there's nothing to stop her claiming a few lives on the way back. Maybe we'd have done better to stay home and knuckle down to Halfdan the Black.'

Next to Gardar he was their leader, and they respected his opinions, but all mention of them was kept from old Heidi. When things were going well only a fool or a hero would show his doubts to a witch. You never knew if the Norns were watching, ready to cut your thread on their weave of life.

Then, early one morning, before the extended dawn had given way before the advance of true day, Heidi disappeared. At first they thought nothing of it. She was always going off on her own to sit and glaze her eyes. But this time she had crossed the fjord and started off along the west bank, into territory which had yet to be explored and declared safe. Eventually, despite his misgivings and the inner promptings to leave her alone to get on with whatever she had chosen to do, Grim set off with a tracker to follow her progress and guide her back to their camp. Despite everything she was still Gardar's mother, and if anything happened to her Gardar would be looking for a head to nail the blame to.

For the better part of that day they followed her progress across the gently rolling countryside. Occasionally they paused at a stream whilst the tracker interpreted whatever signs she had left, and then they would continue, exchanging their litany of search as they went.

'Are you sure we're still on her track? Couldn't she have gone another way?'

'This is the way the signs tell me, Grim. We're still on her trail. We're still following old Heidi.'

'I hope to Odin you know what you're doing, for all our sakes . . .'

They continued westwards, towards the lengthening shadows of the dusk. The only really remarkable thing about their progress was that Heidi appeared to be moving almost in a straight line, as if there was some definite purpose to her wandering, a purpose which was concealed from her pursuers by their ignorance.

Occasionally they would find a blade of grass, a twig, deliberately broken, as if she knew that they were following, as if she wanted them to follow, to bring her safely back. At first it puzzled Grim, but then, with the true fatality of the Norseman, he simply shrugged and continued to follow.

'If we had some horses we'd make better progress,' he muttered.

The tracker looked at him but made no reply. They both knew what his silence represented. It was a form of dumb insolence, a way of saying that they didn't have the horses, and that the speculation was idle, to no purpose. Grim simply tightened his lips and continued to follow the trail.

Then, in the twilight, they came across a little valley. A stream, crystal clear and swift-flowing, reflected the lurid orange of the sky above them. Beside it, the first structure they had seen since landing at Hornafjord, stood an unmistakable stone hut, its ruined thatch of dried grasses mostly fallen in. Within the hut burned the uncertain light of a lamp with a floating wick.

'She's in there,' the tracker muttered.

'But why did she come here?' Grim demanded. 'She came straight here, without hesitation or deviating more than the terrain dictated. How did she know where to come?'

They both knew the answer, but neither was willing to voice it, to acknowledge that perhaps there was more than just talk to Heidi's second sight. Instead they made their way down towards the hut in the valley, fording the shallow stream in the fading light of a tiring day.

The wooden door had long since fallen from the rotten leather hinges and now lay on the ground outside. As they stepped over it and stooped at the low entrance they saw old Heidi, sitting cross-legged on the ground before a sinister huddling of brown rags and glistening whiteness. She did not look round as they entered, but merely continued to squat upon the earthen floor, smiling ironically to herself.

'You've led us a tiring chase, old woman,' Grim snarled, effectively concealing his relief at finding her.

He was about to add a string of oaths based on the innate lack of consideration she had displayed, when the breath caught in his throat. There was something unnatural, ungodly, about the rag-draped skeleton on the other side of the hut. For the most part it was a collapsed pile of bones wrapped in the tattered remains of a monk's robe. From his travels Grim knew it for the habit of one of those fanatical Irish Christian hermits, madmen who would journey to the ends of the earth in search of the solitude which would perfect their quested sanctity. Yet there was a wrongness about its attitude, a strangeness which raised questions within his suspicious pagan mind.

The hood had collapsed because there was no skull beneath it. The rest of the weathered white frame appeared intact, if fallen in, but the skull was missing. Yet that wasn't the only thing. Defying the laws of both gravity and natural decay the left arm and hand was extended, almost in a straight line. The bony framework, whitened and bare though it appeared, could still support the rotting fragments of habit draped about it. The hand, intact except for the bones of the thumb which had fallen away, was slightly cupped, as if it should have held something. And Heidi, opposite, was grinning contentedly and nursing a bundle of the same brown cloth, a bundle which was large enough to contain a fair-sized loaf, or a death's-head.

Suddenly the extended hand and arm dropped, collapsing into a jumble of shreds and bones which stirred the unhallowed dust from the floor of the hut. Grim jumped and cried out inarticulately. The tracker, outside the tiny structure, reached out and clapped a hand reassuringly upon his shoulder.

Old Heidi simply laughed. 'Tonight we rest here,' she ordered. 'In the morning we will start back.'

Grim swallowed hard. 'What's in the bundle, old woman?' he demanded. 'What are you nursing, there in your lap?'

Heidi turned her head to look at the Viking. Her eyes were fever-bright and shone with reflected light from the lamp at her feet. At least, they should have done. But the rays of the lamp, whilst they illuminated the side of her head and hair, could not reach into the hollows of her orbits. Yet the light was there, burning through the crepuscular darkness into Grim's eyes.

'Nothing that need concern you,' she replied with a smile. 'Merely the fragments of a faith we have forgotten.'

He turned his head away, unable to endure that forbidding light. Gardar would eventually return and they would journey back to Norway. Heidi would sit in the prow of her son's ship, holding her mysterious bundle all the way, singing and talking to it in a tongue which none of them knew. Eventually Floki Vilgerdarson, the one they called Raven Floki, would sail for and colonise Iceland, but Grim would not be with him. He would be at home, brooding darkly to himself, knowing that Heidi's bundle contained the skull of the nameless Irish hermit, and wondering what had lain in the palm of that outstretched, fleshless hand.

14 APRIL 939

Noon

Mordecai walked slowly down the valley, picking his way between the fallen rocks which had settled amongst the flattened grass and over the bodies of the fallen. All that mattered to him was that the trap had been baited, had been sprung, and had caught its prey in deadly, crushing jaws.

These had been the most powerful, the most vicious raiders he had ever encountered. Out and out pagans, they had seen in the holy objects nothing more than loot to be taken to assuage their greed. It was only right that the Lord had seen fit to grant him vengeance, that his plan for the deliverance of Christ's people had met with total success. It was unthinkable to Mordecai that it could have been otherwise, after all the planning and ingenuity which he had expended.

The one thing which saddened him was that the Holy Relic of St John which these heathens had taken during an earlier raid would never be returned. As their priest he was the only one who had opened the golden casket and examined its contents. The tiny bone fragment, allegedly dropped as a result of a careless swing by the executioner, was precious beyond gold. Whether it was real or not didn't matter. It needn't even have been human. All that was important was what it symbolised.

When Salome had danced her erotic, lustful gyrations before Herod, St John the Baptist had been alive. Only at the end, when legend proclaimed that the seventh veil had been removed and the shameless pagan harlot stood naked, the foul juices of her filthy exertions running down her unblushing flesh, had St John been decapitated at her request by an executioner who had witnessed her sexual gesturing. The man had trembled with the effects of his own barely-sublimated lust, and the first swing had failed to sever the saint's neck. A second blow had been needed, a blow which had completed the decapitation and left a splinter of holy bone upon the stone flags of the courtyard. That fragment, that Holy Relic, had been snatched up by one of the burgeoning faithful and preserved to become their own testimony to the Truth of Christ. To Mordecai it had looked suspiciously like an astragalus, the ankle-bone of a sheep, but he alone had seen it, and there was no reason to cloud the clear belief of his flock by a confession of his own misgivings.

And now the relic was gone, lost for ever because of the depredations of these pagan Vikings. They had pillaged and plundered this coast before, killing the men, laming the elderly with their hamstringing blades, and taking the women and children to Christ knows what sexual depravities and slavery across the grim, grey seas. Oh yes, Mordecai knew all about the Vikings. He knew of their savagery and moral laxity. He knew of their foul heathenism and worship of strange, degraded gods. And now he strode amongst the slain and the dying, listening to the dismal hymnody of their screaming where they lay amongst the rock-strewn grass of the valley.

He had plotted long and hard for this, motivating his people to carry the heavy rocks up the valley and pile them where they might be hurled upon the invaders. He had threatened and cajoled and begged for the gold which had been nailed onto the seaward door of the wooden church as a lure for the seaborn killers. He had known that, sooner or later, the sun would catch it as a longship passed, that the raiders would see it and mount an expedition to plunder the easy pickings of the Christians. And he had made them ready against that expedition; he had ensured that the invaders would meet death as their reward, the crushing, plummeting death of jagged, hurtling rocks as they advanced up the little valley.

And now it was over. The few survivors had fled back to their longships in chronic disarray. Word would spread throughout the north and it would be a long time before these godless pagans mounted another expedition against Mordecai's flock. They now knew them not as feeble victims, but as powerful and unremitting enemies and adversaries. It was a triumph for Mordecai, and for Christ. Primarily, though, it was a triumph for Mordecai the priest, a means by which his grip upon the faithful might be strengthened and extended.

Even in his planning he had been subtle. There could be no doubt that he was a perceptive, intelligent man. His people would be strengthened by the weapons they could take from the fallen Vikings; their faith would be heightened, which in turn meant a corresponding increase in his personal power, by their proud victory; and in addition he could realise a personal ambition.

Each time they had come the Vikings had burned the little wooden church in the valley. Each time they had departed the faithful had dug new foundations and rebuilt it. Now, with their faith renewed and the Lord their salvation, and the stones which they had cast down upon the pagans scattering the floor of the little valley, they could build an enduring church of stone as a thank-offering for their deliverance. A proper church, with only the roof of wood, and with a vault beneath in which the holy fragment of St John, if it was recovered, might be enshrined.

And that was where Mordecai's subtlety and plotting excelled itself. If they had never seen the Holy Relic they would not know that the item Mordecai was about to recover was not the original. Hidden beneath his robe as he picked his way amongst the fallen was a piece of bone. All he need do was take it out as he bent over a fallen Viking and announce that it was the original, returned to them by the power of Christ. It was that simple, that easy. It would strengthen their faith still further, giving them a reason to fight again if the need arose, and drawing yet more of the faithful to him, to Mordecai, the monk who would one day become the bishop of this part of Scotland. Maybe the relic was a lie, but it was at least a holy lie.

He paused as he reached the burning ruin of the wooden church. At his feet, crushed by a rock against the north wall, lay a fallen Norseman. He had no way of knowing that this blond warrior, his lines charred by the heat and studded with rock-splinters, who stared into the noonday sun through sightless eyes, was a descendant of that same Gardar Svarsson who had found Iceland from Naddodd's account. Nor was he to know that the object about the dead Viking's neck, the object which he now was about to claim as the Holy Relic of St John, abandoning the bone fragment hidden beneath his robe, had once lain in the outstretched, fleshless hand of an Irish monk. What it was he did not know, for there was a strangeness, an alien quality about it which he could never begin to understand. All he knew was that it would serve his purpose; it would play the part he had determined upon for it.

He tore it from the dead man's neck and held it up. 'See here,' he called to his flock, to those same Christians who were descending the valley, gutting those fallen foes who still retained some trace of life, stripping their armour and their ornaments. 'Here is the power of Christ!' Mordecai called. 'Here is the Holy Relic of St John returned to us!'

They flocked to him, eager to see the wondrous fragment, thrilled and delighted by this bonus in victory from their god. The righteous grinned and wiped the blood from their stolen blades. Then they clustered about him, pleading for a sight of the relic.

Their pleas were in vain. Perhaps none but he had seen the original, but Mordecai was taking no chances. It would remain hidden from the eyes of the profane, just in case one of them might know enough to call him a liar. After all, there was no reason why all his good work should be undone by some vague mischance, some know-it-all peasant who could sabotage his hopes for the future.

He was smiling to himself as he told them about his plans for a stone church. In the exultation of victory they listened gladly, gratefully, and committed themselves to the backbreaking work of constructing his visioned thank-offering.

And from the gold nailed to the door, the gold which had lured the Viking raiders to their timely and ultimate destruction, they fashioned a new reliquary, a new golden casket in which the sacred object might lie throughout eternity. They knew nothing of its origin, of its discovery by Heidi after a night of trance and visions, of its resting through the deserted years in the dead palm of a dead hermit, of the vanished, forgotten power it represented.

The land of Thule was a myth unknown to Mordecai's flock. It had been forgotten through the years by all but a handful of its hereditary servants. Those who knew the legend, those who might have told Mordecai what the relic really was, were hundreds of miles away, or dead beneath a rock against the northern wall of the smoking wooden church. And Mordecai himself, the future bishop, neither knew nor cared about the object which he had chosen as the Holy Relic of St John. All that mattered to him was doing his work, and Christ's, to the future glorification of them both.

Even if there had been one there to tell him of Thule, the monk's ears would have been closed against such blasphemies. And what did it really matter anyway? By the time the relic emerged from the obscurity and secrecy he was assigning it to, he would be, like his flock, nothing more than time-sharded fragments in a centuried grave, a forgotten page of history which had crumbled into legend in the turning.

3 AUGUST 1540

Shortly before dawn

The townspeople huddled in their beds. They had seen enough of the strange things which were happening in the Karlsburg's ruins. First that mad clockmaker, Ugo da Dondi, who claimed to be a Master of Time, had entered their community through the Stadt-tor Gate. Then he had begun to build some gigantic machine in the shattered castle which towered above them – only broken walls surrounding the main hall, and that one tower, still stand-ing. Little Heidi, the innkeeper's mad daughter, had spent so much time there with him that they had begun to wonder if he was forcing his unnatural attentions upon the child. One man had tried to sneak up to the Karlsburg to see, but the little things with the sharp teeth, the ones Heidi called Nachtmäuser, night-mice, had seen him.

Yes, it was mad. Yet it was not so insane as what was to come. Some had witnessed the arrival of the Prince-Bishop von Bamberg and his retinue. They had watched the ascent to the Karlsburg. Some had even been aware of the presence there of that Doktor van Meeres and the lady who called herself Baroness Fassenham, the widow of an English Lord, yet who spoke with a southern German accent.

And then, in the darkness of the night, they had heard that monstrous machine of wood start up. They had heard the slow, ponderous booming as its rhythm began to pound through the walls of the ruined castle and down into the streets of the town beneath. It was a rhythm like nothing they had ever heard before, a rhythm which, whilst it might have been the work of some human drummer, carried with it an intimation that something sinister, something which contravened both the laws and the intentions of nature, was to result from its obscene sounding in their darkness.

And now, from those final, frightful sounds, they knew what that something, or at least a part of it, had been. When the morning came and they dared to venture out once more, they would find their priest, his clothing in unholy tatters, gibbering about those luminous, blood-red globes which had hung above the ruins in the night, those globes which had persisted until the blue light came from the north to drive them back to whatever hell they had emerged from. For now, though, there was only the illusory safety of their beds and the thunderous crashing which signified that the remaining fragments of the Karlsburg had shivered and collapsed still further as the massive machinery they housed had erupted beneath the influence of some unknown and unknowable power.

The few who had ventured to glance from their windows, to see the collapse and the blue fire in the sky for themselves, had drawn back shuddering and returned to the haven which sleep might yet promise. There they had sweated out their nightmares, shivering, bathed in the cold sweat of panic fear, awaiting the sanctity which daylight might offer them, if only they could stay alive that long.

Yet the collapse, the bright, wickedly-luminous globes and the fires in the sky, had been shortly after midnight. With the coming of dawn, with the coming of a new and more terrible day than the citizens of Karlstadt had seen for any length of time both within and beyond the memory of any still living, there would be the dead to find and the missing to search for. Little Heidi was gone from their midst. They would never find her body nor understand how its disappearance had come about. And the others . . .

They would explore, of course. It was impossible to view the sharded wreckage of that most incredible and monstrous machine without wanting to explore it, if even only out of curiosity. But there was a great deal that would need explanations they were unable to offer. What those others, the soldiers and followers of the Prince-Bishop's train, were doing, strewn amongst the rubble like so many fire-stained dolls, would remain a mystery. And they would never find any of the night-mice. They were gone, for ever, the living carrying away the dead in the names of both order and secrecy.

Beneath the rubble of the ruins, where the dust still rose in mote-streams upon the air-currents, beneath the fragmented oak beams which had held the massive cogs of the device, which had never quite been an enormous wooden clock, in position, there was still life in those moments before the safety of the dawn. A small, dark, foreign figure, its robes in shreds, hauled itself from the material chaos and began to call out for the one it loved.

'Erzebet!' it called. 'Erzebet, are you there? Are you alive?'

Amsegi waited as his voice echoed back to him from what

remained of the broken walls of the Karlsburg. Here and there a part of the machinery creaked as it settled beneath the weight of rubble pressing down upon it. A groan reached the small man's ears and he clambered towards it, his hands cut and splintered as he sought for the one whose life he wanted to preserve. He found one of the Prince-Bishop's guards, his chest a bloody ruin, impaled.

He discovered the remains of the Prince-Bishop Franz-Alberich Carolus von Bamberg, Erzebet's cousin and enemy, fearsomely transformed by the scourge the prelate had sought to unleash upon mankind, a scourge thwarted by the destruction of Ugo da Dondi's huge machine. Da Dondi was also there, his body as shattered and broken as the framework of his creation.

'Erzebet, can you hear me?'

Another groan, lighter in tone than the one he had heard before. Amsegi made his way towards the sound, towards the life which clung there, desperate and transformed though it might be.

'Are you here, Erzebet? Here?'

He began to dig with his tortured hands, to lift the heavy blocks of stone and seek the love which lay buried, yet still alive, beneath it. Working with what haste he could muster, though it felt incredibly slow and painful because of his own injuries, he delved deeper towards the sound buried beneath him. If she groaned, she still lived. And if she lived she might be saved, restored to him. There were still frightened horses, tethered outside the ruin, upon which they might make their escape. There was still, for a little while longer, the darkness which might cloak that escape and hide it from the eyes of any who might be watching.

As the pain in his fingertips became unendurable, Amsegi broke through to the cavity which, miraculously, had formed in the rubble above the one he sought. His eyes strained in the darkness, eventually making out the beautiful, grimed features of Lady Erzebet Fassenham.

'Are you hurt?' he called down to her.

'My shoulder,' she moaned in reply. 'I think it's out of its setting. I can't use my left arm.'

'Then give me your right hand. I'll pull you up.'

Her hand reached out to him from the cavity. Before he took it he pulled a further block away, enlarging the aperture, making her ascent easier. Then he took her wrist and began to pull.

Erzebet screamed as the muscles about her good shoulder began to wrench.

'Find something to climb on,' Amsegi instructed, releasing his grip as she cried out. 'There must be something down there.'

He heard the sound of scrabblings beneath him and the laboured grunts of his beloved's painful breathing. She had to live. He must rescue her, because of what she meant to him. She might be treacherous, already a murderess many times over, but Erzebet was the ultimate woman in Amsegi's dark eyes, the epitome and triumph of her sex. Yes, she would probably betray him in their future together, but there would be some time before that happened, and that was enough for the one who would haul her from the ruins of the Karlsburg and give her life again.

'Here!' she called, her dirty, clawed hand stretching up through the hole Amsegi had torn. 'I'm ready. Take my hand.'

He reached down and grasped her wrist again. As he pulled he felt her easing the strain beneath him, finding some way of raising her body as he slowly drew her out of the underground prison which the ruins had built about her. Her dress was torn and stained and her knee showed through its once rich fabric as she knelt before him, all but one leg now out of her confinement.

She emerged in her tattered beauty and stood before him, shaking her tresses to clear the stone-chips and splinters from them. Her hair was the red they had begun to call Titian and her young eyes, bright with hidden fires, brown as a gypsy's, shone with desire despite her pain.

Ah, Amsegi thought, but it is impossible to look upon you without loving you, Erzebet. And to have saved you will at least have made you grateful.

Her left arm hung uselessly at her side, but her smile ignored the pain. 'My cousin?' she demanded, her voice as haughty now in the ruins as ever it had been in hall or palace.

'Over there,' Amsegi gestured. 'Dead and rotten.'

'Then that is just as well,' Erzebet von Bamberg smiled at her rescuer. 'And Johannes?'

The little man felt his brows furrow. 'Johannes?' he demanded. 'Oh, you mean the one who once was Faustus? The one the Prince-Bishop called von Meersburg, the man who called himself Doktor van Meeres?'

Erzebet's smile became patronising. 'Forget his names, Amsegi,' she commanded. 'Is his body here?'

The small man shook his head. 'I've found no sign of it,' he replied.

'Then he's still alive,' Erzebet told him. 'I shall not believe him dead unless I see his body at my feet.'

'Do you want me to search some more?'

She shook her lovely head again. 'Those dead that are here can keep their own secrets,' she replied. 'Ptythonius lives on. He's not here. I know that.'

'Then, what do we do? We should be going, Erzebet.'

Her eyes flamed brightly as he spoke her name, then grew cold. After all, he had saved her life more than once. It was only right to allow him some small liberties, and her body was only one of those. Yet this time she felt that there was something different, something which had altered and left her other than what she had been. It was a sensation which had stolen upon her as da Dondi's equipment had begun its rhythm, that rhythm which had begun to summon the one known as Pudendagora, the one her cousin had desired to meet . . .

'Where's da Dondi?' she enquired, her voice as imperious as ever Amsegi had heard it.

'Over there,' he gestured.

'And his documents?'

Amsegi shrugged. 'In his pouch, I assume.'

'Don't assume,' Erzebet snapped. 'Find the pouch and examine it. I know what went wrong. It may be decades before we can try again, but I have to make the attempt. And for that I need the plans.'

The little man's dark eyes widened. 'To summon Pudendagora?' he asked her.

Erzebet's smile was disquieting. 'Find the plans, Amsegi,' she instructed him.

20 SEPTEMBER 1540

Late afternoon

They were nearly there. The carriage had rattled and jolted beneath Erzebet for an almost interminable period, but now the gates of Miltenberg, a small town on a bend of the Main between Freudenberg and Klein-heubach, lay before them. Above the gates the sun shone from roofs moistened by the early autumn rain which glistened red like the last rays of a summer sunset.

Amsegi turned upon his seat and peered from the carriage's glassless window, then turned to face the woman whom he had loved both too long and too well. Somehow, from the ruins of the Karlsburg, she had progressed back to wealth and status in a new identity, doubtless drawing upon that ancient, entrancing power which her looks bestowed upon her, and upon that other, less understood ability which had come to her with the first beats of da Dondi's demoniac machine. Her hair framed a face which, despite his store of arcane and forbidden knowledge, and his first-hand experience of her nature, Amsegi might once have regarded as angelic. Essentially feminine, oval in shape and pale in complexion, with a straight nose which somehow was just the right length, it was also strong with a strength that many men might have envied. The eyes, dark and lovely, were alive with her ambitions and desires, burning with the dark fire which both fuelled and consumed her.

Outside the carriage the air itself was noisy with the rattling of harness and the drumming of the horses' hoofs, a drumming both so similar and so different to that which had beaten out its tattoo in the ruins of the Karlsburg to alter their lives and purposes for ever. Inside the thin, dark figure of Amsegi watched Erzebet's eyes flicker closed momentarily. The tired falling of her gold-lashed lids extinguished their burning intensity for a second or so. He thought back over the few brief months they had been together, months replete with plot and counter-plot, with alliance and betrayal. That she was a dangerous woman, perhaps the most dangerous woman he had ever known, he could not dispute. Yet he loved her passionately. For her sake he had betrayed his master, the Prince-Bishop. For her love he would do much, much more. And he was going to. He knew that, if he knew nothing else. Yet inevitably, in the end, she would betray him as well. She had to, in order to follow her destiny. And, in his way, Amsegi was content simply to know his fate.

'Is the mark upon me yet, Amsegi?'

His shifting, drifting thoughts returned at the sound of her voice. It was a question she had begun to ask since their experience at Karlstadt, yet he was unclear as to its meaning. Erzebet somehow never quite managed to explain the significance of her enquiry, and Amsegi, already more than a little afraid of his strange, enchanting, dangerous lover, didn't pry into her words more than affection might require him to.

'I see no mark, Lady Erzebet,' he replied. Not that hasn't always been there, he added inwardly. Amsegi had read and practised much of the dark lore of sorcery. He knew things which, ultimately, derived from pre-human sources and others which no human mind ought ever to have conceived. But in learning he was only, he acknowledged, a beginner. He could not begin to understand the plans which he had taken from Ugo da Dondi's body, plans which had enabled the Italian to construct the fearsome mechanical device which the Prince-Bishop had sought to use for Pudendagora's invocation. Erzebet understood them, though. She had pored over them in tavern rooms by the light of soot-grimed lamps. She had studied the notes and drawings by the uncertain flames of guttering candles as they passed upon their interminable quest.

The quest, Amsegi conceded, only seemed interminable. That it had an end, an object, he couldn't doubt. His companion told him nothing, though, as to what it might be. And so he travelled with her, as lover and accomplice, anticipating that day which would bestow upon him that same ingress to her mind as he enjoyed to her body.

Behind the jolting carriage rumbled a cart bearing their luggage and those books and papers which Erzebet regarded now as indispensable to her studies. Many of these had been stolen in the preceding weeks from her cousin's library at the episcopal palace in Bamberg. Others had been purchased at great expense, without haggling, using funds drawn from a reserve accessed by a letter of credit, its terms valid despite the fictitious name of the drawer, which had bought the carriage, the cart, the horses and the eight liveried mercenary guards as well.

Outside the gates of Miltenberg, nestled in the false protection of the shadow of the town walls, huddled the huts of the poorer workers and craftsmen which had been drawn to the town to find work. Here and there a goat munched along the range of its tether at the sparser grass of autumn. Ragged children played. Wagons in various stages of disrepair revealed the presence of a few wandering gypsies, either there to be hired for the harvest or more than a week early with their catch-pfennig acts for *Michaelitag*, the feast day of St Michael, Patron Saint of the German States, on the 29th. Cooking fires for the evening meal were already alight, their contents steaming their aroma into the afternoon air.

As they drew closer to the gates Erzebet ordered the carriage to be stopped. 'These were Faust's people once,' she told Amsegi. 'Now, I think, they shall be mine.'

Amsegi said nothing. He felt his brows begin to frown slightly as Erzebet continued: 'There was a troupe of *jongleurs* at Freiburg, when I went there to examine Faust's grave. They had such animals, you know. Thirteen dancing monkeys ... or were there twelve? Dancing bears. All manner of creatures. And freaks, Amsegi. They had freaks. There was one I ... saw ... a man, over six feet tall and completely naked. He held something in his arms which at first I took to be a child. But it wasn't, Amsegi. It was another body, headless, growing out of his own. Yet they had quite separate needs, you know.'

She called across to some of the gypsy folk. 'You there, send me your leader.' Turning back to her companion she asked: 'Where are we to go from here? You asked me that once, Amsegi. Now I can tell you. Into the earth, and across the face of the earth.'

She returned her gaze to the people outside the carriage, leaving Amsegi to ponder helplessly upon this latest riddle of their existence. A dark-haired man with curled moustachios and a spade beard was approaching her cortège.

'You are their leader?' Erzebet demanded.

'I am, lady,' came the gruff reply.

'Your name?'

'Ferencz of Bistritz.'

Erzebet nodded. 'Well, Ferencz Bistritz, you have a sad troupe there. A poor troupe, I suspect. Do you have freaks?'

A small crowd began to gather around Ferencz in a semi-circle.

The gypsy scowled and pulled at the tip of a moustache. 'Some,' he muttered.

'I understand your caution, Ferencz,' Erzebet continued. 'Doubtless you're wondering why this gorgio woman wants to know. I have a great deal of money my friend. Certainly enough to transform your little show into the most amazing spectacle in Europe.'

'And why would you want to do that, Lady?'

'I am the Baronne Jeannine Fouriac de Taille-sur-Marne, Ferencz. Do not let the appearance of my cortège deceive you, as I shall not let the dishevelled appearance of your companions deceive me. I have money. You have something more valuable than money. You have the promise of better things to come. You play for pfennigs to the crowd, when you could play for florins before the nobility of the German States. With my help, that is.'

Ferencz scowled at her words, but his dark eyes were greedy. 'Why should you help us to become so great?' he demanded.

'I have reasons. Let it suffice if I say that the money I invest in you will be doubled within three years. Is that the kind of gorgio logic you can believe?'

The gypsy pursed his lips. 'I shall have to consult my people,' he answered shrugging.

'Then do so. I shall be in Miltenberg one hour. When I drive back through these gates I shall expect your answer.' Then: 'Drive on,' she ordered the coachman, drawing her head back into the carriage and dropping the blind on the glassless window.

Amsegi searched her eyes with his own. 'I don't understand you,' he began. 'Why do we need these people? They're riff-raff, scum. How can they possibly be of service?'

'I have my reasons,' Erzebet smiled, 'as I told them. And they will become rich and successful, Amsegi. You can be certain of that, at least.'

The carriage, with its escort and following cart, passed through the main gate and followed the slope of the now-cobbled roadway up towards the market square, a well at its centre, and the castle above. Low, timbered houses leaned down upon them from overhead, their steeply-pitched roofs throwing long, strange shadows in the late afternoon sun. The carriage wheels straddled the central kennel with its rivulets of filth and floating lumps of offal, souring the air in the narrow streets with its stench. At the Rathaus on the market square they paused long enough for the coachman to ask for directions to their destination. Then the cortège continued once more, turning off into a narrow lane with wooden-shuttered shop-fronts between the residential houses. Here the mounted escort was unable to ride alongside the horse-drawn vehicles, so it rode between them instead.

They stopped outside a wide-fronted house towards the further end of the lane. As one of the mercenaries opened the carriage-door and set a short flight of wooden steps beneath it for Erzebet to descend, she turned to Amsegi once more.

'You are certain?' she questioned. 'This man has it?'

Amsegi smiled and nodded. Erzebet was going to be so grateful for this. 'He has it,' he replied. 'And we already have everything else that we require.'

Erzebet's acknowledging smile was tender and gentle. Amsegi felt himself begin to warm in anticipation of the reward to come for his service. He closed his eyes, savouring the promise of the moment as Erzebet stepped down into the lane.

They never reopened. The nearest of the mercenary guards, previously briefed by Erzebet, leaned through the carriage window and skewered Amsegi where he sat. Another rapped sharply upon the door of the house before which they had stopped. Muffled foot-steps, gradually becoming louder, sounded on the tiled floor of the hall within. They heard the scrape of a bolt being drawn back and, finally, a cautious servant opened the heavy oak door and peered around it.

Erzebet smiled enchantingly at the man. *'Herr Doktor Hassen, bitte?'* she asked.

The door opened wider to admit her. A mercenary entered first, placing an arm about the servant's shoulders and driving a poniard up beneath his rib-cage to the heart. Then he lowered the corpse silently to the floor and beckoned for the others to enter.

Erzebet von Bamberg stepped inside, the tapestried fabric of her dress rustling slightly. Her eyes swept about the linen-fold panel-ling of the hall, noting the staircase off to one side and the three doors which led into various downstairs rooms. It was from the centre doorway, the carved portal slightly ajar, that the voice of an elderly, educated man called: 'Who's there, Ernst? Someone for me?'

With a guard to either side of her, Erzebet entered the room which was Edvard Hassen's study and laboratory. Behind her the other mercenaries were lifting Amsegi's body from the carriage and placing it beside that of the murdered servant. Then they began to unload some barrels which had been stowed at the back of the cart and carry them into the house.

Hassen looked up as his visitors approached. His eyes gleamed in the shadow of his face, sitting as he was against a low window which gave out onto a sunlit herb-garden outside. He spread broad, wrinkled hands upon the chart- and volume-littered table before him and rose to his feet in a gesture of courtesy.

'Ernst didn't hear you,' Erzebet answered, noting the tall, gaunt frame of the Doktor, a frame which reminded her of another man in another place. 'Do you know me, Doktor Hassen?'

The guards closed the door behind her, shutting out all sight of the bodies and preparations in the hall beyond. They stood to either side of it, their weapons sheathed but their attitudes those of men prepared to act quickly and decisively. Hassen moved aside from the window, permitting its light to fall upon Erzebet's features. 'You are a lovely woman, madam,' he remarked, feeling the penetrating gaze of her eyes returning his own. 'But I do not think I know you. May I have the honour of your name?'

'I am the Landgravine Erzebet von Bamberg,' came the reply. 'You have something for me, I believe?'

That part of Hassen's face which was in the light drained of colour. 'I fear I have misheard you,' he began. 'The name I thought you gave is that of a lady who died at Meersburg some time ago . . .'

'You did not mishear me, Doktor. I am Erzebet von Bamberg and, as you see, there is a little life still left in me. And even more in these,' she added, gesturing towards the waiting mercenaries. 'Now, Amsegi arranged a transaction which I am here to complete. Is the object safe and ready for me?'

Doktor Hassen swallowed hard, then bowed stiffly and began to cross the low-ceilinged room. One wall was shelved with manuscripts and incunabula jostling for space against chemical and alchemical apparatus. Various dried specimens hung from the beams, brushing the old man's hair as he moved beneath them. The wall on the other side of the windows bore an enormous open hearth and chimney-breast with more shelves to either side. Upon one of these, shining like dull ivory in the afternoon light, were ranged the domed crania of more than a dozen skulls.

Hassen reached up and selected one of the skulls, obviously both human and very ancient. He turned to Erzebet, his colour partly restored and a forced smile upon his thin, bloodless lips.

'That is the one, Doktor?'

He nodded. 'This is the one Amsegi wanted.'

'There is no possibility of a mistake?'

Hassen shook his head and began to count along the shelf. 'Woman, aged 80, from Schweinfurt. Young boy. Great African Ape. Man aged 93 from Frickenhausen. Fifth along, male, origin and age unknown, properties . . .'

'Let me see it.'

He handed her the skull. Her fingers hooked into one of the empty orbits and she swung it towards her with an action reminiscent of a peasant with a stone jug of cheap ale. Then, holding it by its temples, she stared into the vacant, timeless eye-sockets. As she gazed she began to hear the whispers beginning inside her own skull, and the tiny figure of an obsidian monkey, one hand raised in benediction, the other grasping its tumescent penis in an unmistakable attitude of masturbation, leered out at her from the depths of the hollow cranium.

Hassen gasped. Erzebet averted her eyes from the skull and the whispering stopped. She glared at Hassen.

'Can you not be quiet, Herr Doktor?' she snapped.

'I . . . I thought I saw . . .'

'Yes?'

'On your shoulder . . . a tiny black monkey. A trick of the light, doubtless.'

Or the mark, Doktor Hassen. Perhaps you have seen what my poor Amsegi never will, now. Perhaps you have seen the mark of Thule.

'The skull,' she said curtly. 'This is the one.' She turned to the mercenaries by the door. 'Pay Doktor Hassen,' she ordered coldly.

They paid him, feeding their weapons upon his blood. As Erzebet re-entered the carriage and began to ride away, clutching the skull in her lap, one of the guards lit the slow fuse which would eventually set the house and the bodies it contained alight.

They left Miltenberg, pausing briefly outside the gates to receive an answer from Ferencz Bistritz. It was the answer Erzebet expected.

Only much later, after they were long upon the road, after the fires had died down in that gutted quarter of the little German town, did the blue light come from the north and hover in the sky above the last charred mortal remains of the late Doktor Edvard

Hassen. The townspeople shook their tired heads in bewilderment. Comets usually presaged disaster, but this one had come afterwards. Besides, it didn't really look like any comet that they'd ever seen before.

11 JUNE 1732

Towards noon

'It would be in your interest to speak with me, Mr Harrison.'

He turned to face the intruder, the dark-clad, middle-aged woman who stood so resolutely in his hall for all that Reuben had tried to get rid of her, to keep his master's time as sacrosanct as Harrison wished it to remain. The rest of the family, including his brother James, were at church, and it was during this quiet time that John Harrison wrestled with both the logistics and finances of his project.

'What do you require of me, madam?' he demanded.

Her shoulders rose in a shrug. 'A few minutes of your time, to begin with. Say, five minutes, at the most, by whatever timepiece you decide to measure it. If you find that what I have to say merits more, then you will, I know, decide accordingly.'

John Harrison, thirty-nine, his hair already grey and half-moon pince-nez perched precariously on his strong nose, squinted to keep his visitor in focus. Middle-aged, had he thought? Perhaps she was younger, though her hair, beneath the hat and veil, wisped out as what he thought was white. The broken weave of the veil disturbed her features, making them seem blotchy and irregular, but her figure was trim enough, though with who knew what aid from any amount of whalebone.

'Very well. Five minutes. In here, if you please.'

He held open the door of his study whilst Reuben escorted the lady inside. The room was a litter of books and sheets of diagrams, rolled, folded and spread across the surface of the one enormous table which occupied its centre. Various models of chronological contraptions, some finished, some only recently begun, stood upon the shelves where books had been swept from their surfaces onto the floor. A bench, similar to a jeweller's, littered with glistening yellow filings that were actually only brass, scattered with arbors and cog-wheels and parts of devious and complex escapements, stood in one corner beneath a small, high window. The main window had an equally cluttered desk beneath it, before which stood a chair appearing too frail in construction to hold Harrison's bulk, although it did so quite competently. The only other chair had its contents swept onto the floor and kicked aside by the chronologist to make room for the woman to perch. For five minutes only.

She sat down and Reuben left them. 'Now, madam,' Harrison began brusquely, 'what can I do for you?'

'Rather you should ask what I can do for you, Mr Harrison,' came the reply.

He felt a growl rising in his throat and, though he was not feeling polite enough to offer his visitor any refreshment as she would not be staying that long, he was mannerly enough to disguise it with a cough.

'Riddles are for children and historians, madam. You have a little over four minutes left. Will you come to the point?'

'As you will. Let me begin by telling you about yourself, Mr Harrison. You are a clockmaker, of sorts. You originally trained as a carpenter and that training has stood you in good stead. As an example I might mention that you are conversant with the effects of friction and have employed lignum vitae in your wooden movements to overcome its effects . . .'

'Indeed. It is regarded as self-lubricating . . .'

'I am aware of that, Mr Harrison.'

'Are you, begad?'

'Mr Harrison, you are the one who has imposed the limit upon my time. I will thank you either to extend it or to leave off your interruptions.'

The chronologist coloured and mentally prepared an oath, though it remained unspoken. Instead he replied: 'Forgive me, madam. Three minutes, uninterrupted, I promise you, remain.'

'Then I shall use them to mention your current project, sir. Together with your brother James you are endeavouring to create the first entirely accurate marine chronometer. By its very nature you are unable to work in wood and must turn to metallic materials. This requires capital, which you are endeavouring to raise.'

She paused, staring at her unwilling host through the veil, her gloved fingers taut about the ends of the document case she held upon her lap. 'You have seen Doctor Halley, the Astronomer Royal, who referred you to George Graham of the Royal Society. Help has been promised from the Board of Longitude, if your work turns out well, but meanwhile you have a loan from Mr Graham's own pocket to help you, and the promise of further funds from the East India Company. You presently require hard cash, Mr Harrison, and hard cash to continue your work is what I am here to offer you, despite your rudeness.'

Harrison turned from his guest and stared at the drive outside the house. He rubbed his clean-shaven chin as he began his reply. 'You know a great deal about my work and my finances, madam,' he said. 'How, I shall not ask. I will simply assume that you are well-connected and have employed those connections to make enquiries. What I shall do, however, is to use an expression that our neighbours, over the county boundary in Yorkshire, would consider to be appropriate. They say that you get owt for nowt, madam. Might I venture to enquire the owt that you would require of me before we discuss the extent of your proposed funding?'

'Hardly, sir, in the thirty seconds which still remain to me.'

He waved a hand dismissively. 'Hang the time,' he snapped, turning back to face her. 'What d'ye want of me?'

She opened the document case and withdrew a set of carefully drawn and folded plans on thin paper. 'Will you examine these?' she asked, handing them to him.

Harrison spread them across the cluttered surface of the table and began to trace the outlines with his fingers. Once or twice he looked over at his visitor, before returning to his examination. The three working clocks in the room, one of them a long-case made by his brother James, which incorporated Harrison's two famous innovations, the grasshopper escapement and the so-called gridiron compensated pendulum, ticked noisily on through the intervening silence.

At length he left the plans and turned the chair at the desk to face the woman who was offering him the finance he required to complete his masterwork. He sat down, stretching his legs before him, his fingers steepled in front of his face and his elbows upon the chair's slender arms.

'It's not a clock,' he ventured. 'There is mechanism to create rhythmic movement and an escapement, albeit verge and foliot-derived, to control its speed. But what is it?'

'That's my business, Mr Harrison. Can you build it?'

'One of my apprentices could build it.'

'Your brother James, perhaps, but no apprentices, Mr

Harrison. I shall not be paying you for apprentice labour.'

'Out of interest, then, might I ask what you are prepared to pay for its construction?'

'As you will have noticed,' came the reply, 'I have a carriage waiting outside. It contains a strongbox which holds five thousand pounds sterling in gold coin. That is your fee, sir.'

The steepled fingers fell away from the chronologist's features in shocked surprise. In later years the Board of Longitude would offer Harrison a paltry £500 to build an improved version of the proto-type, and then insist that it be handed to the nation as it had been financed with public money. This woman in the veil was offering enough to repay Graham, complete the work and re-equip his workshops completely, not to mention refurbishing the family's wardrobes and restocking the depleted cellar.

He paused whilst he composed himself. Finally he said: 'That is a staggering sum, madam, and doubtless far more than the actual cost of labour and materials for a half-dozen such projects.'

His visitor smiled beneath her veil. 'Think of it simply as an inducement to complete it quickly and accurately. You will have noticed the scale of the finished mechanism from the plans, and also that it must be capable of being dismantled, placed into storage and then reassembled. I am aware that this is all extra work and, that too, is reflected in my offer. Now, will you do it?'

'Indeed I shall,' Harrison replied.

There would be plenty of time later to discover the true purpose of the mechanism. During the work the plans could be copied and the copy retained until a duplicate, albeit smaller, was constructed. Yet how could this massive machine, with its outdated verge and foliot escapement, serve any purpose? And why did it have to be so large?

'Then I have taken up enough of your time,' the lady replied, standing. 'My coachman will bring in your fee and then I shall be upon my way.'

Harrison stood up, his eyes seeking to penetrate the veil to her face beneath. 'Two things before you go,' he began. 'The first is that I do not know your name . . .'

'I am the Baronne Jeannine Fouriac de Taille-sur-Marne,' she replied. 'And the second thing?'

A French name, the chronologist thought. French and aristocratic. Yet her English is virtually perfect, as if she had lived here all her life, however long that is. And the lesser French aristocrats I've met don't have the kind of money she's spending on this venture, not for things like this.

'I must be going, Mr Harrison. The second thing?'

'How . . . shall I get in touch with you?'

'You will not need to. I shall know when the work is finished and return to inspect and collect it.'

'It will take several months, Baronne.'

'That is your concern, Mr Harrison. I have a great deal more time than you do.'

He stood aside to permit her to pass as she walked out of his study. She seemed, to Harrison, younger and more interesting than when she had entered. He caught a glimpse of her profile through the veil and decided that she was, in all probability, a fine looking woman. As to her origins and present residence, well, the amount she was paying him entitled her to conceal whatever she wished, though he believed it impossible that the nature of the machinery would remain unknown.

But it did. When the great chronologist died in 1776, at the age of eighty-three, the secret of the mechanism was still unknown to him. Nor did his son William find any trace of either the duplicate plans or a model of the machinery amongst his father's effects.

3 AUGUST 1871

Shortly after dawn

It was intolerable that they hadn't told her what it was all about. For nearly an hour now the strangers had come and gone, rapping at the big door with the large glass panels, gaining admittance and being shown into the large drawing-room beyond the double, sliding doors. Yet Ilsa didn't need to be told. It was obvious from her mother's weeping and her father's absence that something had happened to that huge, friendly, warm man in the heavy tweed suits.

A girl of thirteen is a wiser, more inquisitive creature than most parents are prepared to suppose, and Ilsa was more inquisitive than most. There had been plenty of opportunity for practice in her short life, especially in the year since they had fled Tubingen with precipitate haste and wandered Europe. Just under a month ago, early in July, they had reached a Paris still reeling from the effects of the commune and taken a lease of this suburban villa near the Père Lachaise cemetery. Since their arrival Ilsa had been given plenty of time to sit and reflect on their wandering.

Something told her that it wasn't over yet. Her father's face, seamed and tired beneath the greying beard and moustache, displayed its own tale of hardship and suffering. They weren't short of money, for he had been secretly planning their escape from his mysterious work in Tubingen for some time, quietly converting their assets into negotiable bonds. Her mother, loyal and devoted, told the girl nothing, devoting most of her time to supporting and comforting the man she loved. Even so, Ilsa had heard them whispering. She had caught snatches of the terrible things her father had confided in the dark hours, when none could see and only the hidden daughter could hear, besides the ghosts of their consuming fear.

She had known that the chase was on again. Their servants were packing again, replacing those few items which had been taken during the month from the large wooden cases they now lived from on a semi-permanent basis. For two days the preparations had been going on, whilst her exhausted, dispirited father booked passage for them to England and arranged transport for his family and possessions to Boulogne. Today was the day that they should have left, but Ilsa knew without being told that they would not be going now. She also knew without being told that she would never see that big, loving man with the greying beard alive again.

Grief had not yet laid its constricting hand upon her heart, so she could still watch and listen. She had been watching and listening the night before, when they had come for him. There had never been a time when she could remember seeing him look so defeated, and that was the image her destiny demanded that she carry through the years. The happy times, the days when he was a brilliant professor of organic chemistry, fêted at Heidelberg University, would never return. They were gone with his body and his love.

The knock had sounded in the same way as many others. When the maid opened the door she had bitten her lip in shocked surprise. Ilsa vividly recalled the thin trickle of blood staining the woman's chin as she showed the master's repulsive guests into the drawing-room to wait. Watching was now a compulsion of Ilsa's, and from the shadows she had viewed the two monsters with a stifled alarm uniquely her own. The short one was only about four feet tall, and would have seemed a child but for the heavy growth of blackish beard on its elongated chin. The taller one had a hunched back, and its coat was tailored to disguise the bulging, irregular growth which forced its head over to one side. It was bigger than the usual hump, and extended across the left shoulder into a monstrous thickening of the neck.

She was unable to witness the actual moment when her father saw them for the first time, though she heard his muted expression of alarm and despair. What he could have to do with such creatures was beyond her power to imagine, but there had been so many strange happenings since their move from Heidelberg to Tubingen, and her father's research for the beautiful, ice-cold woman wrapped in furs.

Ilsa had seen the woman only three times. The first had been after their arrival in Tubingen, when the dark beauty had called to welcome them. Despite her pale complexion, a paleness which the girl thought belonged more to a red-haired lady than to one who was dark-haired and allegedly Spanish, she was introduced as Dona Juanita Ferrano, and the well-mannered Ilsa curtsied politely through her instant dislike. The dwarf had attended her then, as he came to her father now, but not the hunchback. Perhaps his talents were less courtly, the girl frowned to herself.

The second time Dona Juanita had visited them was shortly before their flight. On that occasion her mask of polite indifference, so firmly in place during her previous visit, had slipped away, revealing a temper sufficiently fiery to authenticate her Spanish origins. Ilsa's father had flinched before her venomous torrent of abuse, and was visibly shaken when she departed, still casting curses over her fur-clad shoulder.

The third time was three days before, when Ilsa had looked from a window of their new home and seen the pale, deadly creature staring from a carriage window. The lady was smiling that time, but the smile was such as the thirteen-year-old girl hoped never to see again, painted by malice and a suggestion of something worse.

The hunchback and the dwarf said little. Their suggestion that her father accompany them into the night was reinforced by a threat of weapons concealed beneath their outer clothing. For a moment her father's eyes had blazed with anger and defiance, but then the expression faded, and he asked: 'And my family? What does Dona Juanita plan for them?'

'They are of no interest,' the hunchback replied. There was an odd quality about his voice, almost as if it carried its own echo. 'You are the one who has offended the Dona. In many ways she is grateful to your wife and daughter. Had it not been for them, for your concern and determination not to abandon them, you might have escaped her. As it is, Herr Professor, they have slowed you down and placed you once again within her reach. They will not be harmed, other than by your absence.'

Ilsa's father nodded, defeatedly, but with a hint of gratitude lingering in his expression. Then he preceded them into the hall and took his cape from a closet. The maid moved forward to help him on with the bulky garment, but he waved her back with a dignity that was somehow sadly out of place.

'You will tell Madame that I have gone out with these gentlemen,' he said quietly. 'She is not to be alarmed, Félice. Is that clear?'

The maid curtsied and withdrew. Ilsa wanted to rush forward, to throw her arms about her father and plead with him not to go, but as she was summoning her courage to approach the two monsters something happened which kept her in concealment, biting her whitened knuckles to the bone to check her scream. As the hunchback held open the door a button dropped from his coat, permitting it to open about the growth on his neck.

'Shall we be on our way, Herr Professor?' he asked in his curious double voice.

Now Ilsa knew why he sounded like that. His face, for all it was tilted over to the side, was quite handsome. But the same could not be said for the secondary face which projected from his neck. Its glaring eyes were open, sightless. The nose was little more than a shapeless lump, and gave no signs of breathing, no expansion or contraction of the deformed nostrils. But the second mouth, situated just before the abnormality vanished chinlessly into the hunchback's shoulder, was perfectly formed and complete with tongue and teeth, and its movements exactly duplicated those of the upper mouth on the hunchback's true face.

Only when the door had closed and her father was gone for ever did Ilsa give way to her fear and terror. She slid down the wall she had been pressing herself against, her arms folded across her churning stomach. Silent tears slid down her face from her large, green eyes. They clutched at the tangle of yellow-gold hair that framed her young loveliness, trapping stray wisps and darkening them where they stuck to her skin.

And then the memory of the hunchback's unholy growth began to fade, though its diminution brought Ilsa no comfort. Instead it was replaced by the image of another face, cold and pale, and laughing before her inner vision as she had never seen it laugh before. Yet even in the laughter's blend of cruelty and pleasure there was another quality, harder to define for a girl of thirteen, a centuried boredom, wearied beyond the confines of mere, comprehensible ennui.

Perhaps Ilsa fainted then. She had no recollection of how she came to be in her bed, awake, listening to the urgent knocking on the large, glass-panelled door downstairs, her unfocused eyes barely aware of the orange dawn filtering through the room's drawn curtains. For a while she didn't even strain to hear the muted voices. Full wakefulness only returned with her mother's strangled cry of grief.

The few servants were too busy or too shocked to notice her as she took up her position behind the sliding doors and listened. Through a crack she watched her mother, leaning heavily on Félice, move slowly from the drawing room towards the stairs. Her mother would remain sedated for the next two days but Ilsa, younger and more robust, was to cry out her grief that morning, was to cry out her grief and go beyond the agony of her father's murder into an emotion which Dona Juanita understood only too well.

The gendarmes remained in the house for quite some time, discussing between themselves, reporting their discussions and their findings to the grim-faced man who wore neither uniform nor insignia. From them, by listening in secret, Ilsa learned to her horror what this invasion of their domestic privacy by the authorities was all about.

A watchman at the Père Lachaise cemetery had found her father's mutilated remains. His summoning into the house to provide the grim-faced official with the details also furnished Ilsa with a catalogue of the mutilations that kind, comfortable man had sustained in his final moments. She wanted to stop her ears with frightened fingers, but the details forced themselves upon her and she abandoned the effort, replacing it with a morbid curiosity. Dawn had stained the white marble a luminous shade of pink. Her father's blood had stained it a deeper, duller red. The catalogue of injuries, missing fingernails, punctured veins, the mark of a rope tightened across the forehead which had forced her father's straining eyes out of their orbits, was given with a calm detachment, a detachment which should have been reserved for those speaking of someone else. Which, of course, she reasoned later, they were.

The policemen were optimistic. The side of dead meat in bloodied tweeds which was all that remained of her father might still be avenged by the law. They might yet find that pale lady with the dark hair who was the unspoken reason for their flight from Tubingen. And, even if they were unable to, her father's papers would yield their clues to Ilsa, who knew that only by understanding her father's work would she truly learn the reason for his horrible death.

Days passed, then weeks, and finally months. It became clear to Ilsa that the police, for all their searching and optimism, would never discover the dwarf and the hunchback. She told them how they had visited the villa, and how her father had left with them on the night of his murder. It seemed such a simple thing to the thirteen-year-old girl that they should be found and captured. Two such distinctive creatures could hardly hide for long unnoticed, not even in Paris. Perhaps the gendarmes didn't believe her, though. Maybe they didn't believe about the dark lady either. For a while they studied her father's notes, but the documents were returned with much shaking of wise heads, and even a little derisive laughter.

Such things cannot be, Ilsa. Your wise, brilliant father had over-reached himself. He had gone beyond the confines of scientific reality. And you ask us to believe that he was killed by a dwarf and a hunchback with two mouths?

No longer the laughing, outgoing child, Ilsa was to study and search throughout the years to come. That night had altered her life for ever, channelling her youthful energies into the dark paths of superstition and revenge. Her mother would never fully recover her strength and health and would die shortly after Ilsa's twenty-first birthday, a broken, pain- and grief-racked woman of forty-three, her spirit and beauty marred by the monstrous servants of a dark woman with a Spanish name. Her death would leave Ilsa with a small private income, enough to live on and to indulge a little re-search in her consuming quest for her father's killers.

Ilsa kept all thought of love and romance from her life. She was to flourish into a beautiful, desirable woman who would be sought by many, yet all her would-be suitors were fated by her father's death to face rejection. Instead she would search through the ghettos and forgotten alleys of an increasingly alien and unknown Europe, pursuing a quest that few knew of, and fewer yet could even begin to understand.

But that was in the future. Now, at the start of the first day of life without her father, Ilsa could only listen as the police and the doctor unfolded and paraded their catalogue of horrors. The plans for vengeance were still beyond her. She was, after all, only a girl, and she would not lose her faith in the world of adults until the police abandoned their search for the murderers. Until then there could still be moments of pleasure, moments when she would forget her grief for an instant and enjoy the delights her mother strove to tempt her with. The Paris Zoo, depleted during the days of the commune, was starting to reassemble its stock of bizarre and arrest-ing animals. A travelling circus came and went, but the clowns wore smiles painted with sadness, and the freaks in the side-shows were creatures to be shunned, denizens of an arcade triple-ringed by painful memories. Even the acrobats made the air about them gibber with unease as they travelled from platform to trapeze and back again.

In one cage at the zoo, alone and pitiful despite its fierce exterior, a great Carpathian wolf prowled and sulked. Its amber eyes burned with hidden fires, incomprehensible, bestial emotions smouldering behind the bars of its captivity. This creature alone, for all its rank breath and innate viciousness, excited Ilsa's sympathy. One day she asked a keeper why it had no mate, and was told that the she-wolf had died a little while before, on the night of 2 August. From that moment on there was somehow a bond between the girl and the beast, and she could often be found before its cage, lost in an incomprehensible communion, seeing in the amber fire of its eyes some small reflection of the flame within her own.

After her mother's death, when Ilsa left Paris, the keeper found the wolf dead. He wasn't really surprised, for it had been five years old when Ilsa had first seen it, and for a wolf to live beyond nine was exceptional. This old dog, its muzzle grey-white but its eyes still full of fire, had lived to the age of thirteen. All attempts to introduce a new mate for it had been failures. It was almost as if it had found its mate in the girl, now a woman, who had stood through the years before its cage, promising to exact in her own life the vengeance that the creature was denied.

CIRCUZ NADASDY ★ CIRCUZ NADASDY
CIRCUZ NADASDY ★ CIRCUZ NADASDY

GRAND AUSTRIAN TOUR

FOR THE FIRST TIME IN AUSTRIA, BEGINNING WITH A SEASON

IN

VIENNA

THROUGHOUT AUGUST 1881

THE CIRCUZ NADASDY – THE FAMOUS TRANSYLVANIAN ENTERTAINMENT TROUPE
offers the most magnificent spectacles of colour, sound and pageant

IN ADDITION there is the famous NADASDY menagerie of Apes, Wolves, Gorillas and all manner of Reptiles and Giant Insects both safe and venomous.

Many SIDE SHOWS and SPECTACLES including: Lela and Lola Chang, the famous Siamese Twins; Varango the Giant, over SEVEN FEET TALL, Goro and Gorinna, the Gorilla People and much, much more . . .

PRIVATE performances arranged for discerning patrons by appointment.

AS DISPLAYED BEFORE CROWNED HEADS AND NOBILITY THROUGHOUT EUROPE.

Late morning

The setting was idyllic. Stones projected above the clear waters of the little stream, drawing lines in its flowing current. Above the faintly gushing rivulets the trees about the little rustic bridge were panoplied with strong, green leaves, their stems and stalks almost bursting with the heavy sap of summer. In the distance Tyrolean slopes, some still glistening with year-round snow, kept their centuried silence like a geomantic tapestry backcloth. The sun shone golden and dazzling in the cloudless blue of the peaceful sky.

It was a setting for romance, for man and woman to exchange confidences and share their passions. In a sense that was what the man and woman upon the bridge, he with his arms leaning upon the wooden parapet and she with her small bag and one hand ungloved, were doing. His head was turned towards her, watching that gentle, intimate smile which had so unnerved him at their first meeting. Had it not been for her obvious refinement, not to mention the position which went with the name of von Zammerhein, he would have thought it the smile of an artful and accomplished whore. Yet no daughter of Graf von Zammerhein, the famed and respected scion of an ancient house, as well as a Professor of Physical Sciences, could ever be thought of as a whore. There was too much pride, too much breeding, in spite of that frustrating smile.

There was also a coldness which had nothing to do with either the weather or the way in which they were talking. It was almost as if this young woman belonged to another, alien world. Her eyes promised pleasure and delight. Her lips invited crushing in the passion of meeting flesh, and yet something about her spoke of a danger beyond anything Klaus Villagar could ever imagine.

His eyes wandered slowly down, studying the figure which was both disguised and displayed by the green velvet dress with the black lace trimmings. It clung to her torso, mimicking the curve of breast and gentle swell of rib-cage. At her waist it became a distorted cone where the bustle and full skirt bowed away, hiding still further the rapture which her eyes invited.

'You know,' he said, 'I was never aware that the Graf von Zammerhein had a daughter, let alone one as beautiful as you are.'

Her smile persisted. One perfectly manicured hand played listlessly with the fastening on her bag. The other, the one which held it, was still gloved in black, and as well as the handle it held the glove she had removed.

Behind them, a few hundred yards away on the road, the closed carriage awaited her return. The grey geldings in its shafts stood erect and eager, almost as if they were conscious of the purpose and loveliness of their passenger. The caped coachman kept his back to the figures on the bridge. He wasn't there to see what transpired. He was being paid too well to watch, let alone interfere.

'You have paid me a kind compliment,' Ilsa replied. 'But it is out of place, Herr Villagar. There is only one thing I need to hear from you. We have already discussed it, and you have also been made aware of what I offer in exchange.'

Her voice might have enchanted him, had he not been listening to the words. It was a gentle, musical voice, but it had an edge almost as sharp as honed steel.

'That is the one thing I cannot tell you,' he said softly, his tones reluctant and his eyes downcast. He stared at the little stream, but the image of the banker's draft she had offered, all those figures and zeros written upon it in a copperplate hand, was all he saw. It could, as she had said, make him rich for life, but Klaus Villagar was a man motivated by something even stronger than greed. Yes, he would desperately like to tell her what she wanted to know. His words were worth a fortune, but it would be a fortune he could never live to enjoy.

'All I require from you is the location. You need tell me nothing else. Just the location, Herr Villagar.'

She knew that he had the knowledge. There was no doubt about that. Yet to impart it would raise several questions that he was not even prepared to contemplate. His own complicity, the possibility of a police action against him, and disloyalty, probably fatal disloyalty, to the most powerful person he had ever known.

'Is there nothing I can do to persuade you?'

He wanted to laugh bitterly, to curse the fate which kept his lips from hers. There was no ambiguity in the invitation. Her clear, green eyes told him that. Her darting tongue promised pleasures he

could only guess at, even as the thumb and forefinger of that ele-
gantly manicured hand released the clasp upon her bag.

'I'm sorry,' he replied, his frame shaking with the effort of his
self-control. 'Even if I was foolish enough to tell you, do you think
she'd leave me to live out my days in peace? We both know I'd be
dead before the end of the month.'

'So you will continue to serve her, if only by your silence,' Ilsa
remarked, a trace of sadness mingling with the frustration in her
voice. Her pale fingers probed the interior of the bag as she spoke.

'I have no choice,' Villagar muttered. 'She's stronger than both of
us. I want to tell you, Fräulein. You must believe that. I want to tell
you more than I want anything in the world. But if I tell you I
secure nothing but my own death.

'Give it up,' he continued, standing upright and smoothing the
wrinkles from his waistcoat. 'Accept what has happened as inevitable. It is inevitable, you know. Nobody can fight her and live, let
alone win against her. Forget it, Fräulein.'

A muffled click sounded from the depths of the bag. As Ilsa
withdrew her hand Villagar's eyes widened in alarm. The pistol in
her hands was unequivocally lethal.

'Put that away,' he snapped, starting to back away from her.
'Are you mad? You have to be joking!'

His voice, previously reluctant and, at times, a little pitying, was
now edged with a note that could develop into panic hysteria. 'What
about the coachman?' he demanded. 'He'll hear you. Or will you
murder him as well?'

Klaus Villagar suddenly realised how little he knew about the
woman standing before him. Did Graf von Zammerhein really have
a daughter? Yes, there might be some family resemblance, but it
could also be mere chance. The only thing that was certain was the
object of her quest. He didn't even really know her purpose. If she
had lied about her identity, if she was not the Graf's daughter, then
it need not even be revenge.

'You . . . you're insane! Will you really go to such lengths to
secure the information you want? Will you really kiss with your
eyes and kill with your fingers?'

She sighed and levelled the revolver. It was a small bore, single
action weapon, but at this range neither of them doubted its
lethal effect. 'If you will not tell me, then you are protecting her.
If you are protecting her, you are against me. There is too much
danger in what lies ahead for me to leave enemies at my back,

Herr Villagar. 1 offer you one last opportunity to tell me what I want to know.'

'Coachman!' he called. His staring eyes followed the direction of the word, watching it speed through the still, alpine air. 'Coachman!'

The man must have heard. The cry was echoing off the distant slopes. Surely it had reached the ears of the caped figure beside the carriage. Yet he gave no sign of having heard. He neither waved nor turned, his back remaining determinedly towards the little bridge.

Ilsa smiled sympathetically, but her eyes didn't for one moment leave the figure in her sights. 'Goro,' she said softly, 'come here.'

Had he really heard her at that distance? Villagar could hardly believe that he had, yet the distant coachman turned and began to walk towards them. As the distance lessened the man's great height became more apparent, as did the fact that he wore a hood about his head, and not the ordinary chapeau associated with his trade.

Goro. Klaus Villagar tried to think where he had heard that name before. There was something familiar, both about the name and about the general bulk of the caped and hooded figure.

'I think you will know him when you see him,' Ilsa smiled grimly. 'He has a singular appearance.' The pistol in her right hand did not so much as tremor. Its barrel remained perfectly level, aimed at Villagar's heart.

He felt the perspiration break out upon his forehead. Oh yes, there was something familiar about Goro. He realised what it was even before the advancing coachman removed his hood and he saw the deep-set eyes and prominent teeth, both glistening in a face covered in thick hair. Only the area around the nose, the forehead and the lips was smooth and hairless. And if the head was nightmare enough for most of those who had paid their roubles and pfennigs and kroners to see him, the body was something extra. Beneath that cape and the tight trousers Goro's muscles rippled in a frame which stood the better part of seven feet tall, rippled under the thick coat of short hairs which had been both his curse and his unhappy living with the Circuz Nadasdy.

'My god,' Villagar muttered.

'Does your fear of her still overwhelm your tongue?' Ilsa demanded. 'I see from your face that you recognise my companion. And so you should, Klaus. After all, you've done your own work for the Circuz

Nadasdy. What did they tell you, Klaus? Did they merely say that Goro and Gorinna had left the sideshows? Is that it? I expect it was. There would be no reason for you to know how Gorinna died, and how Goro escaped to find others who might wish to take revenge.

'Talk to me, Klaus. You know only too well what the true purpose of the Circuz is. You know why she finances it, what she hopes to gain from its performances, even why she sometimes travels with it.'

He felt the rivulets of perspiration gather and run within his clothes. The girl he might have disarmed, but Goro was something different altogether. He'd seen the act, both in its public and private performances. In private Goro and his simian bride, as much a freak as himself, went through a series of bestial, yet somehow sophisticated, sexual embraces. They would start with each other, ape-fashion, then proceed to employ the specially constructed apparatus the Circuz Nadasdy had created for them. The climax of the performance, for private patrons, was the introduction of one of the Circuz whores, who would be buggered by Goro whilst Gorinna masturbated her. Cardboard clouds then drew back from covering a synthetic full moon, and the screams of the whore would be drowned by the simian howling of her tormentors. But that was the private act.

The public performance was less perverted and erotic, but if anything it was much more impressive. Goro and Gorinna paced their cage, generally behaving like the apes they resembled. They snarled at their 'keeper' as he threw in raw meat for them to gnaw. Then Goro would split the bones with his bare hands to lick out the marrow. To add to the effect the cage was littered with human skulls and dismembered skeletons, together with horrifically realistic representations of mutilated human bodies. At the end Goro and Gorinna would appear to sense the audience and rush the bars. When Goro began to bend them apart with his huge strength the crowd would usually disperse in something approaching genuine panic.

With strength like that he could tear them limb from limb, they thought. And so did Klaus Villagar.

'Who . . . are you?' he asked, hesitantly. 'Graf von Zammerhein can have nothing against the Circuz Nadasdy. You're not his daughter. So who are you really?'

She smiled again, so sweetly, so invitingly. No whore could ever smile like that. There was too much pleasure in it, and too much that was tormenting.

'Does it matter, Klaus? We can find that Circuz easily enough. All we have to do is follow the trail of gaudy posters it has pasted across Europe. But it will not in itself lead us to her. And she is the one we seek. She is the one we have to destroy.'

A pleading look came into his eyes as she spoke. 'Let it alone,' he groaned. 'All you can bring about is your own death, and Goro's. She won't even need to breathe to rid herself of a petty nuisance such as you present. Goro's suffered enough, if Gorinna is really dead. Give it up, Fräulein. Leave it alone.'

The ape-mouth moved. Goro's lips drew back, revealing his yellowed, fang-like teeth. 'You are right, Herr Villagar,' he said, his voice thick and gruff, almost a bark but slower and more distinct. 'I have suffered enough. Now it is her turn to suffer. We know what you have done for her in the past. You didn't find me, but you have found others ... similar to myself. You know what the Circuz requires them for, but still you find them. Should I begin my retribution with you?'

His right hand became a fist, the fingers curling inwards and tightening upon themselves. The fine glove-leather split apart at the seams, revealing the hairy pelt which almost completely covered the fingers, and the dark, clawlike nails at the fingertips.

Villagar's mouth felt intensely dry. Whatever he did now, whatever he said, he knew that his life was over. If he said nothing he would never leave the bridge alive. If he gave them the information that they wanted he would die later. Perhaps, though, there was another way, a way that avoided the truth altogether ...

The Fräulein shook her head. 'We shall know if you lie, Klaus. That will secure your death as surely as your silence. Yet if you tell us the truth I can still provide you with the sum we agreed upon. It is more than enough to flee from her. You can still be safe.'

The temptation was there, and it was growing stronger. The image of the banker's draft persisted, edging her words with a fine band of purest gold.

'You will know if I lie,' he muttered. 'But how will you know if I tell the truth?'

With hardly any diminution of her singular smile the Fräulein stared icily at him, her green eyes suddenly frozen emeralds. As he felt himself begin to quail inwardly she replied, her voice soft, coaxing, somehow alien.

'I will know, Klaus,' she said. 'Do you really believe that you are the first of whom I have asked this question? There have been others, you know. Some remained stubborn, and the world has since forgotten them. Others took the draft and now live at ease, secure from even the darkest of their fears. I come to you not merely for knowledge, Klaus, but for confirmation. You are the last person that I need to ask.'

Was it true? Had others already undergone this temptation and finally yielded to it? If they had, then he had nothing to worry about. His mistress would never single him out as the betrayer, especially if there truly were others. All he had to do was conceal his new wealth until she had sought him out and questioned him. He could survive that.

And yet it could be a bluff. It was possible that the others had said nothing. Perhaps there hadn't even been any others. His instincts, those intangible almost-senses which had kept him alive in his chosen service, warned him that he should challenge the Fräulein. Against that challenge, however, was set the pistol levelled at his heart, and the grim shape of Goro if he tried to take it from the temptress.

'You think I am lying,' the Fräulein continued. 'You believe that I've lied to you in order to persuade you. No, don't protest. You are a clever man Klaus Villagar, even when faced with the threat of execution.'

Even as she spoke she heard again the words of that other, the one she had failed to save. Goro had knelt upon the damp cobbles in that alley in Frankfurt, supporting the dying man's bloody head upon his knees, whilst she strained to catch those final, choking words.

'England ... Fräulein ... She has ... gone ... to England ...'

'And the Circuz? Has she abandoned it? Has it served its purpose?'

'There ... is still ... some need. It will ... follow her ...'

Villagar felt the pause lengthen. It had to be a bluff. If he could get the gun out of her hands, into the stream, perhaps, he might outrun Goro ...

'She is in England, Klaus.'

The words were spoken softly, but with enormous effect. She did know, after all. She wasn't bluffing. Villagar's tensed muscles began to relax again. If she knew about England, then all she had to do was to follow the Circuz Nadasdy on its tour, and watch. Sooner or later she would know everything she needed. The only difference his betrayal could make was to hasten her progress a little. And if he still kept silence, then he would be dead in seconds.

'Will you tell me the place in England, Klaus?'

He shrugged. It was important to appear to remain calm. 'The draft first, Fräulein. A little token of trust. After all, you still have the gun, and I have nothing.'

Her smile broadened. With her free hand she held out her bag to Goro. The ape-man reached inside and withdrew the banker's draft. Then he handed it to Villagar.

Klaus studied the draft again, grinning broadly. She was right. He could live in luxury for the rest of his life.

'Your turn, Klaus. Where is she?'

He didn't look up to reply. His eyes were too busy counting the zeros again. 'At present, in London,' he muttered. 'Five days from today the Circuz begins its British tour at Canterbury. She will join it then.'

'You see?' said Ilsa. 'It was so easy. Thank you, Klaus. And farewell.'

The first bullet tore through the paper of the draft and shattered a lower right rib. It was a bad wound and pain shot down his right side, but it was not enough to rob Villagar of consciousness. He staggered back and leaned against the bridge's wooden parapet, looking up through fear-widened eyes.

'But . . . I told you . . .'

The second bullet tore through his stomach and lodged in his spine, sending a jet of crimson out through his waistcoat. Some of it sprayed the draft, turning the stiff paper limp beneath its weight and dampness. The third bullet found his heart, causing a second spurt of escaping blood. The last three blew his skull to pieces.

Only when all of the revolver's six chambers were empty did Ilsa lower the smoking weapon. As the worst of the blood-flow subsided Goro stepped wordlessly forward and pitched Villagar's body down into the little stream. Then he turned back and smiled at her.

'To London, Fräulein?' he asked.

She shook her head and replaced the pistol in her bag. 'No. We would have too much difficulty in finding her there, and only two days to do it in after our journey. It's best that we go directly to Canterbury and wait for her to join the Circuz Nadasdy there.'

She forced a smile in return to his own. 'He would have warned her, Goro. I had no choice. No sum of money could really have secured his total betrayal. She does that to her hirelings . . .'

'There's no need to explain, Fräulein,' the ape-man replied. 'I know only too well what she can do. If you hadn't killed him I would probably have done it myself, only far more slowly.'

They left the bridge and walked back to the carriage. As the last of his blood mingled with the once-clear waters of the stream, Klaus Villagar stared up at the noon sun through his one remaining death-glazed eye.

27 JULY 1884

Shortly after noon

They had bought tickets for the Circuz Nadasdy's first performance on British soil and watched the show the previous night. Goro, heavily muffled, sat beside Ilsa with silent tears trickling down the fur of his face. The display held too many memories for him to detach himself completely, the way Ilsa seemed to have succeeded in doing. She watched avidly, applauding as loudly and well as the rest of the enchanted audience, cheering the lion-tamers and fire-eaters and gasping with surprise at the performance of the vampire magician as he drained mock blood from the neck of his levitated victim.

'She has a very thin neck,' Goro explained later. 'Because of this they can conceal a flesh-coloured hollow collar between her gorget and her hair. That is what Polidori punctures with his teeth.'

Ilsa nodded. 'And the levitation?' she asked. 'How does he get her to rise into the air like that? It can't be on wires or the hoops would never pass over her.'

The man-ape shrugged. 'Some things I didn't learn,' he replied. 'Where *she* is concerned you never really know what is trickery and what may yet be some secret science.'

The warmth of the audience left them in no doubt that the Circuz Nadasdy was about to embark upon a highly profitable tour. That would please Madame Jancisca Ferencz, as Dona Juanita was now calling herself. Yet they both knew the true reason why that lovely, ageless, dangerous woman maintained her troupe of freaks and performers, and it had nothing at all to do with entertaining the public, either in Canterbury or anywhere else. It was for her own demented reasons, half research and half entertainment, and Ilsa suspected shudderingly that she would never be able to understand those reasons fully whilst she retained her sanity.

Goro had seen Madame Jancisca the night before, though he was so used to hiding himself from the ordinary people around him that he was reasonably sure she hadn't noticed him. After she left the Circuz he followed her to a hotel, The Archbishop's Mitre, just beyond the West Gate. After that it had been comparatively simple to discover which suite she was occupying and to report back to Ilsa.

'And with a new identity,' he confided, 'has come a new appearance. Her hair is now yellow gold, lady. The same colour as your own. I think that perhaps the gendarmes did seek Dona Juanita after all, and if not for your father's death, then at least for other crimes in other places.'

'But did you see the dwarf and the hunchback?' Ilsa demanded. 'They were not in the Freak Arcade last night.' She knew that only too well. She had paid the extra coins required and steeled herself to enter that marquee of pitiful creatures. There had been horrors there to turn the strongest stomach, creatures scouted from tiny, forgotten hamlets across the European continent by filth like Klaus Villagar. Whispered rumour even claimed that Madame Jancisca supervised their mating, creating ever more horrible mutations for the public to gawp at, and for her own private delectations.

Goro shook his head. No, the dwarf and the hunchback had not been at the Circuz. Perhaps she had them hidden at the hotel, or — a more terrible thought perhaps — they were executing some grim mission for their inhuman mistress.

It didn't really matter. If they were lucky, if all went well in Canterbury, there would be time enough to find those two later. After all, they were simply the weapons of her father's death. The knives could be blunted when the killer was dead. The important thing was that Madame Jancisca didn't escape them, now that their quest appeared finally over.

Ilsa and Goro had followed Madame Jancisca's devious trail through the years, together seeking the circus as it crossed and re-crossed the European mainland, finding their trail grow suddenly cold as both the circus and Madame paused in hiding to assume fresh identities. Ilsa had used up a great deal of her precious inheritance on the quest, travelling from city to city and country to country in her search.

Cuttings from all the major newspapers had been forwarded to her, scraps of newsprint which might offer some clue to the whereabouts of the Circuz Nadasdy, or whatever it was now calling itself. On one occasion Ilsa had actually succeeded in tracking it down, only to find the dwarf and the hunchback, and Madame, somehow missing . . .

She met Goro in Prague. Initially she was wary of so monstrous-looking a creature, mistaking the outward sign for the inner being. And he, too, was content to hold this lovely woman at arm's length until he knew her better, until he learned that her initial, superficial resemblance to Madame was no indication of her true intentions. Yet gradually, drawn closer together by their mutual need to avenge the wrongs they had suffered at Madame Jancisca's hands, friendship and mutual trust strengthened their relationship, each finding in the other an attribute which would ease his or her solitary searching.

Goro knew the circus as only an insider could. Ilsa's dwindling funds enabled them to track it with greater hope of success. Yet still they knew that finding the circus wasn't finding its mysterious owner. For that they needed the help of someone who knew, someone who was willing to say where she was. Or could be persuaded.

The freak-scouts, Goro reasoned. Ask the freak-scouts.

And so, ultimately, they had come to Klaus Villagar. He talked. He died. He led them to Canterbury.

Ever since she had vowed vengeance for her father Ilsa had dreamed of the moments that would soon be upon her. Ever since she had met Goro they had planned and thought out the few precious seconds that would soon be theirs. They had given their lives to the quest, like the mythical knights of old. Yet their grail was of flesh, not precious metal, and the blood it contained, the blood they sought to shed, was the blood of evil, not of Christ.

The circus itself didn't matter. Madame's thralls would rejoice at her death almost as much as Goro and Ilsa would. The performers, the animals, were only tools to be used and discarded by their hellish mistress. No tears would be shed for her passing. There would be relief, yes, as at the fading of some dread fever, but no tears. No vengeance for Madame.

Perhaps she wouldn't even bother to visit the circus after it was over. There was no need to, and it would be painful for Goro, even if they were hailed as liberators. But Ilsa had read such of her father's papers as she had been able to, and his work, a mixture of alchemy and what today would be known as biochemical engineering, had fascinated her. Goro, in their time together, had told her everything about the performers, the animals, the keepers and ring-men. And he had told her about the *glebulae* as well.

The word was Latin, meaning *little clods of earth*. In itself it was of no interest, but in its implications it was staggering. That Madame Jancisca had been interested in her father's experiments, interested enough to force him to share his knowledge, belied the idea that they were simply some unknown species imported from abroad, like lions or tigers or elephants . . .

Yes, perhaps she would visit the circus, afterwards. For now, though, Ilsa lunched early, settling the fluttering wings of panic in her stomach, whilst Goro watched the hotel beyond the turreted bulk of the West Gate. The Archbishop's Mitre was old, even by Canterbury's standards. Its gables tilted crazily and the timbered façade leaned alarmingly out over the street. Some upper windows, open in the summer warmth, leaned out above the pavement, unwilling to close because of the irregular angles of their metal frames. Inside the floors and staircases of age-polished oak went their own ways, rarely completely flat and often sloping noticeably.

She joined him in the shadowed arch of the West Gate, a place he had chosen despite the passing carriages because its darkness hid his appearance, as well as offering a reasonably unobtrusive view of the hotel entrance. Beneath his coat something hard and straight bulged, cradled beneath the fabric by his folded arms. Ilsa carried her bag, and the weight of the revolver tapped against her as she walked.

'Is she still there?' Ilsa asked.

Goro answered softly, his head motionless. 'I've not seen her come out. There's no reason for her to show herself before tonight's performance. If she wants to see anybody they can be summoned to an audience in her suite.'

His companion sighed. 'It's strange,' she muttered, 'but now that it's almost over I'm unwilling to finish it. What do we do when she's dead, Goro? What comes after the deaths of Madame and her murdering freaks? I'm twenty-four. I've sacrificed love and most of my youth on this search. My body is still young, yes. But what about my mind? There's a fire in vengeance which consumes whoever sets it alight, Goro. In a few minutes, when it's done, there's going to be nothing left but the taste of its ashes.'

Goro shook his head. 'Don't think of it as revenge, lady,' he said. 'Think of it as a purgation. By our actions we shall cleanse this world of something foul, something which should never have seen the light of day in the first place. She killed your father, and she killed my wife. But they're not the only ones. She trails blood behind her in her wake like slime from a snail. Her mind harbours thoughts that would send ordinary, decent people reeling from her presence. And that's why we have to kill her. Not because she has harmed those we love, but because she has also harmed countless others we shall never know about.

'We're hesitating, lady, and that is dangerous. I think it's time we finished our work.'

Without so much as a glance, Goro stepped out into the sunlight and crossed to the side of the road, walking determinedly towards The Archbishop's Mitre. For a moment more Ilsa watched from the shadows of the arch, then she set out to join him, her right hand inside her bag, slipping the safety catch from her revolver. She didn't need to check its load. She had already done that several times during the morning, running her fingertips across the percussion end of the six bullets in its chambers.

Most of Canterbury was still at luncheon. Pilgrim and native alike were washing Canterbury lamb or other choice courses down with claret or Moselle. In the distance the cathedral clock chimed a quarter hour.

Their feet rang on the cobbled pavement. No-one looking from the upper storeys of the hotel could see their approach because of the overhang and the narrowness of the path. Goro, supporting his burden with one arm, unbuttoned his coat with his free hand and reached inside, feeling the twin triggers of the shortened ·12 bore inside the trigger-guard. They walked in shadow, just out of the brilliant sunshine.

'To kill a creature of darkness,' Goro had once said, 'you must first learn to get out of the light.'

They entered the hotel walking normally. Had anyone seen them there would have been no reason to suppose them other than guests or visitors. The tiny reception desk was unmanned, and Goro glanced behind it for a sight of Madame's key.

'Not there,' he grunted. 'It means she's either in her room or in there.' He gestured towards the closed doors of the hotel dining-room. 'We go up.'

'And if she's not in her room?'

'Then we wait.'

They saw no-one on the stairs or any of the landings. Goro led the way with a firm, relaxed stride. Ilsa, her hand closed firmly about the pistol hidden in her bag, followed closely, turning her head from side to side, her eyes probing the doorways and corridors for hidden watchers. It was all beginning to feel too easy.

'I don't like this, Goro,' Ilsa muttered. 'We should have seen someone by now. A guest, or a servant. It's too quiet.'

'Let's just be grateful, lady,' the man-ape replied in a whisper. 'The fewer that see us now, the fewer to guess what we were about afterwards.'

They stood before the door of Madame Jancisca's suite. Goro reached inside his coat and cocked both barrels of the shotgun past safety. Ilsa's grip upon the revolver tightened.

So this was it. The years of planning and hunting were over at last. All they had to do was to squeeze the triggers on their weapons a few times and Madame Jancisca Ferencz, Dona Juanita, whatever she called herself, would lie dead before them. Even if the police caught up with them, even if their assassination earned them the death sentence, it would have been worth it. The world of men would be a purer place for Madame's passing.

Goro knocked lightly on the door. Deferentially, he hoped, like a servant unwilling to intrude upon the privacy of a guest. Then he waited.

His knock remained unanswered. He knocked again.

Still no reply.

He glanced at Ilsa, then flicked his eyes downwards, indicating that Madame was downstairs, in the dining-room. Even so, the shotgun was in his hands and Ilsa had taken the revolver from her bag as they charged through the unlocked door.

Once inside they paused to take stock of their surroundings. They stood in a small drawing-room, well-furnished with modern, mid-Victorian furniture. The legs of a small writing table were shrouded, and the skirts of the easy chairs reached down to the thick pile carpet. Bric-a-brac crowded every available surface.

There were no suitcases, but a large leather hat-box stood on the seat of one of the chairs. It bore the worn patches and scuffs of long years of hard service, and the monogram EvB was stamped in faded gold upon its lid.

Goro followed Ilsa's gaze. 'Take a look if you want to,' he muttered. 'I'll cover the door.'

He walked over to the fireplace, from which he could fire at either the suite or bedroom doors. Ilsa walked over to the hat-box on the chair and peered curiously at the monogram.

'It doesn't fit,' she remarked. 'These aren't the initials of any of her aliases. She always seems to use the initials J F. But this is EvB.'

'Open it if you're going to,' Goro snapped. 'She might come back any moment. When she does I want you with your gun in your hand.'

Ilsa lifted the monogrammed lid. As she did so she gasped softly. The hat-box contained a brown, age-shined skull. Beneath it lay a leather-bound volume, its cover heavily tooled in gold but bearing no legend either upon the spine or the cover. With slightly trembling fingers Ilsa removed the skull and opened the book.

It bore no title page. Instead the manuscript volume began with a full page of text, written in faded brown ink upon paper yellow with age.

'This text has been written down by me according to the wisdom received from Caillchen Mac Eamon's skull. The exact means of communication I shall withhold, in case this manuscript should fall into other hands . . .'

She flipped through the mouldering pages. The book ended only a few sheets in, leaving most of the leaves blank. At the end of the text was a signature, semi-illegible. After a few moments' study Ilsa was able to make it out.

'Erzebet von Bamberg.'

The name meant nothing.

Goro felt his nerves tighten. Ilsa dropped the book and took up her revolver. Slowly, creaking upon its hinges as it travelled along its arc, the door to the bedroom was opening. The ape-man raised his shotgun and sighted along the barrels. Ilsa gripped the pistol with both hands, levelling its muzzle at the open doorway.

There was no-one there.

'Cover me,' Goro muttered.

With infinite stealth and caution he approached the open door. The bedroom beyond was decorated with a light blue, satin-finish paper. Its furniture had been carefully painted blue and gold and the draperies were striped with the same blue. Yet here and there dark splashes marred its perfection, and two dark-clad bodies littered the blue-carpeted floor.

He raised his foot and kicked the door hard, sending it crashing back against the inner wall. Its unimpeded progress meant that there was no-one hiding behind it. Grim-faced, he lowered the shotgun and walked into the room. Still holding the weapon he knelt beside each of the bodies in turn.

'The dwarf and the hunchback,' he grunted. 'Both dead. Killed with a shotgun from the state of them, at close range. Somebody's done it for you, lady.'

Ilsa steeled herself to look. Most of the bearded dwarf's face was missing, and a substantial amount of the hunchback's chest. Both mouths were open, frozen in the gaping rictus of a double scream.

And in this room of the suite, as in the preceding one, there were no suitcases, no traces of the guest who occupied them.

No Jancisca Ferencz.

In one corner, carelessly thrown aside by the unknown killer, lay the shredded remnants of the pillow which had been used to muffle the shots. The blue fabric was blackened in places by powder-burns from the discharged shotgun cartridges. A thin trail of broken, liberated feathers led away from the murdered hunchback.

They stood there, their backs to the entrance to the suite, unspoken questions hanging on their lips.

'But . . . why?' Ilsa asked at length.

'Because it was necessary,' said a voice behind them.

They froze at the tones, each knowing who had spoken. Goro knew the speaker from his days with the Circuz Nadasdy, Ilsa from listening at the door of her father's study.

'Necessary, Madame?' Goro asked.

'Throw your weapons onto the bed,' Madame commanded. 'Do not turn around. The bodies at your feet should tell you that I am armed.'

The ape-man forced a laugh. 'You took a shotgun into the hotel dining room?' he questioned.

'I was never that far away,' came the reply. He could almost hear the smile behind the words. 'Now, pick up that pillow and throw it over your shoulder. And if you turn around, I shall kill you where you stand.'

Goro nodded, defeatedly. With leaden feet he walked across to the pillow and picked it up. Then he back-tracked to where he had been standing and tossed the pillow in the direction of Madame's voice.

'Turn around, Goro,' she ordered.

He obeyed, after tossing his own weapon onto the bed. Ilsa, frozen with fear, watched him in horrified silence, then followed suit. As her revolver plumped down onto the bedclothes she began to turn.

'Stand still, Ilsa!' Madame snapped.

Startled, her heart pounding, the girl obeyed. Goro turned slowly, his eyes fixed upon Madame's face. Yes, the colour of her hair had changed, but she was still lovely, unageing, and dangerous. Instead of the shotgun Goro had expected she held a Schulhof 8 mm pistol, a proto-automatic with a ring-pull in front of the trigger which located the next bullet in the breech.

'The latest thing,' she smiled. 'But be assured that it is deadly.'

'I have no doubt of it, Madame,' the ape-man answered. 'If it were otherwise it would be in different hands. But why did you kill the dwarf and the hunchback?'

'I felt that you had to have other victims, Goro. Besides me.'

As she spoke the pillow in her hand moved in front of the Schulhof's muzzle. Moments later there was a dull thudding and flame spouted through the fabric and feathers. Without a word Goro, slightly lifted from his feet by the impact of the bullet, fell back across the body of the hunchback, a neat hole in his forehead trickling blood.

Ilsa, beyond self-control, began to shake.

Madame circled the room. 'Sit down, child,' she smiled, pointing to a chair against the wall. As Ilsa obeyed Madame set down the Schulhof on the bed and picked up Goro's shotgun.

'You've followed me a long time, young lady. Should I remember you for some reason?'

'You had my father killed,' Ilsa replied. 'Professor Ehrmann. Or are there so many deaths to your credit that you can't remember that one?'

Madame ran a pink tongue over her sharp, white teeth. 'I remember him,' she answered. 'Your father was a fool, my dear. He allowed his principles to get in the way of his commerce. I regretted his death, as I also regretted his defection from my service. But he knew too much of what I was doing, as I suspect you may do. Am I right?'

'If you mean the *glebulae*, I pieced together some of the hints in his notes.'

'Nothing more? He didn't tell you about the machine?' As the blank look of incomprehension gave her Ilsa's answer she continued: 'Such a pity. And you're so like me as well. Don't you think so?'

And then Ilsa knew what had added to her unease. This was the woman she had seen with her father, over eleven years before – exactly the same woman. Not a line, not a wrinkle marred that perfect countenance. She was exactly the same age to look at as she had been then, though Ilsa herself had grown from child into woman in the intervening years.

They were both apparently twenty-four. Their hair was the same colour. Their dress sense was similar. Only details of their features kept them apart, physically.

'I regret this, my dear,' Madame said, moving the pillow in front of the shotgun. 'In another place, at another time, you might have rendered me quite different services. You have beauty and knowledge, both qualities I prize. And youth as well. You know, I have forgotten what it was like to be young, Ilsa Ehrmann. You may pity me for that.'

She heard the whoof as both barrels were discharged. Flame and feathers erupted out towards her. For an instant there was a stinging sensation as the first pellets from the cartridges struck home, tearing away the flesh of her lovely face. Then the darkness, the black oblivion of death, wrapped Ilsa in its nighted mantle and she tumbled from the chair.

'You have become me,' Madame sighed, staring down at Ilsa's dead, ruined face. 'Still, no matter. The Circuz Nadasdy can do without me for a while. My business with it is finished. With your help I shall become a murder upon the files of the English police. I was in here, with my freaks, discussing circus matters, when that man-ape, crazy with hatred because I could no longer use him, burst in and killed us all.'

She threw the shotgun onto the floor beside Goro's body. Then she took the Schulhof and placed it in Ilsa's hand. Ilsa's own revolver she slipped into the dead girl's bag, the straps of which were now across her own arm.

'I managed to kill him, even as he murdered me,' she added. 'They will find my bullet in you, Goro, as they will find shotgun pellets in the others.'

Madame Jancisca Ferencz walked slowly from the blood-sprayed bedroom, reflecting upon the vagaries of fate. She replaced the manuscript volume and the skull in the hat-box and tucked it under her arm. Then, a faint smile upon her lovely features, the dangerous immortal descended the stairs and walked from the hotel to a waiting carriage, to vanish from Canterbury's perceptions for ever.

No-one, either in the hotel or in the street outside, saw her go.

As the carriage began its rattling journey towards Dover, taking her back towards the European mainland and away from the scene of her latest crime, the beautiful woman began to cry within the curtained sanctuary of its interior. Her weeping began gently enough, but grew more violent until she was beating her head against the padded sides, her yellow-gold hair tousled and disarranged with the violence of her emotion. They were all gone, now. All of them. There had been so many. So many. Even poor, dead Amsegi wasn't the first to serve and love her. There had been others both before and after, and there would be still others, like the dwarf and the hunchback, creatures who loved and served without ever really knowing that they received back some fraction of the great love of which she was capable in return. How could they know? How could she let them know? Only the one she sought would know the truth. He alone would know that Ilsa's and Goro's questing was but a pale and transient reflection of her own centuried searching.

And when it was over? What then? She had the skull and the manuscript, but she still needed that little Thulean amulet of black volcanic glass. Once the three were united, for the first time in over a thousand years, the dark lords of Thule, the *nightmare* lords of Thule, would be forced to do her homage. The world would hold terrors only for those who failed to serve her, or who displeased her by their service. And Johannes would come to her again.

Ah, Johannes. She wiped the tears from her red-rimmed eyes. They had spent only one night together, only one night in over three hundred years, but the woman in the carriage knew that only he would really lie beside her in whatever centuries remained.

One day she would find him. For now the search for the amulet must go on, though even that search was the search for her lost love. He must have it. He *had* to. How else could it have eluded her for so long? The amulet and Faustus together! Ah, that indeed would be her triumph.

And so she cried alone inside the carriage, weeping for the dead she left behind her as much as for herself. Whatever they called her, be it Dona Juanita or Jancisca Ferencz, or even Erzebet von Bamberg, her loneliness remained.

Only when she found Faustus would she no longer be alone.

13 APRIL 1978

Mid-afternoon

There was something depressing about spring rain, the driver decided. It was all very well for out-of-fashion singers to croon about it growing the flowers for him to cut to sell to her for her to sell to him to give to her, but they didn't have to work in it. If they tried they'd probably get electrocuted, he decided.

He had plenty of time to study the old lady as he helped her out of the Kensington flat with her luggage. Her hair was white and her features, if the lines were anything to go by, marked her as the wrong side of seventy. Her hands too were wrinkled, with heavy veins and liver-spots standing out on their backs. Only the eyes were still young. Only those young eyes belied her dress and general appearance.

Who was paying him he didn't know. All he knew was that it was much more than he could earn in two years, just for fitting a false Hackney licence number and registration plates to his cab for this one trip. He was aware that what he had to do wasn't exactly legal, but the old dear was leaving the country anyway. Chances were she'd never spot him again, not even if she came back in a month or so.

What was so important about a hat-box, anyway?

He managed to pack all the luggage except the hat-box into the body of the cab. Only that last item, the one he was being paid so much to deliver, he had been told to lock away in the boot on the pretext that it might get crushed by the rest of the luggage, in the hope that the old love might forget it. Or, even if she did remember, it would be easy enough for him to drive off without bothering to get it out. That way it would look less like theft and more like an oversight.

'Heathrow,' she said in a cracked, ageing voice. 'I'm flying to Salzburg, so try to deliver me to the right terminal, will you?'

As crabby as she looks, he thought. Nothing special about her or her luggage, except for those eyes, but she's a long way from being the average happy grandmother.

'Holiday, love?' he asked, trying to strike up a conversation as they pulled away from the kerb and waited to turn into Kensington High Street.

'Business,' she replied, in the sort of tone which left the driver in no doubt that any further questioning would be completely useless.

Okay, he thought, that's fine by me. The less we say to each other the less likely she'll be to remember me when she gets home. And if she's got a flight to catch for a business meeting, she'll have less time to worry about her missing hat-box.

Once he'd got rid of her, the instructions from his mystery client were to drive to Kings Cross and deposit the hat-box in a pay locker. Inside he'd find an envelope with the agreed sum in payment for his services, *and he was to leave the key in the lock* and drive away. Then all he had to do was to take the plates off and his life, except for the large amount of cash he'd gained, would be completely back to normal. Really, it was all so incredibly easy.

For a while he speculated about the contents of the hat-box as he drove. Then he decided that he would never know what it really contained unless he opened it, and that meant stopping between Heathrow and Kings Cross. Better to leave things alone, he decided. What you don't know can't hurt you. Best not to jeopardise the payment by not following instructions.

It wasn't quite as smooth as he'd hoped. There was an awkward moment at the terminal when the old dear had fixed him with those young eyes and reminded him about the piece of luggage in the boot. For a moment he'd wondered if it was really worth stealing the hat-box from her; whether it wouldn't be better just to treat her the same as any other fare, even if she didn't seem the sort to bother with a tip. After all, he could lose his licence and end up in jail if he were caught.

'Okay love,' he muttered. 'I'll just get the keys.'

They were in the ignition, and the engine was running. His last doubt vanished as he climbed back into the driving seat, ostensibly to get the keys to the boot. Without looking back he slapped the motor into gear and drove away.

He watched her dwindle in the driving mirror. She didn't shake her fist or even answer his deception with a well-mouthed curse. She simply stood there, staring at him with those young eyes, nodding gently, with a faint smile upon her lips.

A little while later he left the hat-box in the locker and pocketed the envelope full of low-denomination banknotes. A few minutes after that he parked in a side-street and switched back the plates. Then he counted the money, grinning broadly.

When he was found three nights later, his body scarred by torture and the marks of something nasty about the remains of his throat, there was still sufficient left to ensure him a decent funeral.

MONDAY 23 MARCH
LAST YEAR

Mid-morning

Ptythonius Meeres gestured weakly to the chair beside his bed. With a faint smile Ferrow laid his coat across the seat and then sat down upon it. There were still many things about the affair at Wegrimham that he didn't, couldn't understand.

'Listen to me, Robert,' Meeres began. His voice was weak, and the lined parchment of his face made him look all of the eighty-odd years he had endured. They said that he was dying, although his injuries didn't merit such a diagnosis. If he was dying, then it was because of his own iron will, because of a genuine desire to be free of the horrors of the world he inhabited.

'I shall try to make it clear to you,' he continued, his old eyes burning into those of his visitor with a fire which belied the medical prognosis. 'Tell me, what do you think God is?'

At a time like this he wants to haggle theology, Ferrow thought. I always believed there was something more than a little mad about him.

He shrugged. 'The supreme being, I suppose. The creator.' He studied Meeres, half-expecting an argument. Instead the old man nodded gently.

'That's a good place to begin. Now, don't argue with me. Simply listen to what I have to say.'

Ferrow drew a deep breath, then exhaled gently. Whatever Meeres was about to tell him would probably be as incomprehensible as some of the events of the preceding week. All he could really do at this stage was listen, hoping that eventually some of the pieces would come together.

Yet even for a half-way decent detective, which Ferrow believed himself to be, there were things that had happened in the past week that he felt he could never understand. A week. Was it only a few days since he'd first met Ptythonius Meeres? Only a week to have the frights of a dozen lifetimes?

The Wegrimham affair (the name was pronounced Wemmam by the local cognoscenti) began for Detective Sergeant Robert Ferrow with a series of apparently unconnected incidents. Dead farm animals. Gas explosions. Right from the beginning Meeres had seemed to know more than he was letting on, an attitude which both intrigued and infuriated Ferrow. The dead animals had been killed by unknown and, according to the local vet, impossible creatures. The gas explosions had been used to disguise the deaths of researchers working for Meeres. No connection, on the surface.

But once Ferrow began to dig beneath the surface, once the unknown horrors had begun to attack people, once the lights started to come out of the sky, once the unholy rituals performed by Rufus Williamson at the Grange were understood, crime and motive had become secondary. Alone and unprepared, his reason temporarily shattered and only instinct and blind obedience left, Robert Ferrow had found himself a front-line soldier in a war that was even older than mankind itself, allied with creatures that would have shredded him in seconds save for Meeres' influence against an evil so dreadful and malign that he doubted he would ever really understand it.

That he sustained a slight flesh wound in the final conflict with the monstrous being that Williamson served was nothing, comparatively speaking. That he still had his sanity, even badly shaken and with the frontiers of belief widened for ever, was in the policeman's eyes nothing short of bloody miraculous.

Now, with Williamson dead and the Destroying Angel physically destroyed, with the *familiares*, or the few that survived at any rate, back in their burrows for ever, perhaps there was time to try to understand.

And so he listened.

'If this world was deliberately created by a supreme being,' Ptythonius Meeres began, 'it was more years ago than even the fossils can remember. Whoever, whatever that creator was, has vanished from the memory of the universe. But there are others, my young friend. They are not the creators, they are the inheritors. They are not gods, but godlets. Children, if you like. And like the children they are, they squabble about the division of their inheritance. It is that simple.'

Ferrow shifted uneasily on his chair. He had already seen something of the power of these so-called inheritors. Blue lights which filled the sky like flying saucers. Strange creatures that lived on human blood. Demented, intelligent fungi that appeared during strange rituals in hidden vaults. It was almost beyond comprehension or belief, but he had seen and lived through too much that was strange and alien to reject it entirely.

'What is not so simple is their nature,' Meeres continued from his hospital bed. 'There are two factions fighting for this tiny speck in time and space. One faction, the one represented by that creature you glimpsed in the vault at the Grange, once had sole dominion over it. Yet they were, in our terms, though not in their own, destructive. They harmed the planet. From our point of view they retarded our development. Man was their servant and their plaything.

'As I say, they were considered to have abused their inheritance, to have encroached upon the preservation of that equilibrium which is the essence of life's continuance. To prevent their servants performing those rites, or processes, which would render them all-powerful, the other faction gave man a weapon with which he might resist them. That weapon was called religion. The concept of a creator god was deliberately planted as a propagandist act of war. Even so, there have always been those who could not deny service to the older beings, who nurtured what little remained of the rites and kept alive the possibility of man returning to his previous intolerable status. Such a one was Rufus Williamson, or whatever he called himself through the centuries . . .'

Ferrow scowled, as much to disguise his growing realisation of Meeres' meaning as because the copper in him still found it impossible to digest. 'Are you trying to tell me Williamson was hundreds of years old?' he demanded.

Meeres' answering smile was benign. 'He was the bastard son of William Rufus,' he explained, slowly and carefully. 'Yes, friend Robert, Rufus Williamson was the better part of a thousand years old, and the work he attempted stretches back for thousands of years before his birth.'

'But his father . . . the grave in Wegrimham churchyard . . .'

'Open it if you wish. You will find a dead calf to give the coffin weight. When he spoke to Noel of his forebears it was merely to disguise the truth, to prevent the horror of explaining that he himself had been each of them in turn. Oh, he fathered the occasional child. One or two even lived to adulthood. But he has no descendants, for he has outlived them all.'

Ferrow shook his head. 'It's not possible,' he told himself.

Meeres' bright eyes shone up at him from the bed. 'As the light from Thule was impossible? As Pyewacket was impossible? As I myself am impossible? Do you really believe that I am only seventy-eight years old? I told you I was born in Meersburg, and I was. But the year of my birth was 1485.'

He'd already seen enough not to doubt a statement like that, improbable though it sounded. Even so, Robert Ferrow had to be sure.

'You're not well,' he said. 'Your mind is playing tricks on you. I'd better leave you to get some rest . . .'

Meeres' hand shot out and seized Ferrow's wrist in what was easily strong enough to have been a death-grip. 'Don't patronise me,' the old man hissed. 'What I have to say is too important for that. You will believe me, sooner or later. For now, though, listen.

'Do not make the mistake of thinking I am mad. Neither should you believe that Williamson was the last of the worshippers of Thule's evil. There are more, many more, both deliberately knowing and evil and unknowing and innocent. They lie concealed, waiting for the time when they may call out, as Williamson called out, and be answered by their inhuman masters. As the destroying angel was the Thulean parallel of the *Amanita virosa* toadstool, so there is a parallel for every other created thing, be it mammal, or bird, or vegetable, or disease bacillus . . . And they will come, unless the calls can be prevented . . .'

His voice faltered as the last of the colour began to drain from Ptythonius Meeres' gaunt features. Ferrow gently reached down and took Meeres' hand from his wrist, folding it across the Keeper's chest.

'Rest for a while, Ptythonius,' he said gently.

'In a little while,' came the reply. Then: 'Serve the light from the north, Robert. Serve the blue fire in the sky which comes from Thule . . .'

'But I thought you told me that the evil spread from Thule?'

'Everything . . . comes from Thule, my friend . . . Both good and evil. Everything is everything . . . not just one thing, but many . . . as diverse as good and evil . . .'

The ward sister pushed open the door to the old man's room. 'I think you'd better go now, Mr Ferrow,' she began, smiling strangely. 'It's time for Mr Meeres to rest again.'

Ferrow studied her expression carefully, then nodded and rose to his feet. 'I'll call again,' he told Meeres. 'When you're stronger.'

He leaned over the bed and extended his hand. The old man was still an unknown quantity, despite the peril they had shared together. There was a bond between them, based on the knowledge they shared of things beyond the comprehension of most of mankind, but Ferrow somehow felt that such a bond could also exist between a spider and the fly it was about to devour.

'Come closer,' Ptythonius Meeres whispered.

Ferrow bent further, putting his ear close to the old man's mouth.

'In the locker. I have left something for you, friend Robert. It is yours when I die . . .'

The policeman grunted and stood up abruptly. 'You're not going to die,' he snapped. 'I know you now, Ptythonius. You're too tough for that.'

'Nevertheless, friend Robert,' came the reply, 'you will be here when I die. Have no doubt of that. And now, goodbye,' he added abruptly, allowing his eyelids to flicker closed.

As Ferrow walked out along the hospital corridors his thoughts were confused. So many strange, terrible things had happened to him during the past week, things that meant that his life would never quite be the same again. Meeres' voice, insistent, insidious, rang through his skull as his feet echoed on the polished lino.

'I cannot name the person behind this conspiracy for you . . . BECAUSE IT'S TOO VAST AND TOO SUBTLE . . . Conspiracies need not be human in their origins . . . A voice which your waking mind cannot hear whispers an idea into your dreams, an idea which can persist into your waking hours as a thought of your own . . .'

He smiled to himself, trying to dismiss the threats and questions from his life. It wasn't his concern any more. Yet the effort was conscious, as if he was willing himself to deny that unheard whispering which he now believed was real.

And there were whisperers, even now, as there had been throughout history. They were there, all around him in time and space as they were all around others. The ward sister could never properly explain how someone with her record of service could perform an unpremeditated murder. Meeres knew, but when Ferrow remembered that his coat still lay across the chair and raced back to the room it was too late. The fatal air-bubble was already racing towards the old man's heart.

It was the voices. It had to be. But it was Sister who was tried and convicted. It was Sister who had been reaching for the package in the locker when Ferrow returned, and who had dropped the empty hypodermic in surprise. At the inquest and the trial, however, the package Meeres had left for his younger friend was never mentioned.

They might have won a skirmish, the detective thought, but the conspiracy and the voices were both still very much alive. And so were the questions, the ones which he had forgotten to ask at the time. Meeres had spoken to him of Iceland, of being some kind of keeper. But keeper of what? And why Iceland? It was as if the detective had been set a puzzle which could only be answered in another time, another place. Perhaps even upon another plane of reality.

THURSDAY 30 APRIL
LAST YEAR

Towards midnight

Black candles burned with a strong, yellow flame in the re-
production Georgian silver candelabra. If it hadn't been for the
dope she'd smoked earlier, Mandy might have found it all very
makeshift. Okay, so the fat of a hanged man was tricky stuff to
get hold of these days. The abolition of the death penalty had
seen to that. If you wanted it you had to grab hold of some
overweight prick and hang him yourself. But at least they might
have melted down some beeswax and mixed it up with pitch, and
perhaps a little belladonna. There were plenty of deadly
nightshade plants around the hedgerows if you knew where to
look.

The dope helped her to forget about that, though. Commercial
black candles from the occult shop looked right until you lit them.
Then they burned yellow. No sputtering blue flame and unholy
stench. Just dinner-party yellow.

The candelabra stood upon the makeshift altar, really a table
pushed against the wall and draped in a few yards of black draylon. Ranged between them were a variety of odd items. At the
back, against the wall, which was partly-covered by an H.R.
Giger poster now some years old and decaying around the edges,
stood a large, hand-made plaster figure of Satan, horns and penis
erect, chipped wings spread out to either side. It was garishly
painted in bright reds and gold, in contrast to the plain wooden
crucifix, sawn off its base and stuck back upside-down, directly
in front of it.

The other items were all, in their way, equally bizarre. A home-
made cat o'nine tails, a chrome trophy-cup, now detached from its
ebonite base, a large bottle of home-brewed cannabis wine (from
Geoff), a Tibetan incense-burner reeking dried henbane, datura and
myrrh (also from the local occult shop), and, last but not least, the
book and the box.

The book was Geoff's. At something over fifty the bank clerk was head of the *Ordo Satanas Northamptoniensis* (Northampton's Satanic Order), and didn't give a shit whether the Latin was right or not. To a non-Latinist, which he was, it looked both right and impressive, and that was all that counted. He made as sure as he could that he looked right and impressive on occasions such as this as well. His voice came out high and reedy through the effort of holding his sagging stomach in. His grey hair was swept back away from his forehead in a Draculine widow's peak. His eyes, dilated by the grass and brightened by a few drops of his own potion prepared from belladonna, shone with an appropriate Satanic light, even if he had to half-close them in a squint because he had left his glasses off. His fingers were covered in magical rings and half a dozen talismans (he always said 'talismen') hung about his neck. The final touch, though, the very essence of his priesthood of the Lord of This World, was in the black-dyed pubic bush and the projecting object, well-rubbed with a mixture of pepper and after-shave and brightly rouged, which waggled, half-erect, at its centre.

The others didn't know Geoff's secrets. Mandy did, because she was his favourite, and because the sacred mixture had stung her badly the first time they'd performed the Great Rite, making her insist that he washed before they tried it again. She put up with the charlatanism, though, as lovers have done from the days of Faust onwards, because she believed that there was something deep, some-thing genuine and clever, underneath. Previously they had drawn their rituals from Aubrey Melech's *Missa Niger* (Sut Anubis Pub-lishing, £9.99), but since he'd discovered this other book in a catalogue and paid a quite phenomenal amount, by his standards, for the text, they had worked its rituals faithfully, finding in them a frisson which could well suggest the genuine satanic article.

The book was bound in a dark, discoloured leather which Geoff claimed was human skin. It didn't have the traditional clasps to keep it shut. Nor did it stink of age and decay as malevolent gri-moires are traditionally supposed to do. But it was hand-written, and Mandy had seen a so-called Dane-skin in a glass case on a church door somewhere north-east of Birmingham which looked about the same as the binding.

In contrast to the macabre exoticism which was the book's most prominent feature, the box was plain and uninteresting. Cheaply-made, cheaply-varnished, its appeal was in the methods employed to obtain it and in its powdery, gritty contents. That it stood upon the altar at all was due, in part, to the book. Geoff claimed to have found within the mysterious text some elaborate coded instructions which had resulted in his setting the test which Neophyte Paul had now successfully completed. The small wooden container, eleven inches long, nine wide and a little over seven inches high, had been stolen by Paul, during the last dark of the moon, from the soulless, red-brick, domed bulk of Milton Crematorium. The theft was a part of the initiation process which Geoff believed he had devised to separate potentially useful members of his order from the cowardly and illiterate dross which usually applied. Paul's youth, for he was still only seventeen, was an asset, as was his rumoured bisexuality. That he had successfully completed his ordeal was also in his favour. Thus it was that, this 30 April, *Walpurgisnacht*, he was to be initiated into the OSN.

He was waiting outside the room, blindfold and, like the eight people already assembled and awaiting his entrance, completely naked. Had it not been for the dope, Mandy, looking around at the others, would have found them a pretty nondescript bunch. Were it not for the inordinate amounts of jewellery they wore they wouldn't have looked out of place in the pages of Health and Efficiency. Two of the girls might have been described as pretty, but none of the men was handsome, or even good-looking by any stretch of the imagination. She only bothered with Geoff because he had the magnetic, mysterious power of a leader to enhance his otherwise uninteresting persona. Paul, though, was tasty. Being a neophyte she'd not seen him naked yet, and her thoughts were filled with anticipation to the point where she didn't care whether Geoff saw what her hands were doing or not.

The door opened, a shaft of light from the hall outside spilling across the carpeted floor and illuminating Geoff's ankles where he stood before the altar. He turned, his bright-red penis waving towards the open doorway as an initiate conducted Paul into the temple.

'O thou who standeth on the threshold between the pleasant world of men and the domain of our Lord Satan,' Geoff began, 'hast thou the courage to make the crossing?'

Paul, nudged in the ribs by his escort, replied: 'I . . . have.'

They all grinned. Geoff had explained to them what the book directed should happen next, though he had been careful not to do the same to Paul.

'Then come hither and lie down in the presence of your betters to receive the touch of our Master.'

The two men nearest the open door seized Paul, dragging him into the room and forcing him down onto his back before the altar. His previous escort closed the door behind him and then removed the blindfold. Upside-down, Paul beheld the altar of Satan and its furnishings. He also had a superb and not particularly welcome view of the reddened underside of Geoff's member.

Mandy purred, as did several other of the women present. There was much to be said for Paul, now that they saw him properly for the first time. As their hungry eyes travelled down his young body they decided that there was much more to the youth than had previously met the eye.

'This is the way that all were first brought amongst us,' Geoff continued. He turned to the altar and picked up the box, raising its lid as he did so. Then he turned back to Paul, saying: 'You have brought to us the instrument of your own initiation, O neophyte. I am directed by the sacred text to intone the words of restoration as you receive its baptismal cascade. Thus I say: *Quaesivi vultum tuum, Domine Satanus. Perfice observantiae sanctae subsidium.*'

He had no way of knowing the meaning of the text he was citing. Nor did he possess any means of determining what its result would be. Paul's eyes widened as the box began to tilt. Mandy felt herself begin to fantasise about the feel of a lover sprinkled with the ashes of the dead.

'*Quae te auctore facienda cognovimus, te operante impleamus, per Domine Satanus,*' Geoff continued. '*Thulia est omnia. Restitutor, avertantur retrorsum.*' Thule is everything. Restorer, let them be turned backwards.

Out fell the ashes from the box. And Paul, blinded, his open mouth and nostrils stinging beneath the powdery cascade, began to scream.

Mandy's hand found something moist and began to explore it tenderly. Her eyes widened as Paul's body arched upwards beneath the showering powder, thrusting his most intriguing feature into the air. This was far and away the most exciting *Walpurgisnacht* she could remember since joining Geoff's order. And, afterwards, there was always the possibility of her fantasies becoming a pleasurable reality, after they'd drunk that bottle of cannabis wine upon the altar.

And then the change began.

Geoff, looking down through the falling ashes as he was, noticed it first. At first he thought that his eyes, never good, even with glasses, were playing one of their familiar tricks upon him. They did that on occasions, and this was, if nothing else, certainly an occasion. It was as if the ashes, settling like talcum-powder over Paul's features, were beginning to change him into something other than he was. Wrinkles began to form, to age his skin, to dry his lips and set crow's-feet about his eyes. His screams grew louder, higher in pitch, and his body shook with a force which made it difficult for those who came forward to hold his wrists and ankles to restrain him.

It was no trick, Geoff decided. Paul, young neophyte Paul, was actually beginning to grow older. The Satanic High Priest felt his mouth drop open and his legs begin to shake beneath him. In all the years he'd been playing with occultism he'd never witnessed anything like this.

Mandy didn't notice her fingers fall away from their previous occupation. She simply sat where she was, her eyes wide, her mind confused and growing more so with every passing second. Whether it was simply a trick of the candlelight or not she didn't know, but that firm, exciting young flesh held down upon the floor was growing older, sagging, tightening upon the bones. The hair was lightening from dark to an ancient white all over the altering body. It wasn't the ash doing it. The ash wasn't that colour. It was more pinky-brown. And that promising young plaything she'd promised herself was changing as well, shrinking, wrinkling like the rest of Paul. It wasn't possible. Changes like that didn't happen. But they were happening, there, in the temple of the *Ordo Satanas Northamptoniensis*, under the gaze of eight shuddering, frightened watchers whose bodies were now wet with a cold, unremitting perspiration.

'What the hell . . .?' one muttered.

'Shut up!' Mandy hissed. 'Don't say that word.'

If it were not for the physical alterations it could have been an epileptic fit. But epileptics stayed the same age. They didn't grow old before your eyes, not even with their clothes off. Not like Paul.

'I don't believe it,' another croaked. 'It's not real. It's not happening!'

Geoff's eyes widened. His knees were knocking together violently, affecting his balance. The wooden casket, now empty, fell from his trembling fingers and struck Paul a glancing blow across the forehead, drawing blood which flowed sluggishly into the deep-set wrinkles. Geoff fell back against the altar, his hands clutching at the draylon, knocking over the plaster Satan which fell and shattered into fragments across the carpeted floor.

'Jesus Christ,' he whispered, the words more of an invocation than an oath.

Paul's screams became whimpers, though as their intensity diminished his strength grew greater, until he was able to hurl those who held him away towards the walls. As he began to stand up Geoff lurched aside, his grip upon the black altar-covering upsetting the candles and the incense-burner. Glowing charcoal showered out and burned smouldering holes. Three of the black candles went out. The others began to set light to the carpet. The bottle of cannabis wine, still stoppered, fell with a heavy thud and began to roll in an arc towards Mandy.

Paul, still naked and no longer himself, stood up. He was taller as well as older, and his body, downed with white, curly hair, seemed stronger and more muscular than it had been before. His face was like parchment stretched across a skull which was no longer his own. His eyes, blue and too young for his wrinkled, gaunt visage, smiled down at those scrambling away in their panic before him. Even Geoff fled, leaving his precious book half-hanging off the altar. Only Mandy, fascinated despite her fear, stood up and faced the stranger which Paul had now become.

'Find me something to wear,' ordered a voice she'd never heard before.

'There ... will be something ... outside,' she stammered, horrified and yet, at the same time, attracted by the old man's obvious power. 'I'll fetch it.'

She left him alone in the temple. He turned to the altar and picked up the manuscript for which Geoff had paid so high a price, touching its pages to one of the still-burning candles. As they crisped and curled into ash he dropped the text and stood there, facing the door, awaiting Mandy's inevitable return. In the growing flames about him his features, bathed yellow, were both strong and gentle. Had a policeman called Robert Ferrow been there to see them he would have been shocked to find them familiar, though a part of him would not have been surprised.

Mandy returned, somewhat hesitantly, with an armful of abandoned clothing. The once Ptythonius Meeres took the garments from her and began to dress.

SATURDAY 2 MAY
LAST YEAR

Late evening

If only Harry Chester hadn't phoned.

Ferrow stared morosely from the empty glass clutched loosely in his fingers to the large jiffy-bag, ripped open and with its lining spilling out, beside the half-empty bottle of scotch on the coffee table.

'Chester, you're a prick,' the policeman grunted, stretching forward for another drink.

For a moment his hand wavered above the opened package, almost as if he was hesitating between remembrance and another shot of induced oblivion. Then he picked up the bottle and slammed in the Teachers. With his glass recharged he sat back once again and encouraged his memory to persist by the very act of consciously attempting to banish it.

Detective Constable Harry Chester, one of Ferrow's old colleagues from Waventree, had only been doing the right thing by his old buddy. He'd worked with Ferrow on the Wegrimham affair and knew the name of Ptythonius Meeres. And, after all, Ptythonius Meeres is hardly the sort of name that you forget too easily once you've heard it, Ferrow reasoned. So it was hardly surprising that when Meeres' ashes disappeared from Milton Crem, which was on the fringe of the Waventree patch, he'd take an interest in a minor, if ghoulish, offence. And when that Mandy kid had come in off the street with her stoned account of who'd done what with them it was only being a good ol' buddy to pass the tidings along. Even if your old mate was now a uniformed inspector based at Corby.

To describe Robert Ferrow as a different man since those last days at Wegrimham would be both accurate and inaccurate at the same time. Physically he had changed little, save for a slight deepening of his laugh-lines and the scar across his side where Williamson's bullet had clipped him. His straw-coloured hair hadn't turned grey with shock overnight. Nor had the light of the fanatic added an extra, feverish brightness to his blue eyes. Yet inside, where the world couldn't see, he already felt the effects of some strange metamorphosis. He regarded shadows as he had never regarded shadows before, searching them for little bright-eyes and sharp teeth. His eyes swept the night sky for anything even remotely blue which might twinkle and threaten in the northern quarter of the heavens. He ate a little less and drank a little more. And he would never touch mushrooms, or any other fungi, again, he kept telling himself.

He sprawled untidily on the couch, tunic unbuttoned and tie loose, the heels of his shoes digging into the carpet beside the table, drinking his third glass of scotch (neat), and struggled to forget or interpret the events of the day. He should have been seeing June Lowe tonight, but he'd rung and called that off. When he mentioned Ptythonius Meeres there was a heavy silence from June's end of the phone. Somehow that name seemed to come up every time a date got broken.

Ferrow had listened to what Chester had to say. Then he'd simply said: 'I'll be over,' and put the phone down. He made an excuse to the Super and drove straight to Waventree, where Chester was holding Mandy for him. With a woman PC present he listened to Mandy's story in an interview room, his face a mask, his eyes alert. When she finished, crying and shaking at her memories, he made no comment but simply stepped outside to where Chester was waiting for him.

He looked at the DC. 'You believe her, Harry?' he enquired.

Chester shrugged. 'So-so, Bob. With that kinda kid you can't tell right from dope-dream. We know Meeres' ashes went missing. We know this Geoff Butley's been having some kinky parties, though there's never been enough on him to bust him for anything. There is one thing, though.'

'Don't stop.'

'Okay. While I was waiting for you I checked with missing persons. A Mr Cull called in about his son Paul. Young Paul went out Tuesday and ain't back yet. Well, you know these kids . . .'

'Fuck the kids,' Ferrow grunted. 'I know Meeres better.'

Harry Chester eyed his old colleague carefully. Ferrow swore quite regularly, but when he swore in a low voice he really meant it. 'You really think she's telling the *truth*, Bob?'

'Have you talked to Butley?'

Chester shook his head. 'Thought I'd talk to you first.'

'Then get your coat and sign out. Let's go see the creep.'

'What about Mandy?'

Ferrow shrugged. 'Leave her there till we get back, or you get back. Any dope on her?'

'Nah, she wouldn't be that stupid.'

'Well, have her searched anyway before you let her go. Give her a good fright and she might just quit this satanic bullshit. *And* the dope. Now, get Butley's address and let's get moving.'

The headquarters temple of the *Ordo Satanas Northamptoniensis* was in the back room of a large terraced house in Moore Street. The area was mostly flats, and Ferrow found himself shuddering as he drove past a fire-blacked upper window. They'd found the body of one of Williamson's victims there, the remains badly charred after a gas explosion. The window was boarded up and there was scaffolding about the outside of the house. Harry Chester eyed him as they passed, unsure what to make of Ferrow since the events at Wegrimham.

'Look, Bob,' he ventured. 'We know Meeres is dead. We *know* that. You saw him killed. The path boys cut him open for the autopsy. That ward sister confessed and we had the quickest fucking conviction on record. Then we had the remains cremated. There's no way ashes come back from the dead. 'Specially not when the corpse has had its heart sliced open by the pathologist.'

Ferrow said nothing. The kind of logic Harry Chester was facing him with was irrefutable. But so were the devious, dubious powers of Ptythonius Meeres. If *anybody* can come back from the dead, he reasoned, that old bugger can. No rhyme or reason to it. He'd just go out and get it done.

There were so many unanswered questions about Meeres. Where had he been before he came to Wegrimham? What had he been doing? With the resources he so obviously had why had he needed to detail researchers to track Williamson down? And all that shit about being born in fourteen-something . . .

'Eighty-two?' Ferrow queried.

'Yeah. Just over there.'

He pulled to the kerb and cut the engine. The house seemed ordinary enough. Small, paved front garden. Three storeys. Single-fronted. Slate roof. No wiff of brimstone or sinister shadows. Or blue lights.

They got out of the car and crossed the road. The front gate was missing and, with Ferrow's uniform leading, they walked straight to the front door. Ferrow took hold of the Lincoln Imp brass knocker and hammered it hard. Inside the house the echoes rang a long way back.

Footsteps sounded on the uncarpeted, tiled floor, soft at first then growing progressively louder as they approached the front door. A latch clicked and it opened a few inches.

'Geoffrey William Butley?' Ferrow demanded.

'Oh hell,' the figure said weakly. Its grey hair was awry and the pallid face was unshaven. The open-necked shirt was stained at the collar and cuffs and Butley stank of alcohol.

'Open the door, Butley,' Ferrow ordered. 'We're not going to talk out here.'

The High Priest of Satan reluctantly agreed. Ferrow and Chester stepped into the hall and waited for him to close it behind them. Then he turned and, eyes averted, faced his visitors.

'Let's see this temple of yours,' Ferrow snapped.

With a sigh Butley edged past them in the narrow hall and led the way to a door beside the kitchen, at the back of the house. He reached down and, his fingers trembling, turned the handle. As the door swung open he stood aside.

Robert Ferrow shook his head. 'In there,' he commanded. 'Go on, Butley.'

The High Priest's eyes darted wildly. He took a deep breath, surveyed his two unwelcome guests, then complied.

They followed him, barring his exit. 'Have you been in here since Tuesday night?' Chester demanded.

The question was unnecessary. Everything about the Temple of Satan was exactly as Mandy had described it, right down to the abandoned casket which had contained the ashes of the late Pythonius Meeres and the unopened bottle of cannabis wine.

A strange odour, part stale incense, part burnt carpet and part something *other*, still clung in the air. The black candles had burned down to wax stains and puddles. The shattered image of Satan leered up from where it had fallen. The charred boards of the manuscript, the pages and spine little more than a mass of brittle black curls, provided a last confirmation of Mandy's statement.

'So where's Paul Cull?' Harry Chester enquired.

Butley shook his head, his eyes pleading.

'Is that the best you can do?' Ferrow demanded. 'You and your bunch of loonies get drugged up and go stealing dead men's ashes.

You get your kicks drinking that stuff,' he kicked the cannabis wine with his toe as he spoke, making the bottle clunk over to the nearest wall, 'then have some kind of communal jerk-off. There's a youth missing, Butley. No-one's seen Paul Cull since Tuesday night. Where is he?'

'I . . . I don't know. Believe me, I don't know. I didn't see him leave . . .'

'Then I think you'd better come with us.' Turning to Harry Chester: 'I'll take you and this shit-head back to Waventree. Get that analysed,' he pointed to the wine, 'and you'll have a charge. Find the others and talk to them. And give them all the biggest fucking scare of their lives, Harry.'

'My arrest, Bob?'

'Just keep me posted. After all, this isn't my patch any more.'

He drained the rest of the scotch in his glass and set it down beside the diminishing quantity in the bottle. As he did so his hand brushed the opened jiffy-bag. With his fingers tremoring slightly he reached into its spilling guts and took out the contents. The envelope he set on one side for a while. The gun he dropped into his lap, squinting down at it through eyes that were beginning to swim.

It was impossible to reach his present rank, even allowing for some occult conspiracy, without knowing something about firearms. Yet the Bergmann-Bayard was a weapon usually encountered only in books about the history of weapons. A 10-shot self-loader (he preferred the term to the more common but less accurate *automatic*), the pistol was similar in appearance to the famous 'broomhandle' Mauser, though less well known and taking a larger calibre bullet. First manufactured in 1910, it had later been adopted by both Danish and Greek military forces, but by now few enough survived for it to be more of a collector's item than a working weapon.

The first time Ferrow had seen that gun it had been pointing at his head. Sometimes he found himself wondering if Meeres would actually have used it on him. He suspected not, for the old man needed his help and the time-scale involved would have made it impossible for Meeres to recruit anyone else. Even so . . .

He opened the breech and checked again that it was empty. Like the Mauser the magazine was integral, mounted beneath the barrel in front of the trigger. In the remains of the jiffy-bag were twenty of the large 9mm Parabellum rounds the weapon fired. Not, perhaps, the most powerful handgun in the world, punk, but it could easily blow half your head clean off, and even a quarter was more than enough.

With a heavy sigh he tossed the weapon onto a rumpled nearby cushion and reached for the envelope. Something had kept him from opening Meeres' package until now. Probably it was the same something which had prevented him from disclosing its existence to anyone else: a profound wish that once dead and charcoaled it was the last he'd ever hear of the man who called himself the Keeper.

But now, he knew, it was time. Everything has its season, and this was the season for ripping open jiffy-bags.

Ferrow tore open the envelope and took out the folded sheet of hospital notepaper it contained. In an archaic scrawl he could barely read, the single sentence spidered its way across the surface:

You should visit Scotland for your holidays this year, Friend Robert, particularly Fortstown.

The note was signed PTYTHONIUS.

With a grunt the policeman pulled his feet towards him and struggled out of the depths of the couch. Crossing to an untidy bookshelf nearby he pulled out a motoring atlas and flipped through the index at the back. Then he turned to the page headed *Elgin and Aberdeen* and ran a finger down the references. Sure enough, there it was. B9123 out of Banff, turn north at Gamrie.

Fortstown. Just another fishing village on the coast west of Fraserburgh. Middle of nowhere. North Sea fucking cold.

He dropped the atlas and trudged back to the couch, where he sat down heavily and poised his hand over the whisky bottle. He intended to pick it up. He knew that's what he was going to do. That's why he was so surprised when he found the telephone receiver in his fingers and his free hand dialling a number he knew off by heart.

'That you, June?' he asked, hoping he'd been forgiven for his earlier call.

'If you think you're coming over now, Bob, you've another think coming. It's too late for anything tonight. I'm still trying to impress my new employer by being bright-eyed and bushy-tailed a.m.'

'Let's leave your lovely bushy tail out of this for now,' Ferrow grinned. 'Look, I want to ask you something.'

'Okay, go ahead. But keep it quick and clean for once.'

Now how the hell was he supposed to do that with some of the images he had dancing before his eyes? Instead he asked: 'Any holiday plans this year?'

He sensed her mental shrug at the other end of the line. She replied: 'Well, I had been wondering about Scotland . . .'

He could have screamed conspiracy and slammed the phone down. Certainly a sudden surge of panic swept through him as he evaluated June's answer. But he fought it down.

'Sounds a good idea,' he managed, calmly. 'Friend of mine recommended a place called Fortstown to me once. A little village up near Banff . . .'

Almost frightened of her answer he performed the impossible by interrupting himself. '*And* I've thought of a great way to cut down our phone bills,' he added quickly.

PART TWO

The Skull Meditation

Life is for living. The dead have no place in it. They are a taboo which must not be broken. They bring grief to the living and changes to the flesh. Death should have no beauty. Only pregnancy and life should be permitted beauty. In age, the approach to death, beauty fades and withers like a spring flower in the summer, or like a leaf in the autumn. It is gone, for age is the herald of death. For those who have been kissed by the years which have advanced upon them there is no mystery and no surprise when death lays his hand upon their flesh. For those who have yet to feel time's kisses there is a horror about the unexpected, a horror only known by those who feel that skeletal hand upon themselves, or upon those close to them.

For the living there is grief. The mother, radiant in her expectancy, moans with an incoherent grief which expresses wordlessly her inability to comprehend the stillborn child. The husband, helpless and futile by her side, can neither comfort nor understand. Both are helpless before this change which has robbed them of their anticipated future. Both see only death, the death of the child they had expected. Neither can see that there is still life, that there is organic matter which will change in decay and return, in its difference, to the earth.

And why should they? What right have we to expect them to see beyond their grief, beyond the succour given to those who must keep on living? Why should they have to understand as the pathetic little body is laid in a silk-lined coffin, only to vanish from their thwarted sight for ever? Why should they be expected to see the beauty of decay, the subtle, inevitable, imperceptible changes which dew the harvest of their love? Why should they want to look through eyes that they do not, cannot, possess?

Only to a few is it given to see beyond the tragedy, beyond the lowering cloud which mars the loveliness of growing life. Only to a few is the vision granted which transcends the grave. Most only have the contentment which eventually consoles them by placing the little body amongst the ranks of the heavenly elect. That they can understand. The Lord giveth, and the Lord taketh away. Blessed be the name of the Lord.

The living, consoled as best they can be, must pick up the pieces and start anew. They have their memories, but these will fade like the bloom on the becoffined cheeks of the dead. Ritual may preserve the memories and dull the pain. Soon there will be new love, new life, new beauty. Sometime, somehow.

Only for a few does life continue beyond the veil death draws to hide his own. Only for those is beauty truly to be thought immortal, for their eyes see beyond the corruption of the body, rejecting what is. Yet what is their delusion but the same as those who bury their dead and retain them in memory unseen? Why should they want to watch the dissolution, revelling in the catharsis it brings?

Some say their dead call to them, uttering their names in the small hours of the coming day. Some see the loved one standing near, passing a window in forgotten sunlight, laughing at table because they can no longer eat. Some are haunted by the past, some regretful of the banished future. These are little things, tricks of the mind to keep the loved dead near. For a few, though, there is another way.

Suddenly, for Davie Quarry, the night outside penetrated his heart. Walking in the storms which so frequently buffeted this part of the coast had always been a pleasure to him. His heart leaped and thrilled and pounded with the thunder of the waves upon the rocks. His eyes, squinting through the slanting rain, were bright and happy in the blurred and dampened twilight. His feet, upon the slippery path, were certain with the sureness of habit.

There had been times in Davie's life, a long, long time ago, in the legend-haunted years of his youth, when this walk was not so pleasant. They told him the tales of the ghosts who patrolled the coast, the ghosts of drowned sailors who mewed and pleaded with the voices of the surf and the seagulls, the spirits of the pagan raiders who had once met their doom in an ill-fated raid upon a settlement long vanished, the revenants of star-crossed lovers that still plunged, in the dark of the moon, to a bone-shattering death on the rocks beneath the cliffs. And Davie, being little more than a boy in those days, had felt a little fear.

Today night has been banished by the magic of electricity, but earlier this century, in the remoter places of these islands, that magical power was unknown or, at least, unavailable. Legends brooded in the darkness, feeding off its intangible bulk, creeping into the souls and bodies of those who were forced to walk within it. Davie Quarry was one of them, and a walk alone through the darkened places of his myth-haunted youth was not an experience he relished. There was always that temptation to turn your head, to look behind and see if some doubtful denizen of that dark world of legendary was lurking there upon the path.

And yet there never was. Well, perhaps once or twice there had been a scuffling amongst the rocks or a rustle in the sparse vegetation, but it was always a dog, or perhaps a rabbit, or an injured seagull. The drowned sailors remained firmly in their sunken graves, beneath the persistent pounding of the waters. The pagan raiders failed to groan in savage death. The lovers, already doomed and lost, declined to leap.

With the passing of the years the legends were forgotten, submerged beneath the more practical weather and year-lore of the fisherman. Many of the friends of Davie's youth had grown up and left the little village, seeking the more profitable world of the south. In recent years the more adventurous had moved down the east coast towards Aberdeen, lured by the tales of easy money to be made from the burgeoning oil industry. Of those who left only a few, the unfortunate and the retarded, from years of isolated inbreeding, ever returned to Fortstown.

He himself had never tried to leave. His father had fished the waters before him, and his father in the years before that. Besides, he knew the place and he knew the people. He felt comfortable there, amongst the steep alleys and stepped walks of the little village, carved precipitously through the centuries from the face of the cliffs about a natural harbour. He knew everyone, and everyone knew him. Davie Quarry, the old fisherman in the cottage around the point. D'ye ken auld Davie? No? Then ye're nae fra' roond here, mon.

With age came respect, both for his abilities and his outward stoicism. The deaths of his wife and sons, caused by a railway accident on a trip to Aberdeen, had warmed the village to him. In public Davie shed no tears, facing the world with taciturn inscrutability in the face of his adversity which could only be admired. In private, though, his tears flowed without restraint, for his grief was a private thing, something which the others did not need to share, something which properly belonged to him alone.

Before the accident Miles Fournessie, who kept the Fortstown Arms, and was regarded by half the village as a saint and by the other half of the staunch kirk community as the devil incarnate, for that latter reason, had rarely seen Davie Quarry across his bar. Once alone, though, the old fisherman had begun his nightly pilgrimages along the coast to Fournessie's hostelry. He never drank a great deal, nor did he mix to any great extent with the other villagers, but he would reply civilly to those who spoke to him, enjoying a few drams with a beer chaser, and feeling about him the warmth and companionship which fate had denied to him at home. Every night he went there, haunted by ghosts more recent and more tangible than those which had haunted his youth. Every night he returned to his cottage, a little warmer in heart and body for his excursion.

D'ye ken auld Davie? He's no sa' sad in here. He's a good mon, is yon. Will he be in taenight, Miles?

Davie Quarry? He'll nae miss. Neer sixteen year since they died, and he's nae missed a night. There's his chair, in yon corner, close by the hearth. He'll be in. Watch an' wait, friend.

The path beneath his feet levelled out as he left the spray-lashed rocks behind him. Now he crunched upon the grey-red shingle, the grey-black waves of the North Sea pounding beside him, just a few feet away. He had rounded the point, leaving his cottage behind. In the distance, ahead of him, the few lights of Fortstown burned brightly through uncurtained windows, marking his destination through the gloom.

In the sixteen years Davie Quarry had walked along the coast to Fournessie's inn he had never met a single person on the path. He lived alone and walked alone. His was the only cottage west of the village. There was no need for any other to be going his way, around the point and along beside the rocks. Not even a casual walker would venture that way on a post-prandial stroll. Not under the shadow of the old kirk.

St John's was in ruins now, and had been for as long as any of the villagers could remember. A new kirk of brick and flints, built in Fortstown itself, had replaced the crumbling stone structure outside the village more than 150 years before. No-one would have wanted to make the long trek along the cliffs, then down the depression, beside the stream, to where the ancient edifice stood alone in the midst of its little burying ground, even if the legend had not existed.

This was the one place on his solitary journey which invariably raised something of his childhood fears in Davie's life-hardened being. Here, where he crossed the clear, rilling waters which meandered down from the higher ground inland, the fisherman invariably felt a slight chill, even on the warmest nights. Sometimes, having stepped across the stream's narrow mouth, he would stop and peer up through the twilight, as if looking for something in the ruin that he hoped he would never see. And yet, if there was movement amongst the broken outlines of its arches, it was always natural movement, like the rabbits and gulls which had alarmed a younger Davie all those years before. His heart would flutter for a moment, but then it would be still.

In the Fortstown Arms Miles Fournessie glanced at the face of the clock whilst his hands mechanically dried a pint glass. Auld Davie'll soon be here now, he thought.

He stepped across the stream and glanced at the ruins, black against the lighter darkness of the coastline. A seabird wheeled in the night-blue sky above them, its cries echoing through the pounding waves. In the ruins of St John's, though, nothing stirred that Davie Quarry could see. He turned back to his path, surveying the village lights, now closer and brighter, and stepped forward to continue his walk.

Where the figure came from he never knew. Suddenly it was there, beside him, a dark silhouette upon the beach. And his heart was pounding with the half-remembered legends of his youth.

Oddly-dressed, perhaps, but it was solid, natural. No insubstantial wraith, no pale and demented phantom of the night. Simply a solitary, man-like shape upon the edge of the waters, a man, a tall man, in a long coat and wide-brimmed hat.

The features beneath the hat were indistinct, blurred by a shadow falling from the brim in a light that was already far from adequate. From the outline it was a long face above a white collar, and something told Davie that it was old, much older than his own seamed countenance.

Fournessie placed the glass upon the shelf beneath the polished mahogany bar-counter and grinned at Andrew Craigham. 'Did ye heer young Wullie Stover in here last night?' he asked.

Craigham nodded. 'Soundin' off aboot Caspar Locke, ye mean, Miles? I heered the lad. If 'twas nae the only pub fer miles I'd a' said he'd had a wee dram t'over before he came. He's mostly a sound enough young fella, is Wullie. Still,' he shrugged, 'there's little enough roond here to occupy young minds. The auld legends are something tae keep 'em busy wi'.'

'In all my yeers here,' Fournessie continued, 'I've heered 'em a'. An' auld Caspar Locke comes up reg'lar. But there's none I'd credit ha' seen aught at a'.'

The fisherman stood perfectly still as the figure extended its hand, the fist closed about an unseen object held within. It said nothing and made no sound, not even the sound of breathing. From beneath the shadow of the brim, grey eyes, rheumed and yellowed and shot with purpled blood-vessels, burned into his own.

'Take it,' came the voice, deep and sepulchral, tainted with a dialect that no living man still spoke. 'Hae pity on a poor sinner.'

A shudder passed through Davie Quarry's limbs. His hands, thrust deep into the pockets of his overcoat, struggled not to move. Perspiration beaded his forehead beneath the fisherman's cap he wore, perspiration born of sudden fear, forced from the pores with every fevered beat of his troubled heart. He felt a will that was not his own surrounding him as he stood there, a will that reached into his pockets and slowly, gradually, drew his hands from their depths.

''Tis a small thing tae ask, friend Davie. Take it, mon.'

His fingers shook limply, contrasting strangely with the rigidity of his wrist and arm, as he began to reach out towards that outstretched fist.

'He's a mite late,' grunted Miles Fournessie, squinting at the clock through a growing haze of tobacco smoke.

'Aye,' Andrew Craigham agreed. 'If he's no heer soon he'll lose his seat tae me.'

A little further, Davie. Then that fist will open. Then it will be done, and he'll pass by. Just a little further. Then it's yours.

The fisherman suddenly realised that he had not been breathing. In his fright he had held his breath, his body as tensed and rigid as the arm he was stretching out against his will. As the imprisoned air rushed from his lungs the spell dissolved about him. Panting, soaked with sweat, he stepped back and began to circle around the figure in his path. The ancient grey eyes followed his hesitant progress, and the outstretched fist remained, clenched, pushing its unhallowed gift towards him.

'Christ have mercy!' Davie yelled. Then he turned and ran, gripped by blind panic, towards the reassuring lights of the village. As he fled he heard mocking laughter ring out behind him, laughter that was as unhallowed as the gift that the figure had sought to bestow.

'Christ have mercy?' came the ironic, questioning tones of the figure on the path. 'Christ? Have mercy?'

As Davie gained the steps beside the harbour the hollow tones rang on, mingling with the crashing waves and the cries of gulls, disturbed in the night.

'Has he mercy for you, Davie Quarry? Is that it? He has none . . . for . . . me . . . How should a myth hae mercy for a mon?'

With a wry grin Andrew Craigham moved towards the old fisherman's seat beside the fire-bright hearth. As he did so the little wooden door at the further end of the bar burst open, permitting a sudden, savage wind to howl into the inn. The regulars, young and old alike, turned to face the disturbance. Muttering an oath, Craigham set down his dram and moved forward to close the door.

His hand was upon the latch when Davie Quarry pushed against him, his usually ruddy features white as a corpse-cloth. The younger man caught him about the waist as his legs began to give beneath the skirts of his coat.

Another man closed the door whilst Fournessie, grim-faced, poured a generous measure of malt into a glass. Craigham half-led, half-carried the old fisherman to his seat by the fire. The publican came round from behind his counter and lifted the glass to Quarry's lips. When some of the pale, golden liquid had been forced down he set the glass within reach of the old man's trembling, nerveless fingers.

'What is it, Davie?' he asked, gently. 'Ye look as if ye'd seen a ghost.'

Still panting with the exertion of his flight the fisherman reached out and drained the glass.

'Another?' Fournessie queried.

Old Quarry nodded, determinedly, a red flush beginning to stain the unnatural pallor of his weathered features.

Andrew Craigham knelt beside the old man, one hand gripping his shoulder reassuringly. 'It's a' right, mon. Ye're safe as hooses. Wha's frit ye, Davie?'

Fournessie returned with the glass filled again. Quarry seized it and drank half the contents, then returned it to the table. He looked up at the ring of expectant, whispering faces which had gathered about his chair.

'I ... saw ... him ...' he stammered. 'I saw him, Andy. There, on the beach path ... where they allus said he'd be ...'

Craigham squeezed the old man's shoulder and tried to keep overt concern out of his expression. 'Who was it, Davie?' he asked. 'Who did ye see?'

Quarry turned his horrified gaze upon the younger man and reached out, his old fingers digging into the sleeve of Craigham's jacket. 'It could only be ... him, Andy. I've nae seen him before, but it was him. There's nae doubt. It was Caspar Locke.'

He was agitated as he spoke, but there was no hint of anything besides total belief in what he had witnessed, except for the remnants of stark fear. The ring of faces held their silence for a moment, then turned one to another and went muttering away. At the end of a bar a youth laughed nervously and over-loudly, but he laughed alone, and a stern look from a man he respected brought the laughter to an end.

Craigham patted Davie Quarry on the shoulder and stood up. 'Well,' he began, softly, to Fournessie, 'we've laughed at young Wullie and the others, Miles. Do we believe it frae Davie?' His face, as he spoke, was grim.

Fournessie shook his head. 'He's no one for stories,' came the reply. 'If Davie Quarry said he'd seen auld Hornie I'd nae dispute it. If he says tha' he's seen Caspar Locke, then 'twas Caspar Locke he's seen. What you or I would ha' seen I dinna ken, Andy. But auld Davie's seen Caspar Locke.'

The innkeeper walked back behind the bar and opened a door between the rows of optics. 'Marie,' he called to his wife, 'make up a bed. Davie Quarry's no well. He'll stay here the night. Oh, and telephone for Doctor Farquharson as well, woman.'

Davie Quarry sat alone beside the fire, oblivious of the mutterings around him. Craigham leaned upon the bar and played with his whisky, sliding it around in an ellipse against the inside of his glass. When Fournessie closed the door and returned to polish some more glasses Craigham said: 'Ye ken what this means, Miles? It means that there's truth in the auld stories. It means that there is a Caspar Locke out on yon shore.'

Fournessie grunted. 'I dinna ken the meaning, Andy. All we've heered is a few words frae a frit auld mon. Stay later, when I've closed up. He'll tell us more when Doctor Farquharson comes. I'm nae bairn tae tak frit at a few words. Neither are ye. We'll heer more, later.'

He turned away, peering at the floor, keeping his frown to himself. Miles Fournessie had fought in Korea and served over twenty years as a regular soldier. The darkness of the night had no fears for him. He was a local lad, and he'd grown up with the local legends in the same way as Andrew Craigham and Davie Quarry. He knew the story of Caspar Locke but, like the others, paid little credence to it. But now, on this summer evening, after a day when new life had begun to burst from leafless twigs and the grass had taken on a deeper hue, when the best of the shoals were back and every hard-drinking fisherman in Fortstown was briefly a millionaire for a few hours' work, his world was threatening a change. There was a darkness in some of those old stories, a darkness which could clutch with a stranglehold at any heart weak enough to welcome it. And now, in the dim, smoke-hazed warmth of the bar, with customers who spoke now in lowered voices, Miles Fournessie felt his heart begin to open to the darkness.

Why Gerard Covington happened to be in that street he could never really determine. It was not a location he usually frequented. In fact it was almost true to say that he had never walked its length before. Certainly it held for him an unconscious novelty that was refreshing to one in his state of mind.

He was not one who thought of himself as a deep man, nor was he given to introspection and self-analysis. Some things impinged upon him only when there was no means to hand of avoiding them. His education, exceptional for an orphan, was financed by the only aunt he had. Zoë was his mother's sister, younger and more vibrant than the few dim memories he retained of his mother. She had taken charge of Gerard, an awkward, perplexed seven-year-old, shortly after the accident which eventually killed both his parents. Zoë was both mother and friend in those moments she spared from her own life for the pathetic little boy Gerard had been.

The moments Zoë had granted him varied in both degree and intensity, becoming more frequent and intense as he approached and embraced puberty. Her interest in the young boy was minimal, confined solely to those actions required by the provision of essentials, such as the engaging of companions for the holidays, or the exercise given to her right wrist in signing cheques. Whilst his parents had been in comfortable circumstances Zoë, only fifteen years his senior, had married well and early, only to be quickly widowed. There were times when Gerard somewhat uncharitably felt that, had he been a few years younger, she might have contracted a second marriage and ignored him altogether. As it was, the timing had been perfect for both their needs. Zoë was given the opportunity to play with her lovers for the six years it took for Gerard to reach a state of development in which she could interest herself.

He stared into the window of the shop through unseeing eyes, aware of nothing before and about him. Zoë, dear raven-haired Zoë, had been more to him than could ever be expected of a relative.

She had been both his mother and his friend. She had also been his first and only lover.

His thoughts could travel back nearly seventeen years as if it was only the day before yesterday. He remembered in all its momentous clarity how he had described that incident in the locker-room at school to her, how that older boy, though only by a few months, had taken hold of him and forced his development towards maturity. He remembered what it had meant, how she came into his room one night during the holidays and found him masturbating, how she had coaxed and cajoled him, explaining with a mixture of awareness and misconception that his actions might be harmful. He remembered how she had dissuaded him from the practice with a promise of more intense and intimate places and things.

His gaze was focused a few inches before the doors of the chiffonier, its surfaces cluttered with crested souvenirs and ebony elephants, clustered with shells and onyx eggs, as he recalled the fulfilment of that promise and all it had meant to his life. He pondered celebrations and revels enjoyed during three years as an undergraduate. He reflected on the disappointment trapped between young thighs, flesh that belonged to strangers, however well he might know them in the lecture halls. He dwelt briefly upon returning home, to Zoë, and confessing his infidelities, and the probing questions which always accompanied those confessions.

'But was she as good, darling? Did she offer you everything I can offer you? And where did she learn? Can she purse her lips as I do? Do her muscles know how to respond to you like mine?'

Gerard's answers were always the same. 'No, Zoë.' He'd given up calling her 'Aunt' after that first night of experience. At first it had been strange, a boy of thirteen calling a woman of twenty-eight to whom he was related, his mother's sister, by her christian name. 'No, Zoë, she's not as good. She doesn't know how to move in the way you do. Her mouth is too small – too wide. Her teeth stick out. She's too tight – too loose. There's no way she can compare to you.'

Eventually these confessions, questions and answers, developed into a liturgical ritual between confessor and confessed. The penance imposed, a few token tears, seemed always the introduction to that unusual intimacy which time and desire had established between them.

Yet there was no exclusivity in their relationship. Zoë had other lovers both before and after the initiation of her nephew. Gerard, though thrilled by his aunt's attentions, retained a piquant curiosity regarding girls and women of his own age. When apart, especially during his three years at university, they journeyed along their own paths. But never did their mutual desire decrease. It remained for them as fresh and wonderful as that first evening. It was a precious secret, a gift that both cherished and nurtured, a gift from God.

After university there was no question of Gerard having to earn a living in any way. Apart from the financial legacy from her dead husband, Zoë had also inherited a first-class financial adviser. The few assets Gerard's parents left behind were quickly liquidated and the proceeds invested in a trust. The interest thus earned was reinvested, increasing the capital's earning ability. Inside six years the accountant's dexterous manipulations had effectively doubled the original sum.

Whilst Zoë, dear, lovely Zoë, was not overtly jealous, she determined that Gerard should be financially dependent upon her during her lifetime. The accountant inspired her complete confidence by the way in which he managed her own affairs, successfully restraining her extravagances, ensuring that she only drew off the interest. This was not to say that her life-style was modest, for it was not. Until Gerard's initiation, an act completely unexpected by both of them, she maintained herself with friends and furnishings appropriate to her inheritance. In Gerard, however she quickly came to realise, she had a companion who both suited and delighted her, and could continue to do so for the rest of her life. Thus the benefits accruing from Gerard's trust were not to be released to him until his beloved Zoë was dead. At that time he would also inherit the full estate left by her former husband and become an extremely wealthy man.

The home which Zoë and Marcus Fyler had shared during the period of their brief and tragic marriage, Faracres, in Sussex, required a minimum staff of five and an annual outlay, even in the mid 1950s, of several thousand pounds to maintain. Shortly after that decisive evening before Gerard's fourteenth birthday, in the summer of 1965, she decided that it no longer suited her needs. Consequently she began to look, slowly and carefully, for a smaller and more intimate home for them.

It was almost two years later that Zoë called, herself, to collect her nephew from boarding school for the holidays in a car she was driving. The youth remarked on the absence of a chauffeur and was met with a knowing smile. After the school porter had loaded his trunk and cases into the comparatively modest Mercedes estate they began the drive home along roads which struck Gerard as increasingly unfamiliar. As they progressed east their journey veered to the north, away from Sussex, towards Warwickshire. Gerard's increasingly frequent enquiries regarding their destination remained mysteriously but charmingly unanswered. Gradually his suspicions were confirmed by the countryside flashing past outside. When the A5 linked into the new M6 motorway suspicion was transmuted into certainty. Zoë, the enchantress, had changed castles.

They left the M6 where it ended, at Preston, and continued north into Scotland, skirting south of Glasgow and across towards Aberdeen. The Mercedes continued on, through the centre of the granite city, between rows of tall, brown-pink buildings, and then turned north once more. Gerard, too tired to wonder, fell asleep.

At dusk, almost eleven hours after she had collected her nephew from school, Zoë turned off the cliff road which would ultimately have taken them to Banff. The road had been narrow for this last leg of their journey, metalled, but narrow enough to require the provision of regular passing places, like so many northern highways. Now, as the Mercedes turned down the little track which led to their new home, even the smooth German suspension wasn't enough to leave Gerard asleep.

In the middle of a stretch of cliff-top moorland, surrounded by a screen of shrubbery and low, stunted trees, stood Witham Lodge. Its gates stood proudly open and in the headlight beams glistened with fresh paint. Beyond them the gravel drive swept around in semi-circle until it reached the arched porch on the south side of the two-storey building.

Beyond doubt Zoë's accountant had been busy again. Housing here was substantially cheaper to acquire and maintain than in the more popular south, and the lodge stood in almost 100 acres of land, as opposed to the thirty-five of their former home. Naturally there were shooting and fishing rights with the property which, as Zoë wasn't slow to point out, would prove a great draw for Gerard's friends in the holidays.

The house itself, Gerard was disappointed to discover, was substantially smaller than their former home. There were only three reception rooms and five bedrooms beneath its grey slate roof and plain, if frequent, gables. The garage complex beside it, with a separate flat over for a housekeeper, was only large enough for two cars, and there was no stable-block.

Initially Gerard was horrified. By the standard of Faracres, Witham Lodge was minute and poky. Architecturally it was about the same age as the Georgian House in Sussex, but it didn't have the same white cleanness. Built of local stone, grey-brown without the pinky tinge of the Aberdeen granite, it was a contrast in both size and style. As he stepped out of the car he began to give vent to his protests, leaving his aunt in no doubt that he found it a rather painful contrast.

Zoë only laughed and kissed him lightly on the forehead. It was a part of the enchantment she had woven about him that her public displays of affection betrayed not even the tiniest hint of their private relationship. It was also a feature of her spell that such a caress could inspire him with the promise of things to come, whilst inducing patience and trust. No sooner had he received that kiss than he fell silent. She slipped her arm around his shoulders and led him unresistingly towards the iron-studded door inside the tiled, arched porch.

Once inside the Lodge his doubts began to subside. The rooms had all the light spaciousness of Faracres, even if the ceilings were lower. As in their former home, the Regency-stripe decorations were matched to the overall pastel shades of Zoë's favourite colour schemes. And it was furnished with the best of the familiar pieces from the other house.

The accountant had struck again. The sale of Faracres and most of its contents, even after Zoë had selected the best of them for Witham Lodge, had increased her already enormous capital quite noticeably. The smaller house not only required less outlay on maintenance but also less outlay on staff. From five living-in servants in Sussex, Zoë now only needed a housekeeper-cum-domestic, who lived at the Lodge on a permanent basis, and a pensioner from Fortstown, who came three days a week to care for the garden and lawns around the house. Eventually she would need a forester as well, but for the present the scattered thickets of woodland could be left to the dubious, uncertain care of the local wildlife, which consisted of badgers, foxes and rabbits for the most part. For the present though, with a few mechanical aids, old Venner could cope quite well.

Gerard had never been a particularly dedicated horseman, so the lack of a stable-block struck him as more an architectural or status omission than a practical source of distress. His own room was the largest on the first floor and there was an adjoining door into Zoë's.

The housekeeper, Mrs Szorciewicz, had her quarters above the garages on the other side of the house. Despite her name Mrs Szorciewicz was as Scots as they came. During the war she had married a Polish airman stationed nearby. Afterwards they had settled in Fortstown and continued to live there, happily, until Konrad Szorciewicz was drowned in a fishing accident in 1963. The radio on the boat he'd helped to crew had failed shortly before a storm warning, and he and two others had been drowned before they could make the harbour. Their circumstances had never been good, and that meant that his widow, universally called Helen because very few locals were prepared to attempt her surname, went into domestic service on a casual basis. Zoë had heard of her during an exploratory visit to the village and engaged her after an interview.

As time passed Gerard grew to love Witham Lodge, partly because it was not unfamiliar inside, furnished in the same style and with the same items as Faracres had been, and partly because it was Zoë's choice and he loved Zoë with increasing depth and appreciation. Their relationship intensified in many ways as Gerard passed into manhood. They were able to recognize it for what it was, a merging of personalities and interests. No feelings of disgust or guilt ever entered their thoughts. The rest of the world, if it had known, would have called it incest and cast them out as beyond the pale, Zoë as a pederast and Gerard as her tainted victim. The rest of the world would not have understood. But they understood, and the rest of the world never knew. On the few occasions when Gerard's conversation in company slipped and implied an excessive fondness for his aunt it could always be explained away by her caring for him since the tragic death of his parents. Zoë, older and more careful, never slipped.

As his education continued they began to explore art and literature together. At first Zoë showed no predilection for more modern authors and artists, confining her criticisms and praise to the art of the Renaissance, exploring Dürer's use of line and the implicit homosexuality of Michelangelo's nudes. Her literary tastes seemed similarly narrow, her enthusiasms restraining their field to Richardson and Fielding, both authors venerated by the late Marcus Fyler. Gerard could never respond as fully as he would have wished because his own taste was more modern. He flirted with Dickens and toyed briefly with Thackeray before progressing to Baudelaire and the Mann brothers. At university he studied literature of the nineteenth century, returning home after term to expound on Huysmans and Lautréamont, which he read both in translation and in the original French, and the poems and essays of Edgar Allen Poe, which he insisted provided an effective commentary on his short fictions.

In time Zoë came to appreciate, and then to share, her nephew's tastes.

Together their literary and artistic delvings became more and more directed towards the obscure and mysterious. Zoë's enchantment with Dürer's woodcut lines transmuted into an appreciation of the charcoal fantasies of Félicien Rops. The classical purity of Michelangelo Buonarotti did not prevent her surprising sympathy with the death's-head obsessions of James Ensor. She read Pirandello and Rolfe, and eventually enjoyed them.

After university Gerard was able to spend as much time as he wished with his enchantress. Sometimes he would travel, alone, exploring the pyramids and catacombs of Mexico, bringing her back sugar skulls from the feast of the dead. He haunted Paris, tracing the steps of Huysmans' hero Durtal, as he explored the life of Gilles de Rais and progressed inexorably towards the satanic rites conducted by the Canon Docre. But most of the time he spent at Witham Lodge, trying his hand at painting and poetry, living the life of the protagonists of the books he had read, searching for a mysterious something which seemed ever to elude him.

Despite his unarticulated quest he was not unhappy. Zoë had borne no children to age her body. Her breasts remained firm and full, though not large. Her stomach was flat and her thighs firm. Her hair, for all his life black as a raven's wing, defied a trace of grey and her pale skin flushed to the touch of his fingers as it had first done seventeen years before. Even though he was engaged upon a search he did not, could not, understand, he was happy. He had his love and his interests. He had the game they both played to prevent Helen suspecting the truth about their relationship. There were also friends from college, male friends who would stay with them. One of them, Tom Luyner, even tried to sleep with Zoë. Her repulse, whilst emphatic, was gentle and without rancour. They remained friends, though Gerard always puzzled his guest by the way in which he hinted at a hidden joke.

A face appeared beyond the chiffonier. An arm, stained with the reflections from the street upon the window, added a small brass recumbent sphinx to its cluttered surfaces. The face sought Gerard's and smiled at him. He did not see it. His thoughts were a long way distant, in another time, a happier time.

It was nearly a fortnight now. The feeling of a lump of lead pressing down at the bottom of his stomach had become familiar, almost comforting. He knew he was drinking too much and that his shoes, despite Helen's protestations, were unpolished. Briefly he wondered if Venner's wife had felt like this when the old gardener had died.

In the time they had been truly together, many of them the formative years of his life, he had never spared a thought for this happening. Even now, after twelve days' separation, he found it difficult to believe. Zoë was steadfast. He forgave her occasional infidelities because it was part of their game of life, but he could not forgive her leaving him like this, going off with her hand on the arm of that *shrouded gentleman* with the fleshless face.

He saw her still as he had seen her last, her face pale and lovely, ringed with the hair which had defied white intrusion to the last, her hands discreetly folded upon her breasts. The hideous crushing of her abdomen and upper legs where the car had struck her was mercifully hidden by the folds of her dress. She remained a portrait, framed for ever in his mind in a symmetrical hexagon of silk-finished elm. She was still lovely. She was still Zoë, but she was dead, and Gerard was alone.

He knew where she was to be laid, in the little churchyard at Fortstown. His feet had travelled the gravel path and pressed the mown grass to reach her plot so many times before he had seen her lowered into it. He had spoken briefly to the stonemason, blankly taking the man's suggestions as they were given until the desperate craftsman had eventually made the decisions himself. He recalled, though he could not think why, the Yale lock on the flimsy wooden door of the sexton's shed, protecting spades and shovels and a battered motor mower, closeting iron and plastic vases against the coming of bunched flowers.

Tom Luyner had come up from London for the funeral, four days before, bringing Gerard companionship and a grief which was not totally feigned. Tomorrow he would come again, offering a friendly face and a hand to hold another glass, preventing the master of Witham Lodge from drinking alone, trying to guide him back towards the houses of the living. Tom's jokes might not be wholly in place but they were at least an offer, an invitation to lay aside his grief and find a new beginning for his life. He had been a good friend, despite his passion for poor, dead, beautiful Zoë.

Mechanically, without formulated reason for his action, Gerard moved along beside the window of the little shop and pushed open the door. He never really understood why he had done so. There was nothing in the window which caught and held his eye. He had no way of knowing or even believing that he would find anything inside that he wanted to purchase.

The interior was crowded with the pickings of other people's homes. The sign outside which Gerard had not read proclaimed that the owner would clear houses, offering good prices for the contents. Such a man must have taken his parents' furnishings. But for him such a man might have made his fortune out of a sharp deal at Witham Lodge.

His fingers played idly with the corner of a tablecloth of Nottingham lace, feeling the structure of the threads. The cloth was spread upon a mahogany dining-table. At its centre stood an aspidistra in an ornate pot.

'With the death of your aunt both her own estate and the capital and accrued interest of the trust fund devolve upon you, Gerard,' the accountant repeated in his mind. 'I shall be happy to continue to advise you as I advised Zoë. You are now an extremely wealthy man and some measure of financial guidance is required by your circumstances. True, I'll be retiring in a few years, but my son is considerably older than you and has been in the business with me for quite long enough to offer you advice of an equal competence.'

'Are ye lookin' for somethin' special, sir?'

'Mm?' Gerard turned at the intrusion and found himself facing a young woman in a blue dress. Her hair was blond and cropped, and eyes almost the colour of her clothing burned in her deep face.

'Did ye want tae buy somethin'?'

'Oh . . .' He looked around, a tear beginning to form at the corner of his right eye. 'No, nothing special,' he said. 'I'm just browsing.'

The girl subsided before his words and retired to a roll-top desk in a far corner, shuffling invoice forms and occasionally jotting figures onto a pad with a yellow-plastic ball-point. Gerard released the tablecloth and slowly worked his way in from the door, glancing at the huddled bric-à-brac and piled furniture. He studied a Victorian sideboard, ornately carved in the Gothic style, its surface supported by rosewood dolphins. Mounted antlers reared from the walls above him, occasionally draped with a silk shawl or hung with the Kaiser's helmet.

In the shadows of a far corner lurked a plain, glass-fronted cabinet about ten inches deep. His eyes swept its shelves and moved on, only to be drawn back by the round, bony object on a lower shelf. His spine tingled as he stared at it and its vacant sockets, black and sightless, stared back at him.

'There,' he said. 'In there.'

The girl rose from her desk and followed his gently-trembling finger. 'The skull?' she asked.

Gerard nodded. 'How much do you want for it?'

Without replying she walked over to the cabinet and opened one of its doors, reaching inside and hooking her fingers into the nearest orbit to draw it out. She cradled it, surprisingly tiny for something head-sized, in the palm of her hand, extending it towards her customer. Gerard merely stared at it, knowing that her touch was a profanity, knowing that his own would be a caress.

The girl shrugged slightly and set it down, none too gently, on a nearby table. 'It's a mon's,' she began, rehearsing the words she had heard her father use. 'Ye can tell tha' because there's a bony ridge just heere.' She pointed to the bridge of the nose and ran a fingernail across the ridge and up onto the forehead.

Gerard suppressed a shudder. 'Whose was it?' he asked.

The girl scowled. 'How should I know?' she demanded. 'It wa' in a hoose we cleered. Some auld mon wi' a load o' books an' pictures.' Her eyes flitted from the skull on the table to its potential purchaser. 'You a theatrical? Doin' a play or somethin'?'

He smiled to himself. The question was obvious and he had expected it. For that reason he didn't bother to reply.

'How much do you want for it?'

She pursed her lips and he felt his accent push up the price as she thought. 'They're no' cheap,' she replied. 'It's no' one o' those medical ones wi' the top cut an' hinged an' a' boiled white. It's in one piece, 'cept the lower jaw's gone an' there's some teeth missin'. It'll cost ye twenty poond, if ye're interested.'

Gerard nodded and reached inside his jacket for his wallet. 'Will you wrap it, please?' he asked.

She stared at him through those deep blue eyes. Almost pretty, he thought. Almost, but not quite. No, not like Zoë.

'Do ye no hae a bag? A carrier or somethin'? Oh, a' right. I think there's a paper bag aroond here somewhere that'll do.'

He winced as she picked it up again with her thumb jammed into one of the eye-sockets. She transferred the skull to a sideboard whilst she took the two ten-pound notes which Gerard had removed from his wallet. Then she turned the key in a small metal cash-box, opened the lid and folded the money into it. Once the notes were safely deposited she pulled open one of the sideboard drawers and rummaged beneath untidy lengths of dirty string and a torn cellophane packet which spilled rubber bands when it was disturbed. Finally she found what she was seeking and withdrew a creased, folded bag of thick brown paper to wrap the skull in.

'There you are,' she grinned, extending the badly-finished, rounded package.

Gerard was slow to reach out for it, cautious in case his fingers should accidentally find a tear in the bag, unwilling to touch the object prematurely. Eventually, as the girl drew in her breath for a sigh that would have been both tired and impatient, he took the parcel from her, feeling the hardness of the bony object through the paper. Once in his hands it felt surprisingly light. Almost weightless, he thought. Like a ghost. He stood there with it, in the crowded jumble of the shop, unwilling to move again.

'Anythin' else?' asked the girl. This funny man with the skull was beginning to worry her a little.

Gerard shook his head slowly, mechanically. He made the effort and turned towards the door.

'Thank you,' called the girl. 'Sir,' she added, as an afterthought.

He made no reply. He stepped out of the shop, onto the pavement. He felt like a pilgrim must have felt once the pilgrimage was over. The quest was done, the adventure seen through, the shrine visited and now left behind. About him the noises of humanity going about the business of life echoed and whimpered in the street, but Gerard Covington didn't hear them.

He deposited the skull, still wrapped in brown paper, in the study which Zoë had arranged in their third reception room. Helen did not see it. If she had she would have enquired as to its contents and Gerard would have to think of a reason for bringing it home. That, he conceded to himself upon reflection, would have been difficult. He was still unsure as to why exactly he had bought so unlikely an object. Somehow he felt it was connected with his quest, whatever that was.

Helen forced him to eat with her usual motherly insistence. He took a little consommé, toying with it, drawing his spoon across the dish just fast enough to create a few ripples, then abandoned it in favour of spiced chicken with mushrooms on saffron rice. The only part of the meal which merited anything like his attention was the wine, a white Chianti in a plain bottle that was quickly drained. The dessert passed unnoticed and untasted.

'You must eat, Mr Gerard,' she told him. 'I know you don't feel much like it, sir, and neither do I. It's been a terrible shock for me as well. But we have to eat. There's no sense in moping and going without food. That's no good for the living and precious little use to the dead.'

'Later, Helen,' he replied, sighing. 'I'll have something later. I'm not hungry just now.'

'Well, it'll be in the kitchen when you want it. Do try to have some. You have to go on, you know. It's what Mrs Fyler would want you to do. You're only young. There's time to forget.'

There was more. There always was. Helen's impeccable and unvarying philosophy, developed from the sayings of others when Konrad died, had been sharpened and enhanced by Zoë's death. For the most part it was a monologue composed of saws and platitudes, insistent and pervasive, consoling and cajoling its victim into an unhappy but responsive continuance. In its way it brought with it the comfort she intended.

After the grim reaper came the grim repasts, meals forced down in unwonted silence, washed down with bitter wines that seemed so sweet before. Gerard smoked a cigarette at table with a large brandy. Then, as Helen began to clear away, he carried his glass into the study and sank into a club chair.

Why? It was an old question. For Gerard it had been first asked twenty-three years before as his parents' remains slid beneath the soil. Now it was twelve days old and the answer was still elsewhere.

He finished the brandy and set the glass down upon an occasional table, careless of the coaster which protected its leather top. His fingers slid towards his mouth and he found himself chewing at his fingernails, marring their manicured perfection.

Was he producing Hamlet? He mustered a brief, cynical, inward laugh. He might just as well be. To be or not to be . . .

The skull, still veiled in brown paper, rested near the edge of the long table which filled most of the centre of the room, reflecting shapelessly upon the polished surface. He saw Olivier, that Russian whose name he had forgotten or never known, Warner, Williamson, staring at the mud-stained object the clown handed up from the grave he was digging for Ophelia. A whoreson mad fellow . . .

This skull was Yorick's. No. No, it wasn't Yorick's skull. Yorick's skull was lost in Danish history for ever. Skulls didn't come out of the past except for archaeologists. No, this skull wasn't Yorick's. Nor could it be Ophelia's. Not with that bony ridge above the nose.

Gerard stood up and walked across to his purchase. He unwrapped it carefully, holding it with the paper bag. Touching it would come later.

He left it on the edge of the table and crumpled the bag, tossing it into a waste-basket as he returned to the depths of the club chair. The study faced south and in these summer evenings the falling sun stained its walls and furnishings with oblique roseate light. The skull sat in this, a long shadow splashed out behind it like spilled ink.

Who was he, this dead man who survived only as an orb of close-locked bones? Was he related to the old man the girl in the shop had mentioned? The girl had one of these, under her cropped blonde hair. Her blue eyes stared out of orbits that one day would be as empty, or clogged with mud after the grave had cooked her to the bones.

He covered his eyes with his hands as the thought grew up within him that the same was true of Zoë. Even now she lay in Fortstown churchyard, her fair, white flesh radiant with unaccustomed hues engendered by decay, her hair, still growing in the coffin, as black as the darkness supreme about her. Was this Zoë's skull? No matter, one day it would be.

He waited for the skull to speak to him, to tell its story, to thank him for removing it from the gaze of the vulgar. He waited wordless and unseeing, his eyes still covered by chewed fingers. Eventually he looked up again and found the room darker, the shadows longer, the opalescent light from the windows diminished.

Gerard took the skull from the table and set it on his knee in the chair. His fingers thrilled to the touch of the bone in the way his spine had thrilled when first he saw it. He turned it about, smoothing at the slight roughness of its surface with his thumbs, questioning its muteness with his thoughts. He drew his fingertips around the empty orbits, feeling for eyelids which might cover the hardness of phantom eyes beneath. It struck him as heavier now, but perhaps that was because he was tired.

The underside was a mass of configurations of bone, a geological landscape in miniature, riddled with valleys and peaks. Here and there pieces had been chipped away, ruining the symmetry and the feel, marring the visual and textural pleasure that yielded to his examination. Empty sockets stared like Norman arches where the teeth had fallen away. Tiny holes riddled its surfaces like the workings of an ant-mine, pits in which a flea might break its leg.

His eyes glazed with tears. He had come to know the feeling well over the past twelve days and he reached into his jacket for the accustomed handkerchief. It was still too soon for him to recognise that his crying fits were decreasing in frequency.

He wiped his eyes and blew his nose. His eyes hurt with tears and sleeplessness. To sleep, perchance to dream . . .

'Why, Zoë? Why?' Why did it have to be Zoë? Why did it have to be now? He told himself one more time that now hurt because it *was* now, that now was when it would ultimately have happened whether now was this year or in another ten or twenty. Yet perhaps *he* could have died first.

But that was selfish. If he had died it would be Zoë sitting here now, crying tears that marred the beauty of her cheeks, wearing the rings about her eyes like a domino at a masquerade. No, he could not have permitted that. She had supported him in his youth. He owed it to her to survive, if only to grieve.

And that touch. That wonderful touch he loved so well, the touch of fingers now stiffened and contracted into hooks by death's fell mastery of her flesh. Where was that? No matter, for he would never feel that touch again.

Why, Zoë?

He stared down at the skull. It withheld its answer. He knew that it always would. All it could give him was the pleasure of its touch, not Zoë's, and the puzzle of the missing flesh which once had robed it. Its stare was fixed and expressionless and could not dote upon him or scold transgressions with a glance. Its lips were lost with its kisses. Its breath was stilled in a nose that had only a single gaping nostril.

Yet it could give a species of comfort. Perhaps another had mourned the passing of its owner as he mourned for Zoë, poor, lost, entombed Zoë. It could not love or kiss or sigh with pleasure, but it offered a wordless, sightless, passionless consolation. It loved him in its own way, from a distance, like a god. It had a life beyond the life it once housed.

He stared at the bones of the cranium in the dying light. Their joints offered the appearance of meandering rivers on a plain, the letters joined to itself and repeated throughout infinity. Once there were thoughts in there. Once there were hopes and fears and, yes, once there had been love.

The sunlight and the day were almost gone. Zoë haunted him still and would haunt him throughout the years to come. They say, Gerard reflected, that you always remember the one you share love's first encounters with. Had this one remembered? Did he remember still? Was the knowledge of those joys written inside that bony cavity?

Oh, Zoë, for one whose timing was always so good, your timing was terrible. You've left me to survive you. Yet perhaps you were only being cruel to be kind.

Why must I always think in platitudes?

He fell asleep in the chair, turning slightly to a more comfortable position. As he did so the skull dropped from his lap and rolled beneath the table, out of sight.

Helen looked into the study before she retired for the night. Gerard was still in the chair, snoring gently. The widow muttered to herself about the healing powers of sleep and left him where he was. She did not see the skull.

June Lowe was forced to concede that there was a definite strangeness about this part of Scotland. Mentally she compared it with Galloway, in the south-west, where she had holidayed before. Banffshire didn't have the brooding presence, the tumuli and monolithic remains of Burns's country, but this rugged coastline, to the east of Inverness and the Moray Firth, had a grandeur and majesty peculiarly its own.

It was the first real holiday that she and Bob Ferrow had managed together, and the veterinary nurse from Northamptonshire was grateful for it. They had met earlier that year, when Bob was a Detective Sergeant at Waventree, where she had been working for a vet called Widgeon. There were still some things she didn't understand about the case that had brought them together, and probably she never would. The series of mysterious deaths, some, like that of her employer, attributable to an unknown animal or animals, had culminated in the destruction of Wegrimham Grange, the home of a mycologist named Rufus Williamson. The entire house had been destroyed, together with Williamson and his wife, and somehow that had closed the case.

The one thing June could never understand, and Ferrow would never talk about, was the strange blue light which had appeared in the sky, a light capable of blasting a hole in the side of her flat and directing the actions of the ordinary humans it commandeered.

In the intervening months she had closed her mind to the loose ends. Even if her curiosity was never satisfied, something about the case had secured Bob's promotion to Inspector, even though it meant transferring to Corby, on the other side of the county. Once there, he'd managed to find her a job with another veterinary practice, and shortly after they had set up home together he had proposed.

Living with a policeman had taught June not to ask too many questions. That was why, when he'd suggested that they come here for a week or so at the Fortstown Arms, she'd accepted gladly. It was an odd choice for a couple from Northamptonshire. Almost 600 miles away, the little fishing village on the Banffshire coast had little of the appeal of the better-known holiday resorts. The weather was uncertain, even in August, and the nearest town, Banff itself, had little to attract even the most dedicated tourist. There was the Whisky Trail of course, the round of distilleries, each boasting its own exceptional single malt whisky, but in June's view, and Ferrow's, once you'd seen one distillery you'd seen them all.

And yet it was so nice to be away from it all, to walk along the shore, so rich in shells and sea-grass, and listen to the pounding of the North Sea on the shingle. There was little sand as such at the base of the cliffs, but the grass grew down them almost into the sea itself.

If any part of Scotland, to an English mind, deserved the epithet of 'the brave' it was the very earth and rocks they now trod. Fortstown was hewn, as if by giants, from the very face of the cliffs. Banff was nearly fifteen miles away by badly metalled narrow roads. The nearest village, Gardenstown, was only six miles by road, or a mile and a half along the base of the cliffs at low tide.

Here and there along the cliffs their impressive and impenetrable bulk was broken by the more gentle slopes cut by springs, clear, musical waters that had sought their path to the sea through incalculable geological epochs. It was in such a declivity that they now stood, June and Ferrow, together with Miles Fournessie, their host from the Fortstown Arms.

It had started the day before, during a walk along the pebble-covered beach. June and Ferrow could not fail to notice, and be intrigued by, the little ruin which huddled on one of the slopes against the sparsely-grassed rock. That evening, in the bar, they had asked Fournessie how they could reach it, and he had promised to show them. They'd asked him what it was, and how it came to be there. In retrospect, June recalled, she had asked, not Ferrow. Bob had kept quiet and simply let her get on with it, almost as if he had no interest in it himself, or knew already.

Fournessie told them the story of the little church on the cliffs. It dated, he said, from about AD 1100, and had been built as a thank-offering by the inhabitants of the entire coastal region. For some years Vikings were pillaging the area. Men were killed, women and children bound and bundled aboard the longships to begin a life of slavery somewhere in the icy wastes of Scandinavia, flocks driven down to the shore and slaughtered for supplies. Even the holy relic of St John, in its gold reliquary, was taken by the marauding pagans.

June had begun to protest at that point that by 1100 the Scandinavians had all been converted to Christianity, but Ferrow had laid a gentle, restraining hand upon her arm. 'It's his story,' he said softly. 'Let him tell it.'

Those inhabitants of the area who survived the regular depredations of the sea raiders finally acknowledged that they were faced with the choice of moving further inland, away from the sea which was both their bane and their livelihood, or making a stand which the pillaging marauders would take sufficient note of to leave them alone. After much dubious shaking of unshorn heads the Scots eventually decided to fight.

Their plan was simple, but effective. A wooden church was built where it could be seen from the sea and the area was scoured for any gold or other precious substances which the Vikings had so far missed. These were then nailed to the door of the church.

For several months men and women laboured to build the church and haul rocks up to the top of the little valley. They knew that they were fisher-folk, not fighters, and such weapons as they possessed were short-bladed knives which would be no match for the beard-axes and swords of the Vikings. It was thus that they decided to fight the foe from a distance.

All along the coast lookouts were posted beside the piles of driftwood which were to serve as a beacon early-warning system if the square sails of the longships were sighted on their way to the gold-rich church. For months the Scots dwelt in fearful anticipation of what was to come: and then, finally, the day dawned when the beacons were lit and one of the most feared cries in the history of these islands shattered the stillness of the air: 'The Vikings are coming!'

From the moment that the two longships drew up upon the beach below the church they were doomed, although they had no way of knowing that. Tales of this fabulous little shrine with the golden doors had crossed the seas and found ready-listeners amongst the bearded freebooters of the northlands. Great would be the honour of the party that brought them home.

The raiders had fought these people before and knew them to be without mail and poorly armed. They advanced boldly towards the church, climbing up the slope with long, powerful strides. It was only when they reached the fabled doors and saw how thin the gold was beaten, how sparsely it was applied and how flimsily the shrine was constructed, that the first suspicions of treachery were born in their gold-greedy brains. By then, however, they were as good as dead.

Swords, even the most renowned blades of myth and legend, have difficulty hewing rocks. Victory runes might deflect the fastest arrow from link-mail but deflecting tons of stone was beyond their power. As the first huge missiles began their wildly bouncing descent several of the raiders tore handfuls of the gold leaf from the doors and began to run back towards the beach. One almost made it back to a ship, but a stone slab smashed his legs away before bouncing high to tear off the dragon prow he had sought as refuge.

Many sought refuge in the church and died there as the flimsy structure collapsed beneath the avalanche. Those who remained in the open danced grimly in a ludicrous effort to remain alive. The few that escaped were later hunted down and hacked to pieces by the victorious Scots. Even if enough had survived to crew a longship and escape, several of the larger rocks had reached down as far as the beach, crushing one ship beyond repair and seriously holing the second.

The Scots slowly descended the valley, killing those whom the avalanche had merely maimed, stripping them of their arm-rings and weapons, tearing from their throats the devilish pagan amulets which had failed them before the onslaught of true worshippers.

So it was that the victors built the little stone church between the cliffs as a thank-offering. After all, with true Scots economy, the stone was already there, they reasoned. What better use could be found for it? Besides, St John had shown good faith towards them in a miraculous way. Not only had he interceded with the Lord for their victory, which on its own had the appearance of a miracle, but he had performed the impossible. Although the golden reliquary was lost for ever they had found, hung by a leather thong about the neck of a dying Viking, the holy relic that had been taken during an earlier raid.

Fournessie finished his tale and poured his two guests glasses of twelve-year-old single malt. Ferrow sipped it appreciatively, but June added water. They were the only two residents at the Fortstown Arms, though a Scots couple, regulars for many years and, like June and Ferrow, not really married, and a single lady who sounded very English, were expected the following afternoon.

'Just what was the relic, Miles?' June asked.

Their host shook his head and poured a whisky for himself. 'I dinna ken that, June,' he replied.

He drank his own malt in a single swallow, well used to the larger Scottish measure, then washed his glass and began to polish it. 'There's some as say,' he continued, 'that it's still away in Braw Valley, in yon kirk. Others, the auld folk, tell as how the last minister called it accursed by blood, 200 years ago, an' cast it out to sea. E'en so, it would nae leave him. When he awoke the next morn there it was, hung fast about his neck, the way it was round yon Viking sea-wolf's. But I dinna ken. A' I ken is that he were the last, an' after tha' nae minister came tae the kirk, an' it fell tae ruin, as ye see it now.'

They asked him about the best way of reaching the little church and Fournessie told them about the choice. The safe route was to go out of the village by the road cut up the cliffs, then along and down the track to the ruins of St John's. There was another way, much shorter than the five miles by road and track, but it was not an easy route, and non-natives were advised to leave it alone unless they had a local guide. After several more matured single malts and a small financial inducement Fournessie agreed to take them up by the short route the following morning.

They set out for the ruin first thing after breakfast. Fournessie was eager to take them and get back to prepare for the guests who would be arriving later in the day. Even as they started the fishing boats were returning to Fortstown's little harbour, and boxes of fresh fish were being piled up on the quays.

The climb wasn't as smooth as Fournessie's long, powerful strides might have suggested. June felt herself tiring as she stumbled over the uneven ground, the true nature of its surface grassed over, and Ferrow had to help her up on more than one occasion. She smiled at him and he smiled back, but there was something far away, something hidden, in that smile. The wind whipped her fair hair, not quite as yellow-blond as Bob's, but longer than the short crop she had been wearing when they first met in Widgeon's surgery. He was a strange man, even for a policeman. That he was good at his job she couldn't doubt, even if his hair was just a trifle long for his uniform. Yet there was a silence, and a strength within the silence, that sometimes worried her.

After nearly half an hour they stood within the weathered stone shell of the ruined thank-offering. Ferrow almost visibly restrained himself from remarking that if you'd seen one small stone ruin you'd seen them all. It was enough that the others felt him capable of the remark. After all, if they really knew why Inspector Robert Ferrow had come to Fortstown, it would shock June and probably alienate Fournessie. Both were important to him in their way. June was the woman he loved in spite of himself, his anchor in an uncertain, devious world. And Fournessie was still an unknown quantity, despite the research facilities of the national CRO computer.

June appeared to be fascinated by their host's explanations of which wall was which and which niche was what. Ferrow listened too, though he felt drawn to the feature which lay outside the ruin, the little cemetery which surrounded it.

Beneath them sheep grazed upon the slopes of the valley, cropping the sparse grasses which grew underfoot and only seemed to proliferate between the black slate horizontal tombstones, almost as if the roots found fresh nutriment from the bodies of the ancient dead. The stones were all about two centuries old, or even older. They were, for the most part, well-preserved and legible, probably because of the hardness of the material, and because, flat upon the graves, they had been protected from the worst of the coastal weather.

They wandered out of the ruin and into the graveyard. What a morbid lot these old Scots were, June thought as she studied the markers. Every available inch of surface was covered, if not with inscriptions relating the names and foibles of the deceased, then with *memento mori*. Skulls, hour-glasses, crossed shovels, broken columns and cinerary urns all processed about the scattered, dark grey oblongs on the ground.

Dark clouds scudded across the sun, threatening to punctuate the dryness of the morning with unexpected rain. Their inspection of the ruin and the graveyard completed, June and Ferrow began to descend behind their host. June carefully followed the Scot's footsteps, reasoning that long years in the area would guide his feet more surely than she could guide her own. Suddenly he stopped perfectly still, appearing to freeze on the spot in front of them. Ferrow moved down beside him, only to find Miles Fournessie staring wide-eyed over the declining ground towards the beach.

'What is it, Miles?' he asked. 'Are you ill? What's the matter with you?'

Fournessie gave no spoken answer. By way of a reply he extended his right arm and pointed down towards the sea. A dark-clad figure was walking slowly along the shore, so close to the spume-white water that he seemed to have one foot in it as he went. He was too far away for either June or Ferrow to make out his features, but Fournessie's behaviour left them in no doubt that the figure inspired a mortal fear in him. Something about the gait and posture of the stranger suggested a great age. He was bareheaded, and long, grey, tangled hair streamed out in the sea-wind behind him, whipping at the upturned collar of what seemed to be a greatcoat.

Ferrow stared at the figure for a moment or so, sensing rather than seeing something vaguely familiar about it. 'Who is that man, Miles?' he asked Fournessie.

The Scot licked at his wind- and fear-dried lips. 'He's here.' he croaked. 'Auld Davie was right. Caspar Locke is here.'

He crossed himself hurriedly. 'Lord ha' mercy,' he added.

'What did you say?' June asked, stepping down to join Ferrow in front of Fournessie.

It was left to Ferrow to reply. 'Caspar Locke,' he repeated. 'That was the name . . .' His voice trailed off and something approaching a smile spread across his features. 'Wait a minute,' he added. 'I've seen that name today. Wasn't it on one of the markers in the churchyard? Have we seen the local ghost, Miles?' He was grinning broadly as he spoke.

Fournessie's reply took the grin from the policeman's features. It was not so much the words that were sobering, as the way in which they were spoken. With extreme gravity the Scot said simply: 'Aye, Mr Ferrow. That ye have.'

They returned to the Fortstown Arms and June poured their host a large measure of his own whisky. Fournessie, seated in a chair in front of the bar fireplace, gulped it down and held out the glass for an immediate refill.

'Ye'd better hae just the one your sel's,' he mumbled.

June and Ferrow took him at his word and seated themselves beside him. For some moments they sipped the distilled highland fire in silence. Then Ferrow asked: 'So what's it all about, eh?'

He hoped that his question was spoken in a soothing, encouraging tone, and that he didn't sound too much like a policeman.

Fournessie stared into the depths of his glass. Then he drained it and walked over to the bar to pour himself a third. As he came back and sat down again he looked at the puzzled faces of his guests.

'Ye'd better ask another,' he grunted. 'Auld Andy's no seen it. He'll tell ye. But I canna'. Not now I've seen for mysel'.'

Tom Luyner drove up to Witham Lodge in plenty of time for lunch. Like Gerard he was thirty. Unlike Gerard he was fair-haired and not particularly handsome. His nose was a shade too long and broad and a brush with smallpox had marked his cheeks. The most remarkable of his features were his eyes, pale and intense, glittering like ice-water in the sun.

It was Tom's custom always to arrive in time for a drink, and Zoë and Gerard had never stinted to refresh him. So it was that Gerard took his friend into the study as soon as his bags were in his room and opened the cupboard which held Tom's favourite beverages. As he did so Tom looked past him and glimpsed a solid-looking hemisphere of pitted bone.

'Gerard, what the devil's that?' he demanded.

His host turned and smiled at him. 'What does it look like? It's a skull.'

'I can see that, old man. What's it doing in with the booze? New cocktail mixer or something? One of these macabre humidors?'

The smile continued as Gerard measured and stirred the gin-and-it. 'No, 'fraid not. Sorry to disappoint you, Tom, but it's the genuine article. It really is a skull.'

Tom took the glass which was held out to him, swallowed most of its contents, then lowered it and glared at his friend. 'Hardly the best place to keep it, do you think? What have you got it for, anyway?'

'Oh, I just put it in there this morning to tidy the place up a bit. I'll find somewhere for it to live eventually.'

'Best place would be in the ground. Why don't you bury it? Come to that, where'd you find the grisly item, eh?'

Gerard felt himself beginning to flush. Tom was not going to understand. 'I bought it,' he answered, softly, making Tom strain to catch his words.

'You bought it? You bought that? What on earth for?'

Gerard stared at him. His voice was edged with the inflections of an irritated schoolmaster as he replied: 'I don't think you'll be able to understand, even if I tell you.'

Tom drained his glass and held it out for a refill. 'Really, old man, you do a marvellous impersonation of a pompous prig at times. I'm quite sure you have some highly intellectual reason for having that hunk of dead bone about the place. I just wish you wouldn't insult me by implying that the only thing I can understand is tennis. Why don't you give me the benefit of the doubt and tell me anyway?'

His host's features relaxed and he smiled again. 'Of course,' he said. 'I'm sorry, Tom. I've been alone too much, now Zoë's . . . dead.'

He brushed away a half-formed tear. It was painful to speak Zoë's name. Tom nodded his understanding and waited for him to continue.

'It's like this. I was in Banff yesterday. I went in to get some cigarettes from that little tobacconist's in the High Street. Well, I parked the car in Smith Street and wandered about in the alleys. There's a little street runs off there with some junk shops and things. I suppose I must have seen it before, but I didn't remember it at all. Well, I stared in at the window for a while, not really looking at anything at all. I was . . . more sort of thinking about life's tricks, you know . . .'

Tom nodded, then realised that Gerard wasn't looking at him. 'I do,' he replied. 'I know. Go on, Gerard.'

Gerard nodded, then poured himself another drink from the jug. 'Before I knew what I was doing I was inside the place,' he continued. 'I hadn't seen anything I wanted in the window. I just went in. I didn't really expect to see anything, or buy anything. Then a girl came up and asked me if there was anything I was interested in. I said no, and she left me alone after that. Then I saw the skull.'

'Is that it?'

'More or less,' Gerard replied, sipping at his gin. 'I asked the girl where it had come from, and she said that they'd found it in a house they'd been clearing. I just . . . bought it.'

'And that's it?' Tom demanded. 'You just bought it? You're right, old man. I don't understand. Whatever possessed you?'

'Why did I buy it? I can't really answer that one, Tom. All I can do is try to rationalise it a bit. The moment I saw the thing it seemed to call out to me, to tell me that it could help in some way.

You see, Tom, Zoë was so alive, so vital. She and I had an understanding I'll probably never find with any other living being. For her to die the way she did, when she did, was a terrible shock to me because I was so totally unprepared for it. Possibly I felt the loss of my parents just as keenly as I feel her loss, but I was less mature then. I had the chance to grow away from it, to forget it with the passing years. Zoë, though, is still fresh in my mind. She's still an open emotional wound, Tom. I've got two choices at present, you know. One is to try to forget her completely. And that, I know, is foredoomed to failure. I'll never do it. The other choice is to try and control exactly what I do remember, and that's where the skull comes in. It's a sort of *memento mori*. You know the phrase, of course?'

Tom drained his glass again.' "Remember you must die",' he translated. 'I see. It's a sort of therapy object.'

Gerard nodded, slowly. 'Something of the kind,' he said. 'I don't really know for sure. All I do know is that it gives me a species of relief to look at it and handle it. It doesn't help me to forget Zoë, but it does help to channel what I remember of her.'

For the first time since his arrival Tom Luyner saw his friend's features relax into something akin to a smile, albeit one still tainted by the melancholy of his thoughts. 'That's the idea, old man,' he grinned. 'Happy thoughts. To hell with what the rest of the world might think about it. Now, is there any more gin-and-it in that jug, before we pile into Helen's lunch? I'm just starting to loosen up and find an appetite.'

Gerard refilled both their glasses and his friend managed to turn their talk towards more casual matters. Both then and throughout their lunch Tom worked hard to cheer his host and friend, deliberately choosing his words to avoid all reference to anything Gerard and Zoë might have done together. After the meal they relaxed with coffee and cigarettes, still chatting about things of little consequence. Then Tom sprang his surprise.

'Look here, old man,' he began, 'I've been thinking about this all through lunch. If this thing,' he continued, gesturing towards the skull, 'is any good for you, then I'm all in favour of it. After all, I can't be here to cheer you up every day, and Christ knows you need an interest to pull you out of the state you're in. Now, what say we head into Banff this afternoon and see if we can find this shop of yours?'

Gerard eyed his friend over the top of his coffee cup. 'What do you have in mind, Tom?' he asked.

'Well, from what you've told me, they got hold of that skull when they were clearing some old buffer's house out. Now, it seems to me that there might be some more stuff there. If you're determined to stay morbid for a while, with all this *memento mori* rubbish, then it won't do our friendship a blind bit of good if I try to hold you back. So, what say we drive into Banff and see what else they cleaned out of the old boy's home?'

'And if there is more?'

'Then I'll buy it for you. Maybe if you get involved with some stranger's effects it'll take your mind off Zoë. That way you'll soon get back to normal.'

Oh, Tom, Gerard thought. If only you really knew what normal had been for Zoë and myself. There can never be a normal again. Not with Zoë dead.

He was reluctant, but an afternoon rambling the estate, or even fishing, held no appeal whatsoever. In his heart Gerard never wanted to enter that shop again, but a refusal would have been ungrateful. So it was that they climbed into Tom's car and drove the fifteen or so miles into Banff. It was late August, and the sun was shining brightly. Everything, except Gerard Covington, felt unusually alive.

Unsure as to where exactly he had found the little shop, Gerard instructed Tom to park in Smith Street. Then they set out, as Gerard had done the day before, towards the little tobacconist's. Soon a familiar street, almost narrow enough to be an alley, opened out on their left.

'This way,' he said. 'The shop's about half-way along. I remember it now.'

They turned into the narrow opening and began to climb the gentle slope of the cobbled street. Gerard had almost passed it when he noticed the cluttered chiffonier in the window. 'This is it.'

'Well, let's go in.'

Tom looked hard at his friend. Gerard seemed reluctant to enter. He stood on the narrow pavement, staring at the window. Tom followed his gaze but could see nothing that might have arrested his attention.

'What are you looking at?'

'Hmm? Oh, nothing.'

'Well, shall we go inside, then? As you're not looking at anything?'

'You go in. I'll wait for you here.'

'What's the matter?'

'Matter? Nothing at all. I just don't want to go in.'

'That's utter rubbish. Why else do you think we've come here? Come on, old man. Pull yourself together. Deep breath, now.'

Before Gerard had time to realise what had happened he was inside the shop, Tom's hand still clasped to the lapel of his jacket. He heard the door close behind them and looked over at the roll-top desk for the girl who sold him the skull. She was not there.

In her place, rising to greet them, was a man in rolled shirt-sleeves with close-cropped white hair. He was tanned and wrinkled and his upper lip sported a full moustache, most of its centre stained brown against the grey by nicotine.

'G'day, sirs,' he began, moving through the clutter towards them. 'What c'n I do for ye?'

Gerard suddenly wished that the floor would swallow him. He made no response, hoping that the scene would dissolve as in a film and he'd find himself somewhere way away. Beside him Tom sensed his unease and decided to speak for him.

'Was it your daughter who was in here yesterday?' he asked.

'I 'spect it was. Why d'ye ask?'

'She sold my friend here a skull.'

''At's right. She told me 'bout it. Nothing wrong, I hope?'

Tom smiled reassuringly. 'Nothing at all,' he replied. 'Quite the reverse, in fact. Bizarre as it might seem, my friend was delighted with his purchase. Now, the reason we've come back is that your daughter mentioned that the skull was just one item from a whole collection of odd things you'd cleared from some old boy's home. She said that the rest of the stuff was packed up, but that if we came in when you were here we might be able to get a look at it.'

'Did she, now?' The older man rubbed his stubbled chin with a gnarled hand and eyed his customers quizzically. 'She shouldn'a said that. It's not sorted or priced and there's some things I might not be putting in the shop.'

'Because you want to keep them?'

The dealer laughed disconcertingly. 'No, not for that. There's some odd items there, and I mean odd, if you know what I mean.'

'You mean pornographic?'

'Not so much what you said. More sort of blasphemous. Some of they books smack of truck with the devil and suchlike. I don't know who he was but I knew when I saw the stuff why his kin didn't want to touch it. I'd say he were a bit mad.'

Tom was beginning to tire of this verbal fencing. He reached inside his wallet and came out with a five-pound note. 'Can we see it?' he asked, extending the banknote towards the shopkeeper.

'I don't see as it'll do no harm,' came the smiling reply. 'It's out back, if you'd like to follow me.'

They walked behind him through a curtained doorway at the back of the shop and through an inner room jammed with odd items of furniture. The trader unbolted a door in the far wall and they stepped out into the shadows and sunlight of a small yard. This they crossed before entering what had once been part of a stable-block. Its floor was strewn with straw and sawdust.

'Everything on that side was the old man's,' said the dealer, gesturing with a sweep of his gnarled hand towards a tarpaulin-covered pile in a corner of the outbuilding. 'If you don't mind, gents, I'll leave you to it. This is one of my busy days, so I'd best get back to the shop.'

Before Tom had time to thank him he was gone. Gerard, however, had not spoken since entering the shop, and now stood in silence, staring at the irregular pile.

'Let's get this off, shall we?' Tom enquired, walking up to the tarpaulin and starting to lift it. To his surprise his friend made no move to assist him and he looked back at the unmoving figure.

'Come on, now, snap out of it, Gerard. What's the matter with you this afternoon? You were keen enough before lunch. Give me a hand, will you?'

Gerard sighed deeply. Then he seemed to awaken, as if from a rare lethargy or a trance. For a moment he looked uncomprehendingly at Tom Luyner wrestling with the tarpaulin, then he moved towards him, saying: 'Let me give you a hand with that, Tom.'

For a few moments Tom Luyner stared at his friend. Probably much of his odd behaviour could be attributed to his grief at Zoë's death, but there were things which somehow did not seem right. It was as if Gerard entered a different world, withdrew into himself for reasons only he understood. It was all extremely perplexing for those not initiated into the mysteries which Gerard both created and revered. He was on the point of questioning those withdrawals, then he decided against it.

Together they removed the heavy tarpaulin to reveal five or six tea-chests stacked around some newspaper-wrapped pictures and two oddly-shaped and carved pieces of furniture. Three of the tea-chests were packed with books of various dates in various stages of decomposition. Tom picked a heavy volume off the top of the nearest and opened it. A curious odour, nauseously sweet, wafted up from the open pages. He wrinkled his nose and turned his head away. Then he turned back and tried to separate the pages. They were damp and clung together, threatening to tear beneath his fingers.

He closed the book and strained in the dim light to read the worn legend on the spine. Eventually he was able to read aloud: '*De sanguine ultra mortem.*'

Gerard, who had not yet touched any of the items they had uncovered, looked up. 'On the state of the blood after death? Who's the author?'

'Looks as if it's somebody called Paracelsus.' Tom deposited the decaying volume back in the tea-chest. Then he pushed his way through to the tall cupboard at the back. If its wood was not ebony then it was stained black with age. It was a corner cupboard, nearly seven feet high, with open shelves surmounting a closed cupboard with heavily carved doors. At first he thought the design was of interlaced serpents, but a closer inspection showed that the shapes which writhed across its surfaces were too short. They were also banded and not scaled, and carried insect-like mandibles instead of mouths. The same design, in miniature, chased itself along the edges of the shelves above.

'God Almighty!' Tom grunted. 'That's the most morbid thing I've ever seen. Who on earth would want a thing like that?' He turned back to see his friend staring at the blackened item. There was a brightness in Gerard's eyes which did not strike him as altogether healthy.

The other piece of furniture was a battered oak side-table, probably only Victorian, which was remarkable for the supports being carved in the shape of cadavers. Gerard's gaze lingered on this also, then he stepped over to another of the tea-chests and began rummaging through the books it contained.

'There's more Paracelsus in here,' he ventured. 'There are other authors as well. Some theology, such as "Sherlock on Death", and a folio set of Holbein engravings. Why, it's packed with treasures. You're right about it being morbid, though. Everything seems to revolve around death.'

Tom grunted disgustedly and turned away. As he did so the dealer came back from the shop across the yard. Gerard straightened up and Tom turned back to face him.

'How much do you want for the lot?' he asked.

Gerard stared at his friend in amazement. 'You're really going through with it?' he asked.

'I asked you how much you wanted.'

The dealer rubbed his chin, then played with his grey-brown moustache. 'I'd not given it much thought,' he replied.

'Then you can't want much for it. You said yourself you'd have difficulty in selling it. You're not going to find anyone else like me in too much of a hurry, so you'd be wise not to overprice it. Now, how much?'

The dealer grinned. 'Make me an offer?'

'Fifty pounds cash.'

Gerard shook his head despairingly and turned away. The trader seemed taken aback. 'I was thinking more of 200,' he muttered through his hand.

'That's ridiculous,' Tom replied. 'I might go to seventy-five, though.'

The dealer eyed him curiously. Tom's pock-marked face had taken on a decided cast which discouraged further bartering. Even so, the dealer thought he'd have one more try.

'I'll take 100.'

'Ninety. Cash will be waiting when you deliver.'

They crossed the yard back into the shop, the dealer leading the way. Gerard wrote his address on a scrap of paper and delivery was agreed for the following day.

When they had left the shop and were walking back to the car Tom grinned broadly at his friend. 'I'll bet you never thought I'd go through with it, did you?' he asked.

'Not at all,' came Gerard's reply. 'Your scathing comment about therapy objects was only partially true. There are some rare and valuable books in those chests which are worth preserving. Heaven only knows where the old man found them all. They said that they'd cleared his house, Tom, but they didn't say that he was dead.'

'Well, you can ask them when they deliver it all tomorrow. For now, though, let's get back to Witham Lodge. And then, if you like, we can walk down into Fortstown for a drink. The pub should be open by then.'

Perhaps Tom Luyner might not have been so dismissive, or so eager to visit the Fortstown Arms, if he had known what was to come. Nor would Gerard, who had only been in the Arms twice before, have agreed. There are some dangers in life which can be openly recognised, some that remain hidden, and still others that we are capable of suspecting.

And it's remarkable how many of the latter can involve a beautiful and unknown woman. Even in Ferrow's *middle of nowhere*.

June and Ferrow met the beautiful woman at dinner that night. She was the third of the three new guests at the Fortstown Arms. The other couple, Harry and Moira, travelled up from Aberdeen every year for the last week in August and the first week in September. They travelled under Harry's surname, Carmichael, but as Miles Fournessie discreetly explained to avoid any unintentional embarrassment, they were not married.

Harry was a solicitor, white-haired and crinkly-featured, with merry brown eyes that seemed to wink without even a fluttering of his long-lashed eyelids. Like Moira he was in his late forties, tall and well-dressed, even in slacks and a short-sleeved shirt. Moira was one of those fortunate women who never quite catch up to their age physically. She could have easily been taken for five years younger with her dark hair only slightly beginning to grey and her skin still clear and, as proven by a quite exposing frock, remarkably firm and fresh.

They should have been married. Certainly they behaved as if they were, in the nicest possible sense. Harry had been widowed some years earlier and every visit they made to Fortstown brought a fresh proposal to Moira. Yet every time she turned him down – inexplicably he felt – without making any move to abandon their relationship. It puzzled him, infuriated him, and kept him trying in every respect, much to Moira's delight.

In addition to the 'Carmichaels' there was a third new arrival. Jenny Fellowes, by her appearance, was in her early- to mid-twenties, quiet, and extremely good-looking. June automatically disliked her on sight. She was too well-dressed. Her perfume was both too subtle and too expensive. Her long chestnut hair was pinned up, giving the double row of ungraduated pearls about her neck the perfect opportunity to invite admiration for their size and colour. She ordered with expertise, both food and wine. She ate with an almost bird-like delicacy, as if she were somehow afraid that honest indulgence was a contaminant, and she kept herself strictly to herself. Yet her dark eyes roved amongst her fellow guests, the women feeling themselves sharply observed, examined and found wanting, the men finding themselves appreciated and somehow encouraged by her scrutiny.

She seemed to have the knack of generating a faint but distinct air of mystery, which intrigued Ferrow's police mind. He studied her appearance and responses carefully, especially after Harry invited her ('In a place like this you *have* to be friendly, Moira') to join the others for coffee after their meal was over. Her English accent would have cut glass, even in the Highlands where pewter or pottery was more traditional. There was a brightness in her dark eyes which somehow at the same time both suggested and belied the use of drugs. To both June and Moira she was an overt threat, yet to Harry and Ferrow there was an intimidating quality in her studied perfection which made them feel, when they compared notes later over a late drink, like pieces of meat on the end of her fork, not knowing if they were there to soak up the gravy or to be instantly devoured.

'It's a lovely part of the country,' she remarked. 'I don't think that I've been here before. So wild, despite the little villages. And so pretty.'

Ferrow felt his brain frowning. I don't think I've been here before. How old is she? Twenty-five? Twenty-six? How the fuck long has she had to forget if she's been here or not?

Come to that, what am *I* doing here? A dead man says come to Bonnie Scotland for the hols, so up I troll, dragging June behind me. What do I expect to find here? Sweet FA. So why did I pack that fucking gun of Meeres'?

June eyed Jenny with open hostility. Too well-dressed. Too studied. Predatory. 'She's very sophisticated,' she said to Ferrow later, testing his reactions to the lovely stranger.

He restrained his grin on the grounds that it wouldn't have been fair to either of them. 'She's a good looking woman,' he replied. 'But there's something a bit odd about her for all that.'

'Odd, Bob? What do you mean?'

You clever little bitch, he thought. It's perfectly obvious you can't stand the sight of her, and you're trying to make me say the same thing. She's not competition for you, love, but I'm buggered if I'm going to tell you that.

'You're right about her being sophisticated. It strikes me she's just a shade too old for her years. Obviously she's some sort of business executive and doing very well for herself. But she's in danger of doing it at the expense of ordinary human feeling. That girl's too hard too young.'

June tried another few fencing questions, but Ferrow warded them off without giving her the answers she wanted. He was taking a faintly malicious pleasure in teasing her. Besides, it wouldn't hurt her to stay jealous for a while.

They finished their coffee and moved back through the tiny hall to the bar for a drink. Jenny Fellowes created a minor sensation amongst the grizzled, weather-beaten fishermen who made up the native population, and obviously enjoyed every second of it. In addition to the regulars there were two strangers at the bar, better dressed than the locals. One of them, a tall man with a pock-marked face, seemed to be urging his companion to join in more with their conversation.

Andy Craigham, his brown hair beginning to grey, his eyes bored with the *sassenach* talk forced upon him, his features battered and wrinkled from the better part of forty-three North Sea winters, played his trump card.

'Do ye ken there's a circus in Banff for the holiday week?' he asked loudly.

'A circus?' Moira clapped her well-manicured hands together. Because of their annual trip north (well, Fortstown *is* actually north of Aberdeen) both she and Harry had honorary local status. Their regular visits to Fortstown meant that she knew many of these fishermen quite well, and she and Harry maintained a degree of popularity by the number of wee nips they bought for their acquaintances.

'Really?' Jenny Fellowes asked. Her voice was soft and feminine. It ought to have been seductive, but it was marred by a weary restraint, as if she had seen and said everything before.

Gerard Covington looked at his watch. 'We ought to get back, Tom,' he muttered, running a hand across his dark hair. 'Helen will be having to keep the dinner warm by now.'

'You worry too much about keeping that woman happy,' Luyner replied. 'She works for you, remember? That's all, old man. You've as much time as you want, and certainly enough to meet that gorgeous creature over there.' He gestured towards Jenny Fellowes as he spoke. 'It seems to me she'd be a much better therapy than that lump of old bone of yours.'

Harry Carmichael decided it was his round. For a solicitor the craggy-featured Aberdonian was remarkably outgoing, Ferrow had decided. It was also to be counted an endearing feature that he resisted talking shop with the police inspector from England's most Scottish town.

'There's nothing like a wee nip,' he announced. 'And what they serve here,' he added in a conspiratorial stage-whisper, 'is *nothing* like a wee nip. Will you no join me, June? Robert? And where the hell do you get a good Scots name like Robert from?'

Ferrow grinned and relaxed. Reaching down he gave June's hand a reassuring squeeze as they moved towards the circle of guests and fishermen about the fire.

'Andrew tells me there's a circus in Banff soon,' Moira beamed. 'If you're still here we ought to make up a party to see it. I've no seen a circus since I was a wee girl.'

Ferrow nodded. 'Sounds like a good idea. When's it coming, Andy?'

'They were settin' up earlier today. I had to take the missus in for a wee look roond the shops an' I saw the vans outside. She's allus seekin' ways to spend ma money, ye ken?'

He nudged Harry who broke into an uproarious guffaw. Moira and another fisherman joined him. June and Ferrow laughed politely. Jenny Fellowes permitted herself the ghost of a smile.

'Andy,' Ferrow began, when the laughter had died away, 'I'd appreciate a quiet word with you, when you've a moment. Miles and I were talking earlier today and he said you might be able to clear something up that's puzzling me.'

The fisherman studied Ferrow's face through narrowed eyes. 'Aye,' he grunted. 'Miles said ye'd be askin'.'

They moved aside to a corner table and sat down with their drinks. June joined them. Andy Craigham had been the lynch-pin of the group, the link between guests and natives, and when he left it the circle broke up. The other fishermen went back to their talk of nets and marine engines, and the Carmichaels and Jenny Fellowes found a table of their own.

'Come on, old man,' Tom Luyner urged, tugging a corner of Gerard's tweed jacket. 'Time to say hello.'

He walked across to the Carmichael's table, reluctantly followed by his friend. 'Do you mind if we join you?' he asked.

'Ye recall Miles mentioned yon minister o' the kirk,' Craigham was saying, 'and how he tried to throw away the relic o' St John?

Aye, I ken ye do. Weel, his name was what you heard Miles say. Caspar Locke. It's no a name we say round heer, Bob. It's kept close by our folk. We tell southerners an' sassenachs about yon Viking raids, but we dinna talk about Caspar Locke, or the relic. We dinna say what yon relic was, nor what happened when that poor, foolish man said it had been cursed by the blood o' the pagan man.'

Ferrow nodded. A year or so before he would have dismissed Craigham's story as the ramblings of a superstition-riddled society, primitive and cut off from the rest of the twentieth century. Yet since the affair at Wegrimham, when forces beyond the policeman's comprehension had been unleashed in the course of a terrifying conflict he still didn't understand, Robert Ferrow had kept a more open mind. The interior of the Fortstown Arms was warm and comfortable, but there was a chill creeping into Ferrow's bones, a chill which June, though she had not been as involved in the episode which had brought them together, was still able to share.

'So what did happen?' Ferrow asked.

'Ye'll be thinkin' we're a load o' superstitious fools, I ken, but I'll tell you all the same. I doubt ye'll understand our feelin', for ye're educated people, an' perhaps ye'll hae some sympathy fer all that.

'Caspar Locke found he couldna' lose the relic. He once told as to how he came to the findin' of it. In a dream, he said. In a dream the pagan man, the one St John brought to his deeth among the rocks, appeared to him an' told him where it was hidden in yon kirk. Fer three nights, all in a row, Caspar Locke had that dream. Weel, on the fourth night he did na' hae the stomach fer dreamin' it again, so he got himself up from his bed an' went up to yon kirk to look where the pagan man had said. Surely enough it was there, hidden in the floor beneath the altar table. Hidden wi' it was a paper wi' strange writing, so Caspar Locke was heered to say.

'He sent the paper doon to Edinburgh, where a friend o' his at yon university wrote out the words in gude cleer letters that he could read an' sent it back to him. The paper told as how the curse o' blood was upon yon relic frae the devil gods o' the pagan man an' that the relic had been profaned. Before it was taken it healed the sick by its touch, they said. But when it came back, ye ken, it was profaned an' those touched of it died. Only those appointed by the ghost o' the pagan man could hold it, an' they were doomed to spend their yeers seekin' fer the one who would take the curse away frae them and upon themselves.'

'And if they didn't find anyone?' June asked.

'Then they kept it fer aye, or until they did. Quick or dead it was them that was cursed.'

Ferrow forced a grin. Despite his previous experiences he was still prepared to believe that there might be a Scots leg-pull in this somewhere.

'Surely you're not trying to tell me,' he began, 'that the man Miles saw on the beach, the man he called Caspar Locke, is the same man as the minister who died 200 odd years ago, even if that minister did find the relic?'

Andrew Craigham nodded grimly. 'The same man, but he didna' die.'

'But I saw his grave today, up in the churchyard.'

'Aye. But he's nae in it. Fifty yeers ago, when I was a wee bairn, there was a sassenach came here wi' a letter frae Aberdeen University. He called hisself a professor o' somethin' strange, folk-lore I think. He'd heered the story o' Caspar Locke an' used influence to persuade the kirk authorities to let him open yon grave. There was nae body beneath yon stone. Nae bones. Caspar Locke lives on i' the same body as he had when he was cursed. He'll nae die until he finds some poor man to take the relic frae his hand.'

'Antiques?' Jenny Fellowes asked, in a voice which might have approached interest if it had belonged to anybody else at their table. 'I love antiques, Mr Covington. I've done a little dealing. Nothing spectacular, you understand.'

Tom Luyner kicked Gerard under the table. Now's your chance, he thought. For Christ's sake say the right thing, old man!

'Then perhaps you might like to come up to Witham Lodge sometime?' Gerard asked, more to keep his friend happy than for any other reason. 'There's a few interesting items, and we bought an unusual corner cupboard today. Didn't we, Tom?'

Luyner nodded. But don't bring me into it, you idiot. Keep talking to her yourself. God, don't you know anything at all about women? Work at it, man. 'Time I bought another round,' he grinned. 'Same again, folks?'

'A corner cupboard? How old is it?'

'Difficult to say, Miss Fellowes. It is Miss Fellowes, isn't it?'

'Jenny,' she insisted. 'And it's Ms, not Miss,' she smiled.

'All right, Jenny. I'm Gerard. And the cupboard could be Jacobean. It's certainly dark enough, and the style is suitably massive.'

Good man, Luyner thought. He was smiling to himself as he walked to the bar to order another round of drinks.

June laid her hand gently on Andy Craigham's arm. 'Who else has seen Caspar Locke?' she asked.

The ageing fisherman studied her face carefully. There was an openness about this lass he liked. She had none of the abrasiveness which her man sometimes manifested. He looked at Ferrow and saw that he was curious as well. Then he looked at his watch.

'Auld Davie Quarry,' he replied eventually. 'He lives oot past the point. It's about his time to be comin' in for a nip.'

'Anyone else?'

Ferrow's question had a directness about it which seemed to belie simple curiosity. June shot him a glance and saw that a certain hardness had begun to show in his eyes. It was an expression she thought she remembered from their early days together at Waventree.

Aye, he's a policeman, a' right, Craigham thought. 'Young Wullie Stover claimed to have seen the man,' he answered. 'He's no given to lies, but there's precious little heer for the young to do. I'd no gie him too much credit.'

'But you do believe that Davie Quarry saw him?'

'I believe that he thought he did.'

'And Wullie, is he coming in tonight?'

'If he's no away into Banff.'

'But I'd love to come out to Witham Lodge and see them,' Jenny smiled. 'It sounds as if you have some fascinating items out there, Gerard. Are you doing anything tomorrow? Maybe you'd like to show them to me then.'

Gerard Covington flushed. Luyner, returning with a tray of glasses, noticed his friend's colour and grinned as he reached their table.

'Yes . . .' Gerard began, 'yes, that would be nice . . .'

She had seemed so cold, so distant at first, but now Jenny Fellowes was radiating a positive warmth and interest. Her colouring was different, of course, but there was something about her smile that reminded him of poor Zoë, something more than just the quiet, hidden strength behind it.

Moira was about to suggest that she and Harry came along as well, but the solicitor's hand gripped her knee firmly under the table. She looked up at him, only to see a brief, restrained shake of his bald head. 'I think we'll go into Banff on the morrow,' he announced. 'Would you like us to find out more about the circus?'

Andy Craigham looked at his watch again. Yes, it was time that

129

Davie Quarry had come in. He looked around, turning his head so that he could see every corner of the little bar. Other fishermen and locals had arrived whilst he'd been talking to June and Ferrow, but the old man wasn't amongst them.

He looked over to the bar where Miles Fournessie was polishing a glass on a limp white towel. The innkeeper caught his gaze, sharing the silent expression of unease.

'Would ye like to meet Auld Davie?' he asked his companions.

Ferrow nodded, perhaps a little too eagerly. June held back for a moment, her instinct warning her that there was more than simple interest being shown by her fiancé.

'That would be nice, Andy,' she said. Whatever Bob was up to, she reasoned, was because of his background and training. She had to get used to being a policeman's wife sooner or later, so she might as well start now.

'We'll take a wee walk and meet him,' Craigham muttered, rising to his feet. 'It's no a cold night. Ye'll not need your coats.'

Ferrow and June followed his lead. As they moved towards the door June glanced at Miles Fournessie. Their eyes touched across the bar for a moment, then the innkeeper hurriedly looked away.

'No, you don't need to collect me,' Jenny Fellowes was saying. 'I've brought my own car along. Just tell me how to find Witham Lodge.'

As they made their way down towards the beach Ferrow was mentally groaning to himself. Whatever it was, it was beginning. This was the start of it, no fucking doubt about that. Somehow he'd managed to hide the *frisson* from his neck-hair standing when Craigham spoke of Caspar Locke's supposed age. There was something too reminiscent of Ptythonius Meeres in all this, something which told Robert Ferrow as surely as a loaded gun pointing at his head that he was walking on eggshells, even though they looked like pebbles on the seashore.

But Meeres was dead. Harry Chester's logic was irrefutable. Heart stopped by air-bubble. Heart cut out and sliced up at autopsy. Heart and body cremated.

Ashes stolen . . .

Whatever Mandy had seen had been a trick of some kind. Trick of the light; candlelight. Trick of the mind; doped-up mind. Trick of her surroundings; grubby back-room temple full of perverts.

Ptythonius Meeres was dead.

So a dead man's note had sent them to Fortstown for their holidays. So Miles Fournessie had somehow had a room vacant in late August. Curiosity and coincidence, Ferrow tried to tell himself.

And failed.

The pain was almost over.

Old blood, for all it's supposed to be thin and run like water in an old man's veins, flows slowly, thickly, out towards oblivion. They had done with him now. They had gone, taking the worst of the agony with them.

He knew that it was impossible for them to let him live. If he survived he would be questioned, would tell those who questioned him about the things they had asked for. Sooner or later somebody might begin to fit the scattered fragments together, and that would never do. That was why he had to die.

He accepted the fact quite easily. After all, he'd had a full life. He'd done almost everything that he wanted. And to continue now, to survive, would leave him a weakened, disillusioned cripple at best.

They had been thorough enough. The pain only recurred if he tried to speak or move. The little he had known he had told them gladly. The price of his silence would have been the extension, and eventual failure, of a futile gesture. What could one man do against so many nightmares in the dark? What would have been the point of trying?

His fingers moved spasmodically at his sides, feeling the oily, sticky fabric of the blankets beneath him. They were wet, there in the darkness. They were wet and getting wetter with every beat of his failing pulse. Everything was so wet, and the darkness was growing denser, washing over him with a comforting moisture all of its own. Even the distant footsteps, the scrabblings on the rocks, didn't matter any more.

Most of Fortstown was awake. The first sirens, wailing in the night like demented banshees, had broken into the sleep of all but the soundest dreamers. The engines, the whine of police vehicles and the heavier diesel of the ambulance, had been lost beneath the sound-blanket of dismal howling. Most of the houses and cottages showed yellow lights at curious windows, and figures clustered here and there in the brightness from an open doorway.

Heavy steps echoed on the sloping paths and steps which led down to the pebbly beach. The waterfront houses, white and blue in the moonlight, were splashed by the dark shadows of the uniformed figures running past them. The shingle crunched and the telephones were busy, singing along their wires the song of rumour and speculation. All told it was the busiest night Fortstown could remember since that trader had gone down in the storm in 1969.

Just around the point, in the direction the running, crunching feet were taking, the same doctor who had closed Davie Quarry's staring eyes was injecting June Lowe with a sedative. When the ambulancemen had carried the pitiful remains of the old man back to the ambulance they would return for her. For the present though, the sedative would serve to quiet her a little. Statements could come later, the following morning. Even Inspector McAllister would get nothing coherent out of her before then.

Hugo James McAllister wandered about the little cottage, his heavy brow creased in brooding anger. To him it made no sense at all, not at all. Crimes like this just didn't happen in his patch. Glasgow, yes. Aberdeen, sometimes. But not around Banff. Nobody did things like this around Banff.

Lights flooded the cottage. Everything that could brighten the grim scene, candles and paraffin lamps as well as the electric fixtures, had been pressed into service. Really it was a kindness to refer to Davie's home as a cottage. The single-storey dwelling was half derelict, and the old man's few possessions had been moved into one room of the glorified stone hut. Once it had been a decent-sized kitchen, but now it was dining-room, lounge and bed-room as well. Piles of newspaper vied with mouldy, empty tins and bottles on the mahogany table, and patches of mould and damp discoloured the walls. The door stuck badly, and the frame around it was split in places, coming away from the primitive masonry. In daylight or the single electric bulb of evening it didn't matter, but before the harsh glare which now burned, the full decay of old Davie's chosen surroundings stood out with stark disdain.

But his squalid home was not the appalling thing about the scene. What wrinkled Hugo McAllister's forehead, what had fetched him and his men from Banff to this lonely, forgotten hovel on the coast, was the blood which had sprayed onto the walls and soaked through the bed-covers to the ancient striped mattress beneath, and the grim, white, drained corpse of Davie Quarry which had just been carried away.

'Achilles' tendons cut on both legs,' the doctor had begun. 'Veins in both wrists opened by some sharp instrument. Veins, mind you, not arteries. Marks of beating around the face and head. Another mark, which looks rather like a rope-burn, across the forehead. Three nails missing on the left hand . . .'

The list, sickeningly, continued. Outside, not yet sedated, June was shrieking in the strong grip of two ashen-faced constables. A puddle of vomit, Craigham's, had accumulated by the door, and stains and particles still clung to the weathered boards. Ferrow, his arms crossed over his stomach, was squatting uneasily on the un-broken dining-chair, desperately trying not to remember the sight of the vet, Widgeon, who had died just as bloodily at Waventree. Of course you expected to see death if you joined the police force, but there was death and death. Even road accidents, for all they might be gory, were less horrific than the sheer depravity of a scene like this.

Ferrow was by no means a small man, but McAllister, at nearly six and a half feet, towered over the seated stranger like a giant. His large nose, red and bulbous towards the tip, stood out like a beacon on his ruddy, weatherbeaten face. His once gold hair was now streaked pepper and salt with white, and heavy lines had raised folds of skin which threatened to obscure his deep-set blue eyes altogether.

He peered at Ferrow, then turned to the uniformed sergeant with the notebook who stood beside him. 'And this is the poor man who gave the alarm, is it, Harris?' he asked.

His voice was undeniably that of a man well used to his own authority, though in the stark, bright reality of the bloodstained cottage it came across as almost incongruously gentle. The Scots accent was there, but heavily sublimated, leading Ferrow to suppose that the big policeman had spent some time in the south.

Harris opened his notebook. He contrasted strongly with his superior, much shorter and thinner, and with almost jet-black hair. 'Aye,' he began, his voice husky, rasping as it hit the air. 'He left the others heer and went back tae the "Arms" tae phone. Then he came back.'

'Is that correct, Mr . . .?'

'Ferrow,' Harris prompted. 'Robert Ferrow.'

'Is that right, Mr Ferrow?'

The seated man looked up. His face was still ashen and his lip trembled slightly. 'Yes,' he said. 'That's about it.'

'But why were you here in the first place, Robert?'

'He came down with Miss Lowe and Andy . . .'

McAllister glared at his sergeant. 'Let the man answer for himself, Harris,' he grunted with admirable and unusual restraint.

Ferrow sighed deeply. 'Andy Craigham said he was a local character worth meeting,' came the weary reply. 'He was late coming to the "Arms" so we decided to walk down and meet him. We didn't pass him on the beach or in the village, so we thought he must still be here.'

'And so you walked all the way? What happened then?'

'Andy pointed out the cottage. There were no lights showing and Andy wanted to check on his friend, to make sure that the old man was all right. He called and knocked, but there was no reply. Then he opened the door and put the light on . . .'

McAllister nodded. 'Aye,' he began, 'and we all know what you found here. Then what did you do?'

'Andy cried out. I told June . . . Miss Lowe . . . to wait outside while I went in. Andy pushed out past me and threw up.'

'But you have a stronger stomach?'

'Shut up, Harris! Go on, Robert.'

'Well, it was one of the nastiest sights I've ever seen. I told Andy to pull himself together and look after Miss Lowe while I went for the police . . .'

'You said on the telephone that old Davie was dead. Did you examine the body in order to know that?'

'No. His eyes were open and glazed, and the whole place was swimming in blood. He wasn't moving.'

'So why didn't you try to help him?' Harris sneered.

'Because I didn't want to interfere with the evidence, sergeant! Christ, man, can't you understand that?'

McAllister glanced from one to the other and stood back, smiling faintly. For one reason or another Harris thought he had a suspect in this man. Maybe this was a chance to get his self-opinionated sergeant taken down a peg or two.

'It's hardly the reaction of a normal member of the public, Ferrow. And what did you mean earlier when you said that this was one of the nastiest sights you'd ever seen. D'you see things like this every day?'

'Leave it, sergeant,' Ferrow replied, glaring at McAllister. 'You're serving no purpose by this line of questioning.'

Harris began to redden. There was a quiet authority in this man's behaviour, even here at the scene of a particularly foul murder, which he didn't like at all. And Inspector McAllister was just standing there smiling at it.

'Don't you try and tell the police what tae do, laddie . . .'

'For Christ's sake, man!' Ferrow reached into his pocket and tossed a small black folder across to Harris. 'Read that and stop behaving like a prick!'

Scowling blackly the sergeant opened the wallet, then passed it to McAllister. The inspector was grinning broadly when he handed the warrant card back to Ferrow.

'I think you owe the inspector an apology, Harris,' he smiled. 'But for now just leave the questioning to me. Why don't you go back to Fortstown and wait for the forensic team?'

With an inarticulate grunt Sergeant Harris strode out of the cottage. As he left McAllister produced a small flask from a uniform pocket and offered it to Ferrow.

'He's a good man in his way,' he began, 'but he does tend to get carried away. Here, I think you've earned a wee nip, my friend.'

Ferrow took the flask gratefully and felt the fiery malt warming his uneasy stomach.

'After you'd telephoned for the police you came back here?'

Ferrow nodded. 'June had got away from Andy Craigham and looked inside. It's not a sight I'd have wanted her to see, but she's got this thing about a policeman's wife having to cope with all aspects of her husband's job. She's a strong lady, you know,

Inspector. The hysterical woman you saw just now isn't at all typical.'

'I can believe that. Well, I wish we'd met under better circumstances, Robert. You'd better stop calling me Inspector,' he added, extending his hand. 'My name's Hugo.'

Ferrow stood up and they shook hands. He was beginning to like this large Scotsman, and the warmth of McAllister's handshake told him that the feeling was mutual.

'Is there anything else that you can tell me, Robert? Anything unusual that you might have noticed on the way here? The doctor said that old Davie was only a little time dead. Certainly less than an hour, and probably only minutes.'

The Englishman looked down at his feet, then across to the blood-stained bed. The air about them was growing thick with fumes from the paraffin lamps.

'On the way, just as we were approaching the cottage, I did think I heard something in the rocks. Something small, maybe a dog. I mentioned it to Andy, but he told me that Davie Quarry didn't have one, so I thought no more about it. It was probably just a stray.'

McAllister smiled to himself. 'You're probably right,' he remarked. 'Certainly Davie wasn't attacked by an animal. The cuts were too clean. They were probably made with a knife or a razor. Still, we'll know more about that when the forensic laddies have finished and the doctor's performed an autopsy.

'But tell me,' he continued. 'You said that Andy Craigham had told you Davie was a local character worth meeting. Why the interest in us bucolic Scots?'

It was an open invitation to mention the story of Caspar Locke, but something warned Ferrow that his interest might be considered more than just passing. The time wasn't right, as yet. He had to get to know Hugo McAllister a little better before he brought that legend up. After all, when he thought about it, the whole thing was going to sound bloody strange. Here he was, on holiday, picking his way across a rocky shore at night to talk to an old man he'd never met about a legend that a civilised man like McAllister would dismiss as local superstition. If it came from Andy Craigham it would sound better, more natural. Besides, there was no reason to suppose that the legend had played any part in old Davie's murder. Not yet.

'Folklore's a bit of a hobby of mine,' Ferrow eventually replied, hoping that his words didn't ring too hollow. 'I enjoy listening to old men, even old Scots, telling their stories. Nothing too serious, you understand, but our job means you need to know quite a bit about human nature and credibility. If you like, it's a way of combining business and pleasure.'

McAllister smiled. 'Aye,' he beamed. 'There's some brave stories to be told about this coast. The old kirk in Braw Valley, the shipwrecks, even old Caspar Locke . . .'

Ferrow felt his heart jump, then subside. It was only reasonable that others should know about Caspar Locke if they had lived in the area for any length of time. And that could just as easily apply to the inspector.

'If you've the time during your stay you'll have to come over one night and I'll tell you some stories myself. Over a bottle or two of single malt, of course.'

Ferrow forced a smile and nodded. Outside the crunching of feet on the rocks and shingle told him that the forensic team McAllister had conjured out of the night were arriving.

The following morning Jenny Fellowes drove out to Witham Lodge. Gerard was waiting for her beside the tiled, arched porch, smiling gently. He greeted her with a warm, friendly handshake, then showed her inside through the iron-studded door.

'I hope you didn't mind me phoning the hotel,' he began, 'but the new items have just arrived. As you seemed so interested last night I thought you might like to help me unpack them.'

Jenny beamed at him. 'I'd be delighted,' she smiled.

He led her through into the study, where the refectory table had been moved aside to make way for an untidy jumble of packing cases piled around the ancient cabinet. It was all remarkably dusty.

'There are some household gloves over there,' Gerard indicated.

'You don't get the feel of old things properly through gloves,' Jenny answered. 'Sometimes even the dirt on something has a story of its own to tell. That cabinet looks fabulous.'

'I'm afraid it's rather a morbid curiosity,' came the reply. 'When you get closer you'll see that it's been carved with a motif which can only represent graveyard worms. Most of this stuff has some sort of a connection with death.'

Jenny nodded and smiled again. 'Where's your friend Tom?' she asked.

Gerard grinned rather sheepishly. 'When I told him you were coming over he asked me to give you his regards. Then he decided to take a walk in the grounds. I expect he'll join us for lunch.'

'You have a very discreet friend, I think. Now, shall we start unpacking your new treasures? I want to see absolutely everything.'

She declined a cup of coffee before they began and immediately pitched elbow-deep into the nearest of the packing cases. As each item was removed it was carefully dusted with a paintbrush and deposited on the refectory table, to await a more detailed examination later. When they paused for drinks, just before noon, only the cabinet remained unexplored.

'Some of those books look quite valuable,' Jenny remarked as

Gerard handed her a vodka martini. 'There's an original *Chirurgia Magna* in the Ulm printing of 1536, as well as a lot more Paracelsus. But the books don't really interest me. It's too much of a specialist market. This, though,' she added, pointing to a dusty, dirt-grained casket, 'is something else. If I'm right you've found a real treasure.'

Gerard set down his drink and picked up the age-blackened box. The metal felt remarkably heavy. 'It's as heavy as lead,' he grinned.

Jenny shook her head. 'Not lead,' she corrected. 'It's heavy enough for gold, though.'

'Gold? You mean solid gold?' He lifted his glass again and drained its contents, Then he reached out for hers. 'I think we ought to have another, don't you?'

'But of course. Before you go to freshen our glasses, though, do you have a penknife on you?'

He set down the box and reached into his trouser pocket. 'Never without one,' he replied. 'You never know when it'll come in handy.'

He placed the tiny knife in her outstretched palm and left to get the drinks. Whilst he was out of the study Jenny Fellowes turned the heavy casket upside down and scraped gently at the underside. Beneath the encrustation of dirt the metal began to show soft and yellow. As Gerard returned she held it out to him.

'You see?' she asked. 'It *is* gold, Gerard, and the sheer weight of metal makes it worth a considerable sum. But I think it's worth more without taking that into account.'

He allowed himself a low whistle. Jenny put the box down again and they stood back with their drinks to study the find. It was almost twice as long as it was wide, about eight inches by four, and the hinged lid was steeply pitched like the roof of a miniature house. The hinges formed part of twin raised bands which ran all the way around the outside, and there was a suggestion of dirt-encrusted engraving beneath.

'Any ideas what it might be?' Gerard asked at length.

'I think so. I've seen similar items before, but rarely outside leading museums. By its shape and size I'd say it's a reliquary, designed to hold some fragment stolen from the body of a saint. You never know,' she laughed. 'You may have discovered the fifteenth foreskin of Jesus Christ.'

'The *what* did you say?'

'Just a little joke. At one time in the middle ages there were fourteen monasteries around Europe claiming to have as their relic the prepuce of Christ, and not one of them could have been real. At the time Jesus was circumcised it was a duty of the godfather to swallow the severed fragment.'

'That's revolting.'

Jenny smiled at him. 'History frequently is,' she replied. 'But let's get back to the casket. It's hard to tell before it's cleaned, but the workmanship looks as if it could have been tenth, maybe eleventh, century. That makes it the better part of a thousand years old. Quite an age, don't you think?'

Gerard sipped his drink. 'And Tom only paid a few pounds for the whole lot,' he remarked.

'Shall we find out what's inside?'

'Are you sure it won't unleash a plague of typhus on us? If it is a reliquary then whatever's inside is probably organic. And it's been slowly decaying in there for centuries.'

'I don't think there's any real danger of that,' Jenny laughed. 'You forget, I've done this sort of thing before.'

'Well, I'm game if you are.'

She put down her drink and began to lever the centrally-mounted catch with Gerard's penknife. Slowly, very slowly, with flakes and fragments of dirt falling away onto the polished surface of the refectory table, the catch rose.

'Now a little gentle work around the sides. I expect the hinges are jammed, so we'll need to get rid of as much resistance as possible.'

She ran the edge of the blade around the join, taking care not to mark the soft metal more than was necessary. Then she grasped the base firmly, pressing it down onto the table, and used her other hand to push backwards and up on the pitched lid of the reliquary. With a faint grating, the lid rose. They peered inside. With the exception of some dust and the mummified remains of a dead spider the casket was completely empty.

'Well,' Gerard smiled, 'you can't win them all.'

Jenny said nothing and turned away. Her lower lip was trembling and her face was white as she drained her glass. Then she turned back.

'Do we have time for another drink before lunch?' she asked.

Tom returned shortly afterwards and Gerard proudly showed him their find. 'And you didn't want to go into the shop,' he grinned. 'What a stroke of luck, old man.'

The reliquary formed their main topic of conversation through lunch, though Jenny seemed to some extent to have lost interest in the object itself. She now appeared more concerned with finding out how the casket had come into the shopkeeper's possession, and she and Gerard agreed to drive into Banff and ask the dealer for the address it has been taken from.

After coffee, as they pushed their chairs back from the table, Jenny Fellowes suddenly started and raised a hand to her left eye.

'My contact lens,' she snapped. 'I've dropped it.'

Gerard lifted the chairs clear of the table and they bent to look for the missing lens. Tom found it quite quickly and handed it back to Jenny, who still had a hand over her left eye. As Tom Luyner extended it on the palm of his hand he noticed how dark the lens was, and slightly larger than usual.

With a grateful smile Jenny went to the bathroom to wash and replace the offending article. Whilst she was out of the room Tom remarked: 'It's tinted, old man. Your Ms Fellowes obviously changes the colour of her eyes to match her hair. Now that's being fashion-conscious for you.'

They laughed and thought no more about the incident. Tom declined to join them in researching the reliquary's history and instead remained behind at Witham Lodge. 'I think I'll have a flip through those old books of yours,' he grinned.

They entered the little shop a little after three. The dealer looked up in surprise as they closed the door.

'Everything all right with your goods, Mr Covington?' he asked.

'Oh, yes. They're fine,' Gerard replied. 'One thing, though. Would it be possible for you to tell me where they came from?'

'I said that before. Just a house we cleared.'

'The owner had died?'

'Now that I didn't say. No, he's not dead. He just had a lot of stuff he wanted to get rid of. House was getting too big for him, being an old gent, he said.'

'Do you have the address?' Jenny asked, her voice echoing with that same weary restraint Ferrow had noticed the night before.

'Can't do that, miss. Wouldn't be proper.'

She reached into her handbag and withdrew a twenty-pound note. Gerard eyed her strangely as she extended it to the dealer.

'Does this have any effect upon your scruples?'

'I've got it written down somewhere,' the man replied, grinning broadly. 'But you didn't get it from me. Right, miss?'

'As you say.'

The dealer bent over the desk, riffling back through the pages of a large notebook. Finally he left it open at the required place and scribbled something onto a scrap of brown paper with a soft pencil. Folding the paper in half he exchanged it for the banknote. Without a word Jenny tucked the paper into her handbag and left the shop. Gerard nodded briefly to the dealer, feeling rather superfluous in the transaction, then followed her.

He caught up with her in the street outside. 'Well,' he muttered, 'I didn't expect you to do that.'

'Call it a present from me to you,' Jenny smiled. She took the paper from her bag and opened it. Once she had read the address she passed it to Gerard.

'Shall we see if Mr Hogue is at home today?' she asked.

They walked back to Jenny's car and drove out of Banff on the road back to Fortstown. Just before they reached the bridge over the River Deveron the car swung right and started climbing. Above the town proper, in a ridge overlooking the river, stood an area of tall granite-faced Victorian houses, some detached but mostly in close terraces.

'Aberchirder Street, isn't it?' Jenny asked.

Gerard nodded. 'Number eleven.'

The car slowed to a halt. 'That's it,' she muttered, bending her head down to peer out through the passenger window.

Gerard got out and looked up at number eleven. It stood in the middle of one of the terraces, with a short, steeply-sloping garden separating it from the street. From the steps up to the paint-peeling front door and the cutaway at the top of the garden it was obvious that the house had a basement, making three storeys in all. The garden was sadly neglected, littered with rubbish and a profusion of empty milk-bottles, and an upstairs window had been repaired with adhesive tape where the glass had cracked. All the windows were sadly curtained with faded and occasionally-torn material.

Jenny joined Gerard Covington on the pavement. The street was deserted and several of the houses were patently empty. An air of desolation seemed to overhang the whole area.

'Come on,' she said, squeezing his arm. Then she started up the gateless path towards the steps.

Gerard followed her, almost reluctant to meet the old man who had let the priceless reliquary slip through his fingers. Jenny had reached the door and was knocking on it when he joined her on the top step. Her rapping echoed through the empty rooms inside.

'I don't think Mr Hogue is in,' he muttered.

'Don't be such a defeatist,' she replied, knocking again.

After several minutes of fruitless waiting she had to concede that he was right. 'We'll try again,' she smiled as they walked back down the path to her car. 'Sooner or later we're bound to catch him.'

During the drive back to Witham Lodge Gerard was strangely quiet. Whether he was feeling guilty about the reliquary, when its previous owner was obviously living in straitened circumstances, or whether it was something else, something that he couldn't yet put a name to, he didn't know. Yet he felt uneasy, as if a cloud had passed in front of his sun and refused to move on.

Jenny came in for tea before returning to the Fortstown Arms. She arranged to meet Gerard there that evening and, as an after-thought, extended the invitation to Tom as well.

'Sorry,' he smiled. 'But I'd planned to drive home this evening. If I start about six I can be in York before midnight.'

'That's the first I've heard about it,' Gerard remarked.

Tom grinned broadly. 'Oh, didn't I tell you, old man? It must have slipped my mind. Don't worry, though. I'll give you a ring in a day or so. See how you're getting on.

'By the way,' he added. 'I've tucked your friend into the cabinet. You know, your *memento mori*. That old skull.'

'A skull?' Jenny asked. 'Wherever did you find that?'

'It's what put us on to the old man's things in the shop,' Gerard replied. 'It was in with them when the dealer took Mr Hogue's items. He was a bit superstitious about the rest of the stuff, but he had the skull in the shop. A sort of curiosity value, I suppose.'

'How weird. Can I see it?'

'Permit me, Madame,' Tom beamed, rising from his chair. He walked over to the cabinet and opened the upper door. The ancient skull stood out against the dark interior of the cupboard. Hooking his fingers into the orbits, he lifted it out and carried it across to Jenny Fellowes.

'Nice chap, isn't he?' Tom quipped. 'He's becoming quite an old friend of ours.'

Jenny took the death's-head from him and turned it in her hands. Then she lifted it up and peered at it closely, the bony cranium masking her face from the others. After several moments she lowered it again, this time holding it in front of her breasts so that they didn't see how jerkily she was breathing. Then, in her calm, slightly bored voice, she remarked: 'An old friend, you say? Yes, I can see that it might be that.'

She tossed it back to the mildly startled Tom, who caught it and returned it to the cabinet. Then she stood up and extended her hand.

'It was nice meeting you, Tom,' she smiled. 'I hope I'll see you again sometime.'

'Chances are,' he grinned back. 'Enjoy your holiday, Jenny.'

She looked from him to the cabinet, and from the cabinet to Gerard Covington. Both men were smiling and, behind the worm-carved door, so would be the skull.

'I'm sure I shall,' she replied.

Badly shocked by the appalling sight of the night before, June spent that day in her room. Miles Fournessie sent her meals up on a tray, and McAllister and Sergeant Harris called to take a statement during the course of the morning. When they left Ferrow went with them into Banff, still wondering if he should mention the connection which the legend of Caspar Locke seemed to have with the case. At that time he resolved to treat the link as unimportant and, in the event, said nothing. Later he was to wish that he hadn't been so guarded.

During the afternoon, whilst Jenny and Gerard were looking for the absent Mr Hogue, Ferrow took another walk up to the ruined church in Braw Valley. As he approached the broken shell he noticed that there was someone there ahead of him, a dark-haired youth in jeans and a fisherman's sweater, who seemed to be running his hands over the walls as if searching for something. The young man was so absorbed in what he was doing that he failed to notice the policeman's approach.

Ferrow stood beneath one of the ruined arches, watching silently. It was a bright, sunny afternoon and the shadows between the patches of sunlight were starting to lengthen again. The youth moved from darkness into light and back again with a singular dedication. Obviously vision was not important for his search. He was relying on other senses.

'Lost something?' Ferrow asked casually.

The young fisherman snapped around, staring at Ferrow through wide, fear-startled eyes. For a moment his mouth hung slackly open, then his lips began to work and his eyes relaxed.

'I ken ye,' he said. 'Mr Ferrow. Ye're stayin' a' the "Arms".'

'And I think you'd be Wullie Stover. I've seen you in the bar occasionally. But what are you doing up here, Wullie?' Ferrow moved closer as he spoke, watching the youth's face as he asked his question.

Wullie's eyes hardened and narrowed. His face grew blank, becoming an expressionless mask.

'I dinna ken yer meanin'.'

'You know very well what I mean. What do you expect to find in the walls? Something to do with Caspar Locke?'

As Ferrow mentioned the name, Wullie's emotionless mask dissolved. He moved to push past the policeman, out of the ruins, but a restraining hand was laid upon his shoulder, swinging him around to face the newcomer.

'I know you've seen him, Wullie. So have I. Not up close,' he added, 'not the way you saw him. Not the way Davie Quarry saw him. You've heard about old Davie, of course?'

'I've seen nothin'.'

'That's not how the rest of Fortstown tells the story. I want to help you, Wullie. We know the same thing, that there's some connection between old Davie's murder and the legend of Caspar Locke.'

He was guessing and he knew it. He simply hoped that Wullie Stover didn't know it as well. 'Come on, lad. I can help you. It's pointless to deny you were looking for something. I've been here for some time. You just didn't notice me because you were so busy with your search. Tell me, Wullie. Tell me.'

His voice was becoming more insistent. He had to keep checking himself, reminding himself that Wullie wasn't a suspect and hadn't broken the law. Even if he had, Ferrow had no authority in the area. The most he could manage was a citizen's arrest. Anything more was up to Hugo McAllister.

'Why should I? What c'n ye do tae help?'

'I can look with you. I'm not a disbelieving sassenach. I've seen the old man as well. You can do more with a friend than you can do alone. I know I'm an outsider, but I'm the best you've got, Wullie. And that means you have to trust me. Doesn't it?'

The youth eyed him sullenly. For several moments neither of them spoke. They simply stood there, in the ruined church, Ferrow's hand still clamped onto Wullie's shoulder.

At length, Wullie asked: 'Why the interest, Mr Ferrow? Whether ye've seen Caspar Locke or no, it's no yer business. Ye'll be off soon. We've got tae live here. So what's it tae ye?'

There was an answer, but the policeman knew it would be impossible to explain. Wullie was asking a question that he himself had asked, albeit in a slightly different form. Once again Ferrow sat in the rotunda of the Templar church at Wegrimham, listening in the night to the voice of the late Ptythonius Meeres.

'I cannot name the person behind this conspiracy for you.'

'And why not?'

'BECAUSE IT'S TOO VAST AND TOO SUBTLE!'

Even now Ferrow didn't really understand. All he knew was that a role had been marked out for him to play, and he would play that role because he had no choice, because the alternatives were too frightening for him to contemplate. All that remained was to use whatever intelligence he had to fight the conspiracy wherever he found it, or was told to find it. He didn't even know who his superiors were any more.

In the force it was straightforward enough, and he simply answered to the ranks above him, as the ranks below answered in their turn to him. But in this other work, the work he had been committed to by Meeres' death in an English hospital, there were no ranks, no identifiable masters, only areas of responsibility and promptings which could still be figments of his own imagination.

And how was young Wullie Stover of Fortstown going to understand that?

'Davie Quarry is dead,' he muttered, tightening his grip on Wullie's shoulder. His voice was patient but strained, as if he wanted to shake the youth into comprehension. 'He's dead and by now you'll have heard how he died. I've seen this sort of situation before. Not the same, you understand, but similar. My experience tells me something, Wullie. It tells me that old Davie is only the first, that there are going to be others. If you help me I can help you. I can prevent you being one of them. And that's why you have to trust me.'

'Are ye done?' the youth asked, taking hold of Ferrow's wrist and removing the hand from his shoulder. 'Then I'll be awa',' he continued, starting to walk out of the ruins.

When he reached one of the arches he turned and looked back. 'He's a legend,' he said, defiantly, seeking to convince himself as much as he wanted to convince Ferrow. 'He's no real. What I saw was a dream. A wakin' dream. Nothin' more.'

He was breathing heavily, almost panting as he spoke. His eyes had resumed some of the wildness they held when Ferrow had first discovered him, feeling the walls of the old church. They ranged across the ruins, somehow fearing to meet the detective's steady gaze, then up through the broken, fallen roof to the hills beyond. Suddenly his mouth fell open and his face became white.

Ferrow walked across and stood beside him, following the line of his vision. On top of one of the hills bordering Braw Valley, more than a quarter of a mile of uphill scrambling away, stood a dark figure, watching them. Somehow Ferrow knew, despite the distance, that they had both seen that shape before.

He turned to Wullie, but the young fisherman was gone, running down the valley with a leaping, irregular movement which indicated the blind panic of escape. Then he looked up through the roof again, to where the dark figure was still watching, no doubt in his mind as to the watcher's identity.

The dark-clad being would be gone long before Ferrow had finished the ascent. Though they were too far apart to see each other's eyes they both knew that. Then the figure seemed to dwindle, its vigil over, and the policeman was merely looking up through the roof of a ruined church on a summer afternoon, staring at the vacant hilltop beyond.

'That's twice,' Ferrow muttered to himself.

He walked back down the valley, weighing the possibilities in his mind. Whether it was the original Caspar Locke, or whether someone had taken his persona for purposes of their own, didn't really matter. The only thing that was important was that the story of Caspar Locke wasn't over, and that one of the men who had seen him was now dead.

As he returned to the Fortstown Arms to see how June was, his thoughts were obsessed with the legend which was fast becoming a riddle. His decision to come to Banffshire had not been entirely motivated by the desire for a holiday. Anyone who carried Ferrow's knowledge locked away inside would never be truly able to relax and forget.

There were things that he had to check. Somewhere there had to be records dealing with the time when the church in Braw Valley was still in use, records which might yield some clue as to what Wullie Stover was looking for. In addition there were newspaper files to consult, files which would take him back to the event mentioned by Andy Craigham, to the time when professor some-body-or-other had opened the grave of Caspar Locke and found . . . nothing?

He reached the beach and continued walking back towards Fortstown. Occasionally he turned, wondering if he was being watched, his eyes flashing back towards that distant hill where the dark-clad figure had been standing. Of course, there was nothing watching from the hilltop, but the feeling persisted and it made Ferrow uneasy. Since the affair at Wegrimham he knew only too well what might be watching him, and the knowledge gave him the right to be afraid.

The eyes were watching, all right. They had sought him out when he left the hotel and followed him to the ruin. They had seen him talking to Wullie, and they had seen Wullie searching for something in the walls. But they were not the eyes of the little creatures Ferrow dreaded. They were the eyes of something with a much greater potential for evil.

And they would be watching him for some time to come.

As Merry Foster was shown into his office McAllister motioned for her to take a seat. The red-haired, brown-eyed Scots lass was the last thing the policeman wanted at that moment, but she was there, and it was always as well to keep up at least a façade of politeness with people like Merry.

'Now I wonder what you could possibly want to talk to me about?' the inspector began, his tone only mildly antagonistic.

'You know very well, Inspector McAllister,' came the reply. 'I'd like a statement for the *Echo* regarding the death of Davie Quarry. And where else should I come to be given one?'

'Who have you spoken to so far, Merry?'

The silence which followed told McAllister nothing. She could have spoken to everybody in Fortstown, but she wasn't going to tell the inspector that. He suspected, though, that her unwillingness to answer, and her physical presence in his office, instead of at the other end of a telephone, meant that she didn't have much of a story as yet.

'Let me guess, Merry. Andy Craigham was out on his boat. Mr Ferrow and Miss Lowe declined to see you. Am I right?'

'Not at all,' she denied, perhaps a shade too quickly.

'But you haven't spoken to any of them, have you?'

Merry shrugged. 'I almost saw Mr Craigham.'

'But?'

'Oh, all right. He said he was too upset to say anything more than that he'd lost an auld friend.' Like McAllister, her voice showed Scots only with the occasional intonation, a result of her newspaper training on southern provincial papers.

'And June Lowe?'

Merry shrugged. 'Still under sedation this morning.'

'And Mr Ferrow?'

Ferrow was the unknown quantity in McAllister's calculations. He was a copper, yes, but a sassenach for all that. He was also newly promoted and could be looking to make a name for himself at the expense of his northern colleagues.

'Not there,' Merry replied. 'Out for a walk. I waited, but I couldn't wait for long enough, it seems.'

The inspector breathed a silent sigh of relief. If he could keep Quarry's death low-key in the local media it might just miss the nationals and TV.

'And so you've come to me?'

'I've a duty to my readers, Mr McAllister.'

'Yes, yes, of course you have. And I have a duty to the public which on occasions conflicts with your own.'

'So you'll no give me a statement?'

'My dear, of course I'll give you a statement. I'm only too delighted to. But you must appreciate that at present its scope has to be severely limited. Several of the details will have to be excluded, for instance.'

'For instance?'

'I expect you've spoken to the hospital and discovered that the late Davie Quarry was tortured?'

'I have. And I'll print that.'

'I have no doubt of it, Merry. We must all do our jobs as we see them. I would ask, though, that you do not go into detail in your report.'

The brown eyes narrowed and the pretty features turned slightly sideways as they frowned at McAllister. 'You're afraid of copycat killings?' she asked him. 'Here? in Banff?'

'It's a possibility.'

'Not one you've ever mooted before, Inspector.'

'We've no had a murder like this one before, Merry. That's why I have to be so careful with what I tell you.'

There was something in Inspector Hugo McAllister's smile as he spoke to her that Merry Foster, crime reporter for the *Banffshire Echo*, found objectionable. Not patronising, just objectionable.

'So what are you going to tell me?'

'That following the death of Davie Quarry we are pursuing certain lines of enquiry.'

'And that's it?' Merry demanded.

'As close to *it* as I'm prepared to go at present.'

'You're aware that you're turning the most exciting crime in months into a couple of page three paragraphs?'

'Does it do that? I'm sorry. Can't you write up this circus that's coming for cruelty to animals instead?'

'You're being deliberately awkward on this, Inspector McAllister.'

The inspector moved around his desk and stood over Merry where she sat, putting her notebook away in disgust. 'Now you listen to me, Miss Foster,' he began. 'I've a dead man on my hands. A *messy* dead man. And the one's enough. I don't want any of your bored readers going out and giving me another for kicks, or whatever they're called these days. You see these hands? They're stained permanently brown with the shit of the shitty job I do. Not all the perfumes of Arabia, and so on. When I clap these hands upon the creature who killed Davie Quarry you'll have your story, Merry Foster. Until then, what I know *I know*, and you'll do well to keep your readers' noses clean and out of it. Is that clear enough for you?'

The conversation at dinner that evening was muted and restrained. Ferrow and June went down together to the dining-room, June still visibly shaken by the experience of the night before. Ferrow was also quiet, trying to make some sense out of the events of the afternoon. Jenny Fellowes appeared more animated than she had done the previous evening, and Harry and Moira were their usual bright selves, though careful to keep their conversation away from anything connected with Davie Quarry's murder.

Jenny finished quickly and left her seat for the bar before any of the others had finished eating. As arranged, Gerard Covington was waiting there for her. He was still excited about the reliquary, and still wondering what was the best thing to do about Mr Hogue, its previous owner.

Outside the afternoon had deteriorated, and had become a steady drizzle by the evening. The white-painted walls and slate roofs of Fortstown were glistening with moisture, and the steep, cobbled paths had become treacherous underfoot. The hotel, though, remained bright and warm, a small oasis of comfort in the bleak Scottish village.

June and Ferrow finished their meal and followed Jenny into the bar. June had hardly done more than taste the various courses, and her expression showed that the holiday, for her, was becoming a nightmare. They smiled at Jenny and Gerard as they ordered their drinks, then took them to a separate table. There they began to drink them in silence.

'Bob?' June asked at length.

'Mm?'

'Look, this was a good idea, but it can never be a holiday now. Why don't we go home?'

Ferrow offered her what he hoped was a reassuring smile. The question was far from unexpected, and he already had a carefully prepared answer to it.

'As you know,' he began, 'I was talking to McAllister this morning. He'd like us to stay around a bit longer. Just in case he thinks of any more questions to ask us. As soon as he's happy, we'll be back to Corby. Okay?'

'Then you find it depressing too?'

'It's not exactly what I'd planned for our time away together,' he replied. It wasn't exactly a lie. All he'd known before he set out was that there was something ahead of him which in some way connected with Meeres and the work the old man had been doing. He didn't know for sure what it was, or what he'd find when they arrived. The first few days, quiet and tranquil, had lulled him into a false sense of security. Only the brutal murder of Davie Quarry had broken him out of it.

'Let's give it another couple of days,' he lied, 'for McAllister as much as for us. Then we'll go home if he's finished.'

And he won't be, Ferrow thought to himself. Not if this is what I think it is.

June nodded, then looked up at him, smiling gratefully. She was about to thank him for his kindness and consideration when Harry and Moira walked in.

As if by some unspoken but mutual consent no mention was made of the nightmare they had endured the night before. As if nothing had happened Moira said: 'We've found out about that circus. It's the Circuz Ferencz, and tomorrow's the first performance.'

'And we've booked tickets to cheer you up,' Harry grinned. 'And I got one for you as well, Jenny,' he called across the table.

Jenny turned away from Gerard to face him. 'Sorry,' she said, 'what was that?'

'The circus. You recall we mentioned it last night? Moira's bought you a ticket.'

Ferrow had turned his head to watch the exchange between Harry and Jenny Fellowes. Her reaction to the statement wasn't what he'd expected.

She appeared to freeze for a moment, sitting motionless in her seat in total silence. Then she sipped at her drink and turned back to face Harry. 'That's very kind of you,' she said, 'but I'm afraid I've made other arrangements.'

With a smile Gerard reached over and squeezed her hand. 'We can cancel them,' he grinned. 'It would be nice to see a circus, don't you think?'

'Then that's settled,' Moira beamed. 'Tomorrow we all go to the circus. I'm sure we can get a seat for Jenny's young man as well, Harry, can't we?'

They heard the outer door open and close. Then the inner door swung wide and Wullie Stover, wet and bedraggled from the drizzle, marched in. He shot Ferrow a glare as he passed on his way to the bar. Miles Fournessie, pouring a glass of bottled beer for a previous customer, noted the exchange and said nothing.

'It's a foul night, Wullie,' Ferrow called. Despite himself he was grinning. He intended to help the young fisherman, whether Wullie wanted his help or not.

Andrew Craigham came in shortly afterwards. As soon as he had ordered his drink he came over to Ferrow's table and sat down.

'It's the makings of a foul night oot there,' he began.

June tried to laugh, but the sound she made betrayed her unease more than silence would have done. Ferrow had dreaded Craigham's appearance, knowing that it would serve as an additional reminder of the night before and worrying about the effect it might have on June.

Gerard smiled at Jenny Fellowes, feeling a warmth and happiness and promise he had never known before. Suddenly Zoë was far away, nothing more than another decomposing body in the Fortstown churchyard.

'Ye're lookin' better, lass,' Craigham remarked to June. 'Dinna let yer thoughts dwell on it.'

Ferrow leaned over and squeezed her arm. She was still white, still seeing in her mind the blood-spattered hovel where they had found Davie Quarry's mutilated body. Then he turned back to the fisherman.

'Time I bought a round,' he muttered. 'Will you come to the bar and help me carry the drinks, Andy?'

Craigham nodded and stood up. Together they walked across to the bar and Ferrow gave Fournessie his order. Then he looked at Craigham, who was studying him with questioning eyes.

'I saw Caspar Locke again this afternoon,' he said softly. 'And so did Wullie Stover.'

Craigham scowled and looked across to where young Wullie was trying hard to get as drunk as possible. Wullie was too absorbed with his drinking, scowling into glass after glass, to notice.

'The devil ye did,' Andy breathed. 'Where, mon?'

'Up at the old kirk in the valley. Wullie was there ahead of me.

He looked as if he was searching for something in the walls. Whatever it was I must have interrupted him. He left off as soon as he knew I was there. Then we talked for a while, and just when we were going we saw Caspar Locke up on one of the hills nearby. He seemed to be looking down at us. Watching, I suppose.'

'D'ye no ken what Wullie was lookin' fer?'

'No idea. Have you?'

Craigham shook his head.

'Why don't you take me back to Witham Lodge for a nightcap?' Jenny was asking. 'Did you bring your car or walk down?'

'I walked,' Gerard replied, smiling at her. She really was a remarkable young lady. Was this the kind of woman Zoë had worked so hard to keep him away from? If it was, then his aunt had been wrong, very wrong, in doing him such a disservice.

'Then I can give you a lift back. It's a dreadful night to be on foot.'

Ferrow and Craigham carried the drinks back to their table. June seemed to have relaxed a little and was talking to Harry and Moira about the projected visit to the circus.

'The posters make it sound good,' Harry grinned. 'But then again, they always do. Whatever circus comes along it's always the greatest show on earth, if you'll excuse the phrase.'

Jenny and Gerard stood up to leave. 'Going so soon?' Ferrow asked. What little he had seen of Jenny Fellowes had done nothing to eradicate the instant dislike he'd felt at their first meeting. Gerard he had seen even less of, but the young man struck him as a nice enough sort of person, probably too nice for a bitch like Jenny. Still, it wasn't his concern, and certainly not his place to say anything.

June became easier as the evening progressed. Andy Craigham made no further reference to old Davie's death and the conversation turned upon generalities. The bar shut at the prescribed time and Miles Fournessie shepherded the locals out, though drinking for residents continued for as long as they could cope with it. Shortly after the official closing time June declared her intention of retiring. Harry and Moira followed shortly afterwards, leaving Ferrow and Craigham alone with Fournessie.

'Bob was tellin' me earlier, Miles, tha' he's seen Caspar Locke again.'

Fournessie scowled over the bar, then served himself a double malt and walked across to their table.

157

'Leave it be, Bob,' he grunted. 'It's no your concern.'

'Caspar Locke seems to be making it my concern,' Ferrow replied. 'And I wasn't alone when I saw him, either. Wullie Stover was with me.'

'Wullie?' Fournessie looked puzzled. 'Where were ye, mon?'

'Up at the ruin in Braw Valley.'

Fournessie nodded sagely. 'Wullie told me when first he saw the mon. He said he would be awa' tae yon kirk tae find oot where Caspar Locke was livin'. He thinks the sprite has somewhere up yonder he hides awa'.'

'And what do you think, Miles?'

'It's no my concern.'

'But you've seen him. I was with you when you did.'

'Aye. And once is enough.'

Ferrow suddenly fell silent, preoccupied with a thought inspired by Fournessie's bald comment. Every time he'd seen Caspar Locke he'd been with someone else. The ghost, impostor, whatever, had never yet appeared to him alone. He began to feel uneasy, as if that experience was something he had yet to come.

'I think I'll go to bed,' he announced. 'Good-night, Andy, Miles.'

He started towards the hall door and the stairs beyond, his legs feeling the amount of alcohol he had drunk more than any other part of him. These Scots had a different way of drinking than they had in the south. There you drank beer with a whisky chaser. Here, in Banffshire, they drank whisky with a beer chaser, thinking nothing of putting away a dozen nips with three or four pints of beer in the course of an evening.

His head was beginning to spin when he found the stairs. His knuckles whitened as he gripped the handrail for guidance and support. Gradually he eased himself up, mentally remarking with an effort that he didn't want to be sick, no matter how much the world might start to spin. Eventually he reached the landing and stumbled into their room. June, in the bed, looked fast asleep. Outside the windows, their curtains not drawn, rain was lashing at the glass panes.

Ferrow peered out at the night. Beyond the roof of the ground-floor kitchen extension were the cobbled and stepped alleys of Fortstown, winding down to the beach and the North Sea beyond. And there, standing amongst the white-painted cottages of the little fishing village, staring up at the very window Ferrow was peering out of, stood the dark-clad figure he had already seen twice before.

In the instant when he knew that they were looking straight into each other's eyes the policeman's head cleared. He was no longer drunk, no longer incapable, and there was no longer the distance between them that there had been in the ruins that afternoon. Turning rapidly he left the room, retracing his steps along the landing with a greater certainty and purpose. Seconds later he was down the stairs and outside the hotel, feeling the sting of cold rain on his face and hands.

He turned up the narrow cul-de-sac in which the Fortstown Arms was located and started down the little alley at the end. A short flight of steps at the bottom, a right turn onto a path between two houses, another short slope leading down towards the beach, and they would be face to face.

The rain was starting to penetrate his clothing, his light, summer jacket hanging limply as the thin cloth absorbed the falling droplets. His feet splashed carelessly through the puddles and rivulets in the alleyways, soaking the cuffs of his trousers as he reached the end of the alley and turned towards the cottages. Here, on a level stretch of path, the puddles stood full and deep, but Ferrow didn't notice as he rushed through them. Only one thing mattered now, and that thing was called Caspar Locke.

He made the final turn onto the slope leading down towards the beach. From the moment he had seen his quarry from the hotel window to turning that corner had been less than thirty seconds, yet the figure was no longer there. With rain flicking from his sodden hair he continued down the slope towards the seafront, the dull, wet echo of his running footsteps adding to the rhythms of the night.

The road which snaked down the cliffs into Fortstown ended there, beside the sea. In deference to the wild tides of the North Sea the houses beside the road on the seafront stood ten or twelve feet above the beach. At various points salt-eaten wooden steps led down onto the shore. Ferrow reached the road and halted, panting, feeling the dampness trickle down his spine into his underclothes. Desperately he turned his head to either side, his blinking eyes sweeping the length of the narrow carriageway.

There was no sign of Caspar Locke.

And then he thought of the old church in the valley. Finding the nearest set of steps, he half-walked, half-slid down them onto the shingle of the beach. It crunched underfoot and the leather soles of his shoes slipped treacherously on some of the larger stones. Twice he went down, skinning his knee and grazing the hand he put out to save himself. Like all small wounds the graze hurt out of all proportion to its size. Twice he picked himself up and continued his mad scramble towards Braw Valley. Then, suddenly, he stopped.

From the darkness at the base of the cliffs a figure stepped out to meet him, a tall silhouette, a patch of animate shadow upon the beach. Ferrow wiped the rain away from his eyes with a sodden sleeve. Despite his heart pounding with a mixture of exertion and dread he was determined to remain calm. Caspar Locke, whatever he was, might hold the locals in dread, but the locals weren't Robert Ferrow. They hadn't seen the things Ferrow had seen at Wegrimham.

And it was, after all, only a man. He wore a long coat, glistening black like sealskin in the rain, and a wide-brimmed hat cast its shadow across his features. Strange clothes, perhaps, but nothing more than a man inside them, the policeman told himself, even if he did call himself Caspar Locke.

'And I suppose now you're going to hold your precious relic out for me to take,' Ferrow sneered. 'Is that it?'

The figure made no answer. It simply stood there, in the rain, pale hands limp at its side. Suddenly it occurred to the policeman that if his exertions had affected his own breathing then the figure, which must have moved at a similar pace to stay ahead of him, should be breathing hard as well. Yet there was no sound of panting or labour, and the chest beneath the coat remained still.

'Well? Are you going to give me the precious object or do I just stand here till one of us dies of pneumonia?'

'It will be yours quite soon, friend Robert,' came the reply. 'For a little while, at least.'

And then Ferrow felt fear clutch at his heart. The voice was old, old beyond his concept of age or time. It was deep, almost sepulchral, and yet it was also familiar, horrifyingly familiar. There was no trace of the Scots dialect Wullie Stover or Davie Quarry had heard. The accent was almost perfect English, with just a trace of something alien, something European, perhaps German or Dutch.

'Say . . . that . . . again . . .'

'You enjoy hearing me speak? The night is damp, my friend. It will preclude a long conversation.'

Ferrow felt his eyes widening, despite the falling rain. His effort to remain calm and show no fear was crumbling, melting before the eyes that he knew were watching, studying him from beneath the broad-brimmed hat. Yet how could he remain impassive? He knew that voice because he had heard that voice before. Then too it had been spoken by a very ancient man who wore dark clothing, a man who claimed that his date of birth was 1485 . . .

His thoughts whirled. I . . . forgot my coat . . . Sister turned, alarmed, as he spoke. An empty hypodermic needle rattled to the floor.

'You . . . sound like . . .'

'A dead man, friend Robert? Perhaps I do. Yet Ptythonius Meeres is dead. You know that. You saw him die. His body was sliced up at the autopsy. You saw his body encoffined, and that same coffin cremated some days later. No, Robert, Meeres is dead, but I am here. Perhaps I was once a part of Ptythonius Meeres, or perhaps he was once a part of me. Perhaps he is still a part of me . . .'

Ferrow shook his head, as if trying to clear it of confusion. Instead he only succeeded in shaking drops of rain from his dampened hair.

'I . . . don't understand,' he muttered pathetically. 'I don't understand at all.'

The figure, be it Caspar Locke or Ptythonius Meeres, or someone else, smiled indulgently at him. 'Of course you don't, friend Robert,' it replied. 'There is no need for you to understand, as yet. There is still the better part of a day ahead of us.'

Ferrow's expression grew almost frantic. 'This isn't happening,' he groaned. 'This isn't fucking happening. Not to me. It's just a nightmare . . .'

'Certainly it is a nightmare,' came the response. 'And yet it is a waking nightmare, and they are the worst kind because they embrace realities. And this is one of the most terrible realities that you still have left to face.'

'Then tell me how to cope with it!' Ferrow howled, as much to the storm as to the mysterious figure before him. 'And tell me about the Keeper.'

'As you came to know and trust Ptythonius Meeres, friend Robert, so you must come to know and understand me, whether I call myself Meeres or Locke or . . . Johannes. And, when you do, you will know that you have no reason to fear me. I had no part in Davie Quarry's death, but I must tell you that he was only the first, and that others will inevitably follow him.'

'You're making about as much sense as Meeres ever did. So, what are you? Are you the Keeper?'

The figure nodded. 'I am.'

'Then what the hell do you keep?'

'One day you will know it all.'

'Then why not now?'

'Because you're not ready, yet, my young friend. All you have to do is help, at present. I shall make no speeches to you. I shall not urge you to caution or declaim the perils of our work, our continuing work. You already have some idea of the species of evil which are ranged against mankind. All I have to tell you is that you are not alone in your struggle.'

'But what am I fighting, for Christ's sake? What the hell am I fighting?'

'Do you not know the answer to that already, my friend? Did you learn nothing at Wegrimham?'

Ferrow screwed up his eyes against the rain, then opened them, blazing, expecting the figure to have vanished.

It was still there, still asking its question through smiling lips, still making its unspoken demands upon him by its presence.

'I learned about vicious little monsters and men who live far too long,' he replied, his voice strident in the rainstorm. 'I learned about misguided women and witches and monstrous toadstools and blue lights in the sky. Yet I've no idea what I'm supposed to know. And if I don't even know that, then how the fuck should I know who the bad guys are?'

The figure of Caspar Locke raised its head and allowed Ferrow to see beneath the brim of its hat. The eyes were those of a man older than time itself, but the features, whilst they resembled those of Ptythonius Meeres, were much younger, perhaps those of a man of forty. They smiled at him, sending shivers down his spine with their familiar strangeness. 'You are fighting Thule,' came the reply. 'Even as you are serving Thule, my friend.'

He turned away and began walking back across the shingle to the darkness at the foot of the cliffs.

'Why me?' Ferrow called after him. 'Why the hell does it have to be me again?'

The dark figure turned back and stared at him. 'Why should it not be you?' he asked. 'Yet if it is any comfort you are not the only one. There are others like yourself on every continent of this planet. Did you think that our adversaries exist for you alone to fight? You're not that foolish, my friend. You and your kind meet the assaults and fight the skirmishes. You do not see the overall pattern of the conspiracy because you are not yet equipped to perceive it. Perhaps one day you will be as I am, though that is hardly something you will choose to aspire to. It wasn't my choice either.

'The threat didn't end at Wegrimham. Neither will it end here. Whatever the outcome of our present undertaking the struggle will go on. And on. And on. We are at war, Robert. We are at war with something that the ordinary run of mankind cannot understand and does not even believe exists. Like all wars it is hard and bloody and leaves its casualties on the streets of your cities and the beaches of your lands.'

He turned back again. Ferrow called: 'Will you tell me something?'

'Haven't I told you enough?' the figure asked.

'Are you really Caspar Locke?'

The figure shrugged. 'It's a name,' came the reply. 'It will serve as well as any.'

And then he vanished into the darkness, leaving Ferrow alone on the rain-glistening shore.

For some minutes the policeman stood there, his brain numbed by the figure's revelations. Despite what he'd heard his fear had left him and was now replaced by a calm determination. Knowledge would come later, and bring understanding in its wake. For now, though, he would have to be content to be the poor bloody infantry, muddling through as best he could.

At least the affair at Wegrimham had taught him that help might come from unexpected, sometimes unguessable, quarters. Even so, there was no guarantee that he would come out of the battle alive. He was only important while he could be of service, but who or what was he serving? Thule was nothing more than a name with a myth attached, the legendary home of a civilization which had once dominated the world. It was gone, long gone, swept away by some cataclysm or other now lost in the dark millennia of unrecorded history. Yet its influence lingered on, transcending the centuries in a monstrous civil war which made gods look like hired mercenaries . . .

The cold began to bite. Wet to his skin Ferrow began the walk back to the Fortstown Arms. Despite Caspar Locke's assurances the policeman was feeling very, very alone.

Helen, suitably briefed by Tom Luyner before Tom's departure, had retired to her quarters for the night when Gerard and Jenny Fellowes returned to Witham Lodge.

Gerard settled his guest in the lounge and mixed their drinks. That part of him which ached for the physical contact he had been denied since Zoë's death prompted some sort of action, some approach that would lead this beautiful, self-assured woman into his bed. Yet because of Zoë, because of their self-sufficient life together, he had neither the knowledge nor the experience to take the initiative. With his aunt there was the ease of habit and familiarity. With Jenny, though, there was nothing to guide him, nothing to smooth his path.

Eventually she moved to go, and not so much as a kiss had passed between them. They had arranged to meet at the Fortstown Arms the following evening for drinks before the proposed visit to the Circuz Ferencz. He followed her to the door and held her coat whilst she slid her arms into the sleeves. As he released his hold she turned and slipped her arms about his neck. Before he had time to think or resist, or question, her mouth was upon his, her tongue forcing its way between his teeth, spreading his jaws ever wider, pressing the hot, moist rictus of her lips down onto his with a force that was almost frightening. Helpless, confused by the violence of her passion, he embraced her in return, running his hands over the smooth fabric of her coat.

As they released she snapped her teeth onto his bottom lip, biting until it hurt. Then she stood back, smiling archly.

'Good-night, Gerard,' she whispered.

For almost a full minute he could think of nothing to say. By her surprising action she had advanced their relationship in a way that he could never have believed anyone not Zoë to be capable of. There was so much of Zoë in this woman, so much, and yet so little. Physically she was younger, more aggressive, but there was an air of maturity about her that belied her years. And that last bite following their kiss had made Gerard a promise which both frightened and appealed with the threat of its fulfilment.

Gradually he nodded. 'Good-night, Jenny,' he replied. 'Safe journey back to the hotel.'

She turned and blew him a kiss as she walked to her car through the rain. Gerard stood in the arched porch, watching her as she opened the door and slid inside, flicking on the lights and turning the key in the ignition. Then the car roared away into the darkness, and Gerard went back into the house.

His mind was a turmoil of puzzled anticipation as he wandered into the study. The books still waited in piles upon the refectory table and the dirty bulk of the reliquary stood beside them. Without thinking he walked over to the worm-carved cabinet and opened it, only half-conscious of what he was doing. Then he reached inside for the skull.

The cabinet was empty.

Now he looked in earnest, stretching his arm inside to the furthest corner, feeling for the missing death's-head. In desperation he opened the lower half, but that was empty as well.

He turned his attention to the empty cases, then to the piles of books, scattering them aside in case the skull lay hidden behind them, but still there was no sign of the missing skull. He opened other drawers, other cupboards, determined to recover his *memento mori*. Then the thought occurred to him that perhaps Tom had taken it for a joke. He began to curse his friend with a string of half-affectionate oaths, which he might well have restrained had he known what was to happen.

At about nine o'clock that evening, whilst he and Jenny were drinking together in the Fortstown Arms, a motorist north of Edinburgh slowed down as a furniture van overtook him. The car in front, though, the one driven by a sassenach called Tom Luyner, wouldn't give it room, more from the state of the road than from sheer cussedness. It didn't save him, though. The furniture van forced him off the road and his car smashed through a series of concrete bollards before plunging down into a ravine and exploding in a fireball.

The police searched the burned-out wreckage carefully. If there had been a skull, or even fragments of a skull, they would have noticed. That they failed to do so was more because it had passed into other hands than because it wasn't there to be found. And those other hands were far more dangerous than Tom's could ever have been.

Gerard poured himself another drink. Then he went to bed, still muttering.

Wullie Stover left the Fortstown Arms when Fournessie closed the doors on his non-resident customers, with the exception of Andrew Craigham who was deep in conversation with Ferrow. Wullie's home was with an older brother and his wife, in a cottage close by the seafront, and he tramped disconsolately and drunkenly towards it through the slashing rain.

His brother, a merchant seaman, was away on a voyage to the Far East and would not be back for some days. This left Wullie alone in the house with his sister-in-law, a plain, lumpish woman who insisted on trying to force her unattractive carcass into the youth's bed. 'Jus' ma friggin' luck,' he used to mutter. 'Alone in a hoose wi' a fuck-mad woman an' she has tae look like tha'.' No wonder his brother spent so much time away, he reflected.

Annie would be asleep by now. She'd been starting on a full bottle of gin when he went out, having made it perfectly clear yet again before setting off that he had no intention of 'gi'ing 'a one' on that particular evening. Sure enough, as Wullie set his key into the lock and opened the front door the house was in darkness, and he guessed that Annie would be snoring softly in her lonely bed.

He stumbled over something in the little hall, barking his shin. With a muffled oath he reached for the light and flicked the switch. Nothing happened.

'Friggin' bulb,' he grunted, feeling down to see what had impeded his progress. It was one of their three dining-chairs, and belonged in the tiny lounge-diner to his right. That drunken cow of a sister-in-law must have needed its support to get her to the stairs. Well, she could shift it back again in the morning. Right now the only thing Wullie wanted was to get to his bed and flake out.

The world was starting to spin as he hit the mattress, still fully dressed. He was beyond thought and past caring about details like that anyway. For a while he lay still, his eyes open, staring at the ceiling through the gloom. Then, slowly, he became aware of movement on the landing outside his door.

With an inarticulate sound that fell somewhere between a grunt and a sigh Wullie swung his legs over the edge of the bed and sat up. The door was open and he could just make out a dark shape on the threshold of his room. He reached for the light, muttering: 'For fuck's sake, Annie, I've told ye. No' taenight!'

He flicked the switch and bright, yellow light from the unshaded bulb flooded his dingy bedroom. Annie, in the doorway, looked more saggy and lumpish than ever. If only she'd learn how to hold herself. She might not be so bad then, he thought.

And then Wullie Stover's eyes came into focus. Suddenly he knew why she was like that. The blood drenched down the front of her dress and apron told him, even before his eyes travelled further up and riveted onto the gaping slash across her throat. Annie couldn't hold herself at all. Not with glazed eyes and that much blood out of her body. She was dead. She had to be dead. She shouldn't even be upright.

She pitched forward on top of him, limp and wet and heavy. He grimaced with disgust as he struggled free, kicking her body from his bed onto the floor, gasping through a growing band of nausea in his stomach as he watched her leaving her red, sticky trail across everything she touched.

Desperate, confused, his glance darted back to the open doorway. And then he saw what had been holding Annie up.

'We want to talk to you, Wullie,' hissed an evil, squeaky little voice.

Harry held out a handbill. 'I picked this up at the booking office,' he beamed proudly. Here, have a look, June.'

He passed it across to her. The folded, glossy sheet read on its cover:

CIRCUZ FERENCZ ★ CIRCUZ FERENCZ
CIRCUZ FERENCZ ★ CIRCUZ FERENCZ

GRAND SCOTTISH TOUR

For the first time in Scotland, beginning with a week

in

ABERDEEN –

THE CIRCUZ FERENCZ – THE FAMOUS TRANSYLVANIAN ENTERTAINMENT TROUPE
offers the most magnificent spectacles of colour, sound and pageant.

IN ADDITION there is the famous NADASDY menagerie of Apes, Wolves, Gorillas, all manner of Reptiles and Giant Insects both safe and venomous, and the unique *Glebulae*, which have to be seen to be believed!

'Aberdeen last week,' Harry explained. 'Banff this week. Sounds good, doesn't it?'

June was forced to agree. It did sound good. Just the sort of thing they could do with . . .

'But what on earth are the *Glebulae*?' Moira enquired.

'You've done *what*?'

It was hardly McAllister's most friendly expression, and most of its implicit hostility was directed at Merry Foster. It scowled out, though, at the world in general.

'You can't keep *this* quiet, Inspector. No way. No way at all. This is more than a middle-page paragraph. Much more. Both Grampian and BBC Scotland are sending up their teams from Aberdeen, and there's press on the way from Aberdeen and Inverness.'

'And what bloody good d'ye think they'll do?'

Merry set down her notebook and placed her hands defiantly on her plumpish hips. 'Look, Inspector McAllister, there are people dropping like flies out there. Right under your nose. Davie Quarry one night, now five more. *Five* more, Inspector. Of course it's news. D'you know what the population of Banff and its surrounding villages is?'

He had, but he'd forgotten for the moment. 'Naturally,' he replied. 'Do you?'

'Small enough to make five dead look like a football crowd. And with Davie Quarry more like a Nuremburg rally. Of course there's more press coming. And we're going to want to know a lot more than you've been telling us so far.'

Harris poked his head warily around the door of McAllister's office. 'Ferrow's here,' he announced.

The inspector nodded. 'Ask him to wait a moment,' he grunted. 'Miss Foster is about to leave.'

'Oh, no, not without a proper statement . . .'

'Oh, Miss Foster?'

The reporter turned towards the doorway, where Harris was grinning broadly.

'A call for you, Miss Foster. Your editor. Shall I put it through here, Inspector McAllister?'

McAllister shrugged, then saw his sergeant's sly wink. 'A good idea, Sergeant Harris,' he beamed.

He sat down at his desk and watched as Merry Foster lifted the receiver, greeted her boss, then listened, the colour slowly falling away from her cheeks. Her mouth sagged. Then her brown eyes blazed with furious frustration.

'A D-Notice?' she repeated, incredulously. 'Murders in Banff and some Whitehall moron slaps on a D-Notice? All right . . . all right, Joseph. I'm coming in.'

She slammed down the phone and glared at the seated inspector. 'That's mean, McAllister,' she growled. 'It's also unfair abuse of your authority.'

McAllister smiled up at her. 'Aye, Merry. It would be. But it's none of my doing. I've no had notification of it myself, as yet. And I don't want it,' he continued, getting up. 'I don't want those intelligence boys coming up here and marching all over my methods and systems and coming up with some half-arsed top secret solution that even I'm not allowed to know. But if it's there, it's there, and there's nothing you or I can do about it. Now, I intend to get as much as I can done before those Whitehall morons of yours turn up, so I'd be glad if you'll leave me to it. Good day, Miss Foster.'

She nodded defeatedly and picked up her notebook. As she turned and left the office Harris escorted Ferrow into McAllister's presence. The two of them eyed each other briefly as they passed, Ferrow taking little notice of the reporter, Merry Foster seeing something more than just a simple witness in the English policeman's face.

Once inside Ferrow and McAllister shook hands. 'Did I hear right, Hugo? There's a D-Notice on this affair?'

The inspector sighed and nodded. 'Aye, Robert. For their eyes only, I'm afraid.'

'But that doesn't make any sense.'

'A lot of things about these deaths don't make any sense.'

'Deaths? There's more?'

The Scot forced a smile. Ferrow briefly noted how tired and drawn McAllister was looking, as if he was denying himself all rest and sleep until his patch was calm again. His blue eyes were almost entirely hidden by heavy bags and drooping lids, and he sat slumped in his chair with his elbows on the arms and his fingertips peaked beneath his chin.

'Didn't you hear us again last night?' he enquired.

Ferrow nodded. 'Another death?'

'It was, I'm sorry to say. This part of the world is becoming a little crime wave.'

'Who was it this time, Hugo? Anyone I know?'

'One was,' McAllister replied. 'The others you probably haven't met. Besides, they were here in Banff, not at Fortstown. The one you'd have met was a young fisherman called Wullie Stover.'

Ferrow felt his eyebrows rise in startled surprise. Then a pang bit into his heart. If only he'd told McAllister about Caspar Locke, whoever he really was, then young Wullie might still have been alive.

'Wullie's dead?'

'And his sister-in-law, Annie Stover. But she was only a simple murder, Robert. They just cut her throat. Wullie got the full treatment, though. Just like Davie Quarry . . .'

The Scot paused and wiped a hand across his forehead. 'Can you hear me, man? Can you hear what I'm saying?' He laughed bitterly. 'They just cut her throat. That's all. God almighty, they just cut her throat and she was lucky that's all they did! Can you believe it?'

Ferrow's throat was dry and speech was becoming difficult. Bitter despair was stamped into every line of the local policeman's features and his eyes seemed occasionally to close in silent prayer.

'You . . . mentioned others, Hugo?'

McAllister opened his eyes and looked up. Then he nodded. 'A family of three. Found at home early this morning. Tortured. Mother, father, teenage daughter. All tortured before they were left to die.'

He stood up and made a conscious effort to push his turmoil of emotions aside. 'The preliminary examination suggests that they were killed by the same . . . creatures . . . that murdered Annie Stover. And whoever killed Annie killed Wullie. And whoever killed Wullie killed Davie Quarry. The connection's there, all right. All I have to do is find it and it should lead me straight to these murdering bastards.'

'What can I do to help you?'

It was something more than just a simple gesture from one professional to another. Since his talk with Caspar Locke on the beach Ferrow knew that he was facing something much more dangerous than he had imagined when he came to Banff. Besides, he had now spoken to the mysterious figure in the same way as old Davie and Wullie had. And if someone had been watching, as they must have been watching Wullie and Davie, then he himself stood a good chance of being a future victim.

'You're an outsider, Robert. You may see things that I'm too close to to notice properly. Wullie and Davie Quarry were regulars at the Fortstown Arms. Not related, different ages. The only obvious connection between them is that they were both fishermen. But then again, so is every other man in the village.'

Ferrow forced a smile. 'You'll think I'm mad, Hugo,' he ventured, 'but there is one thing. You remember the legend of Caspar Locke? You mentioned it yourself the first time we met.'

McAllister nodded. 'I do. Go on, Robert.'

'They both claimed to have seen him.'

'Have any of the other villagers?'

'Miles Fournessie, from a distance. I was with him at the time. So was June. But Wullie and Davie both said that he'd spoken to them.

'And there's something else,' he continued. 'Yesterday afternoon I took a walk up to the old church in Braw Valley. Wullie was there, and he seemed to be looking for something. As he left we both saw Caspar Locke again. He was some way off, at the top of one of the hills above the valley, but he appeared to be watching us.'

McAllister peaked his fingers again. Then he said: 'It's not much, Robert, but it is some kind of a connection. Periodically someone or other sees Caspar Locke along that stretch of shore. About a month ago a gentleman living here in Banff was out walking that way. He gave an account to the *Banffshire Echo*. Well, you know that this is what the press calls the silly season. Parliament's in summer recess and real news is a little thin, so even the nationals tend to pad out their pages with any odd scraps they can glean. I believe the *Daily Telegraph* picked it up from the *Echo*, or maybe the *Echo* gave it to a press agency. No matter. However they got hold of it, the *Telegraph* gave it a few column inches on an inside page.'

'Do you know who the man was?'

'I do. The local folklore's a bit of a hobby of mine, too. I cut the story out for my scrapbook. It was an old man called Jimmie Hogue, and it won't do any harm to ask him a few questions. Harris!'

The sergeant opened the door and pushed his head into the office.

'Is Merry Foster still here?'

'No, Inspector. She's awa'.'

McAllister groaned to himself. Bloody typical, he thought. That girl's a pain in the arse most of the time and then, just when she could have been useful, she's still a pain in the arse, just for good measure.

'Then ring Joseph McFee and ask for the address of the man Hogue who gave them an update on the Caspar Locke legend, about a month ago.'

Harris offered a token salute and withdrew. Ferrow eyed McAllister with a slightly puzzled expression. 'Suppose Hogue has been killed too,' he began, 'and that there is some link between Caspar Locke and the killings. Where does that get us? Do we start looking for a 200-year-old priest to arrest?' An icy hand was clutching at his heart as he spoke. 200? Why, if only a fraction of what he'd lived through with Meeres was correct it could just as easily have been 2000 years.

'And how do the others fit into it, Hugo? A family, you said?'

'That's right. The Macreedy family. Father, mother and teenage daughter. They keep . . . kept . . . an antique shop, they called it. A second-hand shop would have been my own description. Stocked from house-clearances. You know, Coronation mugs and Holman Hunt prints. Barometers and mock-Georgian coffee-tables. The shop's off Smith Street, down a bit from Hays the Furnishers. Now, we've a connection via the MOs, and our doctor estimated that the killers could have finished Wullie and Annie and been here in Banff from Fortstown . . .'

McAllister continued to list the details, but Ferrow was no longer listening properly. If Wullie and Annie had died at the estimated time, then the killer couldn't have been Caspar Locke. Ferrow was talking to Caspar Locke on the beach, giving the old man the perfect alibi.

Harris rapped sharply on the office door and intruded his head again. 'That address is 11 Aberchirder Street, Inspector. Do ye want yer car?'

'That I do, Sergeant. Aberchirder? That's up on the old South Rise area.' Then, to Ferrow: 'Feel like coming along for the ride, Robert?' He was beginning to struggle into a heavy melton coat over his uniform, despite the evident warmth of the summer morning.

'If I can be of some help.'

'Don't be so formal, man,' the inspector replied. 'After all, you're in this up to your neck already. You found the first body, and these killings have only started since you arrived on your holiday. If I didn't know who you were I'd be asking you where you were when young Wullie Stover was being butchered.'

Ferrow forced a laugh, hoping that the sound wasn't too uneasy. He was beginning to feel trapped, unable to explain what he knew about Caspar Locke. And that meant that when the killers came for him he would be completely on his own.

He followed Harris and McAllister down into the street where the plain blue Ford Escort was waiting for them, its supercharged engine purring to itself. He climbed into the back seat and, with Harris driving, they followed the road out of Banff, back towards Fortstown, then turned off into the dismal, Victorian streets of South Rise.

The odd-numbered side of Aberchirder Street faced north, presenting a bleak, grey façade rising above the road. Number eleven presented the same forbidding emptiness to this day's visitors that it had done to Jenny and Gerard. Leaving Harris in the car Ferrow and McAllister climbed the steps and knocked on the paint-peeling door. Once more the knocking echoed through the empty interior. Once more there was no answer.

They walked slowly back down the steps to the street. 'Round the back?' Ferrow asked.

McAllister removed his peaked hat and smoothed his hair with a gloved hand. In his casual jacket and slacks the Englishman felt quite comfortable amd wondered why his companion should so patently feel the cold.

'We've reasonable cause,' he replied. 'Round to the back it is.'

He walked around the car and muttered to Harris. Then he rejoined Ferrow on the pavement and they walked along to the end of the terrace and up beside the end house. A narrow alley separated the back-to-back Victorian homes, and they started up this, counting the houses as they went.

'It's a pity they never thought of numbering their back gates,' the Scot remarked.

Despite the size of the house there was no back garden as such, only a once-paved, weed-grown area beside the path which led past the built-on outhouses. The back windows were as uncurtained and in need of repair as the front. The steps leading down to the basement were badly cracked and the iron guard-rail was brown with encrusted rust.

'Back door, Robert?'

Ferrow checked the door and found it secured by a comparatively modern Yale lock. Looking around the yard he found a length of four-by-four timber with a squared end.

'Stand away,' he grunted. He rammed the end of the timber against the lock, feeling it jar and shudder in his hands. At the second blow a loud crack echoed into the kitchen beyond. At the third the whole house seemed to roar its disapproval as the frame split and the door flew inwards.

He tossed the timber away and stood back, grinning at McAllister. The Scot had been peering through the windows on the ground floor. Here and there an item of cheap furniture remained, covered with dust and cobwebs, but there were no carpets or other floor coverings, and the desolate air of the exterior seemed to pervade the interior as well.

They entered together. The kitchen, beneath its coating of dirt, was orderly, with all the saucepans in their places and the pantry shelves, with their meagre burden of basic provisions, mostly tinned, neatly arranged. Mouse droppings were everywhere.

From the kitchen a door led into the hall. After a rapid survey of the ground-floor rooms Ferrow and McAllister ascended to the bedrooms. Everywhere there was the same layer of dust and neglect, as if the house had been untenanted and deserted for years.

The sun had moved around and was slanting into the south-facing rear bedroom as Ferrow opened the door. Just inside, beyond the doorway where he stood, footprints showed up in the dust. McAllister moved to brush past him into the room, but Ferrow held him back and pointed. Then he knelt down and ran his finger across the inside of one of the prints. When he lifted it again it was clean.

'Freshly made,' he commented. 'Someone's been here recently.' His pointing finger followed the circle of prints into the room a little way and then out again. 'Dust gathers quickly in a place like this. Whoever was here, and by the size of the footprints it looks as if it was a child, was here either late yesterday or this morning.'

McAllister shrugged. 'Kids broke in and used the house as a playground?'

'I doubt it. Kids are curious. They'd have gone to the window and looked out. Whoever this was only wanted to see into the room itself.'

Just like we're doing, he thought.

'Do you have a torch, Hugo?'

'There's one in the car.'

'Can you get it?'

McAllister walked back along the landing and down the stairs to the front door. It opened easily.

'Harris,' he called, 'bring the torch in here.'

Ferrow followed him down the stairs into the hall, peering at the disturbed dust around his feet as he did so. If only we'd thought of it earlier, he thought. Unless . . .

He walked back along the hall to the door which led down into the basement. Harris handed the torch to McAllister and returned to the car as the inspector rejoined Ferrow. Slowly the Englishman reached down and turned the handle, pushing the basement door open.

'Shine the torch down there, will you?'

McAllister turned on the beam and shone it down the wooden steps. Each bore its own covering of grey dust, in the centre of which small footprints stood out fresh and brown on the wood.

'We're going to have to disturb these,' Ferrow muttered, 'but the ones in the bedroom should remain intact. Do you think you could get a photographer along to record them? You never know, they might have something to do with all this.'

McAllister nodded and walked back to the open front door. He called to Harris to radio for a photographer. 'And a couple of constables as well,' he added. 'Let's make a house-to-house whilst we're about it.'

Ferrow tried the light-switch just inside the door. 'The juice is off,' he remarked to his companion. 'We'll have to use your torch.'

With the Scot leading the way they descended into the basement, following the trail of tiny footprints. At the bottom of the stairs was another door, wide open, leading into the basement proper. This consisted of a single large room, almost divided into two by a heavy joist across the middle. And, after a fashion, it was furnished.

A bed, made up but not slept in, stood against an inner wall. Across from it was a pine table and a single upright chair, above which some crudely-made bookshelves had been screwed to the wall. On the floor, extending between the table and the bed, was a length of thick-pile carpet over the dusty red quarry-tiles. Just beyond this stood a paraffin heater.

Ferrow walked across to the table. Its surface was covered with books and papers, and an oil-lamp was balanced precariously in one corner. The policeman picked it up and shook it, listening to the liquid slosh inside.

'Have you got any matches, Hugo?'

McAllister tossed a pipe-lighter across. Ferrow raised the glass cover and struck a light to the wick. Slowly a dim yellow light began to illumine the table area.

The writing on the loose sheets of paper caught Ferrow's eye first. The ink had begun to turn brown in the basement's damp atmosphere, but that wasn't the source of their fascination. Some of the letter-forms, though clearly written, appeared alien, and it was only when he tried to read the script that Ferrow realised it was in German.

From its layout it seemed to be a set of notes or comments, and the policeman's attention progressed to the open manuscript book beside it. He fully expected that this would be in German as well, but he was wrong. It only took a classical scholar to read Latin, not to recognise it. Slipping a sheet of blank paper between the pages to mark the place he closed the book, then opened it at the title page.

In the dim light of the oil lamp he easily made out the single word which was the title of the book. Then he shuddered.

'Are you all right, Robert?' McAllister asked.

'Just cold,' he replied, forcing a grin. 'Maybe I should have followed your example and worn a coat.

'Well,' he continued, 'your Mr Hogue doesn't seem to be here, Hugo, either alive or dead.'

The Scot nodded. 'Even so, Robert, there's something going on around here. What's those papers you've got there?'

'Hard to say,' Ferrow fenced. 'It looks as if they're in foreign languages. Some German, some Latin.'

'Then we'll get them taken back to the station. This could be nothing to do with our case, but we won't know until they're translated.'

Ferrow smiled weakly and dropped the book back onto the table. Only then did he realise how blind he'd been. Whilst there was thick dust on the bed and the top of the paraffin heater, there was only a little on the seat of the chair and the contents of the table. And that was when his brain began to work again.

Children, if children they were, had left their tiny footprints all over the house. They went into an upstairs bedroom, but didn't bother to go right to the window. They came into the basement, where there was only a table, a chair and a bed. They went to the table.

Ferrow lifted the top sheet of paper carefully. The one beneath it was blank, yet despite being covered it bore a coating of dust.

So, they examined the papers. They sat down to do it, hence the lack of dust on the chair, so it wasn't just casual interest. How many children could there be in Banff that read Latin and German and were old, or young, enough to go with the size of the footprints? *And* broke into old houses?

Broke in?

How?

The house had been secure. He and McAllister had forced an entry. If someone had broken in ahead of them then surely they wouldn't have bothered to secure the place again afterwards? And surely children didn't bother with details like that . . .?

'Do you think you could get this stuff on the table finger-printed, Hugo?'

'What do you have in mind?'

'We know from the footprints that someone's been here, and I think that, children or not, they were looking for Hogue. Tell me, did you get any prints from any of the murders?'

'Nothing any good. They were all smudged.'

'Anything odd about the size?'

'Not particularly.'

So it wasn't killer children, Ferrow smiled to himself. But there were worse things, things in nature that perhaps he hadn't even guessed at yet. Wegrimham had taught him that. He still had nightmares, several months later, about that moment in the church when Meeres had flicked on the light to show the pews alive with small, deadly furry shapes, shapes with half-human faces that killed for blood with their vicious little teeth . . .

And if they existed, unknown, unguessed, then there could well be others.

He backed away from the table, carrying the oil-lamp with him. It looked as if Hogue, wherever he was now, had used the house only as somewhere to work occasionally. That he hadn't been there for some weeks was evident by the dust. Yet he had given the place as his address when he told his Caspar Locke story to the *Echo*.

Something was missing. He'd spent time here. He'd bought food. He'd had milk. The front garden was testimony to that. But only enough to keep him going on the brief occasions he'd used the house. Yet there were no bills on the mat. No circulars. No shopping lists or receipts. Not anywhere . . .

And if he'd moved out, he would have taken that Latin manuscript with him.

Nothing under the bed. Nothing in any of the pieces of cheap furniture upstairs. Only a drawerless pine table down here. An old kitchen table by the look of it.

But they had drawers.

He knelt down and inspected the bottom of the table. Sure enough, the runners were there, and between them was the familiar shallow box-shape of a drawer. Outside it was just a plain piece of wood. No handle. The lip at the bottom served as that.

With a grin he stood up and wrapped a handkerchief over his fingers. The he reached down for the lip and pulled the drawer open.

Old gas bills. Electricity overdue and disconnection notices, dated a couple of months before. Receipts for camping equipment from a local store. And a sheet of badly typed paper with a receipt scrawled across it in biro.

'"Miscellaneos furnitur receved from Mr Hogue, 11 Aberchirder Street, £25,"' Ferrow read aloud. He turned to McAllister and grinned broadly. 'I've found you your link,' he muttered. 'Look at the letterhead.'

He passed it across to the Scot, still grinning. McAllister took it from him and glanced at it in the beam of his torch. Then he too began to smile.

'The same Macreedys that were killed last night?' Ferrow enquired.

The Scot nodded. 'The same Macreedys, Robert. This ties Hogue to them. And the *Echo* story ties Hogue to Caspar Locke. And what you told me earlier ties Caspar Locke to the murders at Fortstown. So, the circle's complete. Now all we need is a way into it, or out of it. And that means finding Jimmie Hogue.

'I think you're right,' he continued. 'We'd better get those papers finger-printed before the translators get to work on them.'

They walked back up the stairs, out of the basement. McAllister continued towards the front door whilst Ferrow re-entered the kitchen. 'We didn't check the outhouses,' the Englishman called. 'I'll do that and meet you back at the front.'

He left the house at 11 Aberchirder Street by the back door and opened each of the outside doors in turn. One was a toilet, and the second, by the state of the walls and condition of the floor, had once been used for storing coal. Ferrow's hand was on the back gate when something he had seen earlier, something that hadn't registered at the time, occurred to him. Turning on his heel he walked back towards the rear door of the house.

They were there, on the outer face of the Yale lock. The end of the timber was too smooth and too damp to have caused them, and an untrained eye would have missed them altogether. Tiny bright scratches, tiny marks on the weathered face of the metal. Not large. Little more than a hair's breadth in width, and only around the actual key-slot.

The sort of mark you might leave if you were trying a selection of skeleton keys in the dark.

Children? Children not more than nine or ten who read Latin and German? Children who broke into houses at night? Children who went looking in the dark for a man who might well be a multiple murderer? Children who possessed, and knew how to use, skeleton keys?

He walked back around the terrace. Outside the front of the house another panda car had drawn up and a photographer and two constables were being briefed by McAllister. Harris stood outside the front door of number 13, talking to a fat, middle-aged woman in a short-sleeved dress and an apron. As Ferrow approached, the sergeant finished jotting in his notebook and turned away. The door closed as he descended the steps to the street again.

'Anything interesting?' Ferrow asked.

Harris looked at him dourly. 'Well, it canna hurt tae tell ye, Inspector Ferrow. Tha' lady said she saw two people tryin' Hogue's door yesterday afternoon. A man an' a lady. She also claims she heered noises in the night, like someone was inside the hoose.'

'What did the man and woman look like? Could she give you a description?'

Harris nodded. 'Aye. The man was early thirties, wi' dark hair. Gude lookin', she said. The lady was younger, early tae mid-twenties. Long chestnut hair an' well dressed. She was drivin'.'

'What sort of car?'

'Foreign, she said. Wi' a sort of star inside a circle on the front. Sounds like a Mercedes tae me.'

'Colour?'

'A sort o' deep red.'

Ferrow nodded absently. It was only when McAllister finished with the photographer and the constables and rejoined them, and Harris repeated the description of the car and its occupants, that he began to recognise the details. There was a car like that in the car-park at the Fortstown Arms. And it was driven by a girl with long chestnut hair. Jenny Fellowes.

And the man could well be Gerard Covington.

But how did they fit into it? And where was the mysterious Jimmie Hogue? And, most importantly as far as Ferrow was concerned, why did Hogue write notes in German that were observations on passages in the book which had been behind the affair at Wegrimham? Why did he own a manuscript copy of the volume which was something of a bible to both sides in the terrible, unknown war humanity was fighting?

Why did Jimmie Hogue possess the *Thulia*?

Using June as his excuse he left McAllister shortly after their return to the station. Instead of going back to Fortstown he went directly to the public library. Once again he had a distinct impression of being watched, though occasional visual sweeps of his surroundings yielded no intimation as to who the watcher might be. When he asked for the back files of the *Banffshire Echo* he was directed to an alcove where a vaguely familiar woman was already seated at a table examining heavy bound volumes of yellowing newsprint.

'Well, well, Mr Ferrow isn't it?' asked Merry Foster. 'Have you developed an interest in our local history?'

'You have the advantage of me, Miss . . .?'

'Foster. Merry Foster.' She stood up and extended her hand, which Ferrow grasped. 'You're not a local man are you, Mr Ferrow?'

'What makes you ask?'

'Oh, polite conversation. And curiosity. I work for the *Echo*, you see.'

Do you, now? he thought. So that's why you left McAllister's office muttering about the D-Notice. Well, I've done a bit of muttering about that myself. It shows an interest by the authorities that's both surprising and downright unfathomable. Terrorists are one thing. But supernatural terrorists? How do they recognise such a threat, let alone act on it?

'I *do* see,' he responded, permitting himself a grin. 'Looking for inspiration for a new story?'

'Looking, certainly. My editor told me McAllister was interested in the Caspar Locke legend, so I thought I'd do a wee bit of research.'

She could have been prettier, with a bit less weight and slightly better make-up, Ferrow thought. Good bones under the flesh, fantastic hair and keen eyes. Maybe not as bright as June, but certainly as interesting. And probably less passive.

'Caspar Locke?' Ferrow enquired ingenuously.

'Come now, Mr Ferrow. You sound as evasive as that policeman I couldn't get anything out of.'

'Probably because I'm a policeman myself.'

'Brought in to help? Are *you* one of the Whitehall whizz-kids?'

'No way. I'm here on holiday. I'm staying at the Fortstown Arms.'

'So how do you fit in with all this?' she enquired, ingenuously.

It can't hurt to tell her, Ferrow reasoned. After all, she can't print any of it. And she might just be some help, maybe.

'I found Davie Quarry. That is, my fiancée and I, and a man called Andy Craigham.'

Fiancée? Well, I should have known. Blue eyes. Blond hair. Quite good features. They don't last long on their own these days. So, let's try a different approach, Mr Ferrow.

'Are you interested in mysteries, Mr Ferrow? Silly question,' she laughed, 'as you're a policeman. But real mysteries? Those less of crime than of sheer baffling power?'

He eyed her carefully. Not brighter than June? Those dark eyes were stabbing into every corner of his being, seeking . . . what? Not weakness. No, she didn't want him to be weak. She wanted him to be . . . understanding?

'You sound as if you've found something worth knowing about,' he answered with studied casualness. 'And as if you want to share it.'

'Maybe I do, Mr Ferrow.'

'Then you'd better tell me what it is.'

She did better than tell him, She showed him. One volume of the *Echo* was open at the article describing Professor Rumsey's examination of Caspar Locke's grave in Braw Valley. In itself the piece added nothing to Andy Craigham's account, but the photo which went with it forced an involuntary gasp of astonishment from Ferrow's lips.

There was no doubt about it. Almost fifty years had passed since that photo had been taken. Age should have withered him. After all, Professor Michael Rumsey, if he was still alive, would have been about forty then and by now must be heading for the up-side of ninety. He certainly wouldn't be as young as the photo, as young as the man who *now* called himself Caspar Locke, the man Ferrow had spoken with on the beach at Fortstown just the night before.

'Toothache, Mr Ferrow?' Merry Foster smiled up. 'D'ye have a raw nerve somewhere?'

It was impossible, he knew. Quite impossible. But the features in the photograph were unmistakable. Michael Rumsey was Caspar Locke.

He pulled himself desperately together. 'Have you found the latest article?' he asked her.

Merry nodded. 'Here you are.'

Ferrow didn't need to read it. He just looked at the picture. Hogue was getting on for ninety, and his photo showed the man that Professor Rumsey would have been that summer. Old. Lined. Skin stretched like parchment over his skull.

But the eyes were still young, and they were the same eyes that stared out of Rumsey's photograph.

He had been standing, bending over the heavy volumes, to that point. Now he sat down heavily, as if his legs had suddenly collapsed beneath him, Merry's eyes burning up into his own.

It wasn't possible. Perhaps Hogue and Rumsey were the same man. That was possibly just conceivable. But Caspar Locke as well? No way.

Except that Caspar Locke, or at least a part of Caspar Locke, was also Ptythonius Meeres. And with Ptythonius Meeres, Ferrow groaned deeply to himself, almost *anything* was possible.

Including the creatures in Wegrimham Church. Including blue lights in the sky. Including fungi from Thule that wanted to dominate the world. Including the immortals.

Merry Foster was almost purring with anticipation. 'I think you ought to tell me about it, Mr Ferrow,' she instructed.

He swallowed hard to lubricate the dryness in his throat. 'Do they . . . keep a record of who asks for these files?' he asked her.

'No, but they remember sassenachs. They remember, for instance, a young lady with red-brown hair.'

'Long?'

'Aye, it was long.'

'Recently?'

'Within a day or so. And now it's your turn, Mr Ferrow.'

Is it, by God? 'I'm not sure what you mean, Miss Foster.'

'Of course you are. I saw your reaction to those pictures, don't forget. As I'd done the work for you I think you owe me at least an explanation.'

And there's no D-Notice on the Caspar Locke story, she added, mentally.

'I . . . thought I recognised one of the men . . .'

'Is that the best you can do?'

'I don't follow you . . .'

'Of course you follow me. I've been following you, you know. Come on, Ferrow. Let's have a bit of honesty, even if there's nothing I can print. How about it?'

Long, red-brown hair. Jenny Fellowes. It had to be Jenny Fellowes. But was she after Hogue, or Rumsey, or Caspar Locke? Or all three?

Was it possible all three of them were the same?

'You recognised both of the men. I was watching your eyes. You know both of them, somehow. If you hold back on me I can't help you, and one day soon you just might need my help . . .'

McAllister said it had all started since I came here, Ferrow struggled to reason. Or since Jenny Fellowes came here? And what about the children? Children? Or something else?

'I . . . maybe I've seen Hogue about the town . . .'

'More than I have, Ferrow. And I've been looking. Now, will you start to make some sense?'

Sense? I should start to make some sense? Why me, all of a sudden? Why poor fucking bemused me? Why not the rest of this forgotten corner of the British Isles? Or Meeres, maker of mysteries? If only the old bugger would actually tell me what's going on . . .

I do him the credit of assuming that he knows himself. Not that it's much of an assumption, after Wegrimham.

'Come along, Mr Ferrow. Give.'

Ferrow grinned. 'Okay.'

He was seated at the table with Merry standing over him. He reached up and took hold of the back of her neck, turning her face down towards his own. As he pressed their lips together he was both surprised and a little alarmed at how little resistance his tongue met when they kissed.

Keep 'em quiet. Keep 'em interested. Keep 'em helpful. And tell them nothing.

Merry Foster stared down at him, blushing slightly. She was not to know that even as Robert Ferrow grinned mischievously up at her, Moira's voice, at the back of his mind, was whispering something about a circus . . .

It was too early for him to say that it was all beginning to make sense. Perhaps, Ferrow admitted to himself, he would never really know why he was there, why he was straining to assemble the pieces of a jigsaw he didn't understand. As a policeman, of course, he had a duty to keep that nebulous concept called society safe from creatures that murdered for any reason, even for no reason at all. But Ferrow had learned at Wegrimham that he would never be just a policeman again. Now he knew that there were other laws, beyond those framed by parliament and administered through the courts, laws which governed a conflict which spanned beyond humanity, beyond time itself.

They were there, of course, watching him. He couldn't see them, nor could he detect any other physical sign of their presence, but he knew that feeling of being watched by unseen eyes. Well, these things, whatever they were, had to cut throats in order to kill. They used weapons, and that meant that weapons could destroy them. And this time Ferrow was armed.

The afternoon was clear and sunny, but a strong wind was blowing off the sea, bringing with it an unseasonal chillness. This time he'd decided not to start from the comparative cover of the beach, but to walk up through the village and follow the clifftop road to the hill where he had seen Caspar Locke from the church the previous day. He'd chosen that particular route for a variety of reasons. One was that the open ground on top of the cliffs made it harder for anyone to follow him without being seen. Another was that the longer route gave him time to think, time to examine the facts he had assembled so far. The more time he spent worrying them, like a terrier on a kill, the more chance there was that some kind of sense would eventually emerge.

He was wearing a navy car-coat over his jeans and a white sweater. The coat's large side-pockets were deep and roomy, large enough to take a torch and the 10-shot Bergmann-Bayard automatic he had inherited from Ptythonius Meeres. As well as the fully-loaded weapon he was also carrying a reloader, giving him a total firepower of twenty 9mm rounds. A little excessive, perhaps, he grinned to himself, but he wasn't certain of what he was going to find. It might be nothing at all, yet on the other hand it could be something so dangerous that even Meeres' pistol would be useless against it.

Harry and Moira had taken June into Banff to do some shopping. Ferrow was grateful to them for keeping her occupied. Their stay in Fortstown was now irretrievably distant from the holiday she had intended. He was seriously preoccupied with the mysterious happenings in and around the village, and June would be some time forgetting the shock of finding the mutilated remains of Davie Quarry. Eventually, he hoped, there would be time to console her, to help her forget. First, though, there were still some things he had to do.

The similarity of appearance between Caspar Locke, Professor Rumsey and Jimmie Hogue had to be more than just a coincidence. It appeared to act, like so many other things in the puzzle, as some kind of deliberate signal. The same face, in the same newspaper, in stories with the same central theme, though fifty years apart, was almost like the renewal of a message in the personal columns. I'm here. Make contact. But what could continue across half a century? What was strong enough to last through most of a lifetime?

And then there was the legend of Caspar Locke itself. It checked back, all right. Caspar Locke had been the last minister of the little church in Braw Valley, before a newer church had been built in the village of Fortstown itself. An editorial footnote to the account of Rumsey's investigations led to a passage in J. Grant Stewart's *Witchcraft and Folklore of North East Scotland*, published in 1821, which gave an outline account of the legend. Had it not been for that, Ferrow could have believed that Rumsey had invented the whole thing, but he knew that it wasn't so. Caspar Locke and his mysterious relic were known more than a century before Rumsey came onto the scene.

And then there were the murders. Davie Quarry first. He'd seen Caspar Locke and spoken with him. Then something had come out of the night and tortured him to death. Because he'd spoken to Locke? Because something or someone wanted to know what words had passed between them? But why torture the old fisherman to death? Why not just get him drunk enough to loosen his tongue?

Or did they, whoever they were, believe that he knew more than he was saying?

Wullie and Annie Stover. Annie simply had her throat cut. Wullie, though, died the same long, painful death as old Davie. And he'd talked to Caspar Locke as well. So, Annie was just in the way, a lump of live meat to be disposed of before the real business of torturing Wullie began. And that torture had to be for the same reason, to find out if Wullie had learned something in that meeting with Caspar Locke that he wasn't saying.

And then there were the Macreedys. Father, mother, daughter. Tortured, unlike Annie Stover. Why? Like Wullie, had they seen the old man called Caspar Locke? They couldn't have known much. So why bother to kill them at all? Okay, so they'd bought a load of furniture from Jimmie Hogue. And sold it again, perhaps?

He made a mental note to ask McAllister about that when he got back to Fortstown. For now, though, he was approaching the hill where Caspar Locke had stood when he and Wullie had been in the ruins. Wullie had been looking for something, and Ferrow now believed he knew just what it was.

And if Wullie knew, he would have told. He would have screamed and gibbered and babbled it out to his tormentors, so they would know as well. And that was why Ferrow was carrying the gun.

He stood on the crest of the hill and looked down towards the ruin. Then he turned and looked back along the road behind him. There was, of course, no-one to be seen, but the feeling of being watched persisted.

Come on, you bastards, he thought. I'm not dead Wullie or Davie Quarry. This one's ready for you.

Yet had Wullie known enough? Or had he simply guessed? There was nothing to indicate that he'd been back over the archive material Ferrow had studied that morning. It could just have been a lucky or, in his case, unlucky guess. It didn't really matter, anyway. He would have passed on his suspicions to his tormentors, and they might have other sources available to them.

There was something else that gave Ferrow's hunch the edge over Wullie's. Ferrow had seen that receipt for camping equipment in Jimmie Hogue's drawer. As he descended the hill, his eyes sweeping the ground about his feet, he realised what had been worrying him about that receipt. Jimmie Hogue, from his picture, was an old man, well over eighty. What could possibly have motivated him to spend the better part of £200 on camping equipment? A night in the open would probably be enough, if not to kill him, at least to leave him vulnerable to pneumonia or some other serious health condition. So he had to have bought it for a younger man, and probably for a younger man who looked enough like him to be a relative . . .

Ferrow reached the ruins without finding anything along the way. Before he entered the jagged stone shell he turned and looked back up the hill. Something low, perhaps a dog or a sheep, dropped behind the crest of the hill.

Something low, perhaps a dog, had been out there on the beach the night they found Davie Quarry's body.

He continued to watch for five long minutes, but nothing stirred in his line of vision. Finally he stepped through one of the broken arches and entered the ruined church.

Wullie had been checking the walls, but Ferrow knew that the walls were too thin to conceal what he was looking for. If there was a concealed opening it had to be in the floor, and it would be inside the shell of the church, not outside it. Had it been outside Rumsey would have found it fifty years before, and it would have been included in the account written up for the *Echo*.

He stood in front of the altar, looking back down the nave of the little church. If there was an opening, then steps would lead down from it. Chances were those steps would be built into the foundations, so they had to be on one of the side walls. The entrance to the vault wouldn't be in the sanctuary, so that narrowed the area to be searched down a little further. With slow, heavy steps, listening to each of his footfalls in turn, Ferrow began a circuit of the interior.

The north wall yielded nothing, so he crossed to the south and began to work his way back towards the altar. Then, half-way between the south door and the sanctuary, one of his steps rang hollow. He stopped and stamped his foot again, and the hollow sound was repeated.

Ferrow knelt down and tried thumping with his fist. Then he began to work with his fingers, digging at the shallow layer of dirt and grass which covered the flags. Looking about him he saw a piece of stone with a flattish edge which he could use as a scraper. Unaware of the eyes which had moved closer, he worked on, feeling sweat run from his armpits and become lost in the fabric of his sweater. Soon, with the aid of the stone, he had cleared the surface of a plain stone slab and was scraping the dirt out of the cracks surrounding it.

If this was the way down, it hadn't been used for years, perhaps centuries. And the hollow sound from beneath told him that this had to be the way down.

He threw the stone away and hooked his fingers into the widest crack. Squatting on his haunches he tried to channel all the lifting strength of his back into his arms and hands. At first he simply shook and shivered with the strain and the slab remained unmoved. Then, just as he was beginning to think the effort was useless, the heavy slab began to rise. Shifting his balance from foot to foot, leaning back and keeping his arms as straight as possible, he levered the heavy flagstone upwards on its rusted iron pivot. When it had passed the vertical position and entered a slight backward incline he relaxed his grip, allowing himself several heavy breaths to compensate for the effort he had expended.

Ferrow sat there for several minutes, the raised slab blocking his view of the exposed aperture. Then, slowly, he climbed to his feet and, taking the torch in one hand and the automatic pistol in the other, he approached the opening and looked down.

The steps were there, built against the wall. They were old and dank and slippery, but they were there, still intact, still usable. With his heart pounding in his ears, both from the effort of raising the slab and the hideous knowledge of what he could find waiting for him, the policeman began to descend into the vault, feeling the dank, centuried darkness clutching at his ankles and thighs.

The flight was comparatively short and straight, and the eleven worn steps terminated on a level expanse of stone-flagged flooring. In the yellow beam of his torch Ferrow picked out the fat, squat columns which supported the vaulted ceiling. Trading carefully, in case age and decay had rendered the floor dangerous, he began a slow circuit of the hidden chamber. Just as he was about to consider his exercise a waste of time he came upon two objects which added an extra pace to his heartbeats. Both were against the northern wall of the vault.

On their own there was nothing remarkable about either of them, but Ferrow had researched more than just the legend of Caspar Locke that morning. He had gone beyond the *Echo*'s files, seeking information on the little church from older records, and his surprise at finding another door in the north wall of the crypt was consequently less than it might have been. Somehow even the rough coffin lying in front of it was expected as well.

The rope handles on the unplaned wooden casket had long since rotted away. The top wasn't nailed or screwed shut, but hinged with large metal flanges, now rusted to an even, sandy brown. On the opposite side to the hinges the top was secured with a padlock of twentieth-century design.

Ferrow knelt beside the coffin and laid his gun on the lid. With his free hand he tried the padlock, twisting it in his fingers to see if it would come away with a little gentle force. Eventually he stood up and retrieved the automatic. Aiming as carefully as he could by torchlight he fired a single round into the padlock. The vaulting and the pillars soaked up most of the sound of the shot, and as the echoes died away he set down the gun again and wrenched the broken lock from the front of the coffin.

As the lid came up he gritted his teeth behind lips that were firmly pressed together. He already knew what he'd find there, but he still had to look. He still had to be certain that the facts were coming together in the right order. Consciously fighting the tremor which had crept into his fingers he directed the torchbeam at the contents of the coffin.

As the first yellow rays struck the interior Ferrow turned his head away. Then, slowly, with a grim determination, he looked back, forcing himself to take in every detail.

The grinning skull lay on its side, half-way along the coffin. The rest of the skeleton was in scattered disorder, with no two bones connecting as they should have done. Around them were a few shreds of sacking, but anything that might have suggested clothing had long since rotted away, quite probably in another place.

His stomach was beginning to churn as Ferrow released his steadying grip upon the lid of the coffin, permitting it to fall back in place with a heavy crash. As the echoes began to die away they were supplanted by a low growling.

Startled, Ferrow turned and swung the torchbeam. It flashed out across the vault onto dark, merciless eyes in a crazed, bare-fanged face. As he raised his gun to fire his eyes were suddenly dazzled by torchlight from two different angles.

'You can no longer aim your gun, Mr Ferrow,' remarked an evil, squeaky little voice. 'I suggest that you put down your gun and torch upon the coffin very slowly, and then stand quite still. Gyorgy is exceptionally large for a *glebula*, and he's very powerful. If he senses any attempt on your part to escape he will tear your legs off.'

Glebula. Where had he seen that word before? On a circus handbill June had shown him? But what was a *glebula*? 'Who are you?' he demanded, shaking slightly.

'My name is Sodom,' said the voice. 'My dear friend on your other side is called Gomorrah. We want to ask you some questions.'

There was something strange both about the voice and the angle at which the torches were being held. That squeaky quality had the depth and maturity of age about it, but it was too high in pitch to be that of a normal adult. And the torches were held too low down, too near the floor of the vault.

Then Ferrow remembered the circus, and the tiny footprints in the house in Aberchirder Street.

He nodded quietly to himself. Dwarfs, perhaps, but none-the-less deadly for that. They had already killed at least six people, and his own chances of becoming number seven were looking stronger with every passing heartbeat.

'If you gentlemen want to talk,' he began, 'we can be far more comfortable on the surface.'

'It's more private down here,' replied a voice he'd not yet heard, a voice from behind the other torchbeam. That must be Gomorrah, he thought.

'So . . . what can I do for you?'

'We want to know where Caspar Locke is,' Sodom answered. A low growl from Gyorgy accompanied his words, as if to reinforce them.

'He's here,' Ferrow replied, signalling towards the coffin with his still-dazzled eyes. 'There's Caspar Locke, or whatever's left of him.'

'And what is that supposed to mean?' Sodom snapped.

'I'm afraid it's true. Whoever you're looking for isn't Caspar Locke. His name might be Hogue, or Rumsey, but the original Caspar Locke is in there. When Professor Rumsey opened Locke's grave he didn't find the body because it had already been exhumed and brought in here, probably by Rumsey himself on a earlier occasion. Someone wanted to bring the legend of Caspar Locke back to life, and they've been doing a pretty good job so far . . .'

Keep talking, he told himself. If there's an opening it'll come soon. Just keep talking till it turns up.

'So, you see? Whoever you're looking for isn't Caspar Locke.'

'In that case, Mr Ferrow, what are you doing here?'

'Like you, Sodom, I had to be sure . . .'

'And that door?' Gomorrah snarled. 'What's down there? Do you know?'

Ferrow shrugged. 'My guess is that there's a cave down there, and a hidden passage to the beach. I believe that whoever's been playing Caspar Locke, and I don't think he's been doing it for the benefit of the locals, has been living down there. You went over Hogue's house, I believe. Did you find that receipt for camping equipment in the table in the basement?'

Gomorrah's torch wavered fractionally, then the beam flashed back into place on Ferrow's features.

'I will hold Gyorgy back, Mr Ferrow,' Sodom hissed. 'You will turn and open that door. Once it is open you will stand away from it. Do you understand me?'

Ferrow nodded.

'Do it, then.'

Slowly, still aware of the automatic lying on top of the coffin, Ferrow turned towards the door. Standing against the side with the hinges he reached across and grasped the handle. It turned easily in his fingers. Slowly, conscious of the horror called Gyorgy panting just a little way away from him, the horror they called a *glebula*, a 'something' he had yet to even really glimpse, Ferrow began to pull the door open, swinging it out into the vault. As it travelled along the arc of its axis one of the torch-beams left him and flashed around the edge of the wooden door.

Gyorgy's snarling rush was terrifying. Ferrow caught a glimpse of teeth that shouldn't have belonged to the planet's largest carnivore, short fur and baleful eyes. The impression was one of total obedience emitting total viciousness, of stumpy, pig-like legs and pointed ears, of foul breath and utter, soul-devouring horror. Knocked off balance he fell back against the coffin, feeling the palm of his outstretched hand connect with the butt of the automatic. As his fingers closed about it an orange flash, accompanied by a deafening explosion, lit the *glebula* in the doorway.

He glimpsed the fur, which was flying apart. He glimpsed the wicked canines and incisors as they shattered. He caught a brief impression of something unearthly ripping into shreds and tatters of synthetic, dying flesh, veering in mid-spring to crash heavily and messily against the doorframe. In the same moment the two torches went out and Ferrow heard scuttering footsteps across the vault in urgent haste. As he scrambled to his feet he glimpsed two small, misshapen silhouettes against the daylight at the top of the steps.

'Well,' snapped a familiar voice, 'move! Get after them!'

He didn't need telling twice. With the dark figure hard on his heels he raced up the steps and into the sunlit ruin above. About fifteen yards away, running down the valley with remarkable speed and agility, were the distorted shapes of Sodom and Gomorrah. Bracing his feet and holding the pistol in both hands Ferrow sighted the weapon on Gomorrah's back. His finger was closing on the trigger when his companion placed a hand on his shoulder.

'Fire over their heads, Robert,' he commanded. 'They have to escape this time. I simply don't want them to think they escaped too easily.'

He raised the weapon and, as instructed, loosed off three high rounds which fell spent into the hillside above. Then he clicked the safety-catch back on and returned the Bergmann-Bayard to his pocket, before they returned to the vault.

Ferrow studied the figure beside him. 'I think it's about time you told me just what's going on,' he began brusquely. 'And we can start with that thing,' he continued, gesturing towards the bloody remains of Gyorgy. 'Come on, Hogue, or Meeres, or whatever your name really is. What the fuck is it?'

The figure smiled gently, then broke open the shotgun and removed the spent and smoking cartridges from its breech, replacing them with live ones from the pocket of his greatcoat. 'Do you really want to know?' he asked, smiling.

'I . . . have to know, don't I?'

Whatever his name, if he truly had one, really was, the Keeper nodded sagely. 'I suppose you do, friend Robert,' he replied. 'That is . . . that was . . . a *glebula*.'

'I've gathered that much,' Ferrow snapped. 'Now, what the hell's a *glebula*?'

'Have you heard of a *homunculus*?'

'A what?'

'Question answered, my friend. Now, there were two artificial life-forms known to the ancient alchemists, Robert. One was the *homunculus*, a sort of artificial man. The other was the *glebula*, which falls somewhere between a sheep and a wildcat in the evolutionary scale. That is what we have here. A *glebula*.'

He prodded the remains of Gyorgy with his toe. They didn't move.

'There is a thin wall between fantasy and reality,' he continued, staring down at the creature he had killed. 'It is built of the bricks of ability, of technological know-how. That which can be conceived can exist, if only we know how to turn a concept into a reality. That is what has been done here, you see? The *could be* has become the *is*. And it is not a very pleasant *is*, is it? An animate killing machine. Totally obedient, totally loyal, and totally effective.'

He wanted to throw up. Gyorgy alive was bad enough. The remains of Gyorgy, shredded by a close-quarter shotgun blast, were something else. 'Is that the best answer I'm going to get?' he demanded, resignedly.

'It's the best answer I can give you at present, friend Robert.'

'Then let's try another question, friend thingummy. Who are you? Will you tell me that?'

The figure shrugged. 'Who I am you might find a little difficult to believe at present. I was Rumsey, yes. And Meeres. And now I'm Jimmie Hogue. And Caspar Locke.'

Ferrow felt his mouth hang slackly open. 'But that would make you . . . about ninety . . .' he protested.

'Instead of the seventy-eight I was as Meeres? Ah, that I should be so young, friend Robert. You see? I told you it was fantastic. I also told you the date of my birth. 1485, remember? But it's all so unimportant.'

'Don't ply me with more of your riddles,' Ferrow snapped. 'What the hell should I call you, anyway?'

'For the time being, Robert, call me Johannes. It was my name, once. There is still one alive who has called me by that name.'

'Then stop feeding me riddles, Johannes. I want straight answers to straight questions. Christ knows I've taken enough from you on trust. I think it's about time you levelled with me, right?'

Merry Foster checked the court-lists for something worthy of her attention, though the check was more for something to do than with any thought of earning her salary. The times they were a-changing, and on this particular day they were a-changing faster than she had ever known them do before. It wasn't every day you had a D-Notice slapped on your best story ever. It wasn't every day that you got kissed in a library by an out-of-town copper.

She could have used the *Echo*'s library to research Caspar Locke, but that would have meant explaining her interest to Joe McFee. Instead she'd used the public library and seen Ferrow again. Not that she'd got anything out of him . . .

Merry blushed and mentally reassessed her morning. For now, though, there was an afternoon to be worked through, and she still didn't know how Caspar Locke fitted in with the murdered second-hand dealer and the two fishermen.

Still, a few questions around Fortstown would be a start.

She stood up and reached for her coat. Somehow the late August day seemed to be getting colder, not warmer, as it progressed. She was about to sign out of the office when Joseph McFee called her into his office.

'You're no still on those murders, are ye, Merry?' he enquired, his crinkly face mildly concerned that she might be ignoring the Whitehall prohibition.

'Not at all, Joseph,' she replied. 'I thought I'd try a bit of local folklore as there's nothing doing at the courts.'

'Why no try a little natural history?' the editor countered, holding out a circus handbill to her.

Oh shit, she thought. McAllister told me to do the circus. Now Joe's telling me to do the bloody circus as well.

'It's not my field, Joseph,' she answered. 'Isn't there someone else who can check the elephants' pedicures?'

'Harry's off sick ye ken. And Emma's on a half-day, Merry.

You're the only one I've got for this. Besides, there's bound to be a free ticket in it.'

Bloody great. A free ticket to the circus. She snatched the handbill irritably and glanced down its contents. She looked up.

'What're *glebulae*?' she demanded.

McFee shrugged. 'Ye ken? Ye've a story already, lass.'

Gosh. Really?

'So, what're ye standin' there for, Merry?'

With a groan she crumpled the handbill into her coat pocket and left the office. Whilst the afternoon wasn't that warm it was at least dry, so the reporter decided to leave her car in the car-park and walk up to the circus grounds. She could always ring back for a photographer if she needed one. *Glebulae*? she asked herself. Some under-exposed desert-rat, probably. Still, it took care of the afternoon for her. The only real regret was that it also slowed down the Caspar Locke angle on the *real* story.

She climbed the hill towards where the Circuz Ferencz had raised the big top on the open space close by the Deveron estuary. Workmen were still erecting tents for the side-shows and the painted hardboard façade for the 'Arcade of Freaks' still lay on the grass beside coils of rope and folded sheets of canvas. She shuddered at the depictions of misshapen monsters and twisted skeletons.

Men in jeans and grimy T-shirts were struggling to erect the sections of metal bars which eventually would connect the big top to the animal trailers. Merry approached them and tapped one on the shoulder, showing him her press card. He looked up at her from where he was working with a spanner on the ground, his eyes appraising what he could see with disturbing frankness.

'Can I take a look at the *glebulae*?' she asked him.

Something in his face was lined, beneath the actual surface of the flesh. He should have been about thirty, but Merry felt that his true age would be much, much more if she cut him open to look.

'You want see glebulas?' he asked in a thick, mid-European accent.

'Got it in one,' she replied, unsmiling, wondering if the short hairs at the nape of her neck were really beginning to rise.

'I take you,' he answered, standing up.

Merry Foster wasn't short. Well, not really, she told herself. Yet this Czech, or whatever he was, towered a good foot over her. He had hands like hams that could have crushed her skull without even trying, and his broken English added the sinister dimension of imperfect understanding to his physically threatening proportions.

She followed him over to where a trailer was parked with several others. As he swung open the door at one end he reached inside and pulled out a short flight of wooden steps. The stench that came with them was both overpowering and difficult to identify. Eventually Merry likened it to an odour she'd experienced before, whilst she was doing a story about the trade in meat unfit for human consumption. A sealed unit with its refrigeration gone had been opened after several weeks of being impounded. It had stunk like this, only less so, if anything.

The foreigner climbed up inside the trailer and extended his massive hand to help Merry up. 'You come here alone?' he asked her.

'My driver's waiting over there,' she lied, following him up into the darkness.

She stood in a narrow, stinking corridor between the outer wall of the trailer and the barred interior. Only the daylight from outside offered any illumination as her giant companion padded along the metal floor to the further end. The *glebulae*, whatever they were, were scratching amongst the straw in the barred enclosure, stinking and occasionally making strange snuffling sounds, part-way between a pig and a game-dog on the scent. Merry glimpsed something about the size of a sheep. It was staring at her through black eyes that were somehow luminous, even in the darkened interior.

Her companion flicked on the light. The breath caught in Merry's throat as she saw the serried ranks of the *glebulae* watching her.

They neither cowered nor crouched. They simply . . . waited. Their fur varied in hue from reddish-brown to wolf-grey. Their eyes were dark, expressionless, like rodent eyes, and all the more intimidating for their total lack of expression or feature. Their ears stuck out to either side like tufts of fur, and their pointed muzzles, like furry koala-bears, opened to display wickedly-sharp, slavering teeth.

'Glebulas,' the foreigner announced.

Oh, hell, Merry thought. And then her mind divided.

These things are fantastic, she told herself. Utterly fantastic. They're like nothing I've ever seen before. *What* a story, and it's all mine. And then the other half of her cut in.

She saw them, for only an instant, as what they truly were. She saw them as creatures alien to the world of man, creatures bred for the servitude of a destroyer, for one who wanted mankind enslaved before their terrible teeth. She smelt the rankness of dead flesh that walked with them. She saw the cold, amoral destructiveness which glared like bale-fire from their midnight eyes. She saw the claws and heard the eager panting.

Merry Foster shuddered to herself. Beside her the giant European noted her reaction and shook with silent laughter.

'Time I feed them,' he announced. 'You want to help?'

The light in Johannes' grey eyes was faintly disturbing, Ferrow decided completely without surprise. There again, everything about Johannes, or Meeres, or the Keeper was disturbing. Not surprising any more. Nothing about this ... man? ... was surprising any more. Except perhaps the sheer depths of horror which his activities could expose.

'I take it that you feel the time has come for me to explain things to you?' Johannes asked mildly.

'Now that's what I call an understatement. Here I am in the wilds of Bonnie Scotland, almost murdered by dwarfs and their gruesome killing-machine, surrounded by corpses and up past my arse in another of your bloody mysteries. Too fucking true I want some answers. Right now.'

'And will you believe them when you have them?'

'That's up to me. You just give, okay?'

'As you wish. Where would you like to begin?'

'This Rumsey and Hogue business will do for starters. All right, I'll buy for now that you can live almost indefinitely for some unknown reason. But I don't follow how you could look the same as both Hogue and Rumsey, especially if you were *both* Hogue and Rumsey. The only thing I can think of is make-up, but that doesn't fit your style. There has to be something more to it, something I don't know about yet.'

Johannes nodded. 'You're right, my friend. It's a small trick, but it's one I think you might appreciate. Now, watch my face.'

Johannes removed his broad-brimmed hat, revealing dark hair streaked with grey. As Ferrow watched, the hair slowly began to lighten, becoming grey all over. It lightened even more, turning almost imperceptibly from grey to a snowy white. As it did so the face beneath it aged correspondingly, the lines deepening and multiplying, the flesh beneath the skin falling away, shrinking inwards upon itself.

Ferrow felt his eyes widening in surprise and alarm. He was about to cry out when, in less time than it took to blink, Johannes' face returned to normal.

'You see? I was Rumsey, and I am Hogue.'

'Can . . . you grow younger . . . as well?'

A faint smile played upon the old man's lips. 'What age would you like me to be, Robert?' he enquired, his voice gently humorous. 'Shall I be a youth? Will that answer your question, or will two demonstrations not be enough for you?'

'But . . . how? How the hell do you do it?'

'It has nothing to do with hell, or heaven, my friend. Let it suffice if I tell you that I was once subjected to a process which altered the structure of my body with regard to the effects of time upon it. There was another also,' he continued, sighing to himself, 'who was with me. I suspect that she too has this ability. And yet . . . the process was imperfect. Oh, it gave me this ability, certainly. But it was designed to do something totally different. And it may yet be repeated, you know. That is why I have come here. That is why I must offer the bait to Erzebet, and hope that she comes here to take it.'

'Erzebet?' Ferrow queried, his world becoming more confusing with every passing moment.

Johannes nodded slowly. 'Perhaps I had better tell you about Erzebet,' he began. 'To begin, then, Erzebet von Bamberg is the loveliest woman I have ever known, and you will appreciate that I have known a great many in a lifetime such as mine. She was born, let me see, in 1518, the only child of the Landgrave Frederick von Bamberg and his wife, the Landgravine Elena. Her father, I recall, had a magnificent library for the time, which I once took the liberty of consulting. From quite an early age Erzebet was both mentally and sexually precocious. She read. She absorbed. She *experimented*. It was inevitable that, being so pretty, she should attract the attention of her cousin, the Prince-Bishop Franz-Alberich, who subsequently debauched her.'

Ferrow scowled, keeping his lowered gaze away from Gyorgy's still-bleeding fragments. *Glebulae*. Five-hundred-year-old beauties. It just didn't happen. Not here in the land of the Whisky Trail, as the round of distilleries was called. Not anywhere else . . .

'Patience, friend Robert. Your belief is not as important as your understanding,' Johannes continued. 'Yet Erzebet is real, and she is still alive, as I am still alive.'

'How well did you you know her?'

Ah, the police mind is clicking into gear once more. Very good. A suspension of disbelief, if nothing else. 'We passed one night together,' Johannes sighed, 'but only one. It was, I recall, *Walpurgisnacht* 1535, and the place was Ingolstadt. She was seventeen, then, and my servant Wagner had procured her to play the part of Helen of Troy in a small charade of mine. And she had played her part very well . . .'

'But . . . what has this got to do with the relic?'

'Patience, my friend. We will arrive there soon enough. We each chose our paths, Erzebet and I, though they were very different. She took the path her cousin had followed, whilst I became the Keeper. We diverged, yet always knew that one day, no matter how far in both our futures it might be, we would meet again. And now I come to the relic, friend Robert. It is the bait to lure Erzebet to me for that final meeting. Its powers may be used to unlock forces better left alone. You already know something of the powers of Thule, of the conflict which has raged unseen throughout the centuries between the devotees of the opposing factions. Each has its own, opposing aim. Some, like myself, require only the maintenance of the *status quo*. Others, like Erzebet, have become infected with that power-hunger which characterises those who would use Thule to restore the banished powers, the powers which are essentially inimical to man. You can have no concept of what that restoration would be like, Robert. Man rules this planet. He may not do it wisely, and there have been moments when he has come perilously close to his own destruction. Yet believe me when I say that even that destruction would be preferable to the alternative Erzebet's faction would present. Can you conceive a world where man is nothing more than a plaything for his superiors? And, more than that, a source of both spiritual and physical sustenance for them? He would be farmed like cattle and eaten like a bar of chocolate. There would be no dignity, no peace of mind, no privacy. Nothing but total servitude to egos so vast that he could not even begin to measure or comprehend them.

'I have guarded that relic through the years, Robert. If it fell into her hands it would be used as a key to unlock the prisons of those Erzebet serves. When first I knew her she was nothing more than a lovely, spoiled, wayward child. But throughout the centuries she has deepened in her knowledge of evil, and her aspirations and powers have strengthened accordingly. Now at last a time has come when she can no longer be allowed to develop further. A time has come when she is no longer my inferior. She is now my equal and, if I hold my hand any longer, I may soon find that she has surpassed me and can no longer be thwarted or destroyed.

'You have been quite right in what you've been thinking. I assumed the identity and the legend of Caspar Locke to bring her here. I made sure that my photograph, both as Rumsey and as Hogue, appeared in a sufficient number of papers for her to be sure of seeing it. I had to lure her here, and in order to do that I had to make sure she knew the relic was here for her to take. She has reached a point in her development now where the powers which have supported her require a service, and the relic will enable her to provide that service. She knows I have it. Now she must take it.'

'And it's up to you to stop her?' Ferrow asked.

Johannes shook his head. 'No, friend Robert,' he replied. 'It's up to you to stop her. I may no longer have the power.'

Ferrow groaned and turned away. When he looked back his eyes were angry. 'Why the hell does it have to be me?' he demanded. 'Just because I was in the wrong place when you were Ptythonius Meeres and you needed someone to help you sort out that shitty mess at Wegrimham? And now, all of a sudden, you can't run your game without me?'

'There's more to it than that,' came the reply. 'I would not have used you if you'd not been suitable. There were others I could have called upon. But I sensed in you a capability which is rare, friend Robert. You have a good mind, a mind that is both prepared to wrestle with difficult concepts and yet capable of direct physical action. Tell me, why did you come here at this time?'

'I . . . we wanted a holiday . . .'

'You delude yourself. That's not the reason and you know it. You came because you were summoned. You did not understand the summons, but you recognised it and obeyed none-the-less. You see, you already serve Thule, Robert. At present you serve without understanding, but if you live through the next few hours, if you survive to become the *guardian of the relic*, then you will begin to have understanding as well.'

'Will you tell me something, Johannes?'

'If I can.'

'What did you, as Hogue, sell to the Macreedys that got them killed? And where did it go from the Macreedys?'

'In order to answer that I must tell you the story of the relic and, to some extent, of Thule itself. Well then, here it is.

'You know that Thule is no longer a place, in the physical sense, that it is now a concept embodied with certain powers. Once, in the days before history, the Thulean empire covered the globe in a unity, a harmony, which today we would envy. Those who controlled it had evolved beyond simple humanity, and in their evolution the dualism which is now perpetuated by the unseen conflict began to develop. Eventually the anti-human faction was suppressed and religion was deliberately implanted in the souls of men to prevent the recrudescence of that dualism. That is why the official religions have always resisted dualist heresies so vigorously.

'The few true Thuleans left after the conflict concentrated their attention upon re-establishing the empire. In order to do so they were forced to abandon man to his own unsupervised development, and they withdrew and consolidated upon a newly-formed volcanic island in the north. That is why the ideas of Thule and Hyperborea have always been inextricably linked. The island of Thule which became both their base and their grave is today called Iceland. The Romans landed there briefly, though what they found was never recorded. After them came Irish monks, seeking a remote land in which to refine their spirituality. What these found there is unknown, with one single exception.

'The Irish already had good reason to fear the Vikings when they discovered Iceland for themselves in the ninth century, and they hurriedly abandoned the island to the Norsemen. With one of the early Norwegian expeditions, though, sailed a woman who was gifted with the ability to look into the past. It was her fate to find the cell of an Irish monk who had once entered the ice-cavern of the Keeper. Somehow she was aware of the power which the monk had gained access to, and when she left she took two other things with her.'

'One of which was the relic?'

'Correct. The other was the monk's skull.'

'What on earth for?'

'We pay a price for the veneer of sophistication which our society prizes so highly, Robert. That price is the loss of certain innate powers which are common to all created beings. Children believe in fairies because fairies exist for them. They are real. I can say that to you and know that you will understand me. Only as we grow older are we dissuaded from our belief in alternative and truly valid realities. Our Viking forebears did not have the same degree of sophistication. They understood things that we may now never know. They called certain of their priests by the title Thul, a title derived from the name of Thule itself.

'From the skull itself the woman learned a technique by which it could be made to relay knowledge of the two Thules. From this she learned something of the so-called relic's power. At her death the skull and the relic were kept together, though the relic degenerated in status and became a simple amulet, eventually transforming into the lost relic of St John. As such it came into Caspar Locke's possession over 200 years ago.'

'And the skull?'

'It maintained its reputation through the centuries and eventually came into my possession. Without the relic, though, it was useless. Only the two together can have any value or purpose. Unfortunately I didn't destroy them when I had the opportunity, and the skull fell into Erzebet's hands. My oversight, though, all those years ago, has given me the means to lure Erzebet here. I have deliberately fostered the legend of Caspar Locke so that she would know I have the relic. A few years ago I arranged for the skull to be stolen from her, knowing that she would pursue its recovery. And this is where I answer your original question, Robert.

'A recurring preoccupation of Erzebet's is death. It is a state that she has herself managed to transcend, yet its infliction and effect upon others holds a strong fascination for her. Well, I assembled a collection of items, books, furniture, some drawings, which reflected that preoccupation. With them I included the skull, and the original reliquary from the church of St John. Though naturally I retained the relic itself. That is what I sold to Macreedy at a nominal price.

'One as skilled as Erzebet will have had no difficulty in tracing and reclaiming the skull. I regret that she has seen fit to cover her trail by a series of murders, but you will appreciate that they have been her decision, not mine . . .'

'It's still left six people dead, Johannes . . .'

'It has indeed. I mourn for every one of them. But I will mourn even more for the countless numbers who will die if she recovers and uses the relic. And that is what she wants above all else. That's why her two creatures followed you here today, as they have followed and questioned any who might lead them to me. And that is why we had to let them go, Robert, so that they can lead Erzebet back here to claim the relic from me.

'She will come soon, you know. She dare not delay now that she has the skull back and her creatures have tracked me down. She has to come tonight.'

Ferrow looked down and scowled at the ground between his feet. 'Two things, Johannes,' he began. 'Assuming you'll give me straight answers that I can understand.'

'You can only ask me, friend Robert.'

'You said that the process you went through with Erzebet was designed to accomplish something other than what it did.'

'That is correct. I did.'

'Erzebet seeks to recreate the process, and needs the relic?'

Johannes nodded. 'You are right again.'

'Then what does she hope to gain? You mentioned countless numbers dying if she's successful. Does she plan to release something that's like that horror at Wegrimham? Is that it?'

'How many questions have you asked me so far?' Johannes enquired.

'This is my first,' Ferrow snapped. 'You want me to help? OK, I'll help. But only if I know what's going on. Fair enough?'

'You make your point well,' came the reply. 'Yes, Erzebet seeks to release a force which her cousin, the Prince-Bishop Franz-Alberich Carolus von Bamberg, dedicated his life to. They were enemies, you know. Had it not been for the Keeper the Prince-Bishop would have destroyed both of us . . .'

'I thought you said you were the Keeper?'

'I am, but explaining that would only complicate things still further. You want to understand, and you shall. But for now your last question must remain unanswered whilst I continue to explain the one before. The force he served was much the same as that Velaeda you faced at Wegrimham, the avatar, if you like, of the toadstool *Amanita virosa*. I told you then that all created things had their Thulean parallels, that they might even take the forms of disease bacilli. Very well, the force which the Prince-Bishop, and now Erzebet, sought to release was called Pudendagora. It was the Thulean equivalent of a scourge of our modern world, friend Robert. You will know it as syphilis.'

Ferrow's eyes narrowed slightly as he thought over the old man's words. OK, syphilis, the clap, whatever you called it, was nasty, but modern medicine had it under control. There was nothing as bad about it as there had been about that Velaeda creature in the vault beneath Wegrimham Grange.

Johannes seemed to read his thoughts. 'Was there anything so terrible about the toadstool *Amanita virosa*, Robert, that you could have suspected what it served? Now you are thinking that there is nothing so dreadful about syphilis, and you are right. Today it is well-contained and containable. It no longer, with treatment, leads to a mad death as it eats its way through the brain of the unfortunate victim. But that is the syphilis of today. It was not Pudendagora's.

'The original disease reached Europe in 1493. Gaspare Torella, a bishop who later became personal physician to the Borgia Pope, Alexander VI, wrote a treatise upon it, noting its effects. One patient he described as having an ulcerated penis which discharged a dense, venomous pus. This seemed to heal, but dreadful pains throughout the body and limbs followed and, eventually, many horny pustules upon the head, face and neck. All painful. All discharging.

'Infants caught it from their nurses and passed it to other infants in their play. A kiss was sufficient to transmit the disease. As well as the genitals, the whole body from head to shin became a mass of scabs and crusted, discharging excrescences, harder than tree-bark, shaped like tiny horns. They stank. They wept into the clothing which became too painful for the victims to wear. They ran mad smearing the filth of their disease upon whatever they brushed against, man, woman or baby.

'Treatment was vain. Paracelsus, that great physician so sadly forgotten today who first gave zinc ointment to the world, pre-scribed the poisonous metal mercury, taken internally. Gaspare Torella, a good son of the Church if a rather incompetent physician, directed that upon their first appearance the primary sores should be sucked out by one of low station whose subsequent fate was of no concern. Such was Pudendagora's syphilis.

'You will notice that I have said *was* throughout this explanation. There is a reason for that. Your belief that modern medicine has syphilis under control is quite correct. Pudendagora could be fought and perhaps even defeated today. *If it had not evolved.*'

Ferrow gulped at his uncomfortably dry throat. 'Evolved?' he queried.

'Most certainly. And into something that is the modern world's greatest fear. An incurable disease, Robert. A disease with an in-cubation period long enough for the sufferer to have forgotten how it was contracted. A disease that almost always kills. A disease which brings a slow, wasting death to the body and the mental torment of living for months and years with the inevitable. Oh, there is no connection between what Pudendagora was then and what Pudendagora is now. It is no longer syphilis. It is worse, friend Robert. Today it is the auto-immune deficiency syndrome.'

The colour drained from Ferrow's cheeks. 'Oh, Jesus,' he muttered. 'Oh sweet fucking Jesus! You're telling me it's AIDS? But why, for Christ's sake?'

'Can you think of a better way to enslave mankind? A better way to compel obedience than with the threat of such a death for those who find disfavour in the eyes of Pudendagora? It will be grateful to Erzebet for its ultimate release. She will be the favoured servant, the vicegerent of the horror upon earth. She will know undreamed-of pleasures, and inflict unheard-of cruelties. For ever.'

His grey eyes burned into Ferrow's. 'You seem lost for words, my friend,' he said grimly. 'I have answered your first question. Now, what's your second?'

The policeman struggled to recall what he'd wanted to ask, but all thought of it was blotted out by the answer to his first enquiry. If he'd not seen the monstrosity which was Velaeda at Wegrimham he'd have been totally unable to believe what the old man had told him. Yet, having seen, he was unable to doubt. He shook his head to try to clear his mind. Then he asked: 'The Keeper . . .'

'I am the Keeper.'

'But . . . *what of*, Johannes? And where does Iceland fit into all this?'

'Iceland is Thule . . .'

'Oh, you've told me that. It still doesn't answer me, though. You were saved by the Keeper, yet now you *are* the Keeper . . .'

Johannes smiled. 'When it is time you will know,' he replied. 'For now, friend Robert, there is Erzebet von Bamberg to be dealt with.'

Outside the last preparations were being made for the night's performance. The barred corridor leading to the big top had been set up and the sections of cage were stacked inside, ready to be hinged together at a moment's notice. Lions and tigers paced in their cages, snarling half-heartedly at the local boys who crowded about them.

In the distance a fire-eater practised his art, making sure that the prepared solution was at the right strength, and the props required for his spectacular finale were ready. In the Arcade of Freaks the pathetic, deformed exhibits were being shut into their cages and the turnstile was being wheeled into position. It was one of the sick high-points of the Circuz Ferencz, one of the things that had made it the most notorious, if well-attended, travelling show in the whole of Europe. Its freak-show was frankly horrifying, and that was why it wasn't given publicity as such on the circus handbills; the circus didn't want to attract unwelcome official notice of its activities.

Inside the mobile home reserved for her exclusive use the old lady sat alone or, at least, without any human or animal companion. Her thoughts might have drifted back to that day in 1978 when, on her way to Salzburg, a part of her luggage had been stolen by a London cabbie. She knew who he had been working for. There was only one other person in the world who could have wanted the contents of that hat-box. Perhaps the cab driver didn't know himself, but she knew. The old lady with the young eyes could have no doubt about that.

She should have known. She should not have put down to imagination the barely-glimpsed shadows that watched her. She should have been aware that the crisis in the management of the circus which had called her to Salzburg was too easily solved, seeming to evaporate the moment she set foot on German soil, or what should have been German soil if Hitler's Lebensraum had worked out properly.

They were all things she had thought at the time, but they had no place in her present deliberations. All that mattered now was that the contents of the hat-box had been tracked down and returned. It had all been remarkably easy, really. Once she had accepted that there was no such thing as a coincidence or a chance meeting in the twilight world she inhabited, the trail of the missing object had been as obvious as a motorway on a road-map. Yes, very easy.

Too easy, perhaps? Or was it nothing more sinister than modern technology and communications shrinking the world, reducing it to little more than a village?

The questions didn't matter any more. All that mattered was that she was close again at last. The object in the hat-box had almost been handed back to her by the one who had taken it. The ugly little grotesques who had physically retrieved it and held it up, smiling, for her to take were incidental. So was the time and energy and spilled blood they had devoted to covering their trail, and hers.

Soon, now, she thought to herself. Soon it will be over. Soon all the travel and searching of my centuried pilgrimage will be ended for ever. Then they will know my name again. My real name. Then they will know that Jancisca Ferencz and Juanita Ferrara and all the other names were not my own, not the name of the woman who is going to change the way of life of a planet for ever.

I have the skull once more, but that is merely a means of discovering the whereabouts of the relic. That is what I really need. That is the object of my quest. And I alone know truly how it can be used, for I alone have dared to think of using it.

I'm sorry, Johannes. I'm truly sorry. It would have been so pleasant to have you with me, to keep you as my consort and my companion. Of all the men I have met, of all the men who have served me through the centuries, you are the only one who can truly love me as I need to be loved. But we cannot be together. Only my surrender could bring us together, and that would bring the fury and vengeance of Pudendagora down upon us both.

And you, my hard, round friend, she thought, turning her attention to the object on the table. You're home, now, home from your wanderings. Did you tell anyone else anything, Skull of Caillchen? Did you tell Gerard Covington your secrets? Or Johannes? Did Johannes speak to you, with you, as I have done?

She stared at it in the dim light, projecting herself through both vacant orbits at the same time. It was a hard technique to master, but Erzebet had done it many times, and this time it was easier than she ever remembered before. The skull itself had told her how it should be done, concentrating at first upon one orbit, then upon the other, then flicking her concentration back and forth until it both divided and united, sending her through the eye-sockets and deep into the cranium itself.

Again she floated, feeling herself no more than the minutest speck of dust, yet dust eternal and unchanging, inside the cranial cavity, seeking to read whatever runes the brain of the dead monk might have inscribed for her therein. It was always an end and a beginning. Always a renaissance of her quest, her pilgrimage, for she never read the same runes twice. There was ever some slight difference, some new symbol, as there always must have been, for she could never have entered the skull twice in the same moment, let alone in the same place at the same moment. A sorcerer long dead had taught her that.

Is he close, little skull? Is he near by, Skull of Caillchen, fragile relic of long-dead humanity?

He is close, Erzebet, it responded. You know who he was, and who he has now become.

Will I find him soon?

The runes inside the skull seemed to congeal, to run together in demented spider-shapes to furnish an answer to Erzebet's enquiry. They writhed and wriggled upon the bones of the cranial cavity, then settled into new patterns, into a new message for the woman old in evil who sat and stared through eyes which should have been too young to have been her own.

You will find him tonight, Erzebet von Bamberg, the skull told her. Tonight your searching will at last be over.

How must I draw him to me?

He will come to you. Your preparations are known to all your helpers, both those who are manifest and the other, who yet stays hidden. They will also be known to the one you have desired for so long. Your ancient, sometime lover will come to you, and he will bring with him the form of that which you have sought. Take my warning and act accordingly.

Now let me go, Erzebet. You have it all, now. There is nothing left for you.

'Nothing?' she snarled aloud, a wrinkled hand rising in a threat to smash the skull from the table in her anger.

Only dust, Erzebet, it replied, Only that dust which falls through the centuries from a decay which is no longer there. I've served you well, Erzebet von Bamberg. Better than I should have done, perhaps. But the time has come when I can serve *you* no longer.

'But . . . I still need you. I still need you!'

You only need the relic now, Erzebet. That's all. Only the relic.

And the one you knew as Faustus has that small obsidian monkey, Erzebet von Bamberg. And you know who Faustus is . . .

PART THREE

The Guardian
of the Relic

The guests from the Fortstown Arms drove in convoy to watch the circus in Banff. Ferrow and June travelled with Harry and Moira, whilst Jenny Fellowes left her Mercedes at the pub and accompanied Gerard, a little way behind them. Passing the head of Braw Valley on the twisting road they noticed a large removals van pulled into a lay-by, the cab tilted forward to expose the engine beneath.

'Not the best place to break down,' Harry grinned at his rear-seat passengers in the mirror. 'It's a long walk to a telephone.'

For a moment Ferrow wondered if Harry intended to stop and offer help, but their driver had only slowed down for the bend and speeded up again once they were through it. The policeman had his own reasons for wanting to reach the circus as early as possible.

After the incident at the ruined church with Sodom and Gomorrah that afternoon, Ferrow had telephoned McAllister and passed on his suspicions regarding the dwarfs, the house in Aberchirder Street and the murders. The Scot had reacted well, saying that he'd obtain a warrant to search the circus for the dangerous little swine, and for anything else that might be useful to their investigation. That search should now, Ferrow believed, be in progress, and he intended to be in at its conclusion if there was any way possible.

In the car behind them, Gerard Covington was feeling good. Jenny Fellowes had arrived in his life at exactly the right moment. Her interest and encouragment were the best therapy he could have received, he decided. Finally he was able to acknowledge to himself the unhealthiness of his life with poor Zoë. With Jenny's help, he hoped for a normality which for him, because of his childhood, would be a new experience. He smiled across at her as he drove, his happiness only tainted by suppressed thoughts of his old friend Tom Luyner's death in that stupid, senseless accident. She, in turn, smiled back, the epitome of a warm, loving companion.

The cars reached the outskirts of Banff and drove along beside the river before crossing the bridge and heading through the town centre towards the circus ground where McAllister's search was taking place. They parked and began walking towards the big top, its pennants flying against the darkening twilight of the sky, its striped canvas sides lit by spotlights set upon the ground around it. As they passed the owner's mobile home Ferrow saw McAllister, once again muffled in his heavy coat despite the warmth of the summer evening, standing outside its open door.

'You go on inside,' he told the others. 'I just want a quick word, then I'll join you.'

Harry and Moira agreed and carried on. June paused, her eyes searching her fiancé's, her mouth working as if there was something she wanted to say. Ferrow flashed her a quick smile. 'Go on,' he repeated, softly. 'I'll see you in a minute.'

Reluctantly she followed Harry and Moira towards the huge marquee. Ferrow watched her go for a moment, then walked across to McAllister. As he did so Harris came down the steps out of Mrs Flanagan's trailer. From inside the big top the sounds of drum-rolls and applause began.

'Anything?' McAllister asked his sergeant.

'Nothin',' Harris replied. 'And nae skull either,' he added, looking pointedly at Ferrow. 'And nae dwarfs called Sodom an' Gomorrah.'

McAllister commented, 'It's very odd that the woman who's the proprietor of this show isn't around for its first night.'

'Not from the folk I've been ta'kin tae,' Harris muttered. 'They say she's only heer on rare occasions.'

With a quiet smile McAllister turned to his sergeant. 'Then we'll have to see if we can find her. Did you get a description?'

'Aye. Old, wi' grey hair and young-lookin' green eyes. Mrs Joanna Flanagan. Shall I put out a call for her?'

'It would be as well. Apart from anything else she's the nominal employer of those two murderous little midgets. We'll want to talk to her about them.'

Ferrow was about to remark that the description might not be as accurate as his colleagues believed, but he changed his mind before the words left his lips. There were too many complicating features to this case already that he'd had to skate over in presenting it to McAllister. The thought of a suspect who could age or grow young again at will was simply one more outré detail which was best, at that time at any rate, ignored.

'One thing I dinna ken,' Harris added, his face puzzled. 'There's a copy o' yon manifest from when the circus entered the country. Nineteen lorries in a'.'

McAllister shrugged, though the bulk of his coat masked much of the movement. 'It's a large concern,' he replied. 'Nothing unusual in that.'

Ferrow looked from Harris to the inspector. Something at the back of his mind was beginning to make sense out of this puzzle. He turned about his own axis, his eyes flashing through the twilight as he looked around, counting.

Harris nodded and gave Ferrow a rare smile. 'There's no' nineteen lorries here,' he stated. 'I mak' the count eighteen. One short.'

'He's right,' Ferrow agreed. 'Eighteen it is.'

'One missing?' the inspector asked. 'Well, we can easily chase that up. Probably off the road in a garage or something. We know where the circus has been, so it's easy enough to ring round and find a missing circus wagon. And we'll have the patrols keep an eye out for it as well.'

That's making an assumption, Ferrow thought to himself. That's assuming that it's painted like all the others, that it actually looks like a circus lorry. If it doesn't, if it just looks like any one of a thousand other trucks on the road, then it could be anywhere, complete with missing dwarfs, missing circus owner and . . . what?

Yet it was only a wild speculation, and Robert Ferrow decided that it was time for him to change the subject before his imagination took over completely. 'Did those papers we found in Aberchirder Street tell you anything?' he asked. 'Have you had a chance to get them translated yet?'

McAllister waved a gloved hand vaguely in the air. 'Some of the wildest superstitious ramblings I've ever come across,' he said, dismissively. 'Our Mr Hogue must be fairly well off his head. One thing was more of a puzzle than the rest, though, Robert. The German passages were written on modern paper with a modern pen, but the text and some of the letter-forms showed that the words themselves more properly belonged to the sixteenth century than the twentieth. It was an unusual affectation, to put it mildly. However, I'm inclined to dismiss it as the manifestation of a symptom of a much greater mental disorder.'

'What makes you say that, Hugo?'

'The signature on some of the notes. Our Mr Hogue may be a clever man, but he's also stark mad. In some places the notes were signed J.F. In others it was Johannes F. And just occasionally, about twice in the corpus of material we removed, there was a full signature.'

'Which was?'

'You'll like this, Robert. It shows a certain flair, even in a schizophrenic. The signature was Johannes Faustus. Doctor Faustus himself.'

Ferrow felt the silence growing denser about him. Was it possible? Was it really possible that the man in the ruins who called himself Johannes was the legendary Doctor Faustus? Physically, after the transformation he had witnessed that afternoon, he could believe anything of the strange Thulean. It even made sense that Faustus' alleged devil-worshipping could be misunderstood by the ecclesiastical authorities of the time, and was really the study of Thulean doctrine. Yet leaving aside the question of how he had survived down the centuries there was another, larger question to be answered. Why had he protracted his life for over 450 years? What was so important that he alone could be trusted to achieve it?

'Did you say . . . Faustus?'

'The same, Robert. On a par with Napoleon, perhaps, but a little brighter, all the same.'

So Mrs Flanagan . . . Erzebet . . . whatever her name was, had the skull. Johannes . . . Faustus . . . had the relic. Sodom and Gomorrah knew where Faustus could be found. That they'd told Erzebet was evident by the fact that she wasn't at the circus . . .

'We're wasting time here,' Ferrow snapped. 'She'll not be back, and I doubt if the dwarfs will either. They want Hogue, or Faustus. And I think I know where they'll find him.'

'Then why the devil didn't you tell me sooner?' McAllister snapped.

'I had to be sure, Hugo. I don't understand all of this yet, but I think I'm getting closer. Will you trust me until it's over?'

'Do I have a choice?' McAllister scowled. 'I want these killers before they can do any more harm. They're not here, so if you've any idea where they might be, no matter how you've got that idea, I want to hear it. I need arrests, Robert. I've got pressure from the Chief Constable and, would you believe, he wants *me* to tell *him* why there's a D-Notice on this affair. I should know? So, I'll try anything you can suggest that's going to give me a result.'

'Then leave a couple of men here with radios, just in case I'm wrong, but get the rest of them into cars. Hogue is the man who's been playing Caspar Locke over the past few months. It's him they really want. That's why Davie Quarry and young Wullie were tortured. They were known to have seen him, so it was only logical that they might know where he was. And that's also how I know about them, because I found Hogue this afternoon, when Sodom and Gomorrah found me.'

'That makes a kind of sense, Robert,' McAllister muttered. 'So, we patrol the beach at Fortstown, do we?'

Ferrow shook his head. 'Not the beach. That's only where he showed himself. He's in the ruined church. Or, rather, he's not in the ruined church, but he will be.'

'You're not sounding very clear,' the inspector said thoughtfully. 'Either you know where he is or you don't.'

'Trust me, Hugo, will you? I know where he was, and I know where he will be. He'll be in those ruins tonight, sooner or later. And he'll have Sodom and Gomorrah and Mrs Flanagan there with him. And whatever's in that missing circus trailer. We passed it on the way in, looking like any furniture van. It appeared to have broken down above the ruined church, but I'm willing to bet there were men I couldn't see, or dwarfs, carrying its contents down into Braw Valley.'

He stared into McAllister's eyes, hoping that the Scot could believe at least enough to take the necessary action. There was one thing Ferrow still needed to know, but his instinct told him to make his own enquiry rather than depend upon the results of others. Besides, something which nagged away at the back of his skull told him to hold back now as he had to some degree held back all along.

McAllister spoke into his walkie-talkie, calling his men back to their cars for a return to the station to be briefed. The transceiver crackled with their acknowledgements.

Ferrow began to walk away towards the big top. 'I'll join you later, if that's all right,' he smiled.

'And in the meantime?' McAllister demanded.

'In the meantime, I'm going to be short one fiancée if I don't catch at least a part of the performance, so I'm going to watch the circus. After all, Hugo, I'm supposed to be on holiday. And I don't think anything's going to happen until the performance is over.'

He'd reached the ticket-booth before McAllister could ask him anything else. As he handed in his ticket he leaned forward against the window and asked: 'Tell me, what kind of car does Mrs Flanagan drive?'

The woman in the booth scowled, so he produced his warrant

card. The woman's scowl deepened even further as she saw it, but she replied: 'A red one. Foreign.'

'A Mercedes?'

The woman nodded. 'That's the make.'

As he entered the marquee, Robert Ferrow's heart was pounding with more excitement than that of any little boy at the performance. At last he knew that Joanna Flanagan and Jenny Fellowes drove the same car and were the same person. He also knew that the discrepancy in their apparent ages was far more than he could ever begin to explain to Hugo McAllister, unless there was something approximating evidence to back it up with. What he needed was Jenny Fellowes, with Sodom and Gomorrah, in the ruined church in Braw Valley, trying to take the relic from Johannes.

It had to be the church, not the beach. They could have driven their damned van right down to the beach if they'd wanted to, but the lay-by was as close as the road could take them to the ruins. But what was in it, for God's sake? What had they shipped across Europe for Christ knows how long to set up in the pile of broken masonry which housed Caspar Locke's bones? And then there was the old man, be he Meeres or Hogue or whatever. Johannes. Was he really Johannes Faust, the legendary sorcerer?

Johannes: JF. Jenny Fellowes: JF. Joanna Flanagan: JF. And doubtless there had been other JF aliases in the past. Throughout history she had used the initials as a beacon, calling out across time and space through a variety of false names. As Ferrow made his way to his seat he passed the place where Jenny and Gerard Covington were sitting together. Outwardly there was nothing to see, other than two young people enjoying the performance. There was still time for him to be wrong, and Ferrow found himself hoping that he was.

Yet the trap had been prepared and baited by Faustus himself. Whatever happened later, in the ruins of the little church near Fortstown, the centuried searching of two immortals would be over. They had to come together, drawn to each other by that strange relic which was both a symbol and a key, a means of unlocking a strange new universe, a new time and a new order of being, where man was little more than a plaything, and the dark side of Thule held dominion over him for ever.

Ferrow had been too intent upon his enquiries, both with McAllister and at the ticket office, to feel the eyes watching his movements. Yet two pairs of eyes had been upon him, watching his movements, seeking to interpret snatches of overheard conversation. The owner of one pair he had yet to meet, though fate had decreed that he should, eventually. The owner of the other pair he had kissed that morning in the Banff Public Library.

Contrary to her worst and most lurid expectations the giant European hadn't fed Merry to the *glebulae*, but simply produced two heavy buckets of raw meat and handed one to her. He grinned, almost like a simpleton, as he opened a small hinged section in the bars and tipped the contents of his bucket into the cage. Then he nodded for her to do the same.

They snuffled and grunted over the scraps, buffeting each other with their short legs and vicious snouts to gain access to a favoured morsel. Merry wondered if they were like jackals or hyenas, then realised she didn't know enough about either to answer her own question accurately. There was no point in asking her host. His fractured English would have rendered both his understanding of her enquiry and his response hopelessly incomprehensible. And so Merry Foster kept her questions to herself.

They finished with the *glebulae*, a little slowly for the reporter's taste, and the European showed her around the rest of the circus, offering the occasional gesture and the even more occasional monosyllable by way of explanation. From her limited experience of such matters the animals seemed to be well cared-for, and as she didn't have a tame RSPCA inspector to call on for back-up even that aspect of her story had to drop. As the time for the performance drew nearer the giant led her to the ticket office and grunted: 'Show card.'

'Huh? Oh . . .'

She pulled out her press card and held it up.

'Give ticket,' the giant instructed. Then to Merry: 'You see show. You like.'

'That's very kind,' she tried to smile, timidly holding out her hand for a massive ham to crush. 'Won't you tell me your name?'

'Gregor,' he grinned back, taking her hand with surprising gentleness.

'Thank you, Gregor.'

He began to stride away from her to where last-minute preparations were in hand, leaving Merry to feel relieved and, suddenly, hungry. A hamburger stand was just opening up so she strolled over and bought a cheeseburger. As she was eating it a familiar car drove onto the circus ground and parked haphazardly. Unescorted, Inspector Hugo McAllister got out and looked about him, as if expecting to see someone, or something.

Merry turned her face away and bit into the cheeseburger. When she ventured to look back McAllister was nowhere in sight.

She finished the burger and looked round for a litter-bin to take the greasy paper she'd held it in. Something brushed past her leg and she looked down. For a moment her heart, and the burger, began a race towards her mouth as she thought she recognised a *glebula*. Then both subsided again as she realised it had only been a stray dog, probably attracted by the smells of cooking meat and onions.

Well, no point in going back to the office now. Might as well hang around until the show starts. Besides, what's McAllister doing here?

Merry found herself a patch of shadow and settled down to watch. The other police vehicles arrived shortly afterwards and an obvious search of the circus began. McAllister reappeared and handed a carrier-bag to one of his men, who deposited it in the inspector's car.

The public began to arrive. A queue formed at the ticket office. Groups of people, families mostly, wandered around the side-shows, effectively masking Merry from those she was watching, but also, from time to time, frustratingly masking them from her. A group of six adults came into her line of vision. She took no notice of them until one of them detached himself and began to walk towards McAllister and his men.

Merry felt her dark eyes widen. 'It's . . . Ferrow,' she whispered to herself.

Intrigued, she edged nearer. So did the other watcher, though she didn't notice him.

'So we patrol the beach at Fortstown, do we?' McAllister was enquiring.

She saw Ferrow shake his head. 'Not the beach,' he replied. 'That's only where he showed himself. He's in the ruined church . . .'

He's in the ruined church? Who's *he*? God, if only these people would keep their noise down a bit. Whoever he is, he'll no be on the beach . . . Caspar Locke! He has to be talking about Caspar Locke. That's it. That's the connection. Caspar Locke, or whoever's taken his identity, is the killer. It *has* to be that.

Well, D-Notice or not, Merry Foster was going to be in on this. Her one regret was that she'd left her car in the *Echo*'s car-park.

'. . . I'm going to be short one fiancée if I don't catch at least a part of the performance, so I'm going to watch the circus . . .' Ferrow stated.

Great! Merry thought. That gives me time to go back for the car. Then I can follow Mr Ferrow from here to . . . wherever it takes.

She slid through the shadows until she was clear of the police presence and then began the walk back to the *Echo*. There was no way Merry could understand what was going on. All she could do, as she walked, was to turn over in her mind the features of this strange affair which presented themselves to her. Point one: Caspar Locke, figure of legend, is our mysterious killer. That's why McAllister and his men are going to be in the ruins beside Fortstown to catch him there.

Point two: Our Mr Ferrow, bestower of strategic kisses, out-of-town copper and, he says, not responsible for the D-Notice, looks to me as if he's somehow directing the police end of this deadly mess.

Point three: Somehow the Circuz Ferencz is involved. Otherwise they wouldn't be here to be searched and I wouldn't have stumbled across a hot lead. And if the circus is involved, ten to one those bloody *glebulae* are as well. Now, why hasn't anyone written those nasty little horrors up before? They had a week in Aberdeen before they came here. We have the Aberdeen press in the office, the *Citizen & Advertiser*, the *Evening Express*. They both carried reviews of the circus, but neither mentioned the *glebulae* at all. *Is this the first time anyone's seen them?* If it is, why is it? What do they have to do here that they didn't have to do in Aberdeen?

Point four . . . is probably a sub-paragraph of point three. Ferrow, what are you up to? If you didn't slap the D-Notice on, who did? And why, for God's sake? What's to be kept secret in a half-dozen murders in a forgotten corner of Bonnie Scotland?

She reached her car and drove back to the circus, parking despite protests, with a wave of her press-card, close to the big top. McAllister and his men were gone and Merry rapidly showed her ticket and walked into the giant marquee, her eyes roving the banked wooden seats for a sight of Robert Ferrow. When at last she caught a glimpse of him she permitted the protesting usher to finally show her to her seat.

Now there was nothing left to do but watch the show. At worst there was a paragraph or two of review copy in it, and maybe a piece on the *glebulae* which could get her name more widely known. At best ... well, *if* the Circuz Ferencz was involved with Caspar Locke and the murders, sooner or later she might well be able to leak the scoop of a lifetime, D-Notice, or no ...

The performers crowded the ring in a last, glorious parade. Their animals now once more in their cages the lion-tamers and tiger handlers, elephant trainers and seal trainers marched in their resplendent, pastel para-military finery. Fire-eaters blew their last flames at the applauding audience. Jugglers balanced clubs and trotted amongst the clowns, their multi-coloured balls flashing in the spotlights which wheeled and played amongst them. The crowd roared and the trick-cyclists balanced precariously in a last display of skill. It was a marvellous pageant, a triumph of human skill and ingenuity. And then it was over.

So much drama, so much breath-taking finery and talent, the Circuz Ferencz had completed its first triumphant performance in Banff. There would be other performances as well, on the following nights, and the crowds would be drawn to the splendour and spectacle by word-of-mouth. What the audience here tonight could not know, would never see, was the lighter, more joyous note which would underline those future performances: the freedom which the circus had earned, and finally received, after centuries of servitude to the whims of Erzebet von Bamberg. Whatever was to happen that night, both the searching and Erzebet's use for her creation were to end. If she succeeded, if the relic was hers, then there would be no need for the circus to cover her activities, for she would be above such things, the undisputed priestess of a hierarchy that had pre-judged and doomed mankind even before its ascendancy upon the earth. If she failed, then again there was no purpose that the circus could serve for her. But she wasn't going to fail. There was no way she could fail. Her servants were too well-placed for her to be thwarted now.

The crowd dispersed to wait for buses, walk to their cars or simply walk home. Thrilled children ran about their parents, riding imaginary unicycles or cracking their whips at invisible tigers. Chaos and terror had no place in their joy-filled minds, nor in the satisfied smiling of the adults who had gambled the price of a ticket against a few hours of escapist happiness. They were not to know of the conflict which was raging about them. They were not to know of the role which the Circuz Ferencz, its name now that of the Ferencz Bistritz whose ragged gypsy troupe had formed its earliest performers, had played in supporting a woman whose evil was old beyond anything they could conceive. And they were not to know that there was still a role for the circus to play, that there was one last service which Erzebet von Bamberg now demanded of it.

And so the performance ended and the audience went home. Ferrow and June made their way back to Fortstown with Harry and Moira. Gerard drove Jenny back to the Fortstown Arms, where Jenny's red Mercedes was sitting in the car park, for a nightcap. Ferrow was glad that they travelled separately. He'd never have been able to hold down his fear if he'd travelled with the woman he now knew Jenny to be. June, beside him, sensed the suppressed excitement without knowing its cause. She'd known that life with a copper wasn't going to be easy, especially after Wegrimham, but this, she decided, was beginning to get ridiculous.

McAllister phoned the Chief Constable from the police station and received the authorisation he required. Harris unlocked the cabinet and issued side-arms to the men who were to be stationed about the ruins. He understood his chief's reasoning, that they were going after a gang that had killed at least six people, and probably that Caspar Locke as well, but two dwarfs and a looney circus-owner didn't seem that dangerous to him, especially with a dozen boys in blue ready to swoop on them.

And then there was this mad bugger Ferrow, this off-duty copper from the south who seemed to know more about the things going on than the local force did. Harris didn't like Ferrow. The bloody sassenach was too knowing and McAllister appeared a little too eager to please him as well. Still, McAllister was the guv'nor, and the guv'nor's word was law. But even so, it was just as well that he'd made a few enquiries of his own, so that he wasn't completely in the dark . . .

Sodom slid out of the shadows and approached Gregor. 'Everything's ready in the valley,' he squeaked. 'Time for us to go. Hitch up and get your engine started.'

Gregor eyed him uneasily. In the giant's brain a tiny seed of rebellion had been planted by the sight of a slightly-plump Scots lass who wasn't afraid to offer him her hand.

'Come on,' Sodom cajoled. 'You've always known what you

might be asked to do. You've taken the money all these years, Gregor. Now it's time for you to earn it.'

'Thank you, Gregor,' he recalled. Then he challenged: 'You know police here? They look for you?'

Sodom shook his head. 'It doesn't matter, my enormous friend. All that matters is the one we serve. Gomorrah and I. And you. And the *glebulae*. They were her creation, after all. Your pets, perhaps, but *her* creation.'

Gregor reluctantly nodded. 'I come with you, I do what *she* wants. This one time. Then we go free.'

Gomorrah joined his diminutive companion. 'We're all free after this,' he grinned. 'Our lady won't require the Circuz Ferencz any more. She'll have everything she wants.'

Miles Fournessie released the bar on the optic and set the glass down on the tray. Then he backed away and began drawing a pint of lager from the pumps.

In the little bar at the Fortstown Arms the locals and guests were drinking and talking, holding listeners spellbound with their talk of the Circuz Ferencz. June, sipping a martini, smiled at Ferrow, who had an arm about her shoulders. In the corner by the fire Jenny Fellowes and Gerard Covington, apparently unaware of Ferrow's probing eyes, talked softly and drank deep. For Gerard it had been a spectacular evening. The promise of a walk on the beach before Jenny drove him home was both an appealing prospect and a promise of better things to come. Zoë, poor, dead Zoë, was forgotten in his intoxication with this new, enchanting woman, old beyond her years, whose sexuality was both a threat and a delight.

'Astounding,' Harry Carmichael muttered. 'And did you see that wire-walking? When that girl somersaulted between the two men on the cycles I thought my heart was going to stop. I've seen it on television, of course, but there's something about the atmosphere at a live performance that brings you right into the action. It's almost as if you're up there on the high-wire with them.'

'And another whisky, Miles . . .'

Outside, above Braw Valley, gathered in a lay-by beside a broken-down furniture van, McAllister was dispersing his men. A dozen policemen had received and checked their weapons, mostly Smith and Wesson .357s, though one or two had Colt .32s.

'At most I anticipate three targets,' McAllister was saying. 'Two of them are likely to be dwarfs. The third will be a woman called Joanna Flanagan.'

'Are there any distinguishing characteristics about the woman?' Harris asked.

'She'll be with the dwarfs,' McAllister replied. 'But nobody is to fire unless I give the signal,' he added. 'Is that perfectly clear?'

'And the man Hogue?' Harris queried. He was aware that McAllister regarded him as something of a pain in the arse, but he was determined that everything was going to be done properly. If they were to have guns, then they would at least know who to use them on.

'Hogue is to be taken alive for questioning if possible,' came the reply. 'Though Christ alone knows what he'll have to tell us.'

Ferrow paid for the round and carried it across to where Harry and Moira were still talking about the Circuz Ferencz. The panacea to ease the ills of murder, he reflected ruefully. If only they knew. If only *I* knew.

'. . . the way that he ducked and that tiger sailed across over him. And that big cat in the corner,' Moira was saying.

June caught his arm and looked up at him. 'What is it, Bob?' she asked. 'You're nervous tonight. Almost as nervous as that time in Wegrimham before the light came . . .'

He glanced at the corner by the fire. It was empty. Gerard and Jenny had gone for their walk on the beach.

'I'll be back in a little while,' Ferrow muttered.

He stepped out into the evening outside the Fortstown Arms. It was warm, caressing, yet it held a promise of such violence and terror that he had never, despite the Wegrimham affair, known before. Somewhere out there, in the darkness of the late summer night, were two dwarfs called Sodom and Gomorrah. With them . . . leading them? . . . was the woman Johannes had called Erzebet von Bamberg, a woman born in 1518 and, in his way, loved by the Keeper ever since *Walpurgisnacht* 1535.

And the Keeper himself . . . Ferrow still didn't know what, if anything, he kept, except for something purporting to be the Holy Relic of St John. He'd known Meeres. He knew Johannes. Johannes Faustus? Doktor Faustus himself? That made even less sense than a 500-year-old villainess called Erzebet.

The back of his neck prickled. The eyes were there again. He turned on his heel. And stared.

Merry Foster drew deeper into the shadows as she felt his gaze begin to touch her own. Not yet, Ferrow. I have to see it all before you can see me. I have to see it all.

And what else is there, out there? he asked himself. A dozen armed coppers? Okay, so we've done what we could, McAllister and I. But will it be enough to sink Pudendagora? I muddled through at Wegrimham. That's all. I muddled through. But that's not going to be enough here at Fortstown. I have to know. I have to understand.

Yet I don't know, he admitted to himself, despairingly. And I don't understand. Christ, Johannes, why couldn't you tell me the rest of it? Why do I have to try and guess where all the pieces fit in?

He began to wander down towards the beach. His feet moved with a reluctance he had never felt before, making it a conscious effort to place one in front of the other. His path meandered, but it held. It led him through the car-park of the Fortstown Arms, past Jenny Fellowes' red Mercedes, unaware of the dark shape which worked beneath it. Neither did he see the trickle of fluid which glistened in the moonlight, the trickle which meandered in steadily increasing rivulets towards the nearest gutter and the drain which led down to the sewers, and a species of oblivion.

Ferrow looked around again. Once more the eyes had burned into the back of his neck. Once more he sought them. Yet there was nothing to see. The watcher . . . the watchers? . . . were too clever, too shadow-shrouded for that.

He began the long walk down towards the seashore. It had never seemed that long before, but, then again, he had never walked it before with the knowledge that now bowed him down, the knowledge of a Thulean monstrosity which he would have to battle in the ruins in Braw Valley.

Above the valley the policemen began to move towards their assigned positions. As they started away from the road down the rough, rocky, grassy slope they began to see the structure which now towered above the broken shell of the little church, the structure assembled carefully but quickly from the contents of the furniture van. Above the assembly of giant cog-wheels towered the shape of a huge crucifix, each arm carrying a heavy weight in unequally-set positions.

'What the hell is that?' Lambie hissed beneath his breath, not really expecting an answer. Lambie had, like Harris, always wondered about McAllister as their guv'nor. Now, in the darkness of Braw Valley, confronted with a machine like something out of Hieronymous Bosch in the ruins beneath him, ruins in which they hoped to catch three dangerous criminals, he wished that Sergeant Harris was with them, not sent on ahead to tell the sassenach at the pub that they were about to start things off.

Harris looked in at the Fortstown Arms and asked at the bar for Robert Ferrow. Miles Fournessie gestured towards the door by which the policeman had entered. 'You've just missed him,' he explained. 'He's awa' for a walk.'

Oh shit, Harris thought. Still, nothing to be done. I'd best get back to the others and take care of these dwarfs and that Flanagan woman.

And then his mind began to work for itself again. Two dwarfs and a woman, McAllister had said. Two dwarfs and a woman. Just . . . a woman. Not an old woman? Not the ancient Joanna Flanagan they'd been looking for at the circus? Just . . . a woman?

His brow furrowed as the thought turned in his brain. No distinguishing characteristics? Like old age? Just a woman with two dwarfs? What the hell was McAllister thinking of? And as for nobody firing unless McAllister gave the signal, well, what *was* the guv'nor thinking of? They'd left their radios at the station and the assigned positions were too scattered for them to all see the inspector wave. Nor could they all see each other. Och, McAllister had really cocked it up this time.

And where the fuck was Ferrow? Gone for a walk? Knowing what was going down he'd simply taken off and gone for a walk? That made less sense than anything he'd heard so far tonight.

In the darkness, above the waiting policemen, Gregor's vehicle approached the head of Braw Valley. The others, apart from Sodom and Gomorrah, had been nothing, simply mere hands and performers to keep the cover of the circus alive for Erzebet's activities. And now, as he cut his engine on the cliff road, as he glimpsed the nighted shapes and occasional lit windows of the fishing village beneath and to the side, he wished that they hadn't chosen him to keep the *glebulae*. Good money, yes. But even Gregor knew how that money was finally having to be earned . . .

Ferrow descended the worn, salt-crusted steps and stood upon the shingle of the beach. For a moment he thought that he felt eyes upon his back, then decided that the sensation prickling at the nape of his neck was simply nerves. Slowly, deliberately, feeling the weight of the Bergmann-Bayard in the pocket of his coat, he set off along the shore towards the ruins.

'And those clowns,' Harry grinned. 'I expected that auld car of theirs to fall to bits. They always do. But when the pierrot was run over by the front wheels I thought I'd die laughing . . .'

Close by the ruins, staring up at the gaunt stone shell and the peculiar wooden structure it contained, Constable Costello began to feel uneasy. He turned to the nearest man, Frauncie, and pulled a wry face through the darkness. Frauncie grinned back, feeling the coldness of his Smith and Wesson somehow comforting against the sweaty rivulets that criss-crossed the palm of the hand which held it.

Above them, close beside the lay-by, on the cliff road, the cage on the back of a circus-wagon slid silently open.

Gerard and Jenny walked hand in hand, Gerard staring at the waves. The night was young and full of promise and romance. For the first time in his life Gerard Covington felt completely, naturally, normally in love.

The *glebulae* slid into the heather at the head of the valley. They were neither nocturnal nor diurnal, as much at home in darkness as in daylight. They knew Gregor and they knew the demented dwarfs who were with him, controlling him as he controlled them. They knew the ones who could inflict pain and control upon them. And they also knew who were the others, the ones who could be killed without hurt or reprisal to themselves. And they obeyed.

Frauncie looked from Costello to McGowran. Something was wrong. McGowran was grinning from a bloody red mouth he'd not had before, and there was a grim, white-fanged horror between McGowran and himself. With his mouth dry and foul, metallic taste reaching down into his stomach, the sort of taste which comes from sucking honey too hard from a cheap spoon, Frauncie thought to hell with his orders and slowly raised his shaking gun-hand.

Only to feel the gun fall away as powerful teeth crunched down upon his wrist.

Only to feel other, equally-sharp teeth clamp into his throat as powerful jaws bit home, tearing out the unborn, unvoiced scream which might have been his only consolation.

Lower down towards the beach MacGregor thought he saw movement closer to the ruins. He blinked hard, then looked again, then decided that his imagination must be playing tricks upon him. All this talk of dwarfs and circuses had affected his mind. There was no way that monsters could be loose in Braw Valley. He was still thinking this as Sodom's knife caught him between the shoulders. He felt the pain and the reality of the warm blood escaping within his uniform. And that, he knew, in his last few pain-filled seconds, was as real as the *glebula* that was tearing Frauncie's throat out.

Ferrow felt the shingle beneath the rubber soles of his suede shoes. Somewhere ahead of him two young lovers, one perhaps not so young, were walking hand in hand along the beach towards a rendez-vous with two dwarfs called Sodom and Gomorrah, and a man whose name ought not to be Johannes Faustus.

Harris dropped into the rocky depression beside Hugo McAllister. The inspector was grinning quietly to himself with a triumph which totally excluded his companion.

Merrington looked up. Constable Frain wasn't beside him any more. Instead there was a something with demoniac eyes and a frozen, tooth-sharp, almost painted grin, a something short and evil which was struggling to free the cheese-wire from his dead colleague's throat. Before Frain had time to realise and react to what he had seen, the wire was pulling tight about his own.

Besides McAllister and Harris, seven of their force remained alive.

The man on the beach felt the shapes around him in the darkness. He could see nothing. Moments later he could feel nothing, and would continue to feel nothing throughout the eternity to which he had been consigned.

'But I think the highlight, for me at any rate,' Harry smiled, 'was when that girl on the trapeze was about to miss her connection, and no safety-net underneath her either. I really thought that she was going to fall . . .'

Costello fell beneath the same artificially-created teeth which had killed two of his companions. Costain arched backwards, feeling with tormented fingers for the missing section of his backbone. The Colt revolver dropped from his grasp into the grass about his feet, the green grass which, in the darkness, the merciful darkness, he could not see splashed red with his own escaping blood.

The last grim service which the dwarfs and Gregor's *glebulae* could render Erzebet von Bamberg was being discharged with silent efficiency. Eight men already lay dead, and not one of them had been able to offer a warning sound.

Ferrow felt his stride lengthen involuntarily. His walk quickened to a jog as the gravel beach crunched past beneath his feet, masking the sound of his night-wrapped pursuer. Somewhere ahead two young lovers were taking a moonlight stroll towards the ruins, and towards the resolution of a centuried quest.

In the passage beneath the church Johannes waited. He knew of the silent slaughter taking place above him. He knew, yet he both understood and forgave the massacre. He had seen too much dying already to be moved by a few more deaths. Gory it might be, yet it was essential to the working-out of his plan. Only the greater, more fearsome carnage which might result from Pudendagora's release upon the world of man had meaning for him now. He had to remain in hiding, to wait for Erzebet. She would come. She was, even then, coming. She had to come, to demand the relic from him. She had as little choice as he himself, now that the mechanism had been installed inside the ruins.

Harrington felt the knife slice through his throat. Its blade was broad and painful and it carried in its passage a sensation which was entirely its own, a sensation which lasted until his staring, sightless eyes pressed down into the grass. Then, slowly, it began to ease and pass away as death lethargically intervened.

Three men left. And Harris. And McAllister.

And still there was nothing to break the silence. Still the survivors waited, watching through the darkness of the night. Still there was only the quietness of the grave about them, the quietness in which their colleagues were dying one by one.

Ferrow watched as the figures ahead of him left the beach and started up the valley. Behind him, in the Fortstown Arms, June Lowe, more drunk than she might ever have admitted, wavered out into the night to look for her missing fiancé.

Johannes opened the concealed door in the rocks and stepped out into the valley. Keen-eyed, even in the darkness, he saw the men lying dead about him. Grim creatures prowled amongst the corpses, their black eyes turning to look at him as he emerged.

The *glebulae* advanced.

He felt their stares and returned them. They drew closer, even closer as he stood there, waiting for them, his hands palm-in at his sides. He felt the rank, carnivorous, blood-fresh breath as their faces drew level with his groin and stared up at this ancient enemy of the woman they had been trained to serve, this ancient enemy who was also her ancient lover. He offered his hands to their mouths, their sharp-toothed mouths, and rough tongues licked at his palms.

Above him another policeman pitched forward into death.

Gerard Covington was about to cry out as something kicked his legs away from beneath him, tearing his hand free of Jenny's. He saw the flash and felt the cut. Jenny, already a few paces ahead of him in the moonlight, turned back and blew him a kiss. She was smiling as the steel bit through his flesh and the moisture gushed down over his shirt-front. As he choked and pitched over on his side, his throat slashed by Sodom, Jenny was still smiling back at him.

It wasn't so bad really, Gerard thought. At least his beloved Zoë would be waiting . . .

Johannes stood amongst the *glebulae*. Above him, with practised ease, Gomorrah's cheese-wire looped and tugged for the last time. The constable died, falling beside his companion, only the bones of his neck preventing the wire from severing his head completely.

Above Braw Valley, waiting beside the sabotaged van with his empty trailer, Gregor listened in vain for some sound of his charges' labours. He heard nothing. His heart was sick and ill-at-ease at the part he had played in what was happening. His mind struggled to comprehend what was taking place in the darkened ruins, failing to understand or see reason for his creatures' release into the night. That it was for no good purpose was the only certainty for his simple being to hold to, for he had seen *her* around the circus that afternoon, and when *she* came, evil followed, as surely as birth was the first truth and death was the second.

Only Harris and McAllister waited alive beside the ruins, Harris struggling to understand the monstrous wooden device which had been erected there. A handful of fitful torches flamed into life as Gomorrah sighted his tiny wicked companion scuttling up from the beach. Sodom's return could only mean one thing now.

Erzebet was coming.

A silence fell over the valley and the ruined church. No gulls mewed. In the scrub and heather nothing stirred. Even the waves seemed to have ceased their beating at the shoreline in awe at the approach of Erzebet von Bamberg, and the even more dread approach of what was to come after her.

Harris began to rise, but McAllister's hand clamped down onto his shoulder. 'Still, laddie,' he hissed. 'Just watch.'

That's all very well, Harris thought. Let's hope the others are watching as well. I'd hate to have to face those two nasty little buggers on my own . . .

Beneath her feet the shingle gave way to grass as Jenny Fellowes, or the one who had been Jenny Fellowes, began the ascent to the ruins. All trace of her former identities had left Erzebet now. Once more, possibly for ever, she thought, she was the fresh, youthful beauty who had played Helen for Johannes Faust. There was fire and strength in her brown eyes, and breeding and desire. They almost glittered with a light of their own in the darkness, illuminating the pale, oval face with its straight nose and full-lipped mouth. Her Titian hair bushed out and caught the moonlight at its ends, surrounding her shadowed features with a parody of a saintly nimbus.

The time is now, she thought. He will be here, Johannes will be here. We shall meet again at last, he and I . . .

She felt herself beginning to hope. There had to be hope, perhaps even more than there had to be victory. Once they had been lovers, if only for a night.

And then she saw him, there, amongst the *glebulae*.

Watching her approach, taking it as their signal to begin, her dwarfish servitors took their places. Sodom released the lever which activated the massive, drum-coiled spring which formed the only substantial metal part of the machine. Once he had done so Gomorrah slipped the brake from the driving arbor.

Erzebet strained through the night to see the movements as they began. Towering above the ruins, stark as a single crucifix in the blackness of an unhallowed Golgotha, the massive crossbeam of the verge and foliot escapement, its weights beginning to slowly swing beneath it, took up and controlled the power of the spring as it began to power the device which was to summon Pudendagora.

From the carillon of tambours beneath the foliot-beam, a single drum-beat sounded in the death-bought stillness of the dark.

It was working.

Erzebet wanted to hurry, to *be* there. There had always been the chance that the mechanism had distorted through the years, always the chance that it might not have worked properly. By its very nature there was no opportunity of testing it, not until the rest of the preparations had been completed. Yet to hear it, to see it, as she did now, was to make her impatient for the working to be over, for her to taste, to grasp, to bathe in her success. Her feet, though, maintained an even pace. Even though he was there, waiting for her, and the summoning was beginning, she held aloof. After all, with so many years of waiting finally behind her, what could a few more seconds matter now?

Ferrow felt his feet strike something as he followed the line Jenny Fellowes had taken along the beach. He looked down at the corpse of Gerard Covington, smiling in death at the thought of his long-delayed reunion, his blood a dulling wetness splashed about the stones around him.

No more doubts, Ferrow decided. And no more waiting.

With his left hand he vainly tried to check Gerard's pulse for signs of life. With his right he was slipping the safety-catch off the Bergmann-Bayard.

The second beat sounded, though now the background rumble and heavy clicking of the machinery, created to a variation of Ugo da Dondi's plans by John Harrison over 250 years before, added to the echoing sounds thrown back towards the ruins by the sheltering sides of Braw Valley.

Erzebet von Bamberg reached the centre of the mechanism and paused, staring up at the fragments of night which showed above through the arcs and circles of the huge wooden machine. This was the moment for which she had planned and dreamed and schemed throughout the intervening centuries. It was all here: the mechanism, her lover, and the relic, just as the skull had told her it would be.

The carillon sounded its first full cycle of sounds, thudding out into the night like an enormous, irregular heartbeat. Johannes Faust smiled as the *glebulae* relaxed and lay down around his feet. His hand reached into a pocket of his greatcoat and withdrew a thong-tied leather bag. Then he approached the ruins.

McAllister raised his weapon and sighted along the barrel.

Erzebet permitted herself the faintest smile. It was happening. After all these years it was finally going to happen.

Harris, his heart pounding in a rhythm similar, though different, to the dull cadences vibrated by the wooden mechanism in the ruined shell of the church, followed the line of his guv'nor's aim.

Johannes stepped into the ruins. Above him the wide, weighted foliot-beam swung its weights to and fro as the projecting flaps on the axle beneath caught on the teeth of the verge-wheel. With each swing of the beam the carillon sounded, completing and continuing a sequence of beats which none living, except for Erzebet von Bamberg and himself, could ever have understood.

It was like a gigantic artificial heart, beating out the complex rhythm of a creature which both transcended and denied humanity, a creature which would manifest, summoned by its drumming, to the detriment and ultimate destruction of mankind. No simple ritual of words could summon a creature as complex and ancient as Pudendagora from the banishment in which he dwelt. No amount of sacrifice or perversity could hasten his dread appearance amongst men. But the mechanism could. By reproducing that foul, disturbing rhythm by which whatever passed for the monster's life was sustained he could be summoned onto a plane of physical reality. Yet the machinery alone would not suffice. Something more was needed. And Johannes knew that he and he alone was the guardian of that something more.

'This is what you want, Erzebet,' he muttered, extending the bag towards her. 'This is what you've sought me for across the centuries.'

'Get out of here,' she ordered Sodom and Gomorrah. 'And take the *glebulae*. Your part in this is over.'

The dwarfish monsters eyed her, then nodded to themselves. After all, it was her game. They were simply players. They summoned the *glebulae*, which stared at Johannes through their featureless eyes in some unspoken, but understood, salute. Johannes gestured to them and they got up and began the ascent back to their trailer, leaving Sodom and Gomorrah, following, wondering if they still controlled the artificial creatures.

Beneath them in the valley, where it touched the shore of the sea, waves washed in silence at the shingle. Overhead a late gull, mute, wheeled alone, veering away from the steady, mechanical beating of the artificial wooden heart of an awakening terror from Thule.

'Will you take it from me, Erzebet?' Johannes asked her.

She smiled, then looked away. When her eyes returned to the bag, they followed the line of his extended arm up to his face. It was the same face, despite the intervening years, and she could already see by his look that she was still the same woman, still Helen of Troy, and she still held for him that same promise which their bodies had made to one another almost five centuries before.

'Does it have to be like this, Johannes?' she asked him, her eyes pleading. 'Is there no time for a moment in which we two might meet again? Am I not to be your little Helen once more, as I was so many years ago? Is there nothing left to us but victory or defeat?'

He felt himself shudder as he heard her. He felt himself shudder with horror at that which she sought to achieve, but he also felt a thrill of what she had once been, of what they had once been together.

The thudding heartbeat of the machine, irregular and yet still rhythmic, boomed on above them.

'Do you want more?' Johannes asked her. 'Can there be more, for us? For Faust and Helen?'

'I . . . I didn't want it to be like this,' she whispered.

'Could it be any other way, Erzebet? Haven't you chosen your course, as I have chosen mine?'

McAllister's finger began to tighten on the trigger of his revolver. Harris felt his heart speed up. It wasn't right. It simply wasn't right. That wasn't the target which McAllister should have selected . . .

Ferrow knelt beside Gerard Covington's body, his fingers dipping idly into the spilled blood, his mind beginning to numb with encroaching horror. He heard the approaching footsteps behind him and turned where he knelt, feeling the rock press through the knee of his trousers and graze the flesh inside.

'Can there be no time for us, Johannes? No time to remember the love we once thought to share? Is there nothing left to bind us but whatever is in that little leather bag?'

'Go . . . back,' Ferrow ordered, absently. 'Go on, June. Go back to the hotel. This is another one of those things you're not going to want to see . . .'

He heard her gasp as she recognised the pathetic, crumpled mass at his feet, but he no longer had the strength to move her physically away. She could cry out if she wanted to. If she liked she could howl until the darkness dissolved away before the dawn, or the people of Fortstown came out to count the bodies left by the passing night. It simply didn't matter any more. What was the point of one little cry, more or less, when that frightful, demented beating from the ruins was beginning to be answered by another?

Behind her another figure had appeared. 'Ferrow's right,' Merry Foster told June. 'This isn't the place for you. Go on, Miss Lowe. You'd better leave us to it.'

Ferrow looked up at her, his eyes bright with surprised recognition. 'You?' he demanded. 'Here?'

'Where the hell else am I supposed to be?' Merry snapped. 'I saw you at the circus with McAllister.'

June stood between them, mouth agape. As the last of Gerard's blood leaked out onto the shingle she tried to speak, to ask how they knew each other, to ask what was going on, where Jenny Fellowes was, and a hundred other things. Instead her mind gave up and, with a little cry, she turned away. Weeping, picking her path through her tears, she stumbled back towards the Fortstown Arms.

Ferrow stared blankly after her, then the weight of the loaded pistol in his pocket returned him to a terrible and still baffling reality. He glared at Merry Foster.

He pointed up the beach towards the thudding presence in Braw Valley. 'Do you know what's up there?' he asked her. 'Do you?'

She nodded. 'Caspar Locke,' she answered him. 'He's the murderer. I know. I heard you.'

He wanted to laugh, to throw back his head and laugh riotously, hysterically, into the night. God! Even he didn't know which side Caspar Locke was really on. He could even be on his own, using them all for his own particular and unknown purposes. Yet Ferrow's trust of the one Merry had named as the killer was, right then, the only thing which was sustaining the badly-frightened policeman.

'Is that all?' he queried. 'A simple murderer? *That's all* you think there is? What's that sound, woman? What's that fucking sound? A pop concert, for Christ's sake?'

The bag slipped from Johannes' fingers and fell to the floor of the ruins. He backed slowly away from it until it lay equidistant from Erzebet and himself. 'I shan't stop you from taking it,' he told her. 'You've sought it long enough. And now, I think, it's time that it was yours.'

Above them, looking down towards the swinging beam which towered above the broken, ruined walls of the church in Braw Valley, Gregor counted the last of his *glebulae* emerging onto the road. There was blood upon its muzzle, as there had been blood upon all their muzzles, and the giant knew instinctively that the blood was human. He held the back of the trailer open for them to leap inside, his eyes averted from the creatures that he had loved and cared for for most of his life. They obeyed him, as they always did, and he didn't bother to fasten them back inside their cage. He was just closing the door when Sodom and Gomorrah, panting from their climb, came into sight.

Gregor's eyes burned with anger. These were the two that had taken Gyorgy out that afternoon and come back without him. These were the ones who had ordered him to release the *glebulae* into Braw Valley, whence they returned after an unhallowed feeding. They were *her* creatures. Even more than the snuffling horrors he kept for her, the dwarfs were Erzebet's creatures.

They eyed him across the road through the darkness, then began to walk towards the cab of the trailer.

'In back,' he ordered them, forcing a smile to mask his grimness. 'You ride in back.'

The pouch fell and Johannes moved away from it. 'Go on, little Helen,' he told her. 'It's yours, now. Take it and it will all be over. The victory will be in sight.'

Still he calls me Helen, she thought. Still he remembers that one night we shared so many, many years ago.

'I've dreamed of a time when we could be together, Johannes,' she muttered softly. 'You and I . . . are the only ones of our kind now. We should be together, you and I. Don't you find me beautiful any more?'

He nodded, slowly, conscious of the beating overhead and the other answering beating beginning to sound from an undefined point in time and space. 'Still as lovely as ever,' he told her. 'But there's nothing left to us any more. Not now. Our paths have diverged too widely. Look around you, Erzebet. Look at the bodies littering this valley. Our work, my love. Our work. Yours and mine. Yours in the planning and mine in the permitting. But I'm too old now. Too tired of plotting and scheming through the centuries. I can't even be bothered to try to stop you any more.'

She stood just outside the ruined church, watching him, wide-eyed. Johannes set his head upon one side, listening for something beyond the beating of the carillon of tambours.

'Do you hear it, Erzebet?' he asked her. 'Do you hear that sound which is beginning to answer your machine? Do you hear the advance of Pudendagora?'

She listened, as he was listening. And then she heard it, even as he was hearing it. From somewhere above . . . around . . . them a living beat was answering the mechanical summons of the gigantic engine.

Others heard it too. Harris felt the sweat break out anew on his brow. McAllister's pistol momentarily wavered from its target. And Ferrow, still on the beach beside the remains of Gerard Covington, looked at Merry Foster's puzzled features.

'Oh, Jesus,' he whispered. 'It's coming. The bastard's coming!'

'What . . . is it? Come on, Ferrow. Tell me!'

He shook his head wildly, his hair flying. Then he turned and began a desperate run towards Braw Valley. Merry, her shoes unsuitable for shingle, stumbled after him as best she could.

At that answering sound even the Keeper's heart began to tremble. With an effort he bade it be still. There was still time, even if the answer was becoming stronger. The bluff could still work. All it took was a few seconds more . . .

He stared regretfully at Erzebet von Bamberg. 'Oh, yes,' he began. 'You're still beautiful to look at, still my little Helen. I can even feel desire for you. But we need more than that, Erzebet. We need so much more than that. We need what the centuries have robbed us of, more than just that night when I was Faustus and you were my Helen of Troy. We need peace, and time, and neither is there for us any longer. We have fought our way through time, you and I. We have striven and schemed, but never together. And that's why it has to be this way, my poor, lost love. We were ever lovers, but never really friends.'

As he ran towards the valley Ferrow didn't try to attempt to reason out his motives. He knew that if he thought about what he was doing, even for a moment, his stride would falter and his nerve would break. His eyes flashed upwards, scanning the sky for that blue fire which had been there at Wegrimham to help him. It wasn't there, and something told the policeman that it wouldn't be, this time. However, whyever, Meeres had summoned the skyfire before, this time he was fighting his battle without it.

Don't think. Think and you'll be afraid. Christ! Who says I'm not scared shitless already?

Behind him, blindly sensing the story of a lifetime, Merry Foster stumbled along the beach as best she could. Her eyes were wild and her heart was pounding, and for the first time in her life she was beginning to anticipate true terror.

Johannes studied Erzebet's features, gauging the impact of his words. Her eyes were the same, rich brown that he remembered, that had haunted him throughout the intervening years, yet there was something there to mar their beauty, something which he had never seen there before. The lines of age hadn't creased her flesh, and the evil she sought to summon and perpetuate could never have found space enough to register upon her loveliness. Yet still, as he stared at her, as he realised that she had finally heard and believed him, he witnessed the price he had to pay for speaking as he had.

A glistening trail of salty moisture was trickling down each cheek. Erzebet von Bamberg was crying.

Ferrow gained the bottom of the valley, his heart racing and his breath fighting its way to and from his lungs in laboured gasps. He saw the machine, thundering out its beat, dimly lit by the torches in the ruins, and felt the first real waves of panic washing over his being.

She no longer knew what the tears were for. They could have been for herself, for the lost years she had spent searching for something which could never be again. They might have been for the man she loved, the one man she had ever truly loved, the only one beyond herself that she had ever sought to care for. But, as Johannes had told her, there was nothing left to them any more. And that much, at least, she knew to be the truth.

The little leather bag lay upon the broken flagstones between them. It lay waiting for fingers other than her own to take it up, fingers which had already taken possession of both the skull and the manuscript it had dictated.

Erzebet sighed, her tears now flowing freely. When she spoke those same tears had begun to choke her voice.

'Take it if you want, McAllister,' she said softly. 'It's no concern of mine any more. Not any more.' Then she looked back across to Johannes. 'You see?' she asked him. 'There's still one thing that I can do for our memory. Still one gesture I can make for the love that once we shared.'

She turned away from him, walking slowly from the ruins and down the valley towards the beach. Now there was no need for her to try to hold the tears back any longer and they ran freely down her cheeks. Whether Thule was served or not, whether that intensifying beating echoing of the machine which was to summon Pudendagora became a horrifying reality, Erzebet no longer cared. She had sought through countless decades, but the finding was not the conclusion she had built her life upon.

Ferrow watched her approach. That she was there was sufficient proof of her identity. That she had played some part in Gerard Covington's death was beyond dispute. She was the one the dwarfs served. And the *glebulae*. Yet how the hell did you make a case out of what he'd got instead of evidence? How did you present Thule and monsters in a court of law? Without getting yourself shut up in Broadmoor, that was.

He withdrew the Bergmann-Bayard from his pocket and pointed it at the advancing Erzebet von Bamberg.

'Ferrow!' Merry shouted, still struggling to catch up with him. 'Are you mad? What are you doing with that gun?'

Erzebet smiled sadly at him as she approached. 'Shoot if you want, Robert,' she told him. 'Whether you do or not makes little difference. I'm dead already.'

Sodom and Gomorrah heard Gregor shut and bolt the trailer door behind them. The darkness reeked of the *glebulae*, of their diet and waste voided in the straw. The creatures' eyes burned with an unholy light in the darkness. Uneasily Gomorrah made his way forward as Gregor started the engine. He found the light-switch at the inner end and turned it on. The mouths about them, uncaged, were open, grinning, salivating with expectation.

Erzebet's words still echoed beneath the beating in the ruined church. Take it if you want, McAllister.

The policeman stood up slowly, feeling the cramp in his limbs. Besides him Harris, wild-eyed, was surveying the sprawled, blood-stained uniforms which littered Braw Valley. McAllister kept his revolver trained upon Johannes and advanced slowly towards the ruins.

Ferrow lowered his gun as Erzebet disappeared from sight. He looked towards the ruins, to where the machine was beating out its ghastly tattoo, to where McAllister, still covering the gaunt figure which watched his every move, bent to pick the leather bag up from the broken flagstones at his feet. A few paces behind, glancing wildly about as he followed, Harris was trying desperately to reason it all out. It was only when he remembered seeing Frauncie carry that bag from Mrs Flanagan's trailer to the inspector's car that he began to realise the truth.

Thule had not been counting on Erzebet alone.

With a quick lunge the sergeant caught McAllister off balance and snatched at the pouch. McAllister recovered quickly and slammed the barrel of his gun down hard onto Harris' skull. With a loud grunt the clubbed man fell to the church floor. The inspector used his foot to push the unconscious body aside before he bent to retrieve the relic. Johannes, immobile, watched and smiled.

The mechanical rhythm thudded on. The answering beat faltered for a moment then resumed more strongly, more insistently, growing in intensity until it filled the little valley and vibrated against the stones of the ruined church. Merry Foster started forward but Ferrow grabbed her roughly.

'Stay out of this,' he ordered savagely. 'You don't understand what's happening here. Get away. Go on, get out of here while you can!'

'You *have* to be joking,' she told him, wriggling free.

'Then stay still and keep your mouth shut!'

He faced the ruins, watching open-mouthed as McAllister began to back into the machinery. He raised the automatic and sighted along it.

'McAllister,' he yelled. 'Stand still. Stand still or I'll shoot you!'

'No!' Johannes called. 'Robert, no! This has to be. Don't fire your gun!'

Ferrow hesitated, used as he had become to trusting this strange immortal. Ignoring the reporter who stuck grimly beside him he advanced slowly towards the ruins, his weapon still pointing at the Scot.

McAllister was grinning now, certain of success. 'You won't shoot an unarmed man, Robert,' he called, throwing away his revolver. With both hands now free he began to untie the leather thongs which closed the pouch. He looked up at Johannes.

'What do I do with it?' he snapped. 'Tell me! What do I have to do with it?'

'There is a chute beside you,' the old man answered. 'Beneath it is a series of wheels which will grind it to powder and liberate the power of the relic. That is all. Place the pouch in the chute. You do not even need to open it, though of course you may if you wish to. It makes no difference.'

'What the fuck are you telling him for?' Ferrow demanded.

Merry's look was darting from the figures and machinery in the ruins to the man beside her. He was right. She didn't understand. Whatever was going on in Braw Valley was going to take a hell of a lot of explaining to her. Assuming she lived that long.

'Because he has to know, friend Robert,' Johannes called back. 'This is something that has to be.'

'Pudendagora has to be? After all you've told me? You're helping him to unleash one of Thule's greatest horrors upon the earth?'

In the sky above them a shape was beginning to form. Its outlines were vague, nebulous between the stars shining in the sky and the watchers beneath. But they were horribly suggestive. They moved. They *pulsed* with each new beat of the carillon of tambours above the monstrous wooden machine. Faceless, with few features that mortal eyes could even begin to identify, the terrible being known as Pudendagora began to grin.

Merry Foster screamed and fell to her knees. Her scream was the first of many. Ferrow left her where she was, knowing that there were other things for him to do than waste whatever seconds remained in comforting her. He reached the edge of the ruins, his eyes wavering from the old man to McAllister, and then to the terror in the sky above them.

Johannes watched calmly. McAllister had found the chute and held the pouch over it, his eyes glazed, his chest heaving as he breathed.

'Put it down!' Ferrow ordered. 'Down! Now! Or you're dead!'

McAllister, his voice tainted with hysteria, glared at the Englishman. 'You won't fire,' he hissed. 'I'm unarmed, Robert, remember? You won't shoot an unarmed man.'

'The fuck I won't,' Ferrow replied, his finger tightening upon the trigger, his aim certain.

The gun exploded.

The barrel of the Bergmann-Bayard above the magazine buckled upwards before a roar of flame and fragmented lead. Howling with pain as flying fragments sliced into his hands, Ferrow dropped the gun, turning his head to save his eyes.

McAllister dropped the little leather bag into the chute unopened.

The teeth in the trailer drew closer to the cowering dwarfs. Then they began to bite. Gomorrah's cheesewire was useless, and Sodom's knife was little better. The *glebulae* cut the tendons in their ankles first, pitching them down into puddles of their own blood which were forming on the floor. Wicked jaws severed hands which might have used weapons, and other hands which might have become weapons themselves. All the dying monstrosities could manage, wild-eyed, screaming in the brightness of the electric light, howling oaths, pleas and imprecations from throats which would shortly be torn away, as they had themselves ordered so many throats to be torn away, was to flail with their mutilated members at the artificial creatures that had served them for so long.

Until the creatures met Johannes and received their last instructions.

The old man continued to smile. About them the answering beat was becoming thunderous, growing in intensity as the physical form of Pudendagora took on stronger, more demoniac outlines. It was more than just a sound now. It was a presence. Ferrow clapped his injured hands to his ears and shut his eyes in a vain attempt to keep it out. McAllister, wild-eyed, followed suit.

'Get Harris and the girl away from here,' Johannes ordered. Despite the beating of both monster and machine, despite his covered ears and closed eyes, despite the panic which was ravening in his bowels, Ferrow heard him. With desperate haste, his face contorted by his terror and the sounds which echoed through the valley about him, sounds which threatened the shattering of both sanity and the physical stones of the ancient ruin, he reached the unconscious sergeant and began to pull him clear, looking up at the immortal as he did so.

Whatever his real name, whatever his true feelings, the Keeper's features reflected a grim contentment. 'I have to leave you for a while, friend Robert,' he began. 'Do not doubt that I shall return. No, you have yet to see the last of me. In my way, whatever happens here tonight, believe me when I say *I shall be back*.'

He walked into the machinery, confronting the terrified Hugo McAllister.

Ferrow hauled Harris some distance down the valley. Then, despite his terror, he turned and went back for Merry Foster. Once they were both clear he lay on top of them, attempting to shield them from the power of the thunderous cacophony sounding about them. He watched as Johannes faced McAllister and saw a bluish light, a light which was familiar but which had not come from the sky, illuminate them both.

He heard Johannes speak.

Gregor climbed up into the cab. His expression was feverish, though his movements were calm enough. He heard the beating from the valley, though he didn't really understand it. There was only one thing he understood now. That was why, when he started the engine, he didn't bother to turn on the headlights.

He had to be ready. That was all that counted any more.

Pudendagora grew stronger, brighter, firmer. It began to descend towards the ruins.

All over Fortstown lights were flashing on and doors were opening. A D-Notice might keep the press quiet, but it wouldn't stop people talking for years to come about what had threatened them that night. They didn't, they couldn't, understand. But that wouldn't be enough to keep them quiet. Not when they tried to reason out the source of the drumming which thudded through the darkness, a drumming which shattered sleep and reason both together. Even in Banff the dull thudding of the rhythm could be heard, though it was neither so threatening nor so thunderous there.

Erzebet von Bamberg turned the key in the Mercedes' ignition. Her part in this was done. Johannes had rejected her because of her service of Pudendagora. That creature would come for her, she knew. She would die in an agony she shuddered to imagine, despite the pain and terror she had herself inflicted through the years.

Well, the die was cast. After all, she reflected, my life has never truly been my own. Has it, Johannes?

And then she remembered what the skull had told her. Exactly what the skull had told her.

Your ancient lover will come to you, Erzebet. And he will bring the form of that you have sought with him . . .

The form.

Johannes raised his arm, almost lazily. Something arched through the air and landed beside Ferrow in the grass. The thudding of the gigantic wooden machine began to falter.

Johannes smiled at McAllister. 'Did you really think that I would help you to destroy mankind?' he asked gently.

The Scot howled. So did the creature which had been answering the carillon of tambours with its own cacophonous beating.

Slowly Erzebet reversed out of the parking bay at the Fortstown Arms and began to drive up the twisting, sloping road which led out of the little fishing village, passing brightly lit windows and little knots of speculating residents on her way. The tears had been wiped from her eyes and she was nodding gently, a faint smile playing about her lips. Her lover had cheated her at the last and, in a small part of her being, she was glad.

'Guard it well, Robert,' Johannes said. 'It has work still to do, before we all come home.'

The ruins, and the machinery they contained, flew apart.

Ferrow covered his head with his arms to protect it. He didn't see the mingled implosion and explosion which tore through the enormous wooden mechanism and the stone walls of the church. The foliot beam shuddered to a halt, then pitched over and crashed down through the assemblage of cog-wheels. The arbors bucked and buckled, scattering beams and broken wooden teeth splintering in all directions. The church walls pitched briefly inwards before an unknown force hurled them outwards in shards of vicious splintered stone. McAllister screamed as a huge fragment of wood impaled him, entering his chest above the rib-cage and stabbing down to emerge at the small of his back.

The blue light faded. Johannes disappeared from sight in a rush of flying fragments and dust. About the valley something unseen screamed in torment with a force that mortal ears ought never to have heard.

Then all was still.

After the incessant, terrifying rhythm of the machinery, and the creature which had responded to it, the few creaks and fallings of the settling rubble were welcome relief in the weight of the following silence. Ferrow unclasped his head and, slowly, hauled his weary body to its feet. He wanted to laugh, to celebrate his deliverance, but there remained something to be done, and he was the only one alive still in Braw Valley who could do it.

He found the little pouch in the grass and picked it up. With trembling fingers he untied the thong which bound it closed and shook its contents out into his hand. As he looked down at his palm he saw the small figure of a carved obsidian monkey, one hand masturbating, the other raised in benediction, staring darkly up at him.

He slipped the figurine back into its pouch as Harris began to moan. Merry Foster was still groaning slightly. It would be some time before her mind would begin to accept any form of explanation of the night's events.

Erzebet rounded the bend at the head of the valley. Her headlights picked out the shape of something dark and solid that was beginning to travel towards her. Behind the wheel in the trailer Gregor was scowling determinedly. Behind him, in the stark brightness of electric light, the *glebulae* were still devouring the remains of Sodom and Gomorrah.

Harris sat up and felt gingerly at the lump on his skull. He looked at Ferrow and grimaced. 'Sorry, friend,' he groaned. 'I didna' stop acting like a prick in time.'

Ferrow's eyes were upon the settling ruins, searching them for a sign of life he knew he wouldn't find. 'Don't worry,' he responded. 'You did just fine.'

Gregor pressed down on the accelerator. It was all as good as over now, and over was what he intended it should be for ever. For all of them. The circus would be free now. He would buy their freedom, once and for all, with the lives of his *glebulae* and their owner, and himself.

Harris stood up, swaying slightly. Somewhere in the ruins they would find the body of his guv'nor, Inspector Hugo McAllister. Whether or not they would also find the remains of the man Hogue he didn't know, though he suspected they would not. There was something which went beyond simple mortal strangeness about that man. Something which cried out in its mystery about other times and other realms. Harris had never heard of Thule. Perhaps he never would. But he would never forget the man he knew as Hogue, even though he didn't understand just what that man had achieved.

Ferrow stood beside him, still struggling to retain both his memories and his sanity. For now there was only settling dust in Braw Valley, settling dust and a thin, wavering column of smoke spiralling lazily towards the moon.

Erzebet swerved the Mercedes' wheel to avoid Gregor's trailer. Suddenly she realised how close to the edge of the valley she was. Her right foot moved to the brake pedal and stamped down on it.

Nothing happened.

Ferrow and Harris looked up towards the head of the valley as they heard the squealing of her tyres. 'That'll be Mrs Flanagan, or whatever her name is,' Harris grinned. 'When I came looking for ye at the pub I screwed up the hydraulics on her motor.'

Gregor wrenched at the steering to throw the trailer sideways across the road. The momentum would carry him down into Braw Valley, but that no longer mattered. He was going to free the Circuz Ferencz, and he was going to do it in the only way he knew how. By killing Erzebet von Bamberg.

Erzebet stamped on the brake again and again, unconscious of the shining puddles of hydraulic fluid being discharged behind her on the road. All she could see was the solid bulk of the trailer blocking her passage. Gregor stamped on his own brakes in a last, instinctive attempt to preserve himself, but it was too late for both vehicles. As the Mercedes struck the side of the trailer both vehicles left the road and began the plunge towards the ruins. Gregor's mouth opened in a wordless, triumphant howl. Behind him the doors flew open and one of the *glebulae*, nearest the back, jumped for its life. It landed in the heather with a sprained fore-limb and a badly-cracked rib. As the cab bounced, tearing Gregor from his seat and splitting his skull against the inside of its roof, the Mercedes hurtled past it. The doors flew open and Erzebet von Bamberg threw her hands over her face in a last desperate defensive measure. But her flesh was already bruising, and the darkness was closing in about her. A fraction of a second later the car hit the ground and made its first bounce. The petrol tank ignited in mid-air and the fireball which the Mercedes had become, its luxury transformed into a deadly oven, crashed down into the sharded wreckage of the summoning of Pudendagora.

Within an instant of its impact the trailer thundered down on top of it, crushing the machinery and the Mercedes still further, reducing both vehicles to little more than a tangle of blazing metal. As the ruins themselves took fire, two pairs of eyes watched from beneath.

'I reckon I screwed up her brakes real good,' Harris muttered, smiling broadly.

Robert Ferrow nodded. 'I guess you did, sergeant,' he replied.

June had little she could tell the police. Fighting back the shock of her experience, she decided that enough was enough, packed her things and was on her way to her mother's by the time Ferrow was anything like ready to follow her. He told his colleagues what he could, omitting a great deal of matter which they would have regarded as either superfluous or the ravings of a madman. They weren't happy, despite Harris confirming as much as he was able to, but Ferrow's rank stopped them questioning too closely. So did the man in the dark suit they reported to, the man who had been responsible for the D-Notice.

Ferrow met the man briefly at that time. Later he'd meet him again and travel with him through distance and the third reality to unravel the secret of the Keeper once and for all. Yet now, without June, without even any consolation which Merry Foster might have offered him in June's absence, he could only watch as the search of Braw Valley was completed. He could only listen as Harris told him about the findings, or the lack of findings.

No trace of Erzebet von Bamberg. Not surprising, perhaps, in view of the trailer coming down on top of her car.

No trace of Johannes, or whatever the Keeper's name really was.

He didn't mention the so-called relic to them. They'd never have understood, so why bother? Ferrow himself didn't know why a small obsidian figurine was so important. Not yet. When he packed his things and paid Miles Fournessie, the pouch containing it was in his pocket.

The man in the dark suit took a carrier-bag from McAllister's car and appeared to be quite pleased by its contents. Ferrow was being followed, of course, as he left the Fortstown Arms and began to drive towards Banff on his journey back to Corby. He didn't know, and the state of his mind was such that he couldn't even be bothered to guess that he was under observation, much less know why.

As he rounded the bend at the head of the valley he saw the creature sitting in the road in front of him. He braked instinctively, then wondered why he'd not speeded up and crushed it. Instead, for reasons he would only understand in his uncertain future, he stopped the car and opened the passenger door for it.

Moving painfully, its mouth open in an expression he had yet to learn how to interpret, the *glebula* climbed in beside him. He stared at it as it sat on the passenger seat, panting and snuffling. He wasn't prepared to trust it. Not yet.

'I don't give rides to strangers,' Ferrow grunted, 'so I suppose I'd better give you a name.' He searched his memory, shortened as it had been by the past few hours.

'How does Johannes sound?' he asked.

Johannes moved its muzzle closer. It licked his hand.

'Oh, shit,' Ferrow muttered. 'You bloody like me, don't you?'

He wound down his window before he drove on. June had left him and, apart from the threatening presence of the *glebula*, he was alone.

Except for the obsidian monkey, in its pouch.

The car behind him stopped and reversed back out of sight before he could look in his driving mirror. The passenger got out and crept forward, his walkie-talkie open for transmission.

Ferrow took the leather pouch from his pocket. Without even looking to see where it might have landed he tossed it out over the road towards the ruins in Braw Valley.

Robert Ferrow shifted the car back into gear. With the *glebula* beside him he continued his long drive home.

'In the valley,' hissed the watcher, 'He's thrown it into the valley, somewhere.'

The man in the dark suit listened, then turned off his radio. About him a small team watched expectantly.

'Braw Valley,' the man told them.

'And, when you find it, bring it straight to me.'

They went out and searched. They eventually found it, but not before they had annoyed the local forensic boys who were trying to make sense out of the shattered machine for them. The Circuz Ferencz was being detained and questioned, of course. So was everybody who had been in the Fortstown Arms the night before. But what sense there was to be made, was made by the man in the dark suit, not by his underlings.

Robert Ferrow, the Guardian of the Relic, might have abandoned his charge. Yet as he drove on, following the course of the River Deveron along the A97 before turning on to the A96 at Huntly and heading for Aberdeen, with a nightmare creature on the seat beside him as he drove, he knew in his heart that the Wegrimham and Fortstown affairs were simply two episodes in an adventure which had yet to be resolved.

'Ready for what comes next, Johannes?' he asked the *glebula*.

Its dark eyes leered at him, and it panted with something Ferrow could only have described as expectation.

**THE VISIONARY CHRONICLE OF THE ULTIMATE
STRUGGLE TO RULE THE EARTH . . .**

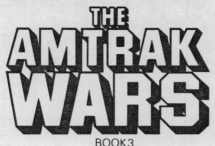

BOOK 3
Iron Master
The third volume of a futureworld epic

PATRICK TILLEY

The year: 2990 AD. The centuries-old conflict between the
hi-tech underground world of the Trackers and the
primitive, surface-dwelling Mutes continues with unabated
ferocity. Steve Brickman, a Tracker wingman whose heart
and mind is torn between the two cultures, embarks upon his
most dangerous mission yet: the rescue of Cadillac and
Clearwater, two Plainfolk Mutes held captive by the
mysterious Iron Masters. It is a nightmare journey into the
unknown . . .

0 7221 8518 9 GENERAL FICTION £3.50

Also by Patrick Tilley in Sphere Books:
THE AMTRAK WARS Book 1 CLOUD WARRIOR
THE AMTRAK WARS Book 2 FIRST FAMILY
MISSION

Out of innocence came forth
unspeakable evil...

NIGHT WARRIORS

Graham Masterton

Henry was the first to reach the body, while Gil
and Susan walked cautiously closer, and then stood
watching. It was the body of a beautiful young
girl, naked like a peacefully sleeping mermaid. Never
in their most traumatic nightmares could they
have imagined the convulsive violence which
followed . . .

NIGHT WARRIORS – they fought an epidemic of pure
evil spawned in the womb of our nightmares . . .

NIGHT WARRIORS – a classic of writhing, inhuman
horror . . .

0 7221 6120 4 HORROR £2.95

From the bestselling authors of
LUCIFER'S HAMMER and THE MOTE IN GOD'S EYE –
the ultimate novel of alien invasion!

FOOTFALL

NIVEN & POURNELLE

It was big all right, far bigger than any craft any human had seen. Now it was heading for Earth.

The best brains in the business reckoned that any spacecraft nearing the end of its journey would just *have* to be friendly.

But they were wrong! Catastrophically wrong!

The most successful collaborative team in the history of science fiction has combined again to produce a devastating and totally convincing novel of alien invasion.

FOOTFALL – the ultimate disaster

GENERAL FICTION   0 7221 6339 8   £3.95

A selection of bestsellers from Sphere

FICTION

THE PRINCESS OF POOR STREET	Emma Blair	£2.99 ☐
WANDERLUST	Danielle Steel	£3.50 ☐
LADY OF HAY	Barbara Erskine	£3.95 ☐
BIRTHRIGHT	Joseph Amiel	£3.50 ☐
THE SECRETS OF HARRY BRIGHT	Joseph Wambaugh	£2.95 ☐

FILM AND TV TIE-IN

BLACK FOREST CLINIC	Peter Heim	£2.99 ☐
INTIMATE CONTACT	Jacqueline Osborne	£2.50 ☐
BEST OF BRITISH	Maurice Sellar	£8.95 ☐
SEX WITH PAULA YATES	Paula Yates	£2.95 ☐
RAW DEAL	Walter Wager	£2.50 ☐

NON-FICTION

NEXT TO A LETTER FROM HOME: THE GLENN MILLER STORY	Geoffrey Butcher	£4.99 ☐
AS TIME GOES BY: THE LIFE OF INGRID BERGMAN	Laurence Leamer	£3.95 ☐
BOTHAM	Don Mosey	£3.50 ☐
SOLDIERS	John Keegan & Richard Holmes	£5.95 ☐
URI GELLER'S FORTUNE SECRETS	Uri Geller	£2.50 ☐

All Sphere books are available at your local bookshop or newsagent, or can be ordered direct from the publisher. Just tick the titles you want and fill in the form below.

Name_____

Address_____

_____

Write to Sphere Books, Cash Sales Department, P.O. Box 11, Falmouth, Cornwall TR10 9EN

Please enclose a cheque or postal order to the value of the cover price plus:

UK: 60p for the first book, 25p for the second book and 15p for each additional book ordered to a maximum charge of £1.90.

OVERSEAS & EIRE: £1.25 for the first book, 75p for the second book and 28p for each subsequent title ordered.

BFPO: 60p for the first book, 25p for the second book plus 15p per copy for the next 7 books, thereafter 9p per book.

Sphere Books reserve the right to show new retail prices on covers which may differ from those previously advertised in the text elsewhere, and to increase postal rates in accordance with the P.O.